Praise for *Not Yet*

"A fresh view of suicide from a new author should be read by anyone affected clinically or personally by suicide. The two main questions, why and how, are explored in detail by Mr. Segall in his work of literary fiction. His poignant account cleverly wrestles with facts about suicide as well as how the main character, a crisis counselor, processes these precarious moments when decisions mean the difference between life and death. Read it and learn. It's a stunning work by a writer with a gift for storytelling."

—Dr. Jody Glittenberg, Professor Emerita at the University of Arizona, Author of *The Promise Seed: Saving Mother Earth,* national finalist for PEN Women of America

"A human story told with fearless compassion, without lapsing into pedantry, Segall's novel demonstrates truths often overlooked in the age of spectacular media, escalating news-cycle and daytime drama, and escapist-entertainment-hounding. First, we do not need talk-show-worthy circumstances to suffer deeply: living itself is psychologically dangerous. Second, that here, as in life, there is true respite to be found—in authentic interpersonal interaction. And foremost, a message not to be missed, when we own our responsibilities we create meaning; and where we find meaning, we find purpose, courage, and personal power. Far more than simply a story surrounding a theme, *Not Yet* lives out distortions of time that trace a mind's path through modern mental illness—ascending anxiety and unqualified depression. Through the gradual revelation of circumstance and character, Segall offers a window opening upon the process of madness, sometimes chilling, often warm or humorous, and always believable. Plus, the Tupac skit is the da bomb."

—Adam Dunham, PhD, *Midwest Book Review*

"Erik Segall's work not only touches the sharp edge of the human existential condition, but also acts a bastion of both hilarity and tenderness around the reality of death and choice. Read his work if you want to be deeply touched by the sacred and the ephemeral."

— Katie Silcox, NYT Best-Selling Author

"The careful reader will discover specific communication skills ...and the snippets of dialogue in NOT YET are full of learning tools!"

—Barbara Hadley MA/LPC, Professor of Psychology at Colorado State University-Pueblo, author of *If Not Joy Now, Then When?*

"An elaborate explanation of suicide with several kinds of fun on every page—grim, offensive, tender and touching. Segall's characters are of a wilder sort; harsh yet loving, suffering yet giddy . . . and left me stunned by the pace, drama, and humanity of his conclusion. This book will travel everywhere."

—Dr. Nancy Regalado, Professor Emerita of French Medieval Literature at New York University

"If the mission of an author is, by creative thoughts, to give us a foreshadowing of a higher reality, then Erik Segall has done just that in *Not Yet*. He strikes all the neurons and emotional cords while directing them to timely images of eternity."

—C. Buck Weimer, Author of *The Darien Jungle Shakedown Cruise*

NOT YET

Erik Segall

Harvard Square Editions

New York

2019

Not Yet
by Erik Segall

ISBN 978-1-941861-67-7
Printed in the United States of America
Published in the United States by
Harvard Square Editions
www.harvardsquareeditions.org

For Coonie

Preface to the Preface

Life as experience in three distinct time frames:

      past,   present,   and future.

Seventeen chronoscopic options contradict *a priori* perspective: past remote, past recent, past-in-the-present, past-in-the-future, past yesterday, past today, non-past → present and still[1] and non-still ← non-future, future today, future tomorrow, future-in-the-past, future-in-the-present, future near, future remote.

Explained in one sentence with the Cast of Characters: (*past remote*) Aaron's nightmare from the age of six about his grandmother Eve drowning on the passenger ship named **Memory**, (*past recent*) which he recounted last week in therapy, (*past-in-the-present*) a conversation troubling him today and (*past-in-the-future*) will probably keep him awake tonight, (*past yesterday*) moreover Aaron couldn't recall if his daughter Zoë came home from school yesterday, (*past today*) yet he was fairly certain his ex-wife Lena had banged on the front door an hour ago looking for their daughter (*non-past*) even though Zoë was never home during the afternoon, (*present*) and Aaron, hiding under the table (*still*) unable to tell the difference between illusion and reality, (*non-still*) realizes fear has nothing to do with his current relapse (*non-future*) because he'll never live without anxiety, (*future today*) and he needs to collect himself and come out from underneath the table by the time Zoë gets home in order to go shopping with his Aunt Jocelyn and select a birthday cake (*future tomorrow*) because they're collecting his grandmother Eve from the nursing home to attend Aaron's birthday tomorrow, (*future-in-the-past*) a party which his mother Marilyn usually forgets, (*future-in-the-present*) and the anticipation of his mother's absence and his ex's banging on the door and Zoë's imminent return and Jocelyn's shopping excursion and Eve's repeated requests to help kill herself are giving him a serious case of the dreads (*future near*) but Aaron feels hopeful about motivating (*future remote*) and spending less time under the table.

Preface

A woman is . . .

— A rabbit in a snare —
"Zeroes, shutting on nothing,
Sliding shut on some quick thing,
The constriction killing me also."
—Sylvia Plath

"The thought of suicide is a great consolation: in that way
one gets through many a dark night."
—Friedrich Nietzsche

A man is . . .

"I stare out
at the horizon
until it gets up
and comes to embrace me.
I make believe
it is my father."
—LeRoi Jones

Prologue

"Help me die."

After ten years at the Suicide Prevention & Crisis Hotline Center, Aaron found his grandmother's request impossible. She held out a pillow and asked again.

"I can't do it alone," Eve said. "My memory is fading."

When Colorado legalized assisted suicide, Aaron's job as a crisis counselor became complicated. Friends and family started asking for help. Prevention turned to permission.

"Cover my face," she said, clutching the pillow. "I won't struggle. Here, let's practice."

Aaron leaned out into the hall of the Poinsettia Nursing Home. The staff was busy serving lunch to a hundred residents.

"Please don't make me," he pleaded.

"My mind is slipping, soon I won't recognize you. I'm ready to go Upstairs."

Aaron knew she meant heaven, but liked to joke with her. "Downstairs is warmer."

"Like this," she said, pressing the pillow down on her face. Her emerald eyes peeked above the edge with a playful sparkle.

As he pressed down slightly, her eyes went flat and gray. Her memory flickered.

Bony hands grasped the sides, nails clawing for life. She forcefully pushed the pillow away from her face. "Honey, why are you trying to suffocate me?"

Aaron couldn't kill his grandmother.

Not yet.

Chapter 1

De-escalating Men as a Means of Survival

The first time Aaron Clifton saved a life, he realized insanity is always original. The call came at midnight. Aaron cradled the land-line receiver in his left hand as he quickly jotted notes on a yellow legal pad. The emergency dispatcher informed him of the vital statistics:

Active shooter, white male, age unknown,
history of mental illness, armed,
law enforcement on scene,
3 people held hostage
shots fired, possible fatalities,
shooter's ex-wife among the hostages.

Aaron learned the shooter and hostages were barricaded in the rear storage room of a local restaurant and hung up the phone. He inhaled deeply and reviewed the items he would need before driving to the scene. Pen. Paper. Folder of color-coordinated brochures from his office at the Suicide Prevention & Crisis Hotline Center—red for anger, blue for sadness, yellow for ambivalence, green for jealousy, orange for the truly deranged and purple for mystical wisdom with conflicting advice for the prevention of suicide like *Hang In There*.

ID badge.
Jacket.
Boots.
Car keys.
Car keys?

Frantically, he searched under a stack of newspapers on the kitchen table then looked between the yellow couch cushions for his car keys and finally found them in his daughter Zoë's jacket, which reeked of cigarette smoke. Aaron hoped she hadn't picked up the habit from her mother, a compulsive smoker. For the moment, he consoled himself by imagining that maybe his daughter had only been hanging out with friends who smoked.

Aaron locked the door behind himself, knocked the snow off his car and was on the road three minutes after receiving the call. With most his experience coming from telephone conversations and hardly any from real-life encounters, maybe less than a hundred hours interviewing people at the intake desk of a local homeless shelter, Aaron suspected he was grossly underprepared as he sped towards the scene of carnage.

From half a mile away, red and blue police lights guided him in. The restaurant turned out to be a Denny's, his favorite back in the day when they had a full-service bar and the smoking section was located merely one booth away from the clean air section. Aaron suddenly craved a *Moons Over My Hammy*, hoping to settle his nervous stomach with plastic cheese, rubbery ham and butter-soaked white bread.

He parked behind an ambulance in the Denny's icy parking lot as a sheriff's deputy eyed him suspiciously until Aaron flashed his badge. With long, unkempt hair and wearing torn jeans and an old leather jacket, Aaron looked more homeless than helpful. The deputy pointed to a white van acting as a command center, surrounded by official looking men.

"You him?" a well-tailored detective asked Aaron. "We've got him pinned down in the backroom. Here's the phone. Bastard's on now." Aaron expected some type of debrief or assessment of the situation to prepare him for his first real-life crack at talking down an active shooter bent on murder-suicide. Aaron's hands shook as he took the cell phone from the detective and pressed the un-mute button.

Aaron could hear the man breathing over the phone. Raspy, he thought, probably a chain-smoker. He began to create an image of the Caller. Over-weight, mid-50s, white male. After ten years of taking Suicide calls, he'd learned how to discern personal attributes based on voice and breathing patterns.

Aaron's automatic introduction kicked in. "Hello, I'm a crisis worker with the local…"

The man interrupted him calmly. "Let me talk."

This initial interaction worried Aaron. He'd suspected the Caller/shooter would be furious, deranged and frightened, yet he displayed none of these traits.

"Ok. Go ahead, I'm here." Aaron expected the man to ramble, to rave, to spout hateful rhetoric and gender-demeaning speech with a bit of queer-bashing. He had a better picture of the man. Bearded, lives alone in the woods, two or three ex-wives, owns at least a dozen rifles.

Instead of launching into an extended diatribe, the man simply said, "Today's the day."

The line went dead.

Aaron handed the phone back to the detective with a defeated expression. "I tried."

The detective handed it straight back to Aaron. "Get him back on. Keep him talking. We're almost in position."

"Position for what?" Aaron asked innocently, redialing the number on the touch screen.

"You're here to distract him as we break through the back door. So…," the sergeant screamed, "DISTRACT!"

Aaron watched as the sergeant turned to address four well-armed and serious looking men. Aaron's failure to connect with the Caller/shooter caused him severe anguish, and in these moments of panic, his mind often collated random bits of cultural trivia. With the snow building on their uniforms, the armored police soldiers reminded Aaron of the white-clad storm troopers he'd partied with at a Star Wars convention where he boldly identified himself as a Trekker rather than a Star Wars geek. This sci-fi persuasion had occurred during his divorce from Lena a decade ago mainly because the run time for all Star Wars movies, not including the Holiday Episode with singing Wookies, is around twenty hours which Aaron managed to polish off in a single day. He needed a longer distraction from his post-marital grief and turned to Star Trek with 79 episodes from the Original Series and Next Generation's 178 episodes and Deep Space Nine's 175 episodes and Voyager's 172 episodes and Enterprise's 98 episodes and a few from Discovery. And this was how Aaron coped with his divorce because watching 700 hours of Star Trek was slightly better than drinking a bottle of Drano.

The Sergeant hollered at his troopers while Aaron counted the number of episodes and accidently said out loud, "A Klingon with a bat'leth could totally take on a Jedi."

The Sergeant looked at his newly appointed crisis intervention specialist and asked, "What are you talking about?"

Aaron shrugged his shoulders. "You told me to distract, so I'm distracted."

"Not yourself, dumb-ass," the Sergeant yelled, pointing to the building. "Him!"

"Oh," Aaron said, "that makes much more sense."

Aaron quickly deliberated whether giving the Caller/shooter a heads-up as the police stormed in the back door would be considered unethical or illegal until he decided the Caller/shooter deserved to die a death worse than a cowardly p'takh. Aaron dialed again and the

Caller/shooter answered. He decided to try a different approach.

"Hey p'takh, wassup?"

The Caller/shooter shouted, "What'd you call me!?"

Aaron intimately knew the rules of de-escalating a tense situation. The first step was to calm the Caller down by having them take a few deep breaths and counting out loud back from ten,

10, inhale

    9, exhale

        8, inhale

            7, exhale

but Aaron never liked rules. He preferred to go straight for the last option. Offend the mentally-unstable and harass the emotionally-volatile.

"P'takh. It means coward in Klingon," Aaron explained. "Or traitor, depending on the translation. Which one are you?"

"Coward? I'm gonna shoot this bitch in the face! She left me and now the courts say I gotta pay her? I'm gonna make *her* pay, you'll see! You think I'm a coward?!"

"You're unhappy, I get it. Your wife left you, not the first time, right?"

"They all left me. They always leave me!"

"And now you're depressed but you don't have the balls to shoot yourself so you're gonna threaten a bunch of waitresses and force the cops to shoot you."

"No balls? I've got huge balls! Here, I'll show you."

The phone chimed with an incoming pic. The shooter had pulled down his pants and taken a dick-pic. In the background, Aaron could see a .30 caliber bolt-action hunting rifle laying on the floor.

Bolt-action, Aaron thought. That didn't make sense. The shooter could maybe get off a shot or two. He looked again at the pic on the cell phone. The man was not over-weight, instead packing a washboard of flat abs.

The Sergeant gave Aaron a thumbs-up. "Nice distraction," he said before turning to his men. "Here we go!"

Aaron coldly spoke into the phone, "You're not a coward. You're dead."

Suddenly, flash grenades exploded and the back door cracked open. Serious men stormed in and shot the man through the head. His bloody brains covered an open bag of hash-brown potatoes like a side of ketchup.

The three employees, including the man's ex-wife, were unharmed. The cops escorted everyone out of the storage room and Aaron stole a good look at the Caller/shooter. White male, mid-twenties, military-style haircut. Not overweight, no beard, not a loner living in the woods.

Sure got that one wrong, Aaron thought.

Yet, Aaron could have talked the man down from his frantic perch had there been more time. When the police found the rifle unloaded, Aaron realized he'd been right about one thing. The young man had held no intention of shooting anyone, including himself. While the police sealed off the back room, Aaron sat alone at the restaurant counter and ordered an egg sandwich.

To his surprise, the manager served him personally. Aaron had learned that the best thing to do in a crisis was to assign everyone a task. After a tragedy, most people heal by going right back to work. The manager had been the only person who stayed behind whereas the waiters, waitresses and customers had fled when the Caller/shooter charged in with a rifle demanding to see his ex-wife. Most people hadn't paid their bill, instead choosing to run out the back door.

Aaron played chess on his phone while waiting for breakfast when a text arrived,[2] immediately followed by a second text from his ex-wife Lena reminding him of a PTA meeting at 7:00 a.m. Aaron looked out the window to the east and the fading darkness convinced him of morning.

Sitting at the counter trying to process the recent events of an angry husband attacking an ex-wife, Aaron thought about his own relationship. Nope, Aaron told himself, he'd never go after Lena like that. They'd been divorced for many years and although he could hardly remember what he'd been mad about, Aaron recalled expressing plenty of anger at her through the divorce. Not with thrown plates or screaming matches, but rather with highly inappropriate and overtly misogynistic remarks that constantly re-enforced the Patriarchy in a way that men tend to do with women they've screwed, no matter how long it's been, as though they have the right to treat their sexual conquests as dominated foes and worse than prisoners of war by torturing them with occasional reminders of *I conquered you, bitch!*

Lena's method of de-escalating Aaron through the divorce was to tolerate his hyper-sexualized tirades for about three months by replying with a simple "Ugh" and a disgusted look on her face which meant, "Stop objectifying me like a piece of disposable meat, and you really need to start treating me like a human being or even possibly a friend because I gave you a kid and I'll always be the mother of your child and you should be *kowtowing* down on your hands and knees to me every time I enter the room because without my ovaries, your semen would only be filling the cement cracks on the bathroom floor."

Aaron knew about de-escalating men because he practiced every night over the phone by taking calls at the Suicide Prevention & Crisis Hotline Center. He listened carefully, then told these men everything would be okay and hung up as soon as possible. His interaction was far different than women who de-escalated men every day of their lives by

flirting with a soft pat on the arm; and,

ignoring stares, catcalls and street harassment; and,

offering one little kiss to prevent getting pinned in a corner; and, enduring belittling words like *girl, hormonal* and *high-maintenance*; and,

tolerating shaming words like *whore, hoe, hoe-bag* and the other 237 synonyms for "sexually promiscuous," which explains why Mrs. Claus reddens in the cheeks when Santa says, "Ho, ho, ho."

Eventually, Aaron had picked up on Lena's subtle cues and halted his continual harassment, although for a while he still found great pleasure in occasionally tormenting her with pseudo-flattery such as, "Hey sweetheart, lookin good today, can I give you my number? … since you took everything else," or "You've lost weight since you were pregnant, too bad your attitude gained it back," or any other jokes about weight which are, although men tend to forget, always offensive even when innocently placed in a stupid Romantic Comedy.

Getting up from the counter, Aaron decided to postpone writing the report about the Caller/shooter until he had returned to his cubicle at the Suicide Prevention & Crisis Hotline Center. Aaron left half an uneaten egg sandwich on the plate and tried to pay the manager who refused to take money for his help in saving the lives of three employees. Aaron calculated the manager's generous gesture at about $2.35 per life.

Aaron plodded back to his car, heels of his untied, heavy black boots dragging on the ground as he slipped away from the crime scene at the restaurant. He drove past the Poinsettia Nursing Home where his grandmother Eve slept soundly, the scent of lavender seeping in through the air vents from Russian sage bushes that poked through the snow. Aaron loved how Colorado's schizophrenic weather could offer blooming flowers in snowfall. A few minutes later, he arrived at the elementary school where his daughter had attended several years earlier. He sat in his car and watched a stream of concerned housewives emerge from their SUVs and minivans. For some reason, Aaron often seemed to be the only man at these meetings. He blamed gender-roles.

Shoulders slumped from exhaustion, Aaron walked towards the front door of the school where he spied Lena leaning against the wall smoking a cigarette and a paper cup filled with orange juice mixed with her morning medicine. She wore a bright blue Canadian goose parka from Neiman Marcus that matched her eyes.

Aaron gave his ex-wife a casual nod. "I didn't know vodka was a breakfast fruit."

She ignored his comment and shrugged her shoulders. "Zoë still sleeping?"

"Probably. I got a call last night, had to go in early. She'll drive herself to school."

Aaron gazed at the paper cup and decided to forgo a lecture on the detrimental nature of morning drinking. Instead, he reached for the cup and took a sip.

Chapter 2

Holidays Suck When Both Parents are Dead
and Friends Keep Calling to Cry About Their Recent Break-Ups

After working for a decade at the Suicide Prevention & Crisis Hotline Center, Aaron Clifton noticed the phone always rang between 10:21 p.m. and 10:30 p.m. Every night, for ten years. Nine minutes of nervous anticipation. He wasn't sure why a call always came in during those nine minutes, but he held suspicions.

Families were winding down after a long day, overwhelmed by the gloom of nightfall and the repetition of tomorrow. The late hour brought the conclusion of sit-coms and people were left holding their remotes like limp dicks and had nothing to occupy their minds for the next few minutes and decided to dial the Crisis Hotline.

Kids were finally asleep and the 41-year-old mom/dad had a moment to reflect on the absurdity of their career choice and they'd been drinking since dinner but once alcohol's depressive phase settled in, they decided that arguing with/threatening suicide to their spouse was the only way to feel again.

Parents were finally asleep and the 15-year-old daughter/son had a moment to reflect on the overwhelming pressure of teenage social life and the nightly anti-anxiety pills had yet to settle in and numbness from the anti-depression pills meant that drawing a razor across their fingertips was the only way to feel again.

Aaron's anticipation during those particular nine minutes of inevitable calls induced within him a crushing anxiety for exactly 540 seconds, not long in the course of a day's eighty-six thousand seconds, but life-changing or rather life-ending if he decided NOT to answer. Every night at exactly 10:30 p.m. even when off-shift, Aaron suffered from heart palpitations, mild angina, dry-mouth syndrome, drowsiness coupled with dizziness, and tinnitus which simulated the ringing of a phone. He also experienced lateral epicondylitis of the elbow not from playing tennis but rather from years of cradling an oversize land-line handset, intermittent symptoms of irritable bowel syndrome from clenching his gut in fear, as well as hives, fever, nausea, retching and contagious suicidal ideation. The symptoms were magically alleviated as 10:31 p.m. passed and Aaron regained the illusion of composure, only twitching with PTSD when someone behind him in line at Gypsy Java had the same classic ring-tone as the Crisis Center's land-line.

In addition to this daily regularity, Aaron also picked up on trends regarding specific dates on the calendar, like holidays and astronomical events and weather-related occurrences, all effecting the collective unconscious of the general population. On average, 105 Americans kill themselves every day. Yet, some holidays are more popular than others.

The season between Thanksgiving and Christmas was always a rough stretch but not for the assumed reason of loneliness. Aaron learned that clinically-depressed persons, as well as those with concealed depression, struggled through the holiday season with forced smiles because no one wants to be the grim-faced downer unwrapping presents on Christmas morning. Their Reason to Live was family. The same family that made unSeasonable demands over the holidays, leveling guilt-ridden expectations from an eager mom and a grumpy dad and deaf grandparents and a gay uncle with cigarette breath and a sweaty aunt with wine perfume and cousins driving in from Toledo with noisy kids.

Aaron never had much experience taking calls on Thanksgiving since he and Zoë were at his grandmother Eve's house, before she had moved into the Poinsettia Nursing Home. He would have been useless on the phone by the early afternoon, having succumbed to a food-induced, Turkey Day coma. However, on Christmas Day he took plenty of calls but not from the Hotline. He reserved Christmas Day for friends.

Christmas makes a Scrooge out of every social worker.

Aaron hated Christmas.

Caller, a dear friend of Aaron's from college, after about eighteen minutes on the phone: "Thanks for talking me down. Gawd, my mom drives me crazy with her constant worrying and my dad's always mean to her. I was seriously about to start slicing my wrist with a butter knife. Ha! Flew back home to be with my parents and since they've gotten divorced, it's really hard to be around them."

Aaron, invested in the call because she's a friend: "Family triggers us like a food allergy. When we go home, we break out in hives, reverting to little kids again, complaining about life, seeking their approval...wait, I'm sorry but can I put you on hold for a sec? I've got another call coming in. Love ya, thanks."

Caller, even more dear friend from high school that Aaron had slept with, which turned out to be awkward because one of her fetishes included hand jobs lubed with blood from her sliced wrist, but they'd remained friends over the years. After about twelve minutes on the phone: "Sorry for crying, I'm stuck in the bathroom at my aunt's house. Remember my -ex, Jimmy?"

Aaron, putting her on speaker while he wiped down the bathroom sink: "You mean your cousin?"

High school friend Caller: "Yeah, don't remind me. Well, he showed up with his two kids and that hairdresser wife, what a slut. Well, they're so stinkin perfect, makes me sick!"

Aaron, flossing his teeth in the mirror: "Saw the pics on Facebook. He looks like a plastic version of Gary Cooper and her hair is Fifties bee-hive without the buzz. Listen honey, you gotta stop obsessing about them…wait, I'm sorry but can I put you on hold for a sec? I've got another call coming in. Love ya, thanks."

Caller, a dear, dear friend from middle school that Aaron had dated on and off over the years and their physical closeness had been cemented by emotionally exposing their darkest fears in the long hours of the night, either that or the sex was really, really good: "I'm sorry to call on Christmas but I'm kinda freakin out here, you got a moment?"

Aaron, trimming his toenails, placing each piece into the wastebasket: "For you, anytime."

Middle school friend Caller: "I know, that's what I love about you."

"Because I cheer you up?"

"No, you actually pick up your phone." After nine minutes of a single-breathed, monologue about her -ex who recently dumped her, she said, "And that's why I'm so over men who can't communicate."

"I hear ya. He's such an asshole, dumping you on Christmas Eve, I mean, who does that? Seriously. He should have at least had the decency to wait until after the first of the year. Like a New Year's resolution."

"Right, like this year I'm gonna stop acting so crazy."

"Oh, you're not that crazy," Aaron said. "I've seen worse."

"Yeah, where?"

"In the mirror. Can you hold on for a sec, gotta finish up somethin. Love ya, thanks."

Aaron clicked back over, quickly Validated his college friend and sent her off with an encouraging word about dealing with family on her own terms. Then he Normalized his high school friend by reassuring her that men still found her attractive and that sooner or later, she'd find a good man. Although he hated stating she could only find purpose in a man, he figured that's what she wanted to hear. Then back to middle school friend with solid advice on how not to pick up men outside of a bar at 2 a.m. on a Tuesday who appear to be bearded hipsters but that actually turn out to be homeless. He was finishing up with her emotional support when another call came in.

"Sorry, but can I put you on hold for a sec? I've got another call coming in. Love ya, thanks."

Caller, a friend from grade school who had dated most of his friends and over the years Aaron had always secretly loved but never worked up the courage to even kiss and treated her more like a sister, after seven minutes: "I'm so alone. Ever since Jerry left, this aloneness consumes me. Every day. I feel empty, not sure what to do now. I'm scared."

Aaron, looking in the mirror at a week's worth of scruff on his face: "But look at your life. Look at the success you've created on your own. The painting you sold last year. And you're raising a kid by yourself, I know what that's like, and it's amazing! You need to acknowledge your successes. Own it, right? You did that, no one else. And the good friendships you've created, friends like me that you can always rely on... wait, I'm sorry but can I put you on hold for a sec? I've got another call coming in. Love ya, thanks."

Caller, a friend he met years ago when she was working as a cocktail waitress/stripper and had confessed many of her woes to him while offering a free lap dance and he had no intention of ever sleeping with her not because the thought had not crossed his mind but he sensed that she dated far above his economic station in life, someone like a sucrose-savior or glucose-guardian or splenda-papa or sugar-daddy, although Aaron secretly hoped maybe someday she'd drink too much and ask him over to console her in person: "Hi, friend. Got a minute? It's been a while."

Aaron: "Of course, let me finish up with another call."

Aaron clicked back to grade school friend, made a few jokes about her -ex Jerry and how she deserved way better and how she's much better off without his alcoholic behavior. This was similar advice he'd given the same Jerry, an old friend of his as well, last week when Jerry called crying about their recent break-up. Aaron often provided this type of schizoid-friend-support, helping out one friend while simultaneously emotionally validating their ex-partner.

Aaron, rubbing the small bald spot atop his head, slightly confused as to which friend he was currently speaking with, but figured the advice was solid for any of his Christmas Callers: "I know you're feeling alone right now, but you gotta stop turning to men as a way to find happiness."

Grade School: "I know, I should only search for happiness within myself. Sounds like some after-school-special BS. But it's easier to steal happiness from someone else."

Before hanging up, Aaron tried to convince her that stealing momentary joy would only deplete her friends and leave her wanting more. Aaron figured he'd use that advice on the next call because the women he chatted with unknowingly helped the next woman in line. He was like an old-fashioned telephone operator connecting those long cords from one broken heart to the next. They were helping each other, he was merely the conduit. A conduit of pain.

Dancing Waitress Caller: "Hey, how are you?"

Aaron instantly heard the weight in her voice. Slow and methodical, as if the effort of speaking was like moving a boulder with a toothpick. Aaron felt exhausted from the rapid arrival of calls but his ears pricked up at her tone. He paused and decided to answer her query with humor as a way of explaining his own depression.

"How am I?" Aaron repeated, hating the question. "I'm always down so I can catch my friends when they fall."

"Well, I'm falling. My parents are dead. About two hours ago. Car crash."

Suddenly, none of the other calls mattered. Asshole boyfriends, abusive husbands, drunken misconduct at an uncomfortable Christmas dinner with ex's and unsupportive parents. They'd been complaining about family whereas Dancing Waitress had none. Aaron knew she'd never be the same, that Christmas for her would be a terrible and dark hole in her calendar, stalking her for months. They chatted for an hour, but she lingered in a state of shock, and Aaron did most of the talking, trying to coax more than monosyllabic answers from her.

In the end, he gave her the number of a grief counselor and recommended a shrink who could prescribe heavy sedatives and mood stabilizers for the next few months.

In the end, she didn't make it very far without her parents. In April, she hung herself on the canvas loop of her mother's apron, dangling from the garage rafter with the fumes of her dad's truck filling the space.

In the end, she wanted to make sure.

Statistically speaking, Christmas and New Year's Eve were not the high points of suicide. Spring was the worst. Nature waking up, flowers blooming, bunnies humping, and everyone falling in love, filled with the vibrancy of energetic life. Everyone except the chronically depressed.

The night before Christmas in Year Two at the Suicide Prevention & Crisis Hotline Center, Aaron received a desperate call which he couldn't shake off until Easter.

Caller, silent:

Aaron, pissed off that Boss Lady had thrown him a shift when his colleague Debz hadn't shown up for work at the last minute: "Hello, is anyone there?"

Caller, female, barely audible: "Not for much longer."

Aaron asked the regular questions. "Are you safe?"

"For now."

"Do you have a plan?"

"Sure," she joked, "but it's not a good one."

"Where are you?"

"Standing on a bridge."

"Are you thinking about jumping?"

She laughed. "Who doesn't?"

Woman on the Bridge responded clearly each time. She certainly didn't fit the profile. She wasn't sobbing, screaming, drunk, stoned, acting out or burdened with sadness. She only wanted to hear his voice, common enough during the holidays for lonely people. Aaron wasn't worried about her because it didn't seem like a Real Call.

That's what Aaron labeled certain calls, perhaps one out of ten. Real Calls. Over the first two years of his ten-year stint, Aaron had taken maybe a thousand calls and most were not the real deal. They were from a third party: an anxious friend of a depressed teenager who had read troublesome remarks on Facebook like *gunna do some cuttin 2nite*; or, a nineteen-year-old lead-guitarist in a punk band receiving late-night suicidal texts from his broken-hearted ex-; or, a worried mother; or, the fed-up wife; or, an overly-concerned and over-educated school counselor; or, even a fellow social worker with a deranged client. These people merely wanted references because they didn't know what to do. Someone had reached out to them, uttered the words, "I want to kill myself" thereby utterly freaking out this third-party member who in turn reached for the nearest phone to dial 1-800-SUICIDE. At this point, Aaron's job was to deal with the caring person in panic-mode, not the suicidal person.

Aaron wasn't sure if the Woman on the Bridge was seriously contemplating suicide. Her voice indicated she might be in her early 40s, the most dangerous age group. However, she could have been older, but Aaron found her age difficult to discern because her voice was muffled. Nothing else about her demeanor indicated a Real Call.

A Real Call was a call that made Aaron's heart quicken and caused him to listen for hints in the background noises. He received plenty of calls from people talking about suicide and Aaron had quickly figured out there was no such thing as suicidal people, only people who pass through suicidal times.

Woman on the Bridge seemed fine. She laughed at her own jokes and answered his questions bluntly.

"Why'd you call us tonight?" Aaron asked. He used the plural pronoun *us* as opposed to *me* because he always wanted the Caller to feel as though everyone at the crisis center was personally involved.

"Just tired, I guess."

"Tired from what?"

"Living," she said.

Aaron pushed a bit. "You got anybody in your life? Anybody that cares about you? Give me something to work with. Got any family?"

"Some."

"Friends?"

"A few.

"Neighbors?"

"None that don't annoy me," she said evenly. "You're a nice boy, really, but I don't think you understand. I'm not calling for any new ideas. I've been through this before and nothing works. For years I've been dealing with this."

"This what?"

"Oh, you know," she said plainly. "I hear it in your voice, too."

She proceeded to list a litany of failed therapy sessions, mismanaged meds and destroyed relationships. It only took a few minutes for the re-cap, a well-practiced speech that she'd obviously given many times. The story sounded oddly familiar.

Aaron let her finish and then said, "Maybe since you've been through it all, you could help others. Might give you a reason to go on, right?"

She laughed again. "Good one, but how can I help others if I can't even help myself?"

"Thinking about others is sometimes the ONLY way to help yourself," Aaron tried. "Since it sounds like you've known a few, tell me what therapist isn't a beautiful disaster." She chuckled dryly as Aaron continued. "Maybe nothing I say is going to help. Like you said, you've tried everything and nothing works. What now?"

The Woman on the Bridge paused before saying, "I just called to say goodbye."

Click.

The sudden conclusion was always the hardest part for Aaron. Unless emergency services were contacted, he never knew what happened after the Caller put their phone away, their voice fading into memory. But that's the thing about painful memories, they don't fade away. Especially when two days later, Aaron read in the newspaper about a female body found in the river a few hundred yards downstream from the 4th Street Bridge.

Easter arrived and her words, *I hear it in your voice, too,* continued to haunt him, lingering like a malignant ghost. He tried to figure out if WomB, the Woman on the Bridge, had been a friend or a foe. Friend or Foe, that's how Aaron segregated a Caller's voice. He could tell immediately when the Caller was a Friend seeking advice on behalf of someone else, their voice cheery, light, seeking knowledge and filled with optimism. A friend of hope.

The other type of voice was the Foe. The first word uttered relayed a Caller's emotional nuance. Not the particular word used, instead the hesitation, dryness, and lethargy of their lips and tongue. The foe of hope, the foe of happiness, the foe of life. Typically, they didn't use their real name and a pause initiated the conversation because shame is a powerful inhibitor.

To the Foe, Aaron had lengthy conversations about childhood trauma and self-destructive behavior, and how to seek professional help and medication. However, to the Friend, Aaron offered concise consolation. He would tell them, "You have to understand that eventually your friend may kill themselves and there is nothing you can do about it."

The Callers who confused Aaron were the ones residing between Friend and Foe. The actors, the one's pretending to call for a Friend but in reality, were the Foe. *I hear it in your voice, too.* Woman on the Bridge's words echoed in the darkness every night after he turned off the lights, nagging him until Easter.

Easter. Aaron hated Easter, not for religious reasons, but instead because call volume steadily increased. April traditionally offers the annual height of self-induced deaths and for every one degree the thermometer rises, the suicide rate also increases precisely by one percent. Also, T.S. Eliot wrote after being married to a manic depressive:

> *April is cruelest month, breeding*
> *Lilacs out of the dead land, mixing*
> *Memory and desire, stirring*
> *Dull roots with spring rain.*
> *Winter kept us warm, covering*
> *Earth in forgetful snow, feeding*
> *A little life with dried tubers.*

April was the worst month for suicide, as Aaron told a woman who called on Denim Day, a day in April to globally raise awareness of sexual assault.

Caller, middle-aged female, angry affect: "I was raped in the park yesterday."

"I'm sorry."

"Don't. That's not why I'm upset."

"Then tell me what happened."

"I passed out under a tree and this guy found me and jerked off into my mouth."

"That's horrible. Sounds like that swimmer from Stanford, Brock something."

"Yeah, exactly. I remember waking up and puking all over him. He tried to run but the cops found him a few blocks away with vomit on his shirt."

"They arrested him?"

"Right, but then they let him go a few hours later."

Aaron, as Listener, troubled affect: "I don't understand."

"Turns out they found a handful of pills in my puke."

"Wait, you were trying to kill yourself?"

"All I wanted to do was die in the park, but I couldn't even do that without getting sexually assaulted."

"And you're upset because they let the bastard go since he saved your life?"

"Exactly! Now I'm afraid to make another attempt because I might get raped again."

Aaron learned an important lesson that day in April. He realized that suicide prevention came in many forms and sometimes fear and anger could be quite effective.

April also had the highest numbers of suicide, as Aaron told another Caller one fine Monday afternoon after Easter, because Jesus killed himself in April and everybody wants to do WJD.

Caller, middle-aged male priest worrying about a member of his congregation: "I'm sorry, what did you say?"

Aaron, having recently moderated a training seminar for Catholic clergy and disgusted by their oppressive views of homosexuality which he felt was directly responsible for the fact that gays kill themselves SEVEN times more often than straight folks, repeated himself to the priest: "You heard me. You shouldn't be asking What Would Jesus Do but rather thinking about WJD, What Jesus Did, and the answer is commit suicide. Why'd you call?"

"Blasphemy! Let me talk to your manager."

"She'd tell you the same thing. She's an atheist," which wasn't true. As far as Aaron knew, Boss Lady had become a social worker in the early 80s due to her Evangelical convictions. He knew that Boss Lady would be reviewing the recorded calls in the morning and wanted to make her cringe in retaliation for forcing him to work the Clergy Convention.

The priest protested. "Our Savior did not kill himself, he died for our sins. Besides, the Jews killed him."

Aaron retaliated by mentioning a Jewish holiday to further irritate the upset clergyman, since Catholics both loathe and adore the Old Testament. "Speaking of Jews, did you know that when they call the hotline around Yom Kippur, the Day of Atonement, they assume the only way to atone for their sins is to kill themselves? Not from the offense but rather from the ensuing shame."

"But suicide is a sin!" the priest exclaimed. "Goes against the Sixth Commandment."

"Call it six point five," Aaron countered, "thou shall not kill yourself. Reminds me of this Psych professor from Brooklyn who told me that Jews are inhibited from taking their own lives because of their religion and that Jews are far too interested in life, creativity and reproduction which prevents suicide."

"Seems reasonable," the priest said, calming down. "Faith often does sustain us."

"But it's not enough," Aaron said. "I had a cousin who hung himself, nice Jewish boy. My father's aunt says I look just like him. And an uncle on my dad's side was a lawyer accused of embezzlement. He was so ashamed that he strangled himself in jail by tying the pants leg around his neck. And my father's older brother was a doctor, shot himself in the head when he broke his hands and couldn't operate anymore. We found him in the study, kids never got over it. And my father's cousin drowned himself in the neighborhood pool."

"You mean to tell me," the priest asked, "that most of the men in your family have killed themselves?"

"That's right."

"I'm sorry for your…"

"Stop. I don't need your sympathy. They've helped."

"How's that?"

"Men have taught me not to follow their example."

"That's bleak," the priest said. "Perhaps if you prayed for guidance. I'm sure your family has provided some fine examples on how to live. What about your grandparents?"

"Well, my great-grandfather came over from Russia in 1904. I always thought he was a rabbi, but according to my aunt Tilda," Aaron said, continuing in a nasally, Upper East Side voice, "*he was a carpenter*, but my cousin Rachel says *he was a street-sweeper*, but Bubbe says *oh, no, he was a drunken bum who drank himself to death*." Despite anecdotal evidence from the Old Country, Aaron knew that once Jews immigrated, their suicide rates matched other Anglo-Americans. Assimilation was complete, Jews had become gentiles.

"Nice story, but I don't…"

"Listen," Aaron said, interrupting the priest, "half my family are Jews, and I've learned that the Brooklyn professor was wrong. Life and creativity are not enough to stop a suicide."

"You also mentioned reproduction. Does not having a child give one a sense of purpose?"

Apparently not, Aaron thought, dwelling on the men in his family who killed themselves in front of their kids. The memory of their suicides bothered him deeply and Aaron lashed out at the priest. "Maybe, but as for the screwing part, that's how Jews have always proselytized. No better way to convert someone than to fúck their brains out!"

The line disconnected, Aaron's reward for vulgarity. The anxiety of remembering his past caused Aaron to create a list as he tended to do when upset. "Don't get pissed, make a list," the best rhyming advice his ninth therapist had given him. For Aaron, this meant compiling history into concise data. Instead of dwelling on the pain of his dead family members, Aaron thought about Masada.

Aaron would have recounted the well-known story of Masada had the priest stayed on the line. A gruesome children's tale that Aaron had never really believed, on a professional level. To avoid enslavement by the Romans, 960 Sicarii Jews slit each others' throats in 73 A.D. Each man murdered his wife and children, then the men drew straws and killed each other until the last man killed himself. Given the Judaic history of violence, Aaron figured they would have gone down fighting. Wasn't every Jewish holiday, Aaron thought, really about the Jews either getting their asses handed to them or kicking the crap out of some other neighboring tribe? Eventually, the Sicarii became martyrs celebrated at synagogues worldwide in youth stage plays because the re-enactment of ritualistic mass suicide is always funnier when performed by kids.

Aaron couldn't imagine how fathers were able to murder their own children and was convinced they drank poisoned wine because over the years, Aaron had learned that drinking and suicide go hand-in-glove like vermouth and gin, like whiskey and puking, like wine coolers and unprotected teen sex. Aaron had read in a journal, either JAMA or Maxim, both about as reputable when it came to publishing accurate data, that one-third of suicide victims are intoxicated. Aaron didn't know the truth of this, but calls certainly increased around holidays when people turned to alcohol in order to cope with family.

Religious holidays offered many opportunities for Aaron to help others, but weather patterns and astronomy also created suicidal rhythms. Any time there was a snow storm brewing or a tropical storm warming or the Sirocco winds blew hot off the desert, Aaron knew he might get more calls than usual. But full moons were the worst. Any trauma surgeon or triage nurse knows that emergency rooms are stocked when the moon shines bright. Cops and firefighters see jails fill up and warehouses burn down. The last full moon, Aaron picked up five calls within two hours from different women—a dumped girlfriend, a jilted fiancée, a distraught divorcee, a drunken wife, and a single mom with three kids.

The single mom had been a tough call, Aaron remembered. He'd blocked it out, had gone directly to bed after his shift ended and he didn't think about it until around lunchtime the next day when he tripped over the land-line phone cord at work.

The cord had triggered his memory. The single mom had called the hotline after failing to strangle herself with an extension cord but climbed off the chair when her throat started to hurt. Or maybe, Aaron thought, the idea of her three kids downstairs had stopped her. Aaron had tried to get a response from her, but she could only whisper by the time she called because her larynx had swollen and temporarily damaged her vocal cords. She had handed the phone to her eight-year-old son.

Caller, boy softly crying: "My momma's hurt. Her neck's really red. She gonna be OK?"

Aaron, stuttering: "Um, I guess. Sure, she'll be fine," kicking himself for making false promises. And he hated to say IT'LL BE OK[3] because often life wasn't. "Listen kid, I'm going to call 911. Stay on the phone, don't hang up," Aaron said reaching for his cell phone.

He managed two calls at once, speaking to Dispatch on his cell while consoling the kid on the land-line. The verbal juggling went smoothly until the kid's mom passed out.

"She's turning blue! Momma's blue!" the boy screamed which agitated his younger sister and brother who started bawling, too. Aaron told the kid to unlock the front door so the paramedics could come inside.

"What's your address, kid?"

"I don't know," the kid sobbed. "We just moved here last week,"

"Alright, go back outside and read me the number on your house."

He heard the kid run down the hall. "Twelve."

"Twelve?"

"Yep, we're in an apartment."

Crap, Aaron thought. In the old days, this job was a lot easier prior to cell phones. When someone called the Hotline, their land-line phone brought up a physical address. Nowadays, even the cops couldn't determine the origin of a call with the locator turned off.

"Tell me the name of your apartment building."

"I don't know," the kid whimpered. "My mom's not movin anymore."

Aaron panicked. He'd forgotten how much he hated Real Calls. "Go bang on your neighbor's door. Quick, kid, run!"

The TV buzzed in the background as the kid's younger sibling screamed in confusion. Aaron heard the slam of a screen door and pounding on a nearby door.

The kid came back on. "Nobody's home! Why won't they answer?"

"Try another one. Hurry up!"

The kid banged on eight doors without success. Maybe since the time hovered at 10:27 p.m. and when the neighbors looked out the peep hole in their front door, no face appeared since the kid was too short. Or maybe in that kind of neighborhood people didn't answer their door at night.

"Alright kid, go find the Super."

"The what?"

"The superintendent. The manager."

"He's in another building."

Aaron lost his cool, "Damn it, kid, you gotta try somethin, your momma's dyin right now! I don't know, run around outside and scream your head off until someone tells you to shut the hell up. Then you can ask them the name of your apartment!"

The kid started crying again and Aaron tried to calm him down while thinking of another plan. Then the kid did what kids tend to do. He put the phone down and walked away.

Aaron could only hear the static of the television. He hung up and frantically hit re-dial but got a busy signal. He repeated his efforts and on the tenth undertaking, the call finally went through and the kid picked up. Cool as ice cream on a summer day.

"Hey, momma's fine. Here, she wants to talk to you."

The woman took the phone and berated Aaron in a raspy voice. She scolded him for scaring her son and having him run around the building late at night. "He coulda been kidnapped!"

"But I thought you were dead!"

"Aw, shiiiit, that weren't nuthin, just passed out is all. I be tryin to hang myself every full moon. Kids outta know by now their momma's stone crazy." And then she did what crazy moms tend to do. She said she had to make a chicken casserole and hung up.

Back at work the next day, Aaron jotted brief notes into the computer and reminded himself to call in sick on the next full moon.

In the middle of Year Seven, on one particular personal holiday, Aaron responded a little differently and distracted a female Caller by interrupting her despair. He accomplished this diversionary tactic with a re-focusing trick to spontaneously trigger a past, joyful memory within the Caller-in-Crisis. Aaron's professional curiosity rather than a desire to provide effective counseling was the inspiration for this random, therapeutic experimentation.

Caller, female, mid-forties, depressed affect: "Hello, is anyone there?"

Listener aka Aaron offering one of his pseudonyms: "Yes, I'm the crisis worker on call this evening, my name is Federico."[4]

Caller, offering the typical background of child abuse and parental neglect known as The Story: "…"

Listener aka Federico-Roberto-Aron: "Your step-dad did what to you? And your mom watched?"

Female Caller Over Forty: "…"

Federico: "Hold on, before you go any further, today is my birthday."

Female Caller Over Forty: "…"

Roberto: "No, I'm not trying to distract you from your problems. I'm not trying to draw the focus onto me."

Female Caller Over Forty: "…"

A-A-ron: "This call is about you, I know that. I'm not trying to silence you, this isn't about female disempowerment. I'm trying to tell you today is my birthday. And you know what? At the end of this call, I want *you* to give *me* a present. I bet you'll give me a gift without even knowing it. I'm only asking for a simple birthday gift."

Female Caller Over Forty: "…"

Listener: "No, I'm not going to tell you what I want. It has to be a surprise, right? Alright, now what were you saying about your mom and step-dad?"

Female Caller Over Forty: "…"

Listener, after twenty-eight minutes: "Nah, don't be ashamed that you were crying a few minutes ago. Better now? Glad you reached out, call us anytime you're feeling overwhelmed, OK? Next time, don't wait so long. We're always here for you."

Female Caller Over Forty: "Thank you. Thank you for the work you do."

Aaron: "Aaaah, and there's the birthday gift I was waitin for. G'nite."

Aaron enjoyed calls that ended well. Selfish, he realized, but the fleeting joy kept him going after a decade. Early in his career, Aaron discovered that most holidays were routine. He could count on domestic disputes around Thanksgiving and Christmas. Yom Kippur triggered regret. Ramadan brought hunger-induced despair cured by hot tea with a touch of sugar. The one holiday that defied prediction was July 4th. He never knew what to expect on the Fourth and calls picked up by Aaron swayed towards the bizarre.

Aaron, a little sad he has to work on a holiday when everyone else is getting drunk and forgetting about the importance of France's role in the American Revolution: "So, you've got a plan to kill yourself?"

Caller: "Hypothetically, if I stuck a firecracker up my ass, like a big one…"

"Your big ass?"

"No, a big firecracker, like an M-80."

"Well, it might go out unless it's water-proof."

"Hey, I'm being serious, man. Are you making fun of me?"

"Well, you said hypothetically. I'm trying to think of other possible scenarios to help you kill yourself. Assisted suicide is legal now. Are you imagining those big, illegal fireworks from Wyoming?"

"Exactly, like Shattered Silence with red and white rings or the one called Titanium Cracker."

"Isn't that a sparkler for kids?" Aaron asked.

"Hey man, seriously, you gotta help me out. I'm hurtin here."

"Not as bad as you will be…"

"I'm only askin if that's one way to go. I wanna go out in a blaze of glory!"

"Then I wouldn't recommend using a sparkler."

*

August was absent of holidays in regards to federally-funded agencies like the Crisis Hotline, and not until mid-October did a holiday occur that brought a confluence of history and shame. Aaron didn't have an opinion regarding Columbus Day although in Year Five he took a call from a guilt-plagued Caucasian male, a botanist by trade and halfway through life's journey, who was convinced his ancestors were responsible for the smallpox epidemic that eradicated 95% of the indigenous population, an estimated 20 million Native Americans. The Caller-Botanist was directly related to Jeffery Amherst,[5] Lord Commander of the British Army during the French and Indian War. This descendent of Lord Amherst had done extensive research against which Aaron could not logically refute.

Caller, male, early fifties, proud of his British linage but horrified by the implications: "My family killed twenty million people! How am I supposed to deal with that?!"

Aaron, tired after taking two calls in a row from panicked teenage boys about their pregnant girlfriends, nonchalant affect: "Wow. That's worse than Stalin."

"You're not helping. Are you even trained for this job? I need professional advice."

"We're not supposed to give advice, we only listen."

The botanist became angry and lashed out at Aaron, a normal reaction from male callers. "Listen? That's it? I need help. This is a Help Line, isn't it? What the hell do they pay you people for?!"

"A few of us are paid less than minimum wage, the rest are volunteers."

"Fùck you!"

After several years of working the Hotline, Aaron had come to realize one important fact. There existed a clear difference, one might say an opposing mode of catharsis, between men and women when in Crisis. Capital C-crisis because even if that little deal in the 60s over missiles is capitalized, as in the Cuban Missile Crisis, then certainly the

Cause of ensuing panic in a life-threatening dilemma

Effects a suicidal finger towards a pistol's trigger.

A crisis vented over the hotline was as dangerous as Khrushchev's finger hovering over the Red Button. To the emotionally disenfranchised, a personal crisis IS the end of the world.

For Aaron, the difference between a woman and man came down to tears. He had found that when a woman calls the hotline, the tears are right up front. She is often sobbing and can barely breathe, making her speech either inaudible or overly loquacious, the words rushing out between gasps before she forgets. When she's quiet with long dramatic pauses, the tears are close, dripping off every word, interrupting her flow. Sobs.

Sobs was how Aaron designated them on his yellow, legal pad when the Caller didn't give a name. Sobs 1, Sobs 2, Sobs 3. In his Fourth Year on Columbus Day, he reached a record of Sobs 12. Usually, Sobs and her fellow cohorts dry up after about eight minutes, her pitch lessening—less alto, more bass. Her tone becomes level as the panic washes away, lifting her head with confidence by raising her mouth up to the phone's receiver. The tears slow to a trickle, the sobbing ceases. After being Validated & Normalized, the woman nods along in agreement, and after twenty minutes is up, both Caller & Listener have a Plan to move forward. The present is less gloomy than the past, the future a bright sun on the horizon, and she offers a gracious parting at the conclusion of the call.

"Thank you, thanks for listening."

Despite his meager pay, Aaron felt this response was his real reward and Completely Worth It. Aaron assigned a pleasant Navajo name for these women in honor of Columbus Day/Indigenous People's Day—*Sobs No More*.

As for the guy, he is strong and sturdy in the beginning.

"Let me explain. I'm not suicidal."

Men always say that.

"I can handle this, I'm only calling to talk." There's sadness lurking in the depth of his voice, and he frequently uses the word *overwhelmed*. For Aaron, the method of extracting information is always an aggravating struggle, draaaagging the memories out of the male Caller.

Slowly, as the story emerges, his voice begins to waver.

"Hey, other people have it worse," he says. "I'm okay."

Men always say that, too.

When Aaron has patience and lets them do the talking, difficult because of the masculine predilection for silence, the cracks appear.

The man's speech slows with even longer pauses. "It's too much," he says, "I've lost too much. How can I go on?"

His voice rises from bass to tenor, then the crack of thunder with a flood of tears.

A guy sobbing proved to be harder for Aaron than dealing with any of the Sobs 1 through Sobs 12. Maybe because he'd become used to a woman's tears. He blamed modern media. He couldn't even think of a movie/television series/RoCo/sit-com where a woman doesn't emote by crying. The same way a white, male, hetro, slightly-balding-with-convincing-hair-plugs movie star proves himself in an action flick by beating up half a dozen thugs[6] in the first two minutes while the intro credits roll. Aaron knew this overly-used device in cinema was called Validation of Manhood.

Inevitably, the man on the other end of the phone realizes that he is NOT okay as he explains the manner in which he lost his wife (*divorce*), lost his two kids (*custody battle*), lost his house (*bankruptcy*), lost his car (*repo*), lost his TV (*power surge*), even lost his leg in Iraq (*IED*). Same explosive device that took out his friend from Gary, Indiana, who had been wearing a flak vest but the sub-standard, Army-issued equipment didn't stop 2200 rounds of double ought buckshot and a few dozen rusty nails from ripping out his friend's intestines. The man hung up while muttering, "Thank You," words that made it all worthwhile for Aaron.

Navajo name for these guys—*Sobs Alone*.

The botanist/descendant of Lord Amherst was not sobbing, instead he screamed into the phone. "I said fùck you! Are you listening now?"

Aaron had heard this sentiment many times. He didn't take it personally, he knew the man needed to exhaust his anger. Aaron decided to help by shaking the botanist even more.

"Sooner or later, you'll have to come to terms with your past. I'm not talking about what some British General did with smelly blankets. You don't have to believe it. Ignore the past, pretend it never happened. Like you're ignoring the real reason you called."

"The real reason?"

"Yes. What did you do?"

"I didn't do anything!" The man launched into a new verbal assault of curses followed by accusations of unprofessionalism followed by threats of vandalism and ending with a childish tantrum by blaming Crooked Hilary for his marital woes. After four minutes, Aaron discovered the botanist had smacked his wife earlier in the day and smothered his guilty feelings of domestic violence by projecting them onto ancestral genocide.

As Aaron pushed for details, the man blubbered about how sorry he felt and how he'd never do it again. Aaron, greatly disappointed the guy didn't make it harder to reveal the truth, wrapped up the call by telling him to take anger management classes, hire a marriage counselor, buy his wife some flowers (which Aaron thought would have been obvious since the man worked as a botanist), and hope she didn't divorce him. In between tiny whimpering breaths, Amherst's descendant tried to utter gratitude but only managed a subdued, "Th...tha...thanks," before hanging up on Aaron.

Sobs alone indeed.

Episode 2.5

ABCs of Suicide

Wednesday, the day after the shooting at the restaurant, and Aaron loathes the mid-week dead day with long hours of sitting by a stationary phone on the early afternoon shift, nobody ever calling because they're either not drunk enough or broke enough or sad enough, only two days until the weekend which instills false hope such as hooking up with someone at the bar on Friday night or trying to score a job by the end of the week, whereas Monday ushers in the depressing hang-over of reality, lyrics explored by New Order in *Blue Monday*, relished by teenage girls after getting dumped by their boyfriends, wholly unlike the desperate deadly calls of a full moon on a frantic Friday at 3 a.m. after the clubs close when girls are crushing boy's hearts by saying *No!*, for without these calls of rejection Aaron is bored, his ass corpse-stiff from the hard plastic orange chairs, so he decides to outline the ABCs of Suicide, resurrecting a few famous **historical persons** who killed themselves and linking them with the word **LIKE** to a **fictional suicidal character**, and Aaron commences the deluge with "A," which conjures the image of Prince Alfred of Edinburgh who assassinated himself in 1899 after abdicating the royal throne **LIKE** Duke Leto Atreides of *Dune* who died by biting a poison gas capsule; which makes Aaron think of "B" is for Eva Braun who in 1945 bowed out by biting a cyanide poison capsule **LIKE** Madame Bovary with arsenic after she was unable to pay her bills; leading to "C" but not Kurt Cobain in '94 singing "Come as You Are" nor Cleopatra by cobra in 30BC but,

ring ring . . . ring ring

and Aaron's flow is distracted as he checks the incoming number to reveal a solicitation call and takes the call anyway, the All-American Insurance agent getting a real shock when Aaron begins nonchalantly, "So, why you wanna kill yourself today?" and the man promptly hanging up on Aaron; allowing him to get back to "C" with Cato the Younger, the Roman councilman, who cleaved himself with a curved cutlass in 46BC, a courageous yet cunning coward **LIKE** Juliet Capulet cracked her cardiac with a coltello upon catching sight of Romeo's cadaverous poison-stained lips; and moving onto "D" with Dana Point

Jane Doe in 1987, and Aaron remembers the article in the newspaper, an unidentified young woman found below Dana Point, California, after jumping off a cliff **LIKE** Thelma Dickinson, the demur Thelma from *Thelma & Louise*, two dangerous dames who drove off the Grand Canyon cliff to escape arrest; proceeding to "E" is for Peg Entwistle, an actress who in 1932 leapt to her death from the Hollywood sign **LIKE** Éponine in Victor Hugo's *Les Misérables*, who sacrifices herself by taking a musket ball on page 1193 in the copy on Aaron's nightstand; and at this point Aaron turns the page on the yellow legal pad that he's writing on, the same pad he uses to take notes on each Caller before inputting them into the computer because there is nothing a Caller hates more than to hear a Listener tapping away at a keyboard while they, the Caller, is Emoting and Venting and Dying on the other side of the phone line; and,

ring ring . . . ring ring

ignored by Aaron, saying out loud to his friend Debz on the other side of the cubicle at the Suicide Prevention & Crisis Hotline Center, "Stop bothering me, I'm on a roll. They're gonna die anyway, so why I gotta listen?" hence onto "F" with René Favaloro, the Argentinian cardiac surgeon known for his coronary bypass surgical finesse whose self-inflicted gunshot to the heart causes Aaron to howl at the heart-felt hyperbole **LIKE** Felix the Cat who drank gasoline after getting his feline heart broken; and the graphic of a gas can ushering in "G" and Aaron thinks of none other than Spalding Gray, the monologist who in 2004 jumped off the Staten Island Ferry gurgling into the grey water for Gray is gone **LIKE** Godric from *True Blood* when he 'meets the sun' which to a vampire is fatal, the gothic euphemism for a death gigantically gratifying,

ring ring . . . ring ring

again ignored by Aaron; who instead hones in on "H" with Nicholas Hughes, son of Sylvia Plath and Ted Hughes, who hung himself in 2009 **LIKE** Brooks Hatlen from *The Shawshank Redemption* who heinously hangs himself and "H" also has Robert E. Howard and Hitler, both shooting themselves ten years apart, one penning Conan the Barbarian, the other acting as Adolf the Totalitarian, but H is for Hanging and so Aaron doesn't include them; and "I" is easy since who can forget Isokelkel, the 17th century, semi-mythical, mostly-mystical conqueror of Pohnpei Island in the Carolines, who bled to death after severing his own penis, not a circumcision at the top but rather at the base of his Easter Island, thereby convincing Aaron that "I" stands for the howl this hero hatched after sudden dismemberment, hollering out a hurtful, "Iiiieeeeeeeeeeeee!"

ring ring . . . ring ring . . . ring ring . . . ring ring . . . ring

picking up on the fifth ring, "This is the Suicide Hotline, what's up?" followed by, "Oh, this is not Pet Paradise on 4th Street, I think you have the wrong number," and followed by, "Well, don't get mad at me for dialing the wrong number, you wanna talk bout it?" and ending with, "It's unwise to bottle up your anger because repressed rage inevitably causes depression," followed by the click of a slammed phone as Aaron hangs the receiver on the base instead of swiping left on a cell phone screen, since he is Listening via a landline, leaving Aaron personally satisfied after the sudden hang-up secure in the fact that he has helped another troubled soul; and switching quickly back to the list, he summons "J" for B.S. Johnson, the English poet-novelist who cut his wrists in the 1970s **LIKE** Dayna Jurgens in *The Stand*, also published in the 70s, who bashes her head against a glass window, smashing in through the solid pane up to her neck and thrashing on the jagged glass edges to open her jugular and carotid; and onto "K" for Allyn King (unrelated to the aforementioned novel's author Stephen King), the Broadway actress pressured by directors to stop gaining weight else she'd be fired causing her in 1930 to panic when she gained literally one pound, jumping from a fifth story window **LIKE** Father Damien Karras in *The Exorcist* who by defenestration found his end; a conclusion dissimilar from "L" for Meriwether Lewis who died not long after exploring the entire West with that other guy even though alphabetically it should have be Clark & Lewis, just doesn't have the same ring to it, and history records that his heavy drinking, debts and opium use led Lewis the Leader to shoot himself in 1809 **LIKE** Leonard 'Gomer Pyle' Lawrence in *Full Metal Jacket*, who died by self-inflicted gunshot wound after murdering that bastard, "Only two things come outta Texas, steers and queers and you ain't got no horns, boy!" drill instructor, which Aaron recites every time he meets someone from Texas; and at this point pauses for "M" since he's halfway through the alphabet when,

ring ring . . . ring ring

before Aaron retreats outside for a cigarette although he doesn't smoke anymore, but enjoys standing with Debz and one of the Brendas and rarely Boss Lady for a smoke out on the corner, exactly twenty-five feet from the entrance as dictated by the law's over-sized lettering on official American Cancer Society placards, the social workers huddled as ER nurses after a midnight rush, puffing gaspers to relieve stress, chatting about anything but work, anything else besides the Callers, talking in unison about Trump's most recent sexual assault accusation, or hairstyles, or nails, or that one romantic comedy starring, "that skinny, pale-faced girl with a page-boy haircut," Debz says, "Oh, I can't tell if it's Wynona Ryder or Kierra Knightly or Natalie Portman," and puff-puff they're done, retreating to their cubicled phones; and Aaron's onto "M" with master Yukio Mishima, Japanese belly-slitter extraordinaire, who in 1970 committed samurai seppuku not for political reasons but for love of country and for love's honor **LIKE** Juliet's Latin-lover Romeo Montague, making a double appearance on this list Aaron realizes—she, also like Mishima, dying for love by Italian seppuku, and "M" also manufactures Marilyn Monroe who at 36 years old combined the sedative chloral hydrate, unapproved by the FDA, with Nembutal, the pharmacologically endorsed barbiturate, although she should belong to "B" for Baker but it's too late for Aaron to go back now; and "N" proceeds with Scott Nearing in 1983, the American conservationist who at 100 died by fasting, eating nothing instead of being eaten **LIKE** Robert Neville in the graphic novel version of *I Am Legend* who takes cyanide pills to avoid being eaten by his vampified/zombified captors after discovering that he is the *real* monster because he's the last human on Earth since everyone else is a vampire/zombie, which reminds Aaron to hurry as 4:30 p.m. approaches, leaving him only half an hour until he's off shift and if he doesn't finish this list now, he knows he never will; therefore "O" promotes Otto Standman, the Estonian Prime Minister who died in 1875 proudly as the leader of his people, a leader **LIKE** Okonkwo in *Things Fall Apart* who hangs himself **out of despair**, but really **in despair** and **out of hope** spurring Aaron to take a quick bathroom break; because "P" releases his favorite category for what would "P" be without, mentioned twice now, Sylvia Plath, the bag-of-bones poet who in 1963 gassed herself in the executioner's chamber of the kitchen yet might have survived had Britain switched earlier from noxious coal gas to the mercaptan, rotten egg-smelling natural gas, but nevertheless she suffocated and perished **LIKE** another Calm-on-the-Outside, Raging-on-the-Inside woman with the mutant name of Phoenix-as-the-Dark Phoenix, aka Jean Grey of the Uncanny X-Men, who telekinetically blasts herself with an ancient Kree weapon, instantly disintegrated in front of the ruby-red eyes of her beloved, Cyclops and no, not Wolverine, despite how the Singer films have mislead us to believe in the intensity of their quixotic bond; leading to "Q" but not as in Q from Star Trek's TNG who tried to kill himself, but then again how exactly does an immortal/omniscient being accomplish such a suicidal task, rather "Q" is for Henry Quastler, the Austrian radiologist, who in '63 overdosed on pills when Quastler's wife was dying of TB, laying down beside her holding hands until they wasted away together **LIKE** Quasimodo who found it unbearable to be separated by death from his true love, searching for Esmeralda's body in a pit filled with dead prostitutes to lay down beside her, his bones only crumbling when years later the grave was exhumed and their bodies finally pulled apart, reminding Aaron that "R" is for,

ring ring . . . ring ring

and he's tempted to answer but ignores the call with only fifteen minutes left until the magical 5 p.m.; hence onto "R" for Roy Raymond, founder of V.S., Victoria's Secret, who back in '93 faced the city and jumped off the Golden Gate Bridge similar to 1,600 other people since the Bridge opened up in 1937 which seems a lot to Aaron but he remembers that in 1935 nearly 1,000 Japanese people jumped to their death into the volcano at Mount Mihara, creating a marketing opportunity for tourist hotels with trinket shops in the lobby selling volcano snow-globes and also providing a shaded patio out back to watch people with the crowd offering encouragement by chanting, "Jump!! Jump!!" which is what people do when gathered beneath a jumper on a building's top ledge but how much more epic for tourists to return home with tales of someone leaping into a fiery volcano **LIKE** Ellen Ripley in *Alien 3* falling into a blast furnace wearing an oil-stained, combat version of a V.S. negligée while clutching an alien baby in her soiled arm; summoning the letter "S" which signals Aaron Swartz, the only person to really figure out the ending of *Infinite Jest* by DFW, who was also as a computer wiz and died by hanging in 2013 right before his JSTOR trial **LIKE** Pavel Smerdyakov from *The Brothers Karamazov* who hangs himself after Ivan tells him that in a world without God, "Everything is Permitted!" and Aaron perceives the end approaching as his wrists begin to burn, frantically scrawling on the pad, pen underlining every other word, his shoulders aching; and quickly onto "T," reviving the name of Hunter S. Thompson, the gonzo maniac's quick death by gunshot, a gunpowder-carbon-copy of Hemingway imitating Ernest in earnest because for both of them, death was preferable to losing their mind **LIKE** Captain Clark Terrell, the Black captain from *The Wrath of Khan* who shoots himself with a phaser rather than have an alien ear-worm take over his mind; and "U" auguring *Ulysses* in the Hades episode when Bloom thinks about his father's self-inflicted death as other men joke about suicide causing a phonetic spasm in Aaron's hand with 'ultimately untimely untellings of untold undulations' jotted in the corner of the yellow pad; then moving next to "V," not V for Vendetta since he died vehemently and violently venting versus vain villains, instead for Vincent van Gogh in a wheat field with crows by gunshot in 1890 who voyaged through the village after vitiating his venture to eviscerate his ventricular organ **LIKE** "de plane, de plane" Hervé Villechaize also dead by gunshot who portrayed Tattoo on *Fantasy Island*, greeting a painter with both ears intact who arrived on the island to paint Michelle Pfeiffer, quite a visceral vagary; but the real fantasy for Aaron is "W," appearing hauntingly with regards to the countless nights wondering what Aaron himself would have said upon this Crisis Hotline if the greatest of W's, the immortal DFW, David Foster Wallace, had called in 2008 before hanging himself off the back porch and Aaron is convinced he would have yelled at him,

"Stop writing! Entertainment encourages suicide!"

and maybe DFW would have laughed through one more night to live for one more day which makes him ponder what he would have said to Robin Williams who died in 2014 by hanging, perhaps a joke about a blue-skinned genie **LIKE** Goethe's Werther whose fictional death while wearing powder-blue lederhosen caused a wave of Werther fever-induced copycat suicides in Europe and Aaron wonders whether Americans will start hanging themselves to copycat Robin who in turn copycatted Wallace who imitated the biggest hanger in history, Judas Iscariot, a simulacra of death with no point of origin, bodies swinging in the wind, and at last with no more ringing to distract Aaron since Boss Lady has rerouted his calls to the Nebraska call center in Boys Town which has a hundred paid volunteers as opposed to the few unpaid volunteers at the Suicide Prevention & Crisis Hotline Center where Aaron earns a measly hourly wage of $10.20; and without interruption Aaron rolls onto "X" with Xun Yu, Han scholar who opposed Cao Cao's ascension to become Emperor, dying suspiciously of forced suicide due to dishonoring the famous General Cao's (T'sao)

Chicken of whom is chronicled in *Romance of the Three Kingdoms* but who the hell, Aaron wonders, has read the Four Chinese Classics on this side of the International Date Line, the other three being *Outlaws of the Marsh* and *Journey to the West* and *Dream of the Red Chamber*, but decency omits *Plum in the Golden Vase* since Aaron can't refrain from making the innuendo, "He put his plum in her golden vase, know what I'm sayin?" to anyone who asks what the novel is about, consequently he decides "X" should be for Malcolm X who didn't kill himself but asked to be killed, knew he would be killed, wanted to be killed, realizing that if a man stands on the shore and refuses to move as the tide comes in, then his actions should be considered suicidal because Malcolm didn't dodge those bullets, he stood proudly in the way, letting the tide of martyrdom wash over him, and Aaron's mind floats back to the *Dream*, as in *Dream of the Red Chamber*, and realizing "Y" is for Dai-Yu, true love of Bao-Yu, but she died of heartache on the night of Bao-Yu's marriage to Precious Bao-chai, and Aaron appreciates how the expanded love triangle is forced onto other characters by linking their names together with either Bao and/or Yu throughout this epic romance; however, since nothing happens plot-wise, his favorite response to people who ask, "What's it about?" Aaron's response has become, "Oh, it's about twenty-five hundred pages!" and finally he's at "Z" when,

ring ring . . . ring ring . . . ring ring

and Aaron stares hard, thinking maybe it will go away, the phone that is, not the ringing, but on the third set of chimes he picks up despite the fact that it's 5:04 p.m., most certainly off the clock, besides it shouldn't be ringing since those paid staffers in a small suburb near Omaha, Nebraska, ought to be picking up but he answers, "Domino's Pizza, can I take your order?" because he knows Boss Lady will be reviewing the recorded calls later and he'll certainly hear about it tomorrow morning, but that's tomorrow and right now he's almost done, at the finish line with "Z" is for Nietzsche's *Zarathustra* who exclaimed, "Die at the right time! Die at the right time!" and so Aaron convinces himself, after years of reflection, that Zarathustra, man-who-cometh-down-from-the-mountain, let himself be killed as in committed suicide, only if he, as Aaron-taker-of-calls, also admits that Socrates, man-who-corrupth-the-youth, killed himself by voluntarily quaffing *conium maculatum* announcing, "Down the hatch!" but in Ancient not Koine Greek and only if he also admits that the death of Jesus is the ultimate Judeo-Christian suicide for did He not say upon the Cross, "Father, into your hands I commit my spirit", and if a Caller spoke those words to Aaron, then he'd immediately link the word *commit* with the phrase *commit suicide* because didn't Jesus utter with his last breath, "It is finished" and if Aaron read that in a suicide note, then he'd know what it meant, and Aaron realizes the Man, the Myth, the Jee-Zeus himself, right before the Son ascended to the Sun, had an epiphany—that He had possessed the power over every single moment in his life, over every detail of His death.

And here's the catch: We All Do.

Chapter 3

Clashing with the Third Caller on a Slow Thursday
before Getting Wasted at a PTA Meeting

The day after the shooting, Aaron answered the ringing phone with a growl heavy from depression's gravity. "Whaaat?"

He was upset that his daughter Zoë had not come home the previous night. She preferred to crash at her friend's house, Thyme and her sister Crow, because they cooked organic delicacies. Zoë had grown tired of her father's two main dishes, nachos and plain spaghetti.

The phone call was the third one for Aaron at the SP&CH Center, Sobs 1 and Sobs 2 having called earlier in the morning. Aaron, deep into *Clash of Clans* on his iPhone, heard a raising pitch in the man's voice, like Mandarin's first tone, indicating optimism.

Caller, labile affect: "Allow me to introduce myself. I am Christopher Highroller, the Almighty."

Aaron, bland affect while upgrading his level 3 Town Hall for 25,000 gold: "Greeeeat." Mandarin's fourth tone, failing away at the end.

Caller, upbeat: "I'm the star of The Truman Show."

Aaron, flat affect: "You mean Jim Carrey?"

Offended: "No, the real person."

"Oh, you mean Truman Burbank?"

Agitated: "No! The REAL real person, I'm living in the show. I'm IN the show!"

Aaron, while waiting to train thirty Barbarians at twenty seconds each, decided to give this lunatic the next few minutes of his life. "Got it. You're Ragle Gumm."

Confused: "Who?" Third Mandarin tone, failing then raising again.

"The main character in *Time Out of Joint*, the Philip K. Dick book on which The Truman Show is based. The book was written in the Fifties but takes place in 1998. Guess what year The Truman Show came out?"

Guessing: "Um, 1998?"

"That's right! Weird, huh?"

Constricted affect: "No! You don't understand, I'm not in The Truman Show, I am living in a reality game-show that is inside The

Truman Show. I'm not the star of the show. I AM the show within the show. My life is a game!"

"Wow, that's pretty cool. PKD would really dig that. Oh, by the way I have to ask, are you feeling suicidal?"

"No, should I be? Suicide is a sin."

Aaron, also training ten goblins at thirty seconds each: "Well, you've called a suicide hotline."

Inappropriate affect: "Shut Up! You need to make more time for the Almighty! Those other callers, those pitiful creatures trying to kill themselves, they are nothing compared to my glory!"

"Your glory? Don't you mean Ragel Gumm's glory?"

"Shut up! In my Game Show of Life, my spiritual journey is like a Dungeons & Dragons adventure, where I gain spirituality and strength as the game goes on."

"What about dexterity? Do you gain dexterity, too?"

Irritable affect: "Noooo." Second tone, a high-level pitch.

"Why, because you're a monk?"

"Goddammit, I'm a priest! Why does everyone think I'm a stupid monk?!"

"What's your hit point level?"

"Stop mocking me!"

"No, I'm monking you."

"Screw you!!"

"Now, is that any way for a priest to speak?"

"Aaaaargh!" All fours tones combined.

Aaron, disgusted that giants take a whole two minutes decides to train only four of them, said quickly, "Thank you Mr. Truman or Gumm or Almighty Highroller or whatever but I gotta hang up now."

"But the Almighty needs to talk!"

"No, you're a man. You need to listen. Bye." Click.

He'll be calling back, Aaron thought. If not tonight, then later this week. A seed had been planted and Aaron knew he'd created a Repeat Caller. Aaron feared that the Caller might be delusional but building a base of weekly callers justified Aaron's job, and the more they called, the more secure his job. Irritating the customers equaled employment preservation. Mass hysteria, contagious suicides, and socially-normalized depression meant job security in the mental health field.

Earlier in the morning, Aaron had argued such a point with Boss Lady during his Evaluation Meeting. She had brought him into her office and asked, "Mr. Clifton, what happened at the end of your shift yesterday?"

Aaron misdirected her questions tactfully by poisoning the well. "You do know that the Rank Theory proposes that depression is a survival tactic? In the animal kingdom, surrendering during a fight prevents further damage."

"Aaron, what's this got to do with your constant, un-professional attitude?"

"You see," Aaron said while squinting, "the loser conveys through painful facial expressions or audible whines that they are giving up, which in turn signals to the victor, 'You've beaten me, and I'm taking it pretty hard, in fact I'm being tougher on myself than you could ever be, and I'm so depressed that I'll never challenge you again'."

Boss Lady sighed. "I need a cigarette."

Aaron, a few days away from his birthday and hitting the big Four-Oh, accepted the realization that he would never be Numero Uno. Like every aging professional athlete knows, there's always a younger punk coming up the ranks that is stronger, faster, cleaner, better, maybe even funnier. Even if that punk is a younger version of oneself because competition with an earlier self only leads to failure. For Aaron, the hardest part of getting older was dealing with the fact that he couldn't achieve the goals once easily accomplished, like the touching his toes or sitting down without groaning or simple arithmetic. The memory of his past accomplishments had usurped his future happiness and permanently left Aaron in a lower rank. This sense of defeat was exactly what Aaron had tried to explain to Boss Lady.

"You will never be the man or woman you used to be," Aaron said. "Your inner voice insures survival. The Rank Theory screams out a single piece of advice."

"And what's that?"

"Give up!"

"Give up?" Boss Lady said. "That's your advice to Callers? Should I write that down on your evaluation?"

"That's not what I'm saying. I'm saying depression has a powerful function for our survival."

"Aaron, you know I like you. I've put up with a lot of shenanigans over the last few years, right?"

"A decade."

"Ten years already," Boss Lady sighed again. "You've been here that long?"

Flat affect: "Tell me about it."

"I don't know why but Callers request you. Maybe because you're one of the few men on staff."

"The only one. Bob quit."

"Really? When?"

"About a week ago, you didn't notice?"

"He just started! Darn Sociology majors, never can commit."

Aaron shifted uncomfortably in the hard-plastic orange chair. He vastly preferred returning to the phones where other people talked about themselves. "Anyway," Boss Lady continued, "the Callers like you. You've got a soothing voice."

I can hear it in your voice, too.

The voice of Woman on the Bridge echoed in Aaron's mind as he re-routed the conversation to the Rank Theory but found himself unable to persuade Boss Lady. Aaron had been deflecting a proper evaluation of his abilities because he despised praise. Criticism he could handle, but praise only raised his expectations. Pessimism meant no surprises and no disappointments.

Continuing the evasion, Aaron told her that depression is the acceptance of a new social position which requires complete surrender, a difficult task since giving up is not an American value. "We are a nation of underdogs and come-back-at-the-buzzer type of people," he explained. "Winning is patriotic even if it means turning a loss into a victory, like Bull Run or Antietam. Like how the South lost the military war but won the cultural war, right?"

"Don't bring the South into this," Boss Lady said, upset by his continual tangents. "We're talking about you, Aaron. Don't change the subject."

"Fine. What about me? Yeah, I'm abrasive and trick the Callers into anger. Gets them outta their heads. For one fúck-ing moment, they're not hopeless!"

Aaron had known he shouldn't curse around Boss Lady because she'd told him repeatedly that bad language violated her Christian values. He had purposefully dropped the F-bomb with a rising "u" and a pause before the "ing" because he wanted Boss Lady to understand. He wanted to convey to her that a deep sense of hopelessness and resigned acceptance were two of the many clues Aaron listened for on the phone to determine a Caller's lethality. Sometimes, a Caller would express constant thoughts of suicide, then intolerable psychological pain, followed by feeling distant from others and the belief that their family would be better off without them. Aaron would also listen for mention of previous Attempts, no matter how insignificant, as well as the recent loss of a loved one from suicide or accidental death. He would try to gauge by slurred speech if the Caller was intoxicated, stoned, tipsy or wasted. He listened for manic episodic behavior indicated by racing speech, or labored breathing of a panic attack, or the voice of despair overwhelmed by life's struggles. Aaron listened for key words that indicated a Caller was out of touch with reality, words like *Conspiracy* or *Aliens* or *Jesus Saves* or *I voted for Trump because he cares about the working-class.* He listened for when a Caller mentioned they had difficulty sleeping, or dreamed every night of killing themselves and had become bored with life like when Hunter S. Thompson wrote out for his wife:

Football Season is Over.
No More Games.
No More Bombs.
No More Walking.
No More Fun.
No More Swimming.
67. That is 17 years past 50. 17 more than I needed or wanted. Boring.
I am always bitchy. No Fun for anybody. 67.
You are getting greedy. Act your old age. Relax.
This won't hurt.

Aaron listened carefully to a Caller when they had a clear plan of when, where and how, like the time the lead guitarist of the rock band *Chicago* played Russian roulette and said, "Don't worry, it's not loaded." Same as Johnny Ace in '54 backstage at the City Auditorium in Houston, who said while pointing a .32 pistol at his temple, "It's okay. Gun's not loaded...see?" Same as the Finnish magician Aimo Leikas in front of a live audience. Same as Christopher Walken in *The Deer Hunter.*

When the four elements of a clear plan including the time, location, method and tools were enunciated by a Caller, Aaron knew what was required of him even though Boss Lady struggled to comprehend. Aaron had only one tactic.

He'd hang up.

Right on the edge, that's where ol' Aaron Clifton would abandon the Caller. He knew they would call back. Usually. Sometimes. Unless he went off shift before they climbed out because Aaron knew the edge wasn't a canyon below but rather a steep cliff upwards and they had better start climbing.

Boss Lady had not been fooled but rather worn down. Exhausted by Aaron's ranting, she excused him from her office and told him to show up on time and stop taking so many days off from work.

"I'll pray for you," she told Aaron as he left. Then she typed into the evaluation report: *Needs Professional Help.*

Later that same afternoon, after Aaron's surreal exchange with Truman/Gumm/Mr. Hightower the Almighty, he received a call from Sobs 3. Midway through the conversation, he remembered what Boss Lady had said earlier about his soothing voice.

Sometimes, Aaron felt as though he worked as an employee of an Emotional Sex-line for Female Depressants. He snatched a blank name tag from his desk that read, *Hi, my name is_____* and wrote E.S.F.D. on it.

Debz, in the next cubicle, peeked over the wall and asked "What's that, Erie-Schenectady Fire Department?"

"Nah," he joked, "Ernie on Sesame street's First Dick."

"Always knew those two were queer!"

"Ernie and Burt were the first gay couple of my childhood."

Debz and Aaron had a strange relationship. She had worked on the other side of his prefab wall for about five years and they harassed each other constantly. She was the kind of friend that made work bearable.

Debz guessed again. "Early Season Friendly Dyke?"

"What?"

"Every cop drama series has one, a butch-not-bitch-kinda-hot-friendly lesbian who pops up in the first few episodes then gets shot because, you know, she's gay and expendable."

"Right." Aaron had no idea what she was talking about but he knew that for Debz, everything centered around gender-biased social structures because she majored in Gender, Politics & Sexuality Studies at Sarah Lawrence college while dating most of the cheerleading squad.

"What's it stand for?" she asked.

He hesitated for a moment because he knew Debz would tease him. "Emotional Sex-line for Female Depressants."

"You're soooo helpful," she said sarcastically, feigning helplessness by clinging to the edge of the divider. She stared down at him with purple eyelash extensions above wide, brown eyes and said, "Tell me more, Mr. Man."

"Knew you'd make fun of me."

"I can't do anything without a man," she continued in a whiny voice.

"Never mind. You wouldn't understand."

"Because you're the only guy here? Must be soooo rough for you. Do you feel, Lawd have mercy, discriminated against? You poor, little white boy!"

"And you da sista I can't resista!" He jumped up and gave her a kiss on the cheek.

"Sexual harassment!" Debz screamed. She turned to the other crisis workers sitting in their tiny cubicles. "Er'body seen it, right? He tried to stick his tongue down my throat!"

"You wish."

"Keep it down!"

"Seriously Debz, enough already."

"Would you two stop it already!?"

The cacophony of outbursts from the other crisis workers was a typical reaction to the antics supplied by Debz. She had the commanding presence of a large woman in a tight-fitting pants suit that made skinny-latte, white girls sit up and listen.

As they got back to work, filling out paper work by checking boxes, Aaron pondered the reality of an Emotional Sex-line for Female Depressants and the possibility that maybe the female Callers-in-Crisis were slightly turned-on by the masculine confidence and calmness reflected in his voice. By actively listening to their problems, he served the role of the perfect husband or caring boyfriend absent in their own lives. Only once was Aaron aroused by a caller. He wasn't a pervert, he had to tell himself afterwards, he simply liked her voice, her desperation, her helplessness. After revealing past sexual abuse, the young lady had blurted out, "Hey, I can't help it. I like to give head," and Aaron's better half responded with an erection. Guilt plagued him through the night and when the same woman called back the next week, he immediately transferred her to a female volunteer. He convinced himself that he had been aroused probably because the young woman's voice had reminded him of Lena.

Aaron finished with Sobs 3, flicked a rubber band at Debz as a farewell gesture and signed off early for the day. He explained to Boss Lady that he had to attend another Parent-Teacher Association Meeting and left before she could protest. He'd listened to enough women for one day and needed to drive.

He chose the long way home, over the train tracks and through the nice part of town. Aaron lived on the poor side, affectionately called the East Side in most American cities because industrial pollution is blown eastward. Like Crown Heights in Brooklyn, and Oakland, Ferguson, East Gary, anywhere on 55th Ave between St. Clair and Superior Avenue in Cleveland, all of Detroit. Aaron took his time, wandering through the neighborhoods with pristine lawns that were not contaminated by lead and arsenic soot from the steel mill. He turned on the radio, listened to an interview on NPR's *Fresh Air* and the culmination of ideas created a fantasy with Terry Gross and Ruth Bader Ginsburg together on tour called *Fresh Laws or How Short, Jewish Women from Brooklyn Can Reform the Clean Air Act.*

When Aaron arrived at home, he found a note from Zoë explaining that she'd be out late. Even in this era of texts, they left each other hand-written notes. He ignored the missed call from the Poinsettia Nursing Home left on the landline's answering machine. If Eve were in trouble, then the nursing home would have called his cell phone. He figured the message was probably an invitation to nursing home's 2nd Annual Party since they had already called many times this week. He couldn't believe Eve had been there for two years. Each day, Eve's memory faded even as Aaron recorded the minutia of her gradual decline.

Unsuccessfully, he had tried to forget the incident with his grandmother when she requested his help in dying. Even though only a practice run, he refused to consider taking the life from her. He clearly remembered the way her hands clutched the edges of the pillow. The hurt in her eyes when she thought he was smothering her. He remembered everything. Except the time of the PTA meeting later in the evening.

His cell phone quacked like a duck which meant Lena was calling. Probably starting her day drinking early, Aaron thought. She preferred *Absolut* vodka only because of the Zach Galifianakis commercials they watched one night while high on kind-bud. This was before he embraced sobriety and in the Stoned Ages when there existed a vast discrepancy between schwag-weed and kind-bud before legal grass brought the homeless in zombie-swarms. Aaron and Lena put ol' Zach on repeat, watching his pseudo-mental collapse on camera which seemed spontaneous but had to be staged, the actor dressed in drag, covered in baking flour, weeping genuine tears of shame with no obvious connection to the global marketing plan of a Swedish vodka distillery. Aaron believed the best humor is often uncomfortable.

He swiped left to ignore.

The phone barked twelve minutes later, but for Aaron only moments had passed. Yet, time had not passed because the past lingered in the present. He was lost in a memory of Lena resting on a yellow couch, his back against the one edge as she leaned into him with his legs wrapped around her waist, his hands on her swollen belly, together laughing at a flour-covered comedian on the television. Or had they sat on opposite sides of the couch, he couldn't remember. She had not shown affection even in the beginning, liquor her only physical comfort. The phone continued to howl.

Aaron had assigned his familial phone contacts a specific animal ring tone. His mother Marilyn was given the sound of a barking dog. The phone fell silent for exactly thirteen seconds then barked again. His mother probably needed a prescription refilled. She suffered from weekly nervous breakdowns. Anxiety attacks. Hysteria. She had lots of names for the residual trauma related to her missionary work in Egypt. Every year, she would spend a few weeks in Garbage City, a town inhabited by the ostracized Christian community that dwelled within the trash dumps outside Cairo. She lived and prayed with the Coptic Catholics, easily identified among the Sunni Muslim majority by a cross tattooed on their arms. Marilyn's latest episode had been triggered by a television commercial advertising Tide detergent. The beige fabric in the commercial reminded Marilyn of a covered woman she'd seen butchered to death at an Egyptian market. The woman's blood had soaked into Marilyn's beige cotton scarf and after many washings, discovered old blood doesn't wash out with time's tide.

Aaron took Marilyn's call only because he planned to steal a few of her pills when he picked up the prescription. The mood stabilizers and pain relievers served Aaron well, but he preferred the sedatives and narcotics that he swiped from his aunt Jocelyn's cabinet. As a psychologist, Jocelyn kept a constant supply of pills for her clients in cases of emergency.

Four minutes passed and the rooster crowed on his phone. Aaron had wanted the chicken chirping sound for Jocelyn, since she owned a dozen chickens on her property, but the rooster seemed appropriate as her ring tone. She had bigger cojones than most men. Whereas Marilyn's wide-eyed enthusiasm could suck the air out a room, Jocelyn could suck the life out of a man with a single look. Her natural beauty in her late 50s made men in their 20s stand closer. She didn't work, she pointed. And men loved her for it. Gave them a purpose, gave them something to do. She'd announce enormous and visionary plans like, "This town needs more trees." Suddenly, men would start digging holes. "These neighborhoods could really use more parks." Within a month, City Council would be purchasing abandoned lots with the intention of urban beautification. "We need more vegetables." Instantly, parking lots became gardens.

The rooster crowed again. How typical, Aaron thought. Lena, Marilyn and Jocelyn always needed him at the same time. Jocelyn probably wanted him to drive her to the mechanic to pick up her car after an oil change. She would never wait the half hour for the car to be done and instead walked briskly home for the exercise and then would call for him like a taxi. Yet, Aaron refused to be tasked and he didn't lunge when she pointed. Even when she brought over a dozen eggs or fresh cinnamon buns or a plate of homemade chili rellenos, he often refused to help her.

Aaron sat on the couch as he usually did after work. The couch was a yellow Victorian chaise lounge, an antique feinting couch made of tufted velvet that Eve had given to Aaron as a wedding present. Leaning against the one side with a raised back, he examined the ring tones of his phone. He was tempted to change Lena's quacking duck, Jocelyn's crowing rooster, Marilyn's barking dog, and if Eve had owned a phone, he would have assigned the lion's roar to her number. However, she had not owned a phone in two years. Hard for her to remember seven telephonic digits when she couldn't recognize the people standing around her bed. Even if Eve managed to locate a misplaced cell phone, when Aaron's picture appeared on the screen, she'd probably hit ignore thinking the face belonged to a long-haired hippie.

Many years ago, all had bowed to her mighty bellow. Sadly, dementia had transformed Eve's roar to a purr. Her mind set permanently at idle made the familiar look foreign, and she learned to fake it. She'd smile at strangers like they were family. While visiting a friend's house, Eve would pretend she lived there, acting as a forgetful host and say, "Now, where did I put those wine glasses?" Forgetting the layout of her own house, she'd ask guests to guide her to the restroom. She had become a stranger in her own home. Although possessing a faithful body, Eve's own mind had betrayed her. Aaron had heard her more than once asking upon seeing her own reflection, "Who's that old woman?"

However, Eve in her prime had been an inspiration to women. Men heeded the commands of Jocelyn and feared the enthusiasm of Marilyn, but men adored Eve. She had a particular talent when speaking to men that managed to be both endearing yet desperate, prideful yet helpless.

When Aaron was a teenager, she told him, "Men want to be needed, and need to be wanted." She also shared a subtle trick with him, which Aaron tried on a few girls while he was in middle school, but the wooing tactic came off as perverted. However, for Eve as a woman working her magic on the martini-soaked, suited Ad-men of the 50s, the trick worked wonders—while walking beside them, she'd lean on them. Ever so slightly, she'd place her hand on their forearm and press down slightly, pulling them into her. Lowered her voice, too, and they had to strain while she looked up at them with Audrey Hepburn eyes and a Jackie O smile. Enthralled they were, but not hooked. She told Aaron that men were not fish to be caught and released. Their attention was her only reward, and Eve would float away to the next man, enchanting every gathering, enlivening even a wake.

Aaron also remembered Eve's roar could be utterly terrifying. In the days when Eve could tell the difference between Verdi and Puccini, they would experience the opera together. Eve loved opera for the music, Aaron because of the suicide. He knew that in one-third of all operas, either the soprano or her love-sick tenor kills themself. Divas complete suicide on stage more often than their male counterparts, but the male characters whine about it more through suicidal ideation. This was an inverse to reality where men complete suicide more than women, yet women have much higher rates of suicidal ideation. Aaron tried to explain this to Eve during *Tosca* after the heroine belted out, "*O Scarpia, Avanti a Dio!*" and flung herself off a cliff. He had looked at his grandmother after the climactic ending and said, "There is a difference between suicidal ideation and suicidal acts. One is a daydream for the dying, the other a nightmare for the living."

Eve had given him a worried look and said, "Don't go getting any ideas. It would kill me," perhaps the greatest reason why Aaron had not made an honest Attempt on his own life since his early twenties with a shotgun while watching Telemundo.

Aaron knew the suicides in opera were always 'predicament suicides' resulting from lost or unrequited love because mental health disorders don't play out well on the stage. The cast may be encouraged to act crazy, or are naturally imbued with an actor's prerequisite insanity, but depression without a cause would be far too boring for a three-hour opera. Dramatic cutting/stabbing of oneself is used most frequently by playwrights, but in reality, this method is one of the least common ways. Starting with the first performance in 1607, Monteverdi's *Orpheus*, four centuries of opera have offered a plethora of suicidal methods, including poisoning, hanging, immolation, and leaping to one's death but only in Massenet's *Werther* does a man imitate reality and shoot himself in the head. Aaron found it odd that even though the Italians may have perfected the operatic art form, sociologist Émile Durkheim revealed that for many years, Italy had the lowest rates of suicide in Western Europe.

A few years ago, on their way to view *Aida* at the opera house, Eve and Aaron stopped for gas. He paid cash, filled up the tank and afterwards went back inside to use the restroom. On his way out, the Egyptian store manager with a thick Arabic accent accused Aaron of not paying for the gasoline. At this point in his life, Aaron thought of himself as a grown-ass man and figured he could handle an irate manager. They argued for a moment, the man's plain white *ghutra* scarf shaking atop his head as he grabbed Aaron while summoning his two large, hairy-armed Egyptian sons. Aaron, not quite a grown-ass man, decided to pay the additional charge instead of risking a foreign ass-whoopin'. He had returned red-faced to the car and pulled away as Eve asked him why he had been arguing with the manager. When the details of his encounter were revealed nearly four blocks later, Eve calmly demanded that he return to the filling station, as she called it. Aaron had seen this stern look on her before and knew better than to dissuade her. Upon their return, she exited the car and smoothed the front of her rabbit fur coat while fixing her short, elegant blonde-tinted hair in the sideview mirror. Aaron followed three steps behind as she parted the two burly sons with a smile, and addressed the manager with a kind twinkle in her eye. He smiled in return, unaware of imminent bluster.

Under a sweet whisper, she asked, "Did you accuse of my grandson of stealing?"

"What? Madam please..." The manager then spotted Aaron hidden behind the larger of his two sons. He pointed at Aaron, "He no pay! See him try to be sneaky."

"Sir, if you don't put that finger down, I will have you arrested for assault," she said with a smile. The manager was confused. Eve explained it to him.

"You have falsely accused my family. You have dishonored our name. We require compensation."

"Madam, please understand, I try to run business..."

Her mouth tightened when she spoke. Like a diva, she paused between each word as her voice raised a notch with each word. "You—will—NOT—interrupt—me—again!"

By the time she reached the final word, the manager's face had paled considerably, his sons motionless, and the other customers stood frozen.

"First, you will suffer a loss of revenue. None of my family nor any of my far-reaching acquaintances will ever frequent your establishment. Next, I will file a formal protest with the Better Business Bureau."

The manager attempted to reply but Eve gently raised her finger. "I'm not done yet. The mayor and I are good friends, we play bridge together on Sundays. Within a week, you shall receive a letter from Mayor Loretta Champion's office. You will most likely be charged under a violation of the General Business Law for price gouging."

The manager shifted his weight from one leg to the other but dared not move. His sons looked at Aaron for help, but he only shrugged his shoulders as if to say, *Good luck trying to stop her.*

Eve continued in a slowly rising tempo. "And lastly, we will be divesting all the stocks owned by our family portfolio from the company which owns this franchise. Later this evening, I will be writing a personal letter to the CEO of the Board of Directors at

Exxon to tell him about this little encounter."

"But we're Chevron," the manager attempted to explain.

Eve leaned across the counter, finger in his face and her voice a commanding roar, "And if you ever touch my grandson again, may the Lord help you because the law won't!"

Eve turned away from the manager without another word, head held high as the two sons cringed. Aaron followed her out and opened the car door. Eve smiled at him as she kissed him on the forehead. "Oh, honey, don't worry. I won't be doing any of that nonsense. I wanted to scare him a little, make him think twice before harassing honest people."

Aaron glanced back at the store and saw the manager still had not moved. "Oh, he's scared alright."

"And don't let anyone call you a cheat," Eve said patting him on the shoulder. "You came into this world with your name and you'll go out with it. That's all we really have."

"I'll remember, Grandma."

"And next time, get a receipt."

*

The phone quacked. Aaron picked up and heard Lena's voice. "Ten minutes, see you there."

He quickly made an organic peanut butter and pesticide-free blueberry jam sandwich and headed off to another PTA meeting. This parental gathering was a continuation of the one held the previous day where several of the moms complained of nutritional deficiency in the school lunches. Aaron couldn't believe only one day had passed since the shooting at Denny's. He still hadn't filled out the paperwork.

After grabbing an old brown leather jacket with holes in the elbows, Aaron lazily strolled to the school a mere two blocks away. After the divorce, he'd picked this neighborhood because of its proximity to a good elementary school for Zoë.

Once again, he found Lena finishing a cigarette outside the brick school building. She'd forgotten her parka and stood shivering in a Dolce & Gabbana dark navy business suit with her blonde hair pulled back in a power bun. They both served on the Board of the elementary school's PTA, a remnant of their old life together when they had plans to improve the public education system. That was until they got a divorce and Aaron sent Zoë to a private Catholic school, encouraged and paid for by his mother Marilyn. Nowadays, he no longer gave a damn about public education. He only showed up at these meeting to scope out the hot soccer moms and to catch up with Lena since they remained friends even after the divorce. After all, they'd had a kid together.

"Sup, how's life?"

Lena tilted towards to him, "Hey, happy birthday tomorrow. You turning the big four-oh, right?"

"Don't remind me."

"Any special plans?"

"Seeing the doctor. Time to put me down."

When Aaron didn't follow up with additional information, Lena offered him a fresh Parliament and asked, "How's work?"

"Oh, work is work," Aaron said, declining the cigarette. Years ago, he had chain-smoked for his health, as in to decrease the amount of years he'd have to suffer on this planet, but gave up the habit because he didn't want to contaminate Zoë's air space. After years of concealing his numerous drug addictions from his family, now that Aaron was sober meant being honest with his daughter even if it meant telling her about all the drugs as a way to dissuade her. He didn't care about being a good role model, he simply figured there was no one better than an ex-addict to convince the youth.

"For a guy who spends his life on the phone, you sure don't talk much."

"Yup."

"Ugh. How's Zoë? Nice seeing her last night for dinner. Tell her to stop by again sometime, OK?"

"I'll try," Aaron said. "Can't tell that girl anything. Haven't seen her much since she got her driver's license."

"She having sex yet?"

"What the…? Where'd that come from?"

Lena shrugged and took another drag, "I don't know, just thought I'd ask."

"We'd be the last ones to know."

"Drugs?"

"Booze or weed? I'm trying to discourage her from both, but I don't know. Why don't you ask her."

"She won't answer my calls."

"It's cuz you only call her when drunk."

"Don't start with me," Lena said.

"Fine." Aaron pointed to a large Dixie cup in her hand. "Is that lemonade?"

"Mostly."

Aaron could smell the vodka and shrugged, "Hell, give me a sip already."

"That's why we're still friends," she said. "You take me as I am."

"No, we're friends because I'm a fabulous enabler," he said after taking a sip.

Waiting for the meeting to begin, their conversation drifted to Aaron's work since Lena had always been curious about his career choice. Never supportive, merely inquisitive. After thirty-seconds, they were fighting again.

"Why do you even care if they kill themselves?" Lena asked. "The world's overpopulated, we'd be better off without them."

Aaron looked at her sternly. "The world doesn't have enough people. We've got plenty of food and water. We can't waste water."

"People waste water every day. Reminds me, I forgot to turn off the hose last night."

"Again? You musta been really wasted."

"I said don't start."

"Water evaporates," Aaron continued. "The Earth is a closed system. The problem is distribution, leading to the exploitation of poverty and starvation as a means of political domination ..."

"Spare me another one of your political rants."

"And the Earth has a way of self-correcting. Not long ago, the human race dwindled to a few thousand people after some big volcanic eruption in like 70,000 BC."

"Not long ago?" Lena swayed, shaking her head. "You're always trying to make ancient history seem recent." She chuckled in a way that Aaron still found adorable.

"That's the one. That volcano was responsible for drastic climate change which lead to genetic bottlenecking. And I can guess what those ten thousand humans said when the Neanderthals showed up."

"What's that?"

"Half of them were probably like, 'Yippee, we've got some new neighbors. Hope they like dogs,' and the other half were like, 'Seriously? Wish some of those Neanderthals would go kill themselves'." Lena laughed again and finished her cigarette, allowing

Aaron to continue. "Soon they'll be ten billion on this planet. This planet could probably sustain a hundred billion if we did it right. Rice fields, soybeans and desalination factories."

"A hundred billion vegans, hmm?"

"Sure, there's plenty of room. Ever driven through Kansas?"

The Elementary School principal approached in a brown corduroy blazer and announced that the meeting was starting soon, frowning when he recognized the two of them. Aaron said they'd be right in as Lena reached into her purse.

"Here, I almost forgot," she said, handing him a check.

"Thanks," Aaron said timidly, placing the monthly alimony and child support into his wallet.

They entered the school's gymnasium and whispered to each other, making fun of the other parents. Moms with bright red lipstick and baseball caps, and the only other father wearing standard garb for a Colorado winter day including cargo shorts, a football jersey and the greatest fashion faux pas, white socks with Birkenstock sandals, guaranteed contraceptive because not even his own wife would have sex with him. Lena and Aaron sat together in the back, like the stoners and actors and artists in high school who have no use for indoctrination.

Laughing together, sometimes Aaron would forget why they had gotten divorced. But with a single slurred word, the reason came back to him. The tone of her voice gave away her drunken state. Aaron remembered how she would ask for a particular object when seated on the yellow couch, lit ash from her cigarette burning tiny holes in the antique recliner. She'd sit down before realizing the remote for the television was on the mantle. She'd yell out to Aaron and he'd have to stop whatever he was doing and fetch it for her. The main problem with being tasked by her was that he struggled to stay focused. Life offered plenty of distractions, and she'd become the type of woman most feared by men. She had become a burden.

Yet, the request wasn't troublesome but rather her tone. "Can you hand me the remote?" Such a simple task but it alerted him to the level of Lena's inebriation depending on the emphasis. "Can you hand me the remote?" was obviously different than "Hand me the remote!" but when *Can* was stressed, elongated to a *Caaaaan*, almost whiney but not high pitched, instead uttered with an effort, indicating that perhaps the device was too heavy for her to lift. Rarely was there a *please* attached to the end of her request, but if present would give him cause for concern. "Can you hand me the remote, PLEASE?" as if she was thinking, *Oh gawd, you haven't done a single thing for me today, so at least do this!* But when she said, "Can YOU hand me the remote?" then he knew he'd done something to piss her off and was certain he'd hear about it later and dreaded even sitting next to her, waiting for a sudden explosion about dirty dishes in the sink, dirty socks left on the floor or dirty magazines hidden under the mattress. When she said, "Can you hand ME the remote?" her selfishness was peaking and he knew later he'd be running errands to the kitchen to get potato chips or out to the store to buy a pack of smokes and a bottle of vodka. He occasionally would refuse to get alcohol, but in the inevitable argument she'd wear him down with the most effective and aggravating technique: Repetition. Aaron never figured out how to de-escalate his enraged wife, and like a sober bartender at closing time, Aaron would hear the same request until finally he'd throw up his hands, grab the keys and drive off to escape her incessant nagging. In the morning, she'd apologize but never remembered what she had done. When she said, "Can you hand me THE remote?" then he didn't know what to expect and idled nervously until she passed out in an upright position on the couch. And when she said, "Give me your remote" then he knew the monthly twinkle in her eye meant he might get lucky, perhaps the real reason he stuck around but he always wondered how unlucky is the man whose wife passes out during sex.

Sitting down next to each other in the auditorium, Aaron switched the wallet from his pants into his jacket to avoid developing sciatica. Looking at his wallet with Lena's financial support, Aaron realized he had become the burden.

The meeting began with the principal introducing the new board members, three moms with similar frosted, shoulder length hair and dressed in spring-hued sweaters and black yoga pants. Each one clutched a grandé expresso protectively.

"I'd like to begin by reading a report from the Treasurer. The school lunch program needs to raise an additional…"

Lena stood up and interrupted. "What are you doing about the leaky roof?"

"We'll get to that, Mrs. Clifton. Please be patient."

Aaron flinched away from Lena as she exploded. "Mrs. Clifton?! Seriously? I haven't gone by that in years."

"I'm sorry," the principal apologized, "but that's how I remember you when your daughter attended our school. Anyway, as I was saying…"

While the principal droned on about fiduciary responsibility, Lena plopped down in the chair and turned to Aaron. "I never shoulda taken your name."

"Hey, your choice. Told you not to."

"But you got me pregnant. What was I supposed to do? We needed family health insurance."

"I know, and I wanted our daughter to have my name. It's a good name."

Clifton was an English surname of Norman lineage. The Clifton's had resided in Lancashire, and the meaning implied a farm atop a cliff. Lady Clifton had arrived in Virginia in 1648, and Aaron had tried to convince himself that he possessed no relation to such noble blood because then he'd have to admit that the ancestors of any Black man or woman he met on the street with the name of Clifton had been owned by his relatives. English, Irish, and Scottish slave-owner names like James and Irving (Cavs' Lebron and Kyrie) or Johnson, Bryant and O'Neal (Lakers' Magic, Kobe and Shaq) or Jordan and Pippin (Bulls' Michael and Scottie) or Russel and White (Celtics' Bill and Jo Jo). Those were not names from the African Maasai, but instead from the Colonial massa.

The Clifton family motto was *Tenez le Droit* and Aaron knew his ancestors had indeed owned slaves whose great-grandchildren later played basketball or football because the motto meant *Right Guard.*

"Screw your last name!" Several of the other parents turned around and stared at Lena, but she ignored them and whispered with a clenched jaw. "What's the big deal? You men, always trying to pass on your name."

"Well, it is kinda important…"

"Ugh, men. Worried about your legacy and your money and your good name!"

"Calm down."

"Your good name? Ha!" she faked a laugh and took another swing. "You should be passing on good morals."

Aaron sat silently and watched as Lena pulled out a tin flask and filled her paper cup. He listened as the principal passed the microphone to the first of the three new moms.

Mom #1, excited affect, fourth espresso kicking in: "What we propose to do is raise money by holding a bake sale. Chocolate chip cookies and apple pies."

Mom #2, Prozac-induced steady affect: "I make a great lemon ménage pie."

Lena laughed and turned to Aaron, "Dumb bitch meant meringue."

The president took the microphone back. "That's a wonderful idea…"

Lena interrupted loudly. "A bake sale? What we'd make last time, ten bucks?"

"Thirty dollars and fifty-five cents."

"Here's an idea," Lena offered. "Hold your silly little bake sale outside the marijuana dispensary on Fourth Street."

The new moms paled as the principal stammered, "I don't think, ummm, that's not the image this school wants to present to the community."

Lena chuckled harshly. "Yeah, but you'd make more cash than a hooker on Colfax!"

Mom #3, aside to Mom #1 and Mom #2, shocked by the dual notion of weed and prostitution but more upset that a woman had interrupted the male principal: "My heavens, the mouth on that woman."

Lena heard them whispering and jumped up. "Stupid-ass housewives, bet you never worked a day in your life!"

Simultaneously, Mom #1 stood up and yelled, "Shut-up!" as Mom #2 joined her with an accusation. "I can smell the booze from here," as Mom #3 leapt to her feet, "Drunk bitch!"

The principal tried to restore order. "Please ladies, everyone please be seated."

Aaron grabbed Lena by the arm. "Come on, let's get outta here."

"Don't touch me!" As Lena pulled away, she stumbled into several chairs and crashed onto the floor.

Everyone drew silent as Aaron helped her up. The three moms and the other board members looked down at her with mixed expressions of pity and condemnation.

"I'm not…not drunk," she muttered.

"Come on," Aaron pleaded. "Let's go. Please."

Lena stood up wobbly and latched onto Aaron for support as he apologized to the principal. "Sorry, it's her medication."

Without further disruption, they left the gymnasium together. Silently, Aaron took her car keys and drove to her house. She passed out on the way and Aaron left her sleeping in the car. He knew from experience that she'd wake up cold in about an hour and move herself safely inside.

Aaron left the keys in her jacket pocket and walked home, his untied boots smacking against the concrete. They lived only a few blocks apart because after the divorce, he wanted to make sure that Zoë could ride her bike back and forth. No custody battle, no 50/50 split for their daughter's time, which allowed Zoë as a little girl to see both her mom and dad every day. Aaron often thought this was one of his better decisions.

Exhausted by the long day's work and from fighting against Lena's various nemeses, Aaron paused several times on the way home and reflected on the disastrous PTA meeting. He wasn't sure why he kept covering for Lena, but figured he owed her both financially as well as some kind of cosmic debt. She'd given him his greatest joy. Bolstered by thoughts of his daughter, he hurried home.

Sadly, Aaron found an empty house. He sat on the yellow and sun-faded couch, devoured an entire thirty-two-ounce bag of Flamin' Hot Cheetos while watching an episode on the History Channel about WWII fighter pilot aces and discovered that every single one of the top hundred aces were German. After an hour, Zoë's absence reminded him that the life of a parent is a life of worry.

With nothing else to do, Aaron transferred the hotline calls from the office to his home landline, cradling the phone base in his lap. The Germans were notching up kills over Stalingrad when the phone rang and Aaron settled into The Process before answering.

The Process was how Aaron dealt with the emotional onslaught of suicidal callers. He couldn't simply answer the phone and say,

"Hi there!" (too cheery); or,

"How are you today?" (too generic); or,

"Yo son, why you down?" (too patronizing); or,

"How's it goin?" (too misleading); or,

"Wassup?" (too dismissive); or,

"Hey bitches!" (too inappropriate).

He had trained himself to rapidly undergo a transformative process of setting up a protective barrier of light & love to guard against negative energy, or at least that's what his eighteenth therapist had recommended in New Age language. At first, the routine had taken him twenty minutes of meditation before going into work. After a decade, he could do it in a matter of seconds. He would take a few deep breathes and imagine himself surrounded by a bright shield of crackling energy.[7]

The Process was a preamble to a verbal engagement, but also involved a tricky imaginative procedure that evolved during the entirety of the phone call. Aaron would picture the Caller not as a voice on the phone but rather as a person directly in front of him. Aaron hated how in television and movies when actors conducted intense dialog or plot development over the phone: one actor would speak into the receiver, then there'd be an editorial cut to the other actor's response. This type of acting didn't create suspense or intrigue or catharsis but rather resulted in a screaming match against an inanimate object. As a moviegoer, Aaron wanted to see and hear people interacting directly with each other, watching for those spontaneous and improvised reactions within the actors. The magic lay in an unscripted bit of human interaction when the actor momentarily lost themselves in the role. Quite different from Stanislavski's Method acting when the actor completely morphed into their role. Rather, The Process required a split personality, one as the actor and the other as the role. This allowed for those little extemporized moments of clarity when Aaron could be the actor (Listener) while empathizing with the role (Caller) and still maintain a protective barrier between the two. The Process was exhausting.

Aaron's disgust of phone-talk driven dialogue in cinema had forced him to visualize the suicide calls as a face-to-face interaction, vis-à-vis Caller and Listener, as if the encounter was conducted on a celluloid split screen, the Listener's comforting/confrontational face on one side of the screen and the weeping/withdrawn face of the Caller on the other side. First, Aaron imagined the Caller in the same room, sitting in a chair across from him. Until the Caller spoke, Aaron created an amorphous humanoid figure lacking facial features, like the default setting of the T-1000 from *Terminator 2* but as a beige, fleshy blob. Once the Caller spoke, Aaron would start to add pieces like gender, age, race, height, weight, hair color, eye color and health conditions. The voice delivered everything.

Aaron skipped the preamble and jumped right in. "Why'd you

call?"

Caller, panicked, labored-breathing, in distress: "Hello? Hello? Hello? I'm okay, really. Don't know why I called." He sounded like a man in his mid-thirties.

Aaron instructed him to take a few breaths and asked him to start from the beginning. Billy offered his name freely, a rarity since most people insisted on being anonymous, a throw-back to the days when suicide was illegal. Billy worked as a prison guard at the State's medium security facility on the east edge of town.

Listening to his voice, Aaron deduced the man was an overweight white guy with short, cropped brown hair and brown eyes at 5'6" with a high school education. Gender and age were usually easy to guess but not always. Sometimes a fifteen-year-old boy sounded like a thirty-year-old woman. Billy's tone and accent gave away his race and his word choice identified his level of education. The information that Billy worked as a prison guard allowed Aaron to picture a military-style haircut, the brown hair and eyes were added as flavor. He knew the man weighed over 250 pounds because he overhead Billy moving around his apartment with effort and labored breathing during the conversation. As for his height, he suspected the man suffered from short-man complex. Aaron inferred most of this information from background noises, and The Process helped him manufacture an imaginary character in the chair across the room.

Billy mentioned that he often stopped by Loaf n' Jug on his way home to pick up a dozen white eggs, quart of 2% milk, pack of Camels and a few scratch Lotto tickets. Billy was quite specific on the line, peaking Aaron's interest. Such detail often indicated the impending revelation of a traumatic event. Aaron knew that people became keenly aware in the moment of crisis.[8]

Aaron put down his iPhone after queuing fifteen archers on *Clash*, allowing him seven minutes until he needed to check his phone again. Aaron decided to give Billy his full attention, at least for seven more minutes. Apparently, while Billy paid for his items at the front counter of the convenient store, some Eastside gang-banger rolled in and pulled a gun. Not on the register, but on Billy.

"You were still wearing your security guard outfit?" Aaron asked.

"Correctional officer. Yeah, I was in my uniform. Gun, too. A forty-five in the holster but that vato had the jump on me."

"How'd you know he belonged to a gang?"

"Chump wore a blue Duke t-shirt and I know he didn't go to college there. Punk-ass bitch probably didn't make it outta middle school. Pants sagging below his knees, and the number thirteen tattooed on his neck."

"Thirteen?"

"Thirteen is for M," Billy explained. "The thirteenth letter of the alphabet."

"I don't get it."

"La Eme. M is for the Mexican Mafia. Don't you know anything?"

"Guess not," Aaron confessed.

"This punk starts yelling at me, right? Cursing me out, telling me that when he did time, some white guy like me used to beat the shit outta him."

"You ever seen the guy?"

"Nah, just some local banger. He went after me cuz of my uniform, I guess."

"Makes sense. He was lashing out, and you provided a target for his anger."

"But you don't understand," Billy wailed, "He made me … he put that gun in my mouth … told me to get on my knees… it's on camera …" Billy broke down. Aaron let him cry for a while. Sometimes silence was the best medicine.

"What else? Tell me, it's okay. You're in a safe place now, right?"

"Yeah, I'm home now. Happened about an hour ago. I'm fine, called the cops and reported it. Didn't tell my wife, she doesn't need to know. She worries enough."

"You're strong, I can tell. That's good. But now you can let it go. Tell me."

Billy's voice remained even, he'd passed through the tears. "Hehe yanked down his pants and the guy behind the register freaked out. I got on my knees. The banger said something like, 'You gonna suck my dick, bitch'. Something like that, I don't know. He pulled out his dick."

Aaron became conflicted at this juncture. He should have responded by validating the man's experience by saying *that must of have been scary for you* or he could have responded empathically with *you must have freaked out, I sure would have.*

Instead, Aaron said, "How small was it?"

"What?"

"His cock. Tiny, right?"

"What the … I don't know!"

"He Army raped you, didn't he?"

"Army rape?" Bill asked confused.

"You work in a prison, right?" Aaron asked. "When men rape each other, what do we call it?"

"Prison rape, I guess," Billy said.

"But men get raped in the Army as often as prison, therefore prison rape should be called Army rape."[9]

"Really?"

"Probably, who knows. Men generally don't report that kind of thing," Aaron said, pleased by his success to momentarily distract Billy. "Tell me again what this kid did to you."

"I don't wanna think about it."

"Come on, focus. There you are, on your knees. He's got a gun in your mouth. You're helpless. He's unzipping his pants, right? And out it plops…"

"Bro, what are you doing? Told you I don't wanna think about it! And no, I didn't suck it. Some people walked in and this wet-back, punk-ass-bitch panicked and ran off. It's over, whatever."

Aaron countered with a rough tone. "No, it's not over. It's not in the past. You're still there, in the present. Out it plops and look, it's shriveled and withered, like he's stepping out of the tub."

"That's disgusting!"

"It's tiny. It's ridiculous. It's the smallest cock you've ever seen."

"Okay," Billy said, confused. "I guess."

"No, don't guess. Picture that in your mind. I want you to see it. Every time you relive this trauma, imagine the world's tiniest penis. You started laughing, don't you remember?"

"I did?"

"Yes, you did! You were laughing, rolling on the floor. Remember?"

"Right, I get it," Billy replied, starting to understand. "Yes, it's so little. That's hilarious!"

"It's so lee-ttle."

They laughed together as Aaron kept Billy talking for another few minutes, going over the experience again and altering history to make him feel better. Happiness is about perspective, Aaron reminded Billy. He also told Billy that he'd probably suffer from PTSD for a few months and need therapy and gave him a referral for a local shrink. He wished Billy good luck.

Caller, relaxed, breathing calmly, relieved: "Thank you."

Done and done.

Or so Aaron thought until the phone rang a few minutes later.

"Hey Es-say, wazzup?"

Aaron was puzzled by the next Caller's tone. He began The Process but struggled to create an image. This seemed like a social call. "Say what?"

Caller, Spanish accent: "Nah, man. Esé."

Aaron queued fifty Level 3 purple-haired female archers on *Clash* before jotting down on a yellow pad that the Caller sounded like a twenty-year-old Hispanic male who offered the name of Carlos. Aaron assumed it to be an alias because most people didn't use their real name.

"What can I do for you, Carlos?"

"Feelin weird n'shit, comprendé?"

"Want to tell me what's going on?"

"Nah Esé, I'm all good. Dis in confidence, yah?"

"Confidential, yes it is."

"Good, cuz I'm up on a burner anyhow."

For the next few minutes, Aaron listened as Carlos rapped into the phone but Aaron couldn't understand a word. Eventually, he picked up a word he'd heard on *CSI: Miami*.

"... down at the spot slingin carga, ya'know, da chiva."

"Hold on, you talking about heroin?"

"Yah, man, hair-juan. Dat's it, bro. Tryin to re-up n'shit, but chica gorda got busted cuz her loco nephew got pop'd at school. Anyways, gotta make some scratch, right? Chillin at the Ln'J earlier today and I sees dis peckerwood roll up, and I'm like fück dis muthafücka, eyein me up n'down, reminds me of this See-oh back in Lobo."

"See-oh?"

"Ya'know, a screw, a C.O., a correction officer, duh. Lookin at his pasty white-ass gets me hot, right, so I bust out a pistola and shit gets real serious, k?"

"What happened? You shoot him?"

"Nah, nah, don't worry bout dat. I just wanna freak'em out un poquito, scare the white outta his bones. I pulled me pena, told him, 'suck it, don't fück it'. White dude was all like *whaaaat*, crapped his pants. Too funny, k?"

"You pulled your dick out?"

"Listen here, holmes, I ain't no cakero, ain't no chava, no maricone."

"I don't care if you're gay or not, that's not the issue. Why'd you do that?"

Finally, Carlos spoke slower while remembering. "Dis peckerwood used to get all up on me, ya'know? Different one but same, right?"

"Alright, the guard you saw in the store, he reminded you of the guy who used to beat you up? Is that what you're telling me?"

"In jouvie. Muthafŭcka would gimme a solid beat-down, like fo'reals, but wouldn't leave a mark."

"Why not?"

"Cuz if you don't leave a bruise, then it ain't abuse."

"That's terrible," Aaron laughed. "I know a hundred battered wives and twice as many cuckold husbands who might argue against that logic."

"Old cock what? He'd didn't do nuthin weird or anything. Beat on me, that's all."

"That's not all," Aaron replied, incredulous that he was Validating and Connecting with this guy on the line. A few minutes ago, he'd been aiding the victim and now he was helping the perpetrator.

"Got tired of his shit. Made me a pico outta a plastic spoon, sharp as hell, thought about stickin em but knew I'd never be makin it out then, k?"

"Murder will get you life."

"No doubt, son. No doubt."

Carlos carried on for a few minutes and Aaron allowed him to ramble. He didn't understand most of the words, but soon enough Carlos broke down and cried. His mom had died of cancer, his dad was serving a double-life sentence for drug trafficking, his baby-momma had hooked up with the general manager of Taco Bell and wouldn't even let him see his baby girl. Carlos shot heroin and smoked meth, he said. Might have AIDS, he said. Looking for a job, he said. Tired of robbing houses and breaking into cars, he said. Aaron patiently waded through a life unfamiliar to him, offering encouraging *hmmmm's* and *that's so messed up*. After thirteen minutes, Carlos finished and Aaron offered the address of a free-clinic for addicts. Carlos said he'd visit tomorrow then hung up.

Aaron called dispatch and told them to have an officer placed at the clinic's front door to look for a young, Latino male with the number thirteen tattooed on his neck. After giving them Billy's phone number as a point of contact, he disconnected the phone. Utterly fed up with everyone's drama, he realized that only silence guarantees confidentiality.

Chapter 4

Nachos de Los Alamos
and Other Top Secrets from WWII like Carrots & Potatoes

Pacing on the hardwood floor, Aaron waited for Zoë to return home late from school. She'd been driving since the summer, her car purchased and the monthly insurance taken care of by Marilyn for keeping up good grades. Aaron was thankful that his mother paid for so much of Zoë's life, but rarely did he express his gratitude. He didn't know how. With her own car, Zoë's independence was now firmly established several months into her junior year of high school. For every day of her life, he'd known her exact location and the circles she traveled in. Suddenly, with the onset of her freedom bestowed by a driver's license, he fell out of the loop.

Aaron heard the car pull into the driveway and met Zoë at the door with a hug. She was dressed in red jeans and a t-shirt with the stenciled phrase, *Hey TSA - I've got a Bomb…in my Pants!* Aaron constantly worried about her catching a cold but knew she wouldn't wear a coat because apparently, no one in high school ever did either. Her shoulder length, light brown hair hung free and she had inherited her mother's crystallized sapphire eyes. After dropping her purse by the door, they greeted each other with a mutual,

"I love you."

Aaron, having been raised absent of men, was the sort of father who could speak his heart. He easily said the words "I love you" and he told his daughter every day.

He didn't say *love ya*; or,
    send a text *luv u*; or,
        like you; or,
            louvre yah; or,
                here's lookin at you, kid.
And when Zoë would say "I love you" to him,
    he never said *me, too*; or,
        back at 'cha; or,
            yup; or,
                ditto; or,
                    the classic Han Solo line, *I know.*

Aaron would say "I love you" to his daughter ten times a day with casual eye contact. They said it as a farewell gesture and a just-checking-in-with-you and is-everything-ok type of greeting. They said "I love you" to each other without cause, for no reason except they were living in the same house without a mother, without a wife, without sisters or brothers, only the two of them, relying on each to make it through the day. He said the same huge words, not three little words, making sure Zoë knew they weren't little, capitalizing them like the end of Kurt Cobain's suicide note to his daughter Frances:

I LOVE YOU!   *I LOVE YOU!*

Their parent-child relationship was clear, Aaron as father and Zoë as daughter, but they were more like partners-in-crime, stealing time together and sharing cleaning and cooking duties. He never had to assign her chores because they both liked to live in a clean house. When he cooked, she did the dishes. And sometimes he did both while she did homework, it didn't matter. They weren't keeping score. He pretended that his job offered enough money to make it through the week, although he had assistance from the women in his life, and Zoë never asked for an allowance. Aaron enforced neither a bedtime nor a dinner time schedule, they simply ate when hungry and slept when tired. She earned good grades while he kept his job, a simple agreement.

Simple, he knew, until boys threatened to start knocking on the door. Much to his relief, Zoë had made it to her junior year without a date to plunder her innocence like what had happened to her mother, Lena. The Huns had not burned Rome. The Horde had not swept through Mongolia. The Blitzkrieg had not descended upon France. Not yet.

But they were coming, and he could do absolutely nothing to prevent the most dreaded fear in a father's heart: Boys. Aaron asked himself frequently why he worried about boys. Because he had been one himself and understood the dark temptations and hormonal urges? No. Because some random boy might knock her up? No. The truth was that someday, a boy might come along and steal her away. And his little girl, the star of his life, the beating in his heart, the breath in his lungs, would leave her father. Willingly. Aaron knew he was on borrowed time when Zoë came home and dropped her backpack on the kitchen table. The barbarians were at the gate.

Zoë arrived home from school hungry with questions and Aaron felt obligated to feed her. As the child of a single father, Zoë had been raised on a strict diet of French toast, spaghetti and nachos, always with a side of answers to her scholastic queries.

She immediately launched her first salvo. "Hey, why did we bomb Hiroshima? And happy birthday tomorrow."

"Thanks, but let's not celebrate until this weekend, everyone's coming over. How was school?"

"Doing a report on World War Two. Mr. P want us to write an essay. He assigned the class a list of questions and everybody selected one."

"You hungry?"

"Always."

Aaron opened the fridge, took out a block of cheese and asked her, "World War Two, huh? What were some of the other questions?"

"Let's see, Cāste got something about the Russians. Thyme is writing about Ethiopia which is cool cuz I didn't know they were involved and Alanis is doing the Battle of Great Britain…"

"Just Britain. Battle of. Lasted for about 100 days. Brits celebrate every September fifteenth. Five hundred RAF pilots were killed versus two thousand German pilots."

"Wait, that's like four-to-one. That can't be right."

"Brits had radar. Told everyone carrots were responsible for better eyesight to spot the German planes. People still believe that lie."

"Wait, carrots don't improve night vision?"

"War propaganda. People can be deceptive when their homes are threatened."

"Like when you kicked that dog that came into our yard last year?"

"It tried to bite you," Aaron said defensively. He took out the cutting board and began grating a block of cheese to make nachos for dinner.

"I was petting him. And you lured him over with a treat."

"Maybe I overreacted."

"You tend to do that," she said, giving him a quick hug from the side.

"Anyway, ask your teacher what we were doing while the world was under siege."

"What *were* we doing?"

"Chillin. The Americans didn't join the war for another year and a half! I mean, sure, eight volunteer pilots snuck through Canada over to

England and eventually swelled to become the Eagle Squadron. And FDR shipped over one hundred and twenty Flying Tigers to help out in China."

Zoë ignored his tangent as she continued. "Anyway, that funny kid in the back row, Cinqué, he gets to do Italy, of course, since Mr. Papino and Cinqué's dad are both in the Sons of Italy. Stinky Finkle threw a big fit in class because he's got to do an essay on the effectiveness of Third Reich propaganda."

"Why doesn't he want to?"

"Well, he's Jewish."

"Ah, I see."

"He wanted to do the Holocaust, but Missy snagged that one already. She'll probably make a poster with happy faces and moonbeam stickers like she did for her *Physics of Probability in the land of My Little Pony* project."

"Sounds awful. You want some guac?"

"Sure," Zoë said as she began to chop up a ripe avocado. She put the pieces in a bowl and mashed them with a fork. "Missy already told Mr. P the title of her project. Check this, she's calling it the *Happy, Healthy Holocaust for the Homos, Homeless and Heathens.*"

"Wait, what?"

"She said the German people were confused and the whole thing was a great, big misunderstanding. They didn't really mean to kill the Jews."

"What, we accidently fell into those ovens? It's called Revisionism. Kinda of, I guess. More like Stupidism. That doesn't even make sense."

"Seriously, I can't even. She's such a freak."

"Anyway, what do you want to know about Hiroshima?" Aaron asked, severely distracted as he grated a block of sharp cheddar cheese. He lingered in shock about the Happy Holocaust idea. He could imagine Neo-Nazi's wearing tiny *Happy Holocaust Day* buttons, marching around town dressed in khakis and button-down polo shirts while holding flaming tiki torches. The Fascist image throbbed so vividly that he scraped part of his knuckle on the grater, adding a bloody flap of skin in with Wisconsin's finest.

Zoë didn't notice. She asked, "Why did the Americans, I mean we, why did we nuke Japan?"

Aaron washed his hand off under the sink to prevent getting blood on the cheese. He didn't want his mild injury to interfere with their conversation.

"Oh, right," Aaron said, "but see, you gotta ask why we nuked them TWICE, that's the real question. I mean, did they try to surrender after the first one at Hiroshima but before the second one at Nagasaki three days later? Why didn't we warn them, right?"

"Hold on. Let me write this down."

"Why not simply test the bomb, say, up in the isolated mountains of Hokkaido or offshore in Tokyo Bay or send them newsreel of Trinity, right?"

"Trinity?"

"Gawd, what're they teaching you up at that school?" Aaron reached into the junk drawer, searching for a Band-aid to place over his knuckle as Zoë grabbed a notebook out of her backpack in the other room.

"You mean what are they NOT teaching me?" Zoë asked as she came back into the kitchen. "A lot, I'd say. For instance, they're not passing out condoms anymore."

"Anymore?"

"Big drama last year in Sex Ed class. Missy's mom got upset because her daughter might see some rubbers and get," pausing before she tossed up air quotes, "tempted by the Devil."

"But that girl's mom is, how you kids say nowadays, cray-cray. And besides, Missy's mom got knocked up at sixteen."

"No way!"

"Way. She was a junior, I was a year ahead of her. Came back from the spring break and she wasn't pregnant anymore."

"Abortion?"

"She never said so, but everyone knew."

"Whoa," Zoë said. She reached into the fridge and pulled out a tub of sour cream and a glass jar of salsa. "Anyway, who was Trinity?"

"The heroine of the Matrix."

"What?"

"Never mind. Trinity is a place. Heard of Oppenheimer?"

"Um, I don't think so. Hold on, I can google him."

"Forget it, can't learn anything that way. And stay away from Wikipedia. That site is like condensed milk. Filling but lacks nutrition."

"Then what am I supposed to do?"

"Research. Look for sites with dot edu instead of dot com. Anyway, Oppie built the bomb. He served as the director of the

Manhattan Project."

"They built the bomb in New Mexico, right? I remember now." Zoë looked around in the cupboard, "We doing beans, too?"

"Sure," Aaron said as he grabbed a quart-sized pan while Zoë opened a can of organic, refried black beans.

Aaron continued. "Oppie helped build it but his daughter fell victim to the atomic age. Her name was Toni and she wanted a job as a UN translator."

"What'd she speak?"

"I dunno, probably French. Private school girls in the 50s learned French so if they ever got knocked up by their boss and fired from their secretarial job, then they could still make a little money as a tutor. Anyway, the FBI denied her security clearance because her dad, well, Oppie got screwed after the war. He didn't want anything to do with the H-bomb and they discredited him, labeled him a Communist. He moved his family down to St. John's Island[10] to get away from the madness."

"The madness which he helped make."

"Right. So, his daughter completed suicide at thirty-two when she didn't get the job."

"That's a little extreme," Zoë said as she stirred a small can of diced black olives into the refried beans.

"…and they donated their beach house on St. John's to the public. Sins of the father trying to repay a debt, I guess. Always suspected Oppie was a little schizophrenic, sure explains a lot."

"Whadda mean?"

"Man's delusion that the ultimate weapon of destruction will bring an end to war."

Aaron wanted to express to Zoë the complexities of Oppenheimer and how the location selected for the Trinity test site in New Mexico had been named *Jornada del Muerto* by 15th century Spanish explorers, appropriately translated as 'The Journey of Death'.

Instead, Aaron said, "When he saw the bomb go off, Dr. Oppie said, 'Now I am become Death, the Destroyer of Onions'."

"Onions?"

"Onions? Did I say onions?"

"Yeah."

"Worlds, Destroyer of Worlds. You want onions in the guacamole?"

"Duh, of course. Red onions?"

"Yup."

"So, Trinity?"

"Oh, right. That's where they tested the first prototype. Of the bomb. They didn't even know if the gadget would work. Thought it might literally ignite the nitrogen in the air or the hydrogen in the water. And they really didn't know how big that first explosion would be. But for Oppie, the real bomb dropped eighteen months earlier when his mistress Jean Tatlock killed herself."

"Both his daughter and his mistress committed suicide? That's rough."

"Hopefully, I'll never have to find out," Aaron said uneasily.

The juice from the sliced onions seeped under the Band-aid and burned his scraped knuckle. The propanethiol sulfer-oxide from the onion also teared Aaron's eyes, which made him think of how the VIPs who witnessed the Trinity explosion wore welder's glasses, Lincoln Super-Visibility Lens, Shade #10, and how they applied sun-tan lotion at 5:30 a.m. before being temporarily blinded by the man-made sun, and how afterwards the physicists patted each other on the back and said, *Now we're all sons of bitches!*

Aaron flushed his eyes and raw knuckle with cool water from the faucet. He turned back to Zoë and since he did not want to continue talking about the possibility of losing a daughter, he lectured angrily. "Since Trinity, we've nuked ourselves more than the Russians ever would have. There have been over two thousand nuclear tests, crazy to think about. Maybe ask that teacher of yours not why we bombed Japan twice but why people have nuked the planet so many damned times! I guess the Earth herself was the real target, irradiating the clouds and cities, the streams and seas, pines and pastures, corn and cattle."

"Real poetic, Dad, can I write that down?" Zoë said sarcastically. She pulled out a history textbook and highlighted words in her notebook. He peeked over her shoulder while stirring the pot of refried beans and noticed none of the ideas he had spoken about had made it into her notebook. Probably a good thing, he figured.

Aaron laid down a layer of blue corn tortilla chips on a large ceramic plate, covered them with grated cheese and then laid another layer of chips, repeating the technique until he had a large pile of chips and cheese, and in his atomic frame of reference, the mound resembled the first full-scale, chain-reacting pile as big as a two-car garage built by Enrico Fermi.

Holding the plate of nachos in both hands before sliding them into the lower rack of the natural gas heated oven, Aaron paused and asked, "Hey Zoë, how long do you think it would take to eat a garage-sized plate of nachos?"

In a voice imitating their favorite sketch from The Chappelle Show's character of Tyrone Biggums, Zoë said, "Hours!"

He laughed, set the timer on the oven, and spied an over-ripe mango on the counter which he thought might compliment the salsa. Holding the mango in one hand, he felt the weight and remembered that the core of Fat Man was a ball of plutonium, the element named after Pluto, not the planet but instead the Roman god of the dead. The core had been about the same size as a mango surrounded by a watermelon-sized uranium tamper weighing one ton. "That's a hell of a mango," he said out loud.

"What?"

"Never mind. What else you wanna know?"

"Well," Zoë said looking up from her textbook, "you haven't been much help." She paused then said, "Says here Einstein had something to do with the bomb. What's up with that?"

"Well, yes and no. He did say *Ich bin Feuer und Flamme dafur* when he left Germany for good, which pretty much implicates him in the destruction of mankind."

"*Ich bin ein Berliner*? That speech?"

"No, that was Kennedy."

"We saw that in class yesterday, something about the Cold War, right? What did he even mean?"

"Kennedy wanted to convey that he was one of them, that he understood the struggles of those living in Berlin, that he identified with their plight. But saying *ein Berliner* changes it."

"Changes it to what?"

"I'm a jelly donut!"

"Really?"

"It's slang." Aaron danced around the kitchen, pointing both thumbs at himself. "Hey, I'm a jelly donut! Check me out, jelly donut, y'all!"

Zoë laughed. "Dad!"

Aaron went back to the cutting board and started dicing the

mango. "Actually, Kennedy was spot on. It's proper grammar. *Ein Berliner* implies having the spirit of a person from Berlin. His audience loved it. You think ol' Jack would mess up a thing like that up?"

"Fine, but this doesn't help me at all," Zoë said pointing to her notebook. "So, back to Einstein."

"Right. Albert's *Ich bin Feuer und Flamme dafur* means 'I am Fire and Flame for it'. Sounds like he was talking about the bomb, right?"

"He wasn't?"

"Nope, he wanted our jelly donuts!"

Zoë rolled her eyes. "Ugh."

"Alright. Einstein burned with excitement to leave Germany in the early Thirties. And Nazi's, that's why he left."

"Cuz they were killing Jews."

"Not on a large scale. Not yet."

"But what about that *Kristallnacht* thing with the broken glass?"

"Right," Aaron said, proud his daughter had been listening in class. "Einstein saw the storm clouds gathering and bailed early. The anti-Jewish laws stripped Germany of a quarter of their physicists, and this is the part that must have really burned the Nazi's. Eleven of those Jews would work on the Manhattan project and earn the Nobel Prize."

"German Jews built the bomb? That's ironic."

Aaron thought the real irony lay in the fact that Japanese physicist Tokutaro Hagiwara at the University of Kyoto first envisioned thermonuclear hydrogen chain reactions but his government refused to consider developing a weapon. Just like gunpowder—Asians invent it, but Anglos changed it into a weapon.

Aaron replied, "Yeah, Oppie built the bomb, with the help of German Jews, two billion dollars and three years of tinkering with gadgets in the desert of Los Alamos."

"How much would it cost today?"

Aaron didn't hesitate since he knew how to adjust for inflation from the early 1940's by multiplying by fifteen. Like most men, the only thing he had trouble adjusting to was the idea of change. "About thirty billion."

"That seems like a lot."

"Not really, considering we spend over six hundred billion on national defense."

"You mean national offense."

"Nice one, kid."

"So," Zoë said, "a bunch of Jews were fleeing Europe. I get that, and they helped us build the bomb."

"Fleeing? You make it sound like they had a choice. Don't get me started…"

"Chill, pops. I know about the Camps, been hearing about it since first grade. And I know we weren't letting them into our country either, I read about the *St. Louis* last week. We doing jalapeños?"

"Sure. By the way, nobody wanted the Jews. They never have. The English kicked them out in the 13th century, booted from France in the 14th and expelled from Spain in the 15th. We had nowhere to go. Nowhere!"

His mind flashed with stats, as it tended to do when adding a little salt to the soup of his mind. The numbers rolled in: 80% of the Jews were exterminated in Hungary. 85% in Czechoslovakia. 90% in Poland. 90% in Greece. 92% in Lithuania. 94% in the Netherlands. 95% in Yugoslavia. The Jewish question had almost been solved. Aaron didn't want to even mention the other Holocaust, the one that started with the rape of Nanjing by a Japanese cock-shaped bayonet and ended with thirty-five million Chinese people dead or wounded, most of them civilians.

Bing.

On the stovetop, the timer ended and Aaron hesitated to remove the plate of nachos from the oven. He didn't want to seem callous to his daughter and speak of the Holocaust and ovens in the same sentence. Zoë was busy scribbling in her notebook as the timer rang for a full thirty seconds. Aaron stood in the middle of the kitchen, a green clothed hot pad in one hand, swaying back and forth on two feeble legs between the oven and the timer. Ovens. Holocaust. Six million Jews. And another number flashed in his mind. Thirty-five million Chinese. Thirty-five million! The number became a sound, echoing in his mind, a deep baritone somber voice, repeating itself over and over. The number loomed large and overwhelming. Aaron couldn't move, unable to decide whether to silence the beeping sound or remove the hot plate out of the oven. The procedure confused him because he wasn't sure where he would place the scorching ceramic plate. The order of how to navigate the world suddenly expanded into an infinite number of complex variations. To commit to one path of action negated every other possibility. He couldn't be held responsible for negating a possible future, and the indecision left him immobilized.

Finally, Zoë raced over and turned the timer off.

"What's your deal? You're gonna burn dinner. Again." She took the green mitt from his hand and pulled out the hot plate, placing it onto a second cooler plate to easily transport the baked dish over to the kitchen table.

Nice move kid, Aaron thought. He shook his limbs to gain mobility. He bounced on his toes to revive the stagnant blood in his legs. I'll be okay, Aaron told himself.

Opening a can of Sprite to give himself a sugar boost, Aaron was relieved that Zoë hadn't noticed his mini-anxiety attack. Sitting down at the kitchen table, she was preoccupied with the large plate of sizzling nachos.

Aaron had lost his appetite, but sat down to join her. He forced the anxiety out of his mind and took another sip.

Zoë snatched a lone corn chip from the top of the pile. "Mommy said she had a dream about you. She was giving you a blow job."

Aaron coughed, spitting up soda water. "Drunk again, hmm?"

"Duh," Zoë said, rolling her eyes. "Wait a second, do married people still give each other head?"

Aaron always appreciated Zoë's direct line of questioning, and didn't want to dissuade future inquiry, which is why he said, "Hell, that's WHY men get married!"

"Anyway, she said fellatio is probably a metaphor for bankruptcy. What's that?"

"You know what a blow job is but not bankruptcy?"

"Come on, Dad, I don't wanna have The Talk. We tried that in the third grade, remember?"

"You were playing with your dolls and started grinding Barbie and Ken's crotches together."

Zoë laughed. "Then I asked you how babies are made."

"I just about died!"

"Remember what you told me?"

"I sat on the floor next to you and said, 'Go ask your mother.'"

They both laughed, Zoë covering her mouth to prevent bits of corn chips from spewing out.

"But then you took me to the library and we checked out a book."

Aaron nodded. "The Birds and the Bees and other Queer Fish."

"Ha!" Zoë giggled. "I remember that."

"Some kinda kid's book on Queer theory and gay sex."

"Good job, Dad. You totally messed me up," Zoë said with a smile. "And these days, it's just called sex."

Aaron knew he'd done alright because beginning at the age of twelve, she had asked him about the two most addictive challenges of puberty: drugs and boys. And over the years, he had answered every question. Truthfully.

Between bites, Zoë glanced at her notebook again and asked, "Wasn't Hitler working on the bomb, too?"

"Sure, Hitler was desperate to make the bomb, but don't you mean Schicklgrüber?"

"Who?"

"Adolf's father. His original name was Schicklgrüber. Can you imagine a bunch of Nazi's running around saluting each other, crying out, 'Heil Schicklgrüber'? Sounds like a Mel Brooks film."

Zoë laughed because they'd watched *Young Frankenstein* about a dozen times together. "How close did the Germans get to making the bomb?"

"Heisenberg took the wrong route. Heavy-water instead of graphite."

Zoë double-dipped into the guacamole, leaving a bit of the sour cream in the bowl, which irked Aaron but he remained silent as the image of an avocado tree sparked a memory of Hitler's family tree. The guacamole dish reminded him that Hitler had become a vegetarian in order to atone for the romantic fling with Geli Raubal, his own niece, who he shot in lover's quarrel and made it look like a suicide. Aaron remembered that most of the six women that Adolf dated ended up committing suicide. Aaron suspected that the *Führer* had been a total manic depressive, a difficult type of person to fall in love with. However, this personality disorder was familiar to Aaron since many of his ex-girlfriends had told him, *Dating you is depressing me.*

As Aaron realized he should probably stop comparing his dating life to Hitler's, Zoë looked up and asked, "What's heavy-water?"

"Well, you see, deuterium replaces…oh, never mind, I really don't understand it either." He wanted to say that in 1944, the last 162 gallons of heavy-water in Europe sank aboard the passenger ferry *Hydro* into Lake Tinnsjo, sabotaged by Norwegian agent Knut Haukelid, thus ending the German atomic bomb project. And how after the war, Knut ended up living in the same town where many of the people had relatives that drowned on the ferry that he'd sabotaged and everyone knew he'd done it, making encounters at the local Starbucks extremely awkward.

Instead, Aaron said, "The Germans really never had a chance."

"So, we developed the bomb first and dropped it on Japan."

"Twice."

"Right, twice. Why exactly?"

"Cuz fuck[11] em, that's why."

"Daddy!"

"Just kidding, but a lot of people thought like that back in Forty-Five."

"But Igo and Kāne are in my calculus class and they're pretty cool. Even the Chinese kids like them."

"You gotta understand, we were at war," Aaron said. "And hell, they started it."

More stats flashed through Aaron's mind, numbers like seventy-eight million dead worldwide and most were civilians, not soldiers. Civilians going to work, paying bills, making love, chewing gum, minding their own business and then boom, a 250-pound Mark I general purpose bomb would suddenly crash through the roof of a Tokyo apartment.

"Maybe they started it, but we sure ended it," Zoë sighed.

The statistics formed a lesson that Aaron wanted to convey to his daughter. "Yes, we did," Aaron agreed. "And many innocent civilians died. During war, it's always been safer to be a soldier than a civilian."

Innocent civilians in cities like London, Hamburg, Dresden, Chongqing, Yokohama, Hiroshima, and Nagasaki, who worked in the war factories, made the bullets, primed the bombs, built the aircraft, riveted the bolts, filled the tires and checked the oil. Civilians fueling the war machine which made their innocence questionable.

Aaron continued. "You have to understand, America was determined to drop two bombs."

As Zoë spilled a drop of salsa on the tablecloth and got up to fetch a rag to clean it up, Aaron's mind wandered. He imagined General Leslie Groves standing in a trench at the Trinity test site and being asked by a reporter if the war was over . . .

Groves: "Yes, but only after we drop TWO bombs on Japan."

Reporter: "But General, why two bombs?"

Leslie Groves lowers the shaded lens, his eyes reflecting the atomic blast, primal affect: "Because those slanty-eyed Nips will never surrender."

The man next to Groves, a Yale-educated statistician: "That's true. When four of our boys are killed in action, one will give up. But we have to kill over a hundred Japanese soldiers before even one will surrender."

Groves: "They're fanatics!"

"Aren't we all?" says someone from behind.

The men turn around and greet Julius Robert Oppenheimer who wears the despondent frown of responsibility.

Oppie, withdrawn affect: "There is traditional Japanese proverb. 'We will fight until we eat stones'. It means they will continue to fight until every man, woman and child lies face down on the battlefield."

Groves: "That's why the official policy of the US Air Force is to firebomb the hell outta the Japs so that not one stone remains atop another."

Statistician: "Pretty sure that's what Rome did to Carthage when they went after Hannibal. Salted the earth and leveled the stones."

Groves: "Damn stones."

Oppie: "What have I done?"

Zoë sat down and wiped up the salsa. She looked down at her notes and asked, "What were we talking about?"

"Something about civilians."

"Right, so why didn't we drop a bomb on their army base?"

"We targeted a populated city because we were curious to see what would happen."

"That's terrible."

"You forget, no one had ever seen anything like this. We bombed Hiroshima mainly because it had been untouched."

Aaron decided not to explain the details of why certain cities were targeted whereas others were left untouched. Secretary of War Henry Stimson refused to bomb Kyoto because of its cultural significance as Japan's ancient capital. Also, Doolittle spared the Imperial Palace from bombing on his famous raid, a decision he said was the best one of his life. Of course, there were continuous firebombings, and more people died on one night in the city of Tokyo than in the immediate blast of Hiroshima or Nagasaki. Ultimately, Hiroshima was targeted because it had been largely unmolested by aerial raids, and contained a large population of industrial factories surrounded by family homes where the Allies hoped the bomb could be used without warning to maximize psychological impact. Japanese civilians were directly targeted during the early morning at 8:16 a.m. when people were heading to work, studying at school, playing at day care, shopping at the supermarket, and lounging in the park.

Zoë reached for another chip, then decided to simply stick her finger right into the guacamole. "So, Hiroshima happened. Didn't they immediately surrender? I mean, come on now. Who would keep fighting after seeing that big mushroom cloud?"

"Hannah Arendt says the Common World was destroyed on that day. But three days later, we did it again. Guess why we picked Nagasaki."

"Because it rhymes with Milwaukee?"

"Close. Nagasaki had the Mitsubishi factory that constructed both the Zero planes and the wood-finned torpedoes used at Pearl Harbor."

"For real?"

"No, but that's a good enough reason. We were sore about Pearl."

"Still are."

"True, true. Heard that we tried to warn the people of Nagasaki."

"So nice of us," Zoë said sarcastically.

"Leaflets were dropped by Allied planes telling them to evacuate and surrender."

"But?"

"But the leaflets were accidently dropped one day AFTER the bomb fell."

"Oops."

"A high-grade military oops. The Japanese surrendered the next day but the Emperor didn't get around to it until about a week later, and during that time, we dropped twelve million more pounds of explosives on them."

"Twelve million? While they were trying to surrender?"

"And four more nukes were being constructed at Los Alamos. Check this out, if the Japanese had not surrendered, then we were planning to use poison gas on twenty-five of their cities, killing up to eight million civilians."

"Wow, we were just getting started."

"Yup. Everyone wanted the war to be over."

Aaron could only think of the writings of Yukio Mishima and how the excitement of surrender hovered like a toy balloon about to burst with everyone in Japan wondering,

Will it burst now?

Will it burst now?

Aaron thought that maybe Yukio foresaw that a nuclear bomb could explode anytime, anywhere in the world,

Will it burst now!

And we've been worrying ever since. Panoizys.[12]

But Aaron didn't want to speak of nuclear anxiety and instead desired only to answer Zoë's original question of why two bombs were dropped on the Japanese people. Despite his numerous and varied tangents, he always tried to answer her questions. But for Aaron, life was a myriad of distractions.

Aaron wanted to explain how the Russians finally invaded Manchuria at the end of the war and were marching for northern Japan. The Americans, in an effort to deter a Russian invasion of Japan, dropped a second bomb.

"You know," he said, "they should have been grateful."

"Grateful for nuking their cities?"

"The Soviets would have occupied Northern Japan."

"So?"

"The communists would have prevented a speedy capitalist rebuilding of Japan's economy. Millions might have starved to death. Like in North Korea."

"I'm NOT putting that in my paper. I swear, sometimes you go too far."

Aaron remained silent while Zoë doodled in her notebook. They both mindlessly picked at the food, switching between the various toppings of refried bean dip with olives, guacamole with red onions, sour cream, and mango salsa. Aaron poked at his finger as the blood seeped through the bandage. He looked up at the depleted pile of nachos and spotted something odd resembling a crispy sliver of an olive. Suddenly, he realized the anomaly wasn't cheese or an olive but rather the missing piece of skin from his knuckle. He'd forgotten to take it out of the shredded cheese.

Aaron gazed across the table at his daughter. "I suddenly know why we nuked them twice."

Zoë arched her eyebrows. "Why's that?"

"Maybe that girl Missy is onto something. Maybe we enjoy killing each other."

Zoë looked at her father with a sudden comprehension. "Happy Holocaust. Fʊck."[13]

*

Intermission in honor of the dead—eleven people murdered at the Tree of Life Synagogue in Squirrel Hill and the fifty people slain at the Al-Noor Mosque in Riccarton.

And almost Temple Emanuel in Pueblo.

Never again.

Never.

Again.

And again.

*

Aaron paused while the nachos began to stiffen, the cheese congealing in fatty pools. He figured it would be beneficial to backtrack, maybe start at the beginning. He'd been bashing Zoë with facts about European genocidal horror and Asian nuclear hell, and Aaron wanted to convey the origins of the Pacific theater. Maybe that would help answer her question.

As Zoë read silently from her textbook, Aaron picked at the few remaining corn chips. The bowl of guacamole was empty, the sour cream had been ruined with streaks of salsa, and the bean-dip smelled rank. Aaron pondered how to explain the forgotten half of the war, the one in the Pacific, forgotten until the light of a thousand suns brightened the horizon. Maybe he'd start with Manchuria in '31? Or the Marco Polo Bridge incident on July 7th, 1937? Too complicated to explain a Japanese-occupied China. Much easier for Americans to start with Pearl.

Aaron decided not to emphasize numbers, dates or battles in order to simplify the complexities of multi-national militaristic engagements and pandemic atrocities contrasted against Japanese logistical brilliance and the American rise to global hegemony.

Instead, Aaron said, "History is not dates. History is not war. History is not linear."

Zoë titled her head, perplexed. "Well, that's a relief. So, then what is it?"

"History is the story of people between the date lines. And the stories repeat themselves."

"You've said that before, stop repeating yourself," Zoë said with a grin.

"We study history to learn about the present."

"And predict the future?"

"Maybe. If we're wise enough."

"If history isn't about war," Zoë asked, "then why do you always tell me war stories?"

"Cuz it's exciting!"

"You mean the rape, pillage and plunder of innocent civilians? You mean violence against the weak? You mean tyranny of the strong?"

Aaron sighed and said, "Damn liberal arts education."

Zoë laughed. "You paid for it!"

Cowardly, Aaron decided not to tell her that Marilyn was footing the bill. He didn't want Zoë to think that he couldn't provide for his own daughter. "Alright then, grasp this. It's the little moments of heroism that define humanity."

"War heroes, like those four bronze statues downtown? Those guys with the medals?"

"Sure, but I'm talking about guys like Dorie Miller."

"Dory, the forgetful fish from *Finding Nemo*?"

Aaron laughed. "Basically. His name was Doris."

"He identified as Trans?"

"No, tough guys usually have girl names. John Wayne's real name was Marion. And *mensches* like Sandy Koufax and Abbie Hoffman. Anyway, during the attack…"

"Which one again?"

"Pearl Harbor."

"Right. When the Koreans invaded the Panama Canal."

"Zoë!"

"Just messin with you, Dad. I know, we watch that movie ever year. The one with Ben Affleck. And that other cute guy."

Every December 8th, Zoë and Aaron watched Michael Bay's *Pearl Harbor*. The 8th represented the actual day across the International Date line in Japan when the planes struck Hawaii and Aaron thought celebrating on December 7th would be like visiting a dead relative's grave on their death day instead of on their birthday.

"Remember the guy played by Cuba Gooding, Jr.? The boxer?"

Zoë smiled. "You always cry when he gets behind the big machine gun and shoots down some planes."

"What? It's the pepper you put on the popcorn, makes me tear-up and sneeze."

Zoë looked at her father in disbelief. "Whatevs."

"Fine," he admitted. "You're right, gets me every time." Aaron wasn't the kind of father who avoided crying in front of his daughter. In fact, he did it at least once a day when she rushed home and told him about acing a test, speaking up in class, sharing lunch with a friend, standing up against a bully, arguing against a teacher, scoring a goal, blocking a goal, or simply kicking the soccer ball.

"Yes," Aaron continued, "that guy. He's a real hero."

"Why?"

"Because Doire Miller never got a Medal of Honor."

Zoë glanced up from the big plate of nachos. "Why not?"

"Because some men get medals for doing the same thing as other men."

"That doesn't sound fair."

"And the medal winners have one thing the other men don't."

"What's that?"

"A witness."

"A white-ness?"

Aaron laughed. "Exactly."

Aaron wanted to explain how during the attack on Pearl Harbor, an officer in the Navy named John W. Finn, the son of a Californian plumber, welded the tripod of a .50-cal onto a bench and blasted away at incoming Japanese aircraft for nearly two hours. The enemy pilots shot off his heel and part of his arm, but literally cursing like a sailor mixed with Irish rage kept him alive and reloading. His reward for bravery amounted to twenty-nine bullet holes in his body and a Medal of Honor.

On the other hand, Dorie Miller who towered at 6'3", a Black and proud American, a fullback and boxing champ from Waco, Texas, was ordered to serve white boys in the Navy's kitchen aboard the *West Virginia*. During his service, Dorie discovered the Navy to be about as segregated as the rest of America. Dorie, a man about as big and black as the famous boxer Jack Johnson, was given the humiliating rank of Mess Attendant, 2nd class, to do laundry for preppy East coast officers and racist Southern ensigns. When those planes showed up with the red ball of a rising sun under their wings, Dorie had stored up plenty of Black rage. A lifetime's worth. With no training, Dorie jumped on a .50-cal and shot down a few of those planes. A nearby soldier said that moment was the only time he'd ever seen Dorie smile. A few months later, Nimitz awarded Dorie the Navy Cross, but not the Medal of Honor like ol' Johnny Finn because that's the Navy. The Admiral pinned the Navy's third highest medal to Dorie's chest and the two shared a private word, and Aaron imagined the scene went down like . . .

Chester Nimitz, stern affect: "Good job, boy, you done real good."

Doris Miller, ramrod straight, chest puffing out, regal affect: "Thank you, sir."

Nimitz: "You should be real happy with gettin the highest award ever given to a Black man. You're a credit to your race."

"Um, thank you, I guess."

"What's that, boy?"

"I mean, sir, yes sir! Thank you, sir."

"Now then, boy, we're gonna promote you and send you around the country to sell war bonds. You're a hero, son."

"Hold on a sec," Dorie replies. "They killed my friends back at Pearl. I wanna fight and kill some Japs, just like every other American."

"No, no. We'll put you on tour to raise money for the war effort, that's where you're needed, son. We'll get lots of cash outta those Black folks now."

Dorie pauses then says, "Sir, with all due respect...I ain't your Negro!"

The gathered crowd of Colored cooks, Mulatto mess mates and Darkie deck swabbers cry out in unison, "Daaaaaaaaaaaamn!"

Aaron knew what happened next because the Navy did what they always do. They stuck Dorie back in the bottom of an escort aircraft carrier and promoted him. Yes, indeed, they promoted him to Ship's Cook, 2nd Grade. From 3rd class to 2nd class. Some white boy unloaded a .50-cal at planes for two hours and received a Medal of Honor whereas Dorie got a shiny 2nd class medal and a 2nd class promotion for those thought to be 2nd class citizens. Aaron could have guessed how the story ended. Dorie's ship was torpedoed off the coast of the Gilbert Islands in '43 and he drowned. Done and done, son.

Aaron couldn't relate any of this to his daughter and instead looked over at Zoë who flicked at the remaining nacho. As the meal closed to an end, terrible guilt swelled in Aaron for not preparing any vegetables. Also, the sliced bit of skin from his knuckle was nowhere to be seen. He hoped that he'd eaten it and not her.

Zoë reached for her calculus homework and Aaron decided to grab her attention for a little while longer. He wasn't ready for the night to be over. Soon, she'd be on her phone.

"Ready for some ice cream?"

"Always!"

Aaron stood up and grabbed a one-pint tub of Ben and Jerry's Hippy-Dippy-Chocolate-Chippy from the freezer. He brought over two spoons to the kitchen table, one large and one small. He wasn't sure which one Zoë would want, and he figured he'd use the other one. He brought both because that's what fathers do.

For the same reason, Aaron knew that's why men wear layers. When out with their families, the guy can shed clothing when the clouds roll in—jacket to one kid, sweater to another, hoodie for the wife. Inevitably, he's left shivering in a short-sleeved shirt. That's what it meant to be a father. Carry the gear for your kids. In Nepal, they're called Sherpas.[14]

As they took turns diving into ice cream, Aaron dropped one last zinger to get her attention. "When the dive-bombers hit Pearl, some of the sailors fought back with potatoes and wrenches."

Zoë looked up in disbelief. "That's not true."

"I can't make this stuff up." Aaron thought about how during the air attack, sailors from the *Oglala* and *Helena* were unable to return fire since the unlit boilers provided no power to operate the anti-aircraft guns. The rifles and pistols were locked up, and the deck officer with keys was passed out drunk. The sailors resorted to throwing potatoes and wrenches at the low-flying Japanese aircraft. "See, that's history," Aaron continued. "It's impossible to understand the global intricacies of a world war, but we can understand the frustration of surprised men."

"Throwing potatoes at a plane? What's that gonna do besides make tater tots?"

"And wrenches! We were so unprepared, asleep in fact. Oh, and this one bad-ass soldier got on a bicycle, pulled out his pistol and chased after a Zero, firing into the air!"

"On a bike? For real?"

"Yup. Well, as true as any war story. But here's a true one. Women, not men, saved our asses."

Zoë exploded, "We learned that in class today!

"Really?"

"Yeah, a woman named Mary Babnik Brown donated her hair for bomb sights. That's why they're called crosshairs."

"Mrs. Brown, you mean Mitzi from the Grove?" Aaron said, "She died when I was teenager, such a sweet old lady."

"I guess."

"She helped out in the war? How come I never heard about that?"

"You don't know everything, Dad. The government needed blonde hair that had never been chemically treated. They wanted twenty-two inches of her hair, but she gave them thirty-four inches. That's Pueblo for ya, always giving more than asked."

"Pretty cool," Aaron said in amazement. He loved it when Zoë taught him something new. "Well, I was talking about Agnes Meyer Driscoll and Genevieve Feinstein. They broke the secret Japanese codes."

"Is there a movie I can watch? Maybe a YouTube clip?"

"Sorry, no best-selling books, no Hollywood blockbusters, they're only footnotes in the back section of history. These two ladies sat in a damp basement for most of the war looking for patterns in a long list of Japanese words intercepted over radio waves."

"Sounds boring."

"Agnes Driscoll, she was the sharpest. FDR called her Madame X. As usual, the smartest people in the room were Jewish women."

"Here we go again," Zoë said, feigning interest as she picked up a mechanical pencil and turned back to her math homework.

Aaron barely suppressed his desire to tell Zoë about how, later in the war, Madame X helped Alan Turing[15] decipher the unbreakable Enigma code. Inspired by her brilliance, Alan named the world's first computer *Agnus Dei*, otherwise known as *Agnes*. Her only reward appeared thirty years after her death when the American government finally awarded her an unnamed star in the Pentagon's Hall of Honor, right next to Felix Leiter, the Black secret agent who always rescued James Bond, written by Ian Fleming.[16]

"Agnes knew about Pearl Harbor," Aaron declared suddenly.

"Why didn't she say anything?"

"She tried. But the Russians knew."

"Say what? Wait, never mind."

As Zoë turned back to her homework, Aaron fantasized about how the Japanese fleet was spotted by the Russian trawler *Uritsky* two days before the infamous surprise attack . . .

On board the *Uritsky* where the crew speaks English with a terrible Russian accent.

Captain Muscovite, sleepy affect after being awoken by two startled crewmates: "Vat is going on? Vhy are you vaking me up?"

Vladimir, sailor from Vladivostok: "Captain, you have to see dis! The Japanese navy is on ze move!"

Oleg, sailor from Odessa: "Holy Mother of Russia! Stalin save us!"

Captain Muscovite: "Calm down you two. Can't be vat bad"

Captain M stands on the bridge, raises a pair of binoculars and shudders at the sight—two bulging battleships, four deadly destroyers, two cumbersome cruisers, a few unctuous oil tankers, six city-sized aircraft carriers loaded with hundreds of pernicious planes, and three submarines slithering beneath the silent sea.

Captain M, pale faced, lowers the binoculars: "Vladimir, Oleg. You have to do dis one thing vor me."

The two sailors look desperately at their captain: "Anything captain! Tell us vat to do."

Captain M, dramatic pause: "Bring me ze vodka."

The men share several shots of Starka. "Na Zdorovie."

Vladimir: "Will zey sink us now because we see them sneaking up on ze Amerikansy?"

Oleg: "We are doomed!"

Captain M: "Maybe, but first we vill send a radio message to Stalin."

Vladimir: "We vill save ze day!"

Oleg: "We vill be heroes!

Captain M: "And ze Amerikansy vill thank us vor saving their tiny island."

Aaron knew how the story played out. Did Stalin say a word to Roosevelt? Of course not. Ze Germans were a mere fifteen miles from Red Square and ze news came as a relief to ol' Joseph because ze Amerikansy vould soon be in ze war.

But the real mystery for Aaron wasn't why the Russians remained silent but by why no one listened to Agnes. Aaron figured because no one ever believes a smart woman.

Aaron focused on his daughter while she scribbled long equations on a piece of paper and said, "Even though Madame X was the smartest one in the room, they didn't believe her."

Zoë rolled her eyes. "Casandra complex, huh?"

"Right, and the same thing happened to the first person who saw the Japanese were about to bomb Pearl Harbor."

"Someone knew it going to happen?"

"Well, thirty-two people knew the Japanese were going to invade, including President Roosevelt. See, Agnes decoded a message…"

"Dad, focus!" Zoë exclaimed.

"Right, sorry. Back to the story. On that clear Sunday morning in December, twenty-two-year-old flying instructor Cornelia Fort spotted a string of Japanese fighter planes headed towards Pearl."

"A female pilot?"

"There were plenty of women who served in the WASP."

"Let me guess, they were all white women."

"How'd you know?"

"Come on, with a name like WASP?"

"Right. I think this stood for Women Airforce Service Pilots."

"Anyway," Zoë asked, "how'd this pilot know the Japanese were the bad guys?"

"Well, they weren't the bad guys yet. In fact, good and bad are such subjective terms. The Japanese considered the attack preemptive, and not a surprise attack, because of the oil embargo. Chomsky wrote a book about the difference between preemptive versus preventive attacks."

Zoë looked at her father. "Seriously? Stay on track, Dad."

"Sorry, the flying instructor. Cornelia was training a teenager how to fly. She immediately spotted the rising sun insignia on the planes and figured out the Japanese pilots were headed for the eight American battleships."

"Ok, I'm with you," Zoë said. "What'd she do next?"

"Well, having no guns on the two-seater Cessna, she played a game of high stakes air-chicken."

"Really?"

"Unarmed, she went straight at em!"

Zoë's eyes grew wide as she cried out, "Nevertheless, she persisted!"

Aaron's pride swelled. These were the little moments he lived for, when his daughter exerted her feminist knowledge of current political affairs. For Aaron, these revelations were exactly why they ate dinner together.

He swallowed a tear and continued. "Ok, so the Nipponese pilots got their first taste of Yankee salt and banked to avoid this furious woman but not before firing a few bursts of machine gun bullets which knocked out her radio."

"Sounds bad."

"She immediately dove the plane into a controlled crash landing, jumped out and told her student pilot to run like hell."

"Poor kid musta shit his pants."

"Zoë!"

"I'm just sayin," she explained as they laughed together.

"Two of the Japanese pilots turned around to strafe her as she ran towards the hanger. With bright tracers and armor-piercing rounds kicking up dust around her heels, she dove in slow-motion, crashing through the glass bay window of the main entrance."

"Dove in slow-motion? Are you making this up?"

"Probably. Some of it. Doesn't mean it's false."

Zoë smiled. "Go on."

"Alright, she rolled to a stop, stood up quickly and brushed glass out of her auburn hair. And a bunch of men stood there laughing at her."

The rest of the story unfolded in Aaron's mind, a flash of narrative conflict . . .

Cornelia Fort, yelling, panicked affect: "The Japs are attacking!"

Six grey-haired pilots from WWI, stiff leather jackets to compensate for a lack of stiffness elsewhere, sitting in the lobby drinking their Sunday morning coffee, bored, listless, unimpressed:

"Who do ya think you are? Pancho Barnes?!"

"Never shoulda given women a license to fly."

"She should be at home making babies, not making aerial acrobatics."

"She's crazy!"

Cornelia Fort, hero extraordinaire: "You dumb bastards! Look up, see those planes? Yes, the ones SHOOTING at me!"

The men explained the obvious to her:

"No, that's just target practice from our Navy pilots."

"Yep, probably some of Bill Halsey's boys."

"Ha! That ol' Bull. You know how those boys can be."

"They're just playin around."

"Probably Wildcats up there."

"Nah, sounds more like Grumman F3F-2's."

"Listen here, missie, no need to get your panties in a wad."

Cornelia, angry yet desperate: "You're the one wearin panties, you leaky-cocked, old cockpit jockeys! We need to call the duty sergeant down at Pearl. Hell, you guys play golf with Short Kimmel, give him a call at home, for God's sake. Tell em the Japs are comin!"

The troop of aged men bristled:

"Pardon me madam, but it's General Short and Admiral Kimmel."

"Hmmm, don't bother explaining it to her. She's a woman."

"Right, those are our planes."

"Practicing war games."

"Dummy rounds, not the real thing."

"Can't be the Japs."

"Japan is too far away."

"No way they could fly here from Japan. Silly woman!"

Aaron blinked twice and noticed Zoë was waiting for him to continue.

"So," Zoë asked, "Cornelia stands up, splinters of glass in her hair and then what?"

Aaron reached his hand out, simulating the circling of an airplane. "Cornelia looked up, saw the Zero coming around for another attack. She ducked behind a cement wall for cover as the fighter plane approached. The men stood together, straining their necks upward and as they sipped from coffee cups. Suddenly, hot lead ripped through their bodies, killing them instantly."

"Really?" Zoë said with surprise.

"And then Cornelia looked over their dead bodies and said, 'Maybe now you'll believe me.'"

"Whoa, that's cold," Zoë said as she stood up and collected her books.

"All done?"

"Thanks for dinner," she said, kissing him on the forehead. "I really gotta finish my homework. Love you, Dad."

"I love you, too," Aaron replied as she marched up the stairs to her room.

Aaron sat quietly at the table, uncertain of the ending to his imaginary scene. And in Aaron's mind, a lone survivor from the troop of old men, gurgling on his own blood, looked up at Cornelia:

"Those ... aren't ... Japs."

Because no one ever believes a smart woman.

Chapter 5

Vasectomy as Voluntary Biological Suicide
and the Ubiquitous Predicament of Male Frontal Nudity

Aaron committed suicide on his 40th birthday by getting a vasectomy, the dreaded sexual lobotomy that would eviscerate the very raison d'être he'd invested much of his existential importance since puberty. For months, he had been deliberating whether to go ahead with the terminal procedure and had scheduled the appointment on his birthday. With his daughter nearly off to college, Aaron had no intention of starting over as a parent. The fear of being 60 years old when his next child left the house motivated him to volunteer for societally-sanctioned sterilization.

Aaron found a handwritten card left by Zoë on the kitchen table with a white rose taken from the neighbor's yard. Aaron hated celebrating birthdays and remained grateful that she wasn't making a big deal out of it. Nevertheless, her thoughtfulness made him cry twice while reading the birthday card. After breakfast, he left the house wearing heavy boots and his thin leather brown jacket and trudged downtown to the doctor's office. Shivering with the jacket drawn tight against his body, he followed a meandering path along the icy river bed, across the railroad tracks and under the 4th Street bridge, a spot where he suspected WomB had thrown herself. He noticed a high point on the bridge where somebody could stand and jump into the water below. Maybe she had stared at the water in morbid desperation and hesitated, Aaron thought. Then again, she probably jumped right in. She had sounded determined.

Lost in thought, Aaron startled a baby deer by the river's edge. The deer looked up as Aaron approached, freezing like its parents along with generations of genetically-instilled survival instincts had taught it to do. The deer and Aaron faced each other motionlessly, their breath fogging in the morning air, hoping the other would make the first move. Aaron clapped his hands but the deer, having discovered a patch of acorn nuts under the snow, refused to budge. Aaron stomped his feet but the deer ignored him, causing Aaron to re-evaluate his decision to receive a vasectomy. He interpreted the encounter as symbolic rather than accidental, as an augury of children, and he realized that although he would soon be unable to have kids, he'd always be a parent. He also thought that since the deer was feasting on acorns, it meant the procedure on his own nuts wouldn't go well. Then again, Aaron told himself, maybe not everything's a sign because the universe didn't revolve around his wishes. Signs implied solipsism.

Without further interruption by spirit-animals, Aaron finished his cold, long walk and entered the office of Dr. Lucy Capon, a physician who ran a downtown teaching clinic. Additional students were always in the examination room, but this was the price Aaron had to pay for subsidized medical treatment. The co-pay of two bucks made the experience endurable if not somewhat humiliating. He sat in the waiting room and rubbed his frozen hands together before filling out forms, the first question a real quandary. After forty years of being a member of the male species, he was fairly certain of his gender but the numerous options confused him. On the intake form, there were 112 options listed for gender which meant Aaron could select a different gender twice a week for the entire year. The choices of Male or Female were offered first followed by Transgender, a process requiring hormonal adjustments and surgical tucks, wholly dissimilar from "tranny" to pejoratively describe the fashion fetish of transvestites; followed by Gender Queer, which he agreed with because the socially-constructed concept of gender had always seemed a little queer to him; and next Gender Fluid, a fairly accurate description because life's experience had proven that lots of fluids were exchanged when genders interacted; and Gender Blank, which supposedly conjured a mental (_____) while envisioning the concept of gender; and Gender Punk, one who actively resists gender norms; and Anxiegender, one's gender effected by anxiety, probably first experienced by Kafka as an anxiegendered cockroach; and Surgender, not Sir Gender, one of the knights of the Phallic Table, but rather when one gender is surpassed by another; and Ambigender, like an ambidextrous dresser who wears jeans under a miniskirt; and Exgender, like an atheist who doesn't believe in the existence of gender; and Verangender, allowing one to shift genders the moment their gender is identified; and Amicagender, changing gender based on your friend group, allowing simultaneous admittance to fraternities and sororities; and Quoigender, when the very notion of gender is non-sensical; and lastly Agender, at which point Aaron was utterly astonished by the abundance of Greek and Latin prefixes that he looked up at the receptionist and said, "Dʊ ɧ fΩck?"[17]

Aaron wanted to check the last option, Intersex, because he was afraid to leave it blank. He mistakenly thought the choice was *Into Sex* and feared that if he didn't mark it then the doctor might snip off more than his tubes.

While deciding on which gender box to check, Aaron closed his eyes and took a short nap in the waiting room . . .

Aaron is sitting in a reception room of a doctor's office. Many non-gender specific persons with blank faces and beige colored jump suits are waiting as well, reading magazines like *Gender Weekly, The Neutered Male, Masculine Mystique,* and *Monthly Masculinist.* The alluring receptionist is comedian Margaret Cho with spiky, flaming orange hair and ruby painted fingernails. She is seated at a wooden desk placed in front of a long wind tunnel.

The words *La Tuñel* are stenciled upon a free-standing sign with an arrow that points to the tunnel, symbolically representing a vagina. Margaret taps impatiently upon another sign[18] resting on her desk that reads, NO ADMITTANCE!

"Why can't I get in?" Aaron begs.

"Nobody gets in without my permission."

Aaron grows desperate. "When can I get in?!"

"You can't just come barging in," Margaret explains. "First, you have to buy me a few drinks."

Aaron hands her a water bottle. "This do?"

"Artesian sparkling?"

"Sure," Aaron lies. "Now what?"

"Sweet talk me, baby. Get me in the mood."

Aaron compliments her nails, her face, her Korean genetic lineage that hides wrinkles. She smiles and Aaron proceeds. "Now what?"

Margaret tilts her head up. "Rub that little sun dial until it turns red."

Aaron sees an almond shaped disk located above the entrance to La Tuñel. He can't quite reach the sun dial and asks several of the blank-faced, non-gendered guests in the waiting room to help him. They form a large cheerleader pyramid and Aaron climbs to the top. He begins to slowly rub the disk in a circular motion with his thumb.

"Faster," Margaret commands. "Now, to the left, wait, back to the right. A little lower, that's it. Right there! Perfect!!"

Talking-suds from the Mr. Bubble commercial in 1974 emerge from La Tuñel and lubricate the sides of the wall with clear foam. The animated suds sing in high-pitched voices, "He's soooo handsome," and "Hope he's a doctor," and "Our kids will look so cute!"

Margaret is very excited and wipes the sweat from her brow with a handkerchief. "You're almost there…"

"Now what?"

"I need to know two things before I can let you in," she pants.

"Fine," Aaron says eagerly.

"When I was twenty, I wanted to know if a guy had a job and a car. When I turned thirty, I wanted to know if he had kids and an ex-wife. In my forties, it got real simple."

"Go ahead with your two questions."

"Can you get it up and do you shoot blanks?"

"Hell yah to the first!" Aaron exclaims, for which he receives rowdy applause and high-fives from the non-gendered cheerleaders. "As for the second, I'm working on that. I'm getting clipped today."

Margaret's flirtatious smile disappears. She dismisses the suds as the walls of La Tuñel dry up. She leans forward in her chair and taps on the sign. "Sorry honey, no admittance. Next!"

. . . "Next!" A voice woke Aaron from his dream. Sitting in the waiting room of Dr. Capon's office, he gathered his belongings and was escorted by a curvaceous Latina nurse into the examination room that also served as the operating room. The nurse explained how the sterile environs of a hospital room were not necessary since vasectomies are a relatively minor procedure. The affable Dr. Capon greeted him with a firm handshake and introduced her students, two young women from the sports medicine program and the other in her second year of med school, all three with brown hair tied back in pony-tails giving the impression that they excelled in sports as well as academics. For Aaron, this meant three chicks he'd never met would be staring at his package for the next hour.

Since this wasn't a hospital and Aaron had not changed into a surgical gown, Dr. Capon indicated for Aaron to drop his pants. "Alright, Mr. Clifton, let's see the goods."

As Aaron stood with his hands on his hips like Peter Pan, the doctor donned a glove and examined his testicles while pointing out the different parts of his Peter. In the moment of being surrounded by women intensely interested in his member for merely medical reasons, Aaron gleaned an insight that,

the penis is public; and,

the vagina is private.

He reflected on the many times in his life, starting in elementary school, that he'd seen a dick drawn in public spaces. Dicks sketched on the inside of a bathroom stall, dicks penciled on notebooks, dicks on lockers in the boy's changing room, dick-themed graffiti on abandoned buildings, dicks as the punch line of every joke, dick jokes in every Seth Rogen movie, drunk guys at a party who rock out with their cocks out, flashers exposing their dicks in the park on a Sunday afternoon, dicks out while coughing at the doctor's office, the ubiquitous and unwanted receiving of dick pics by every woman at some point in her life, dicks, dicks, and more dicks. The first cave painting was probably a dick pic.

In the other hand, the seclusion of female genitalia was quite a contrast. Even at the OB-GYN, a place where a woman is expected to expose herself, there is a sheet or a screen between patient and doctor that allows for privacy. As if making eye contact while inside a woman would be far too intimate. Aaron thought maybe the privacy stemmed from a woman's confusion as to what's going on *down there*, a mysterious region that itches, leaks, oozes discharge and wobbles with an uneven pH balance that is only mildly corrected by cranberry juice. Which explains the popularity of Cape Cods, as in vodka-cran, an intoxicating beverage as well as a preventative measure. And if women are uncertain about their vaginas, then men know nothing. Even Shakespeare called it nothing, as in *Much Ado about Nothing*. What is it that Hamlet loved about Ophelia? Nothing, as in (), the symbolic representation of both labias/labium pressed together. For Hamlet only wished to lay his head in Ophelia's lap and discover her nothing, "a fair thought to lie between a maids' legs." What is it about Desdemona that drove Othello mad? Nothing. What is it that Romeo wanted from Juliet? Ab-so-lute-ly nothing, every night creeping up a vine-laden balcony and risking exile or perchance death to get inside the nothing of, "my only love sprung from my only hate." What is it that convinced Macbeth to murder his king? Nothing, the one no-thing Macbeth focused upon after news of his wife's death,

> *Out, out, brief candle!*
> *Life's but a walking shadow, a poor player,*
> *That struts and frets his hour upon the stage,*
> *And then is heard no more. It is a tale*
> *Told by an idiot, full of sound and fury,*
> *Signifying nothing.*

Nothing. *La Tuñel.* The only no-thing obsessed by men besides their own dicks.

As Aaron reclined on the table, he thought how unfair the biological gods had been to women. For female sterilization, women endure pumping gas into their abdomen and a tubal ligation or the seriously hysterical hysterectomy. Also, Aaron thought, tying tubes is way more invasive than a vasectomy because the ball sac hangs like ripe fruit whereas the Fallopian tubes are buried like cassava tubers. He hoped male sterilization was relatively easy,

> easy like a bee sting, injecting lidocaine into his Nutz!

> > easy like a pinch, poking a small hole in his Nuutz!

> > > easy like taking chicken off the bone, nudging arteries off the vas deferens of his Nuuutz!

> > > > easy like a limp spaghetti noodle, grabbing the vas deferens of his Nuuuutz!

> > > > > easy like Samson's hair and the fateful snip.

Easy like suicide, because once committed the only task left was the cutting. Dr. Capon removed a section of his vas deferens and placed it in a jar to be tested for abnormalities. He tried to relax and accept the idea that doctors were always taking things and never giving them back. For cervical exams and breast exams, doctors took a biopsy of a possibly cancerous, hopefully benign, tumor. Doctors took out an appendix, or a bone spur, a kidney stone, a callus, a mole, a nose too sharp or breasts too large, or even sebaceous cysts. Doctors were so greedy, they *took* his blood pressure, they *took* his temperature, they *took* his pulse. But they never gave it back! Lying on the table under Dr. Capon's scalpel, he feared she would take away the volcano once known as Manhood.

Aaron calmed his thoughts during the vasectomy with a few deep breaths but panic swelled like swollen cajónes when,

like hair burnt in a candle, cauterizing the tubes.

> like grandma sewing a scarf, suturing the ends.
>> like a teddy bear's stuffing, cramming in the fibers.

Dr. Capon lectured throughout the vasectomy, alerting Aaron to the minutia of male reproductive anatomy. About halfway through the procedure, Dr. Capon pointed and said to her three assistants, "His vas deferens are so pretty."

Aaron thought this would be a good time to make a joke to impress the ladies. "Hey, that's my new pick-up line at the club. 'Yo girl, I've got the prettiest vas deferens. Wanna check them out?'"

Dr. Capon laughed and while jiggling her arm, said the worse thing a man can hear when a woman has a sharp instrument next to his balls. "Oops."

Aaron gulped. "Oops?"

She smiled at him. "Just kidding. We're all done." She slapped him on the back like a football coach and said, "Walk it off."

*

Aaron took an Uber home, placed a bag of frozen peas atop his groin, took six tablets of ibuprofen to reduce testicular swelling and slept for the rest of the afternoon. Thankfully, Zoë was gone for the evening and he allowed himself to wallow in masculine self-pity for the remainder of the evening. He watched the entire four-part *Lethal Weapon* film series[19] to boost his testosterone, favoring the sequel for its anti-Apartheid message like the stickers on the Murtaugh's family fridge and because of the greatest line ever delivered in cinema, "Free South Africa, you dumb son-of-a-bitch!" He passed out around 3 a.m.

A dull pain in his crotch and the ringing phone roused Aaron from slumber early on Saturday morning. He noticed the number from the Center and decided to ignore it. Saturday mornings were dedicated to visiting his grandmother Eve.

After ignoring the phone three more times, Aaron figured it might be urgent and answered.

Boss Lady, irate affect: "What did you do now?"

Aaron, innocent: "Could be anything."

"Remember Carlos?" she asked. "He was just a kid."

"Nah, he was a thug. I sent the cops to pick him up."

"He made it up!" yelled Boss Lady. "Now I gotta do all this paper work since he's a minor. Get your ass in here."

Turns out the police picked up "Carlos" at the clinic. Ernesto, the boy's real name, was only in the seventh grade and had pulled a plastic, toy gun on Billy. Apparently, the boy had to scare a cop to gain entry into a gang. An entrance exam for gang-school, an elaborate ritual to reach manhood.

Wow, did I ever get that one wrong, Aaron thought. He suddenly felt slimy for making fun of a seventh grader's penis. Then it occurred to Aaron that the boy had convincingly fabricated quite an elaborate story, probably real stuff he'd heard from his uncles and cousins who had actually done hard time. So, Aaron thought to himself, what part of the story was not real?

Aaron hung up on Boss Lady. They'd sort it out on Monday. Today belonged to Eve.

He swallowed 800mg of Norco to ease the pain of his swollen sac and he also hoped the pills would prevent the sadness that always followed his time with Eve. Seeing his grandmother was never easy. He wished the visit could be routine and ordinary, but there was nothing normal about losing one's mind.

Day by day, Eve's condition worsened, regressing into childhood. Whereas a child grew, she diminished. Each day, she lost a little piece of herself. Aaron heard this loss in the way she played the piano. Even though she practiced every day, her skills progressively worsened. This troubled Aaron because the main purpose of practicing was to improve one's ability. Eve had played for so many decades that she didn't know how to stop. He also noticed the staff cut her food into small pieces at meal time because she had forgotten how to use a knife and the fork shook in her arthritic hands. Aaron suspected that soon she wouldn't remember how to swallow and she'd choke to death on her own saliva.

He entered the main lobby of the Poinsettia Nursing Home and found Eve sitting on the couch with a red and white checkered wool blanket pulled up to her neck in front of a muted television showing a first season episode of *Sponge Bob Squarepants*. Aaron plopped next to her, but her attention never strayed from the cartoon characters. The faint smell of urine and mildew wafted from the cushions as he sat down. Aaron put his feet on a light grey ottoman stained with either spaghetti sauce or red wine or fruit punch. He guessed the stain was food because red dye #5 leaves a bright blemish on cushions but blood leaves a hauntingly maroonish discoloration. Aaron didn't mind the stains, but he was incensed that the drapes didn't match the floral pattern of the expensive and plush IKEA couch. He knew the chaotic décor would have bothered his grandmother had she been more aware of her surroundings. On her behalf, he had verbally complained to the Poinsettia's managerial staff many times, even wrote a letter to their home office in Raleigh, North Carolina, although he never received a reply, even after threatening to remove not only his grandmother but her friends, too. He also threatened to sell off his personally owned stock options invested in their publicly traded company, a tactic he had learned from Eve many years ago when she had made a similar threat after Aaron was dishonored by a gas-station attendant. An empty threat because he didn't own stock in anything. Much to his dismay, the administration had yet to find matching upholstery.

Aaron leaned over to kiss his grandmother on the forehead, the scent of lavender lotion setting him at ease. For as long as he could remember, she'd always smelled of lavender. Her choice of perfume, incense, and body moisturizer had always been marked with a purple flower.

"Hi Grandma, how are you?" He noticed her eyes were cold and grey.

Today was not a good day. She stared straight ahead, unaware of Aaron. He hugged and kissed her again but received no response. Every day, she grew more disconnected from reality, and watching her fade away was painful. Angered by his own selfishness, he knew her condition had nothing to do with him but he felt powerless to save her. She wasn't suffering. She wasn't in pain. She wasn't angry. She simply wasn't here.

His anger also stemmed from helplessness because she dwelled in a non-state of existence, but the decision wasn't his to make. He blamed Eve's daughters, Marilyn and Jocelyn, for keeping her in theological limbo between life and death. Aaron's mother, Marilyn, was the eldest daughter and carried an inherent responsibility. She was the hammer, frequently calling the nursing home to demand fresh flowers by Eve's bedside and fresh fruit for breakfast. Marilyn complained about any unsavory misstep surrounding Eve's care, insuring proper medication and regular check-ups by a doctor. However, her infrequent visits proved filial duty is not automatic since the eldest child is, after all, the closest one to death. A dying parent is a daily reminder of mortality.

His aunt Jocelyn was less of a hammer and more a nail. Unlike her older sister, Jocelyn didn't manage Eve's care from afar, but preferred to fasten her complaints directly. When confronted by a problem regarding their mother, Marilyn would announce and Jocelyn would pounce. When the nursing home failed to deliver the *New York Times* to Eve's room, Marilyn complained to the main office. A few hours later, Jocelyn arrived with a stack of newspapers and showed every nurse the location of Eve's room. When the home messed up Eve's Zoloft dosage, Marilyn ordered a pharmaceutical representative to visit and educate the nurses while Jocelyn personally delivered a large container of transparent pill containers. The nursing home only tolerated Jocelyn's antics because she smiled while making demands.

Naturally, Aaron served as the piece of wood the hammer nailed into. He endured their intrusive demands because he loved his grandmother. Also, because they paid him. Marilyn took care of his mortgage and Jocelyn bought him groceries. On his meager salary, he was unable to afford the capitalistic trappings of modern society for his daughter like private school, a cell phone and a car. On the worst days, Aaron felt his inability to provide for the family was a moral flaw, a shameful trait he buried within. On the best days, Aaron served as a wooden lifebuoy that Eve clung to as she lay drowning in lost memory.

Eve's life wasn't anybody's choice except for her own, and yet she could no longer make that decision. With her mind failing a little more each day, she had lost self-determination and direction in her life. More importantly, she had lost the power over her own death. As Aaron quickly discovered, nursing homes profit by keeping their clients alive. Power had been subverted by what Eve's doctors called Reasons to Live. At this point in her deterioration, only Eve was privy to her personal RTLs.

Aaron had encountered a vast array of Reasons to Live over the years. Some of the socially maladjusted Callers has expressed their personal RTLs, reasons which kept them from killing themselves. Reasons to Live were varied and often convoluted, a sense of responsibility or guilt usually the main RTL that Aaron heard on the Crisis Hotline. In one call during Year Five, Aaron listened to a woman in her mid-50s who summarized all the important Reasons to Live.

"I can't leave my children," she had moaned, "they need me."

Aaron had voiced her greatest fear and said, "Don't worry, you're only a burden on them."

Then she said, "I don't want to hurt my parents. I'll wait until they die," and Aaron had again confirmed her fear by saying, "Your parents never loved you."

Then she had said, "It's gotta look accidental, or else my husband can't collect on the life insurance policy," and Aaron had verified her fear by saying, "He'll just spend it on his next wife."

But Aaron could not provide a decent rebuttal to her final Reason to Live.

"Who will care for my dog?" she had said. "Who'll take him for a walk? Do you think Big Brutus will eat my body if the cops don't show up after a few days? And I don't want to abandon my cats. Who will feed them? Joey and Maurice like salmon paté but Señor José and Mr. Mittens like shreds in beef gravy."

Thinking that maybe choosing the right kind of cat food is often a decent Reason to Live, Aaron laid his head on Eve's shoulder and pulled out a slim collection of Chinese poems. Reading aloud to her softly, he chose random selections from the *Shi Jing*, the Book of Songs. The English translation bothered him with its Victorian slant, but he'd bought the copy for only twenty-five cents at a yard sale. He read about lakes and mountains and red-tailed sparrows and long winter nights of solitude,

> *Deep rolls the thunder*
> *On the sun-side of the southern hill.*
> *Why is it, why must you always be away,*
> *... come back to me, come back.*

"Oh, honey   how lovely," Eve breathed, long pauses between words, uncertain as to what followed. A brightness lingered in her eyes. "How are   you,   my dear Aaron?"

Speechless, he paused and put the book down. She recognized him, which made him happy in a selfish way. He knew time was fleeting and soon she'd slip away. He held her hand and cried.

"What's wrong   my dear boy? What can   I do?" Her words sputtered with long gaps. He knew not to interrupt her for she might get lost by the end of a sentence and would never be able to find her way back again.

"I'm fine," he said slowly.

"Do you need cash?"

"No, Grandma. I'm fine."

"You only say   fine   when you're not."

Aaron placed his head on her shoulder. "I can't hide from you, can I?"

"Here," she said, reaching into her pocket. Even without a purse, she always managed to have money. She handed him a twenty-dollar bill. Aaron resisted, but Eve forced the lavender-scented money into his hand.

"Thanks," Aaron said sadly.

"Oh, honey   what's wrong?"

"I just miss you. Told you I'd be here."

"I know   I know. But when   can   I go Upstairs? Will you   help me?"

Aaron shook his head. "It's not time. Not yet."

She exhaled slowly, a lifetime of exhaustion expelled in a single breath. "I'm tired."

Aaron hugged her closely and gently rocked her back and forth like she did for him when Aaron was a little boy.

When Aaron was six years old, Eve held him after he scrapped his knee and he asked for his pillow in between tiny sobs, crying out, "MY PITOW!" After the bleeding stopped, Eve asked, "Why are you still crying?" and Aaron said with a childish lisp, "I like to cry." He was overcome with a sudden sadness, not yet understanding the depression that would haunt him for years. Aaron felt Eve was the only one who understood him because she had spent a few weeks in the Snake Pits of Camarillo State Hospital and recognized his gloom.

Listening to her steady breath, Aaron leaned back on the stained couch and looked at Eve. She'd fallen asleep. Aaron curled up beside her and closed his eyes. As he drifted off to sleep, the Eve he knew and loved would be gone when he awoke.

Episode 5.5

Cleaning,
or How to Effectively Procrastinate
while Waiting for Everyone to Arrive

Swollen from his recent voluntary sterilization, Aaron limped from the Poinsettia back to his car and drove home to apply ice packs and pain reliever. He was tempted to hide under the table but people were coming over to celebrate his birthday and the house needed to be cleaned. For Aaron, cleaning bestowed purpose.

Marilyn and Aunt Jocelyn were bringing Eve over later in the afternoon with a chocolate birthday cake, probably with a big Four-Oh stenciled in sugary lettering. Zoë invited Lena because kids need both parents on holidays. Aaron had asked Debz to come because she was his only friend from work and she loved chocolate.

Before Aaron could begin his cleaning ritual, Marilyn and Jocelyn appeared early to help prepare for the party. Marilyn, with frazzled grey hair and a furry brown Alpaca coat, entered first without knocking. Jocelyn, wearing an orange feathery double-breasted long jacket and a curly wild bob of dark thick hair, arrived with groceries before going to pick up Eve. Neither one of them wiped their feet at the door and tracked frozen bits of mud into the house. Aaron caught the end of their conversation.

"You saying my son likes to clean?" Marilyn asked her younger sister.

"He might be a little obsessed." Jocelyn placed two paper bags with party favors on the counter.

"He can't help it," Marilyn said. "When Aaron was a little boy, I saw him in the bathroom. He was standing on one leg and holding up the toilet lid up with a knee, while brushing his teeth with one hand and cleaning the basin with his other hand. All while peeing!"

Jocelyn, a social worker herself, made a clinical assessment. "Sounds like chronic and acute Putzfimmel."

Aaron interrupted and feigned distress. "I'm a putz?!"

"No," Jocelyn explained, "you like putzing around the house. *Putzen*, it's German for cleaning."

"Oh, right," Aaron said. "Guilty as charged."

Jocelyn whispered to Marilyn, "Maybe he needs an intervention?"

"Probably," Marilyn sighed, "but what mother would stop her son from cleaning?"

Aaron couldn't properly clean with his mother and aunt in the house. "Gotta get ready for the party. I can't have guests right now."

"We're family, not guests. Besides, it's the end of the month." Marilyn placed an envelope containing a check on the dining room table. Aaron purposefully did not look at it.

"We're not guests," Jocelyn repeated. "Guests are like fish, they stink after three days."

"Guess what else stinks after three days?" Aaron asked.

"What?"

He laughed and pointed to the sky. "Jesus."

"That's awful," Jocelyn sighed.

"You may not believe in Jesus," Marilyn said as she made the sign of the cross above her necklace of rosary beads, "but he still believes in you."

Offended by his irreligious sentiment, the two ladies said in unison, "We'll pray for you."

"Prayers are for the weak," Aaron said while pointing to the door. "Time to go, I gotta clean up before the party."

They ignored him and began putting food in the cupboards. Marilyn opened the fridge but couldn't find room for the large cake and soda bottles. Without asking, she removed three Tupperware containers and handed them to Jocelyn, who in turn threw the contents directly into the trash can.

To discourage the two women from lingering, Aaron announced, "Alexa, play Cleaning Up Before Suicide." The playlist, lasting two hours and twenty-nine minutes with forty songs, was a collection of suicidal classics. Jocelyn and Marilyn busied themselves in the kitchen but after Aaron turned up the volume, they collected their purses as the first song ended.

At the doorway, Marilyn turned to Aaron and said, "I've never understood your obsession with death. Why can't you just be happy?"

Aaron shrugged and looked down at the ground with hands in his pockets. Even after forty years, he would always be a little boy trying to gain his mother's approval.

Marilyn gently placed her hand on Aaron's shoulder and looked him directly in the eye. "If you killed yourself, I'd be okay with it."

Silence echoed between mother and son.

Jocelyn grabbed Marilyn's arm and spoke to Aaron as they quickly rushed out of the house. "She didn't mean that. Now, clean up and we'll be back in a little bit."

The music of Aaron's suicidal playlist evaporated into background noise as the mania of his Putzfimmeled mind took over in the journey to cleanliness. Aaron washed the dishes as the first tune described spilt apple juice in *Adam's Song* by Blink 182, the music summarizing Aaron's own feeling towards Marilyn, "Please tell mom this is not her fault," and next;

Jeremy by Pearl Jam while cleaning out the pantry, listening to Eddie Veder's haunting voice about a boy who "spoke in class today" and shot himself in front of a classroom full of grade school kids as they "try to erase this from the blackboard," and next;

Straight A's by the Dead Kennedys and the pressures of what someone like Jeremy may have faced had he made it to high school, "Sixteen, on the honor roll, wish I was dead. Parents hate me, I got zits and bruises 'round my head. Read the paper, wonder why. It's your fault, you made me die," with the best ending of any punk tune, "Aw, shit!" and next;

A Day without Me by U2 and, "I started a landslide in my ego, look from the outside to the world I left behind," followed by *Spectators of Suicide* by Manic Street Preachers and also *Suicide Journey* by the Church of Misery with an introduction by a reporter on the Heaven's Gate Cult mass suicide, and next;

Revolution by Maynard from Tool and Zach from Rage Against the Machine, busting out a sing-along, "Suicide seemed to be the only way to stop the pain," flowing smoothly into *Gloomy Sunday* by Billie Holliday, waking up depressed on a Sunday morning, "Little white flowers will never awaken you. My heart and I have decided to end it all," and next;

Suicidal Thoughts by the Notorious B.I.G. and his accurate description of a suicidal Caller and a concerned Listener in a call-and-response type of exchange, and if Aaron heard a Caller say, "I know my mother wished she got a fuckin abortion," then as a Listener, there's only one thing to say. "Yo, I'm on my way over there." And if the Caller said, "You see, it's kinda like the crack did to Pookie in New Jack," then as a Listener, Aaron would have to say, "Chris Rock was dope! And trippy how Cop-Killa-Ice-T ended up making a career of a gangster pretending to be a cop pretending to be a gangster," at which point Biggie probably would have hung up, and next;

That Year, Brandi Carlile's reminiscent eulogy to a departed friend, "You should have taken a break instead of a long drop," and next;

Suicidal Failure by the Suicidal Tendencies came on while he vacuumed, occasionally turning off the vacuum cleaner so he could listen to the band's list of failed Attempts, "I have suicidal tendencies but I can't kill myself," a self-referential homage, and next;

CHOP SUEY! by System of a Down because any song that starts with, "We're rolling 'Suicide'," immediately catches Aaron's attention. A song originally titled, "Self-Righteous Suicide" but when the studio balked, the artists changed the name to "Chop Suey," a Romanization of the Cantonese dish *tsap sui* because it sounded like the original tile of "Self-right-chop suey-cide," and next;

Cheap Trick's *Auf Wiedersehen*, goodbye in German but a song mostly in Japanese, "Sayonara oh suicide hari kari, kamikaze, you won't see another evening. Goodbye bye-bye so long farewell see you later suicide," and next;

Why, a country song by the Rascal Flatts, but Aaron frequently confused this with their other song, *Why Wait*, because the title and lyrics matched up with suicide so nicely, "What'aya say girl, we do somethin' crazy. Quit puttin' it off, you know what I'm sayin'. Ain't like it ain't gonna happen, forever's a given. It's already written. Who we kiddin' baby, come on!" Aaron knew they were singing about running off to get hitched, but sometimes marriage seemed like suicide, and next;

Aaron swept the floor to *Suicide* by James Arthur because, "it ain't the gun, it's the man behind the trigger," and James Arthur led to James Taylor's *Fire and Rain* and his heart-wrenching farewell, "But I'd always thought I'd see you again," and James Taylor led to Jamestown Story's *Goodbye, I'm Sorry* and "I'm in a fleshy tomb buried up above the ground, every eighteen minutes somebody dies from suicide, every forty-three seconds somebody Attempts one," followed by a Public Service Announcement which was cut from the radio edit, "If you or anyone you know is suicidal, call 1800 784-2433," spelled out as 1800 SUICIDE, and next;

1800 273-8255 by Logic, spelled out as 1800 APE TALK, the phone number for suicidal humans and the unrealistic expectation of "I don't wanna cry no more," and next;

Aaron took a break from cleaning, sat down on the slightly torn feinting couch and listened to *So Many Tears* by Tupac and how the artist had "lost so many peers, and shed so many tears," and "I'm suicidal, so don't stand near me, my every move is a calculated step, to bring me closer to embrace an early death." 2Pac's hopeful expectation of "Will I survive to the mo'nin, to see the sun," fit nicely with the next song, *Asleep* by the Smiths when they moaned, "Don't try to wake me in the morning," and next;

Suicide Note, Part I by Pantera, an acoustic, soft melody, "Can you tell I'm a man? With these scars on my wrists to prove I'll try again, try to die again, try to live through this night," a song quite different than *Suicide Note, Part II*, with a heavy-grinding guitar and ear-splitting vocals, "Why would you help anyone who doesn't want it, doesn't need it, doesn't want your shit advice when a mind's made up to go ahead and die?" and next;

While folding laundry, Aaron heard, "It's always darkest just before the dawn" by Rise Against in their song *Make it Stop (September's Child)*, causing Aaron to reflect on the popular theme among suicidal songs of surviving through the night and making it until dawn. The song was dedicated to the high number of LGBTQ+ teens completing suicide in September of 2010 highlighted by Tyler Clementi's web-cam outing at Rutgers University. The music video, accompanied by an optimistic promotion of Dan Savage's "It Gets Better" PSA message, tells the story of three kids who decide not to kill themselves after ceaseless anti-gay bullying. Yet, Aaron could never figure out why the actors in the video didn't commit suicide since death is obviously the easiest way to "Make It Stop" and Aaron assumes "It" refers to the emotional pain of being teased, bullied and harassed in middle/high school for your sexual orientation followed by self-doubt, self-loathing and self-hatred with ensuing years of depression; however, the "It" of "It Get Betters" may also refer to life after high school, life after finding your way with friends who are similar in the best way, life after fleeing from a Red-state, homophobic town, life after the bullying and harassment and assault makes you stronger followed by self-confidence, self-respect and self-love with ensuing years of contentment for being exactly who you are. And that, Aaron knew, was the secret missed by every song and video about suicide prevention:

Be your own best friend.

Advice which caused Aaron to take himself out on dates once per week and the reason he spent so much time putzing around because he deserved to live in a clean house.

Only songs about suicide were on Aaron's playlist. He refused to listen to any songs about the prevention of suicide because such tunes inspired false hope in the listener and no one who is depressed wants to hear, "Get over it," or "It'll be okay," like Billy Joel singing, "Don't forget your second wind" or R.E.M.'s lullaby *Everybody Hurts*.

Aaron would occasionally listen to The Fray's *How to Save a Life* only because the narrator, after failing to save his friend and the ensuing sadness combined with experiential counseling, manages to administer good advice on listening to troubled teens. Because staying up all night listening to a friend is sometimes the only way to save a life.

Not great advice for counselors, but good for troubled teens, a funny sentiment because Aaron knew most teens were troubled. Troubled by drugs,

weed for the lazy ones, coke for the ambitious ones; or,
troubled by not enough drugs,

Adderall for the hyper ones, Wellbutrin for the sad ones; or,
troubled by too much sex,

shamed as a slut or man-whore; or,
troubled by not enough sex,

shamed as a virgin and prude; or,
troubled by grades,

fearing an A- will ruin their chances at an Ivy League; or,
troubled by not enough grades,

and taking college classes in high school; or,
troubled by working,

to afford fly clothes and hip sneakers to fit in; or,
troubled by not working,

and unable to afford even a busted-up Chevy; or,
troubled by bullying,

and taking a gun to school for revenge; or,
troubled by not standing up to the bully,

and feeling ashamed for watching.

Somehow, Aaron thought, these troubles are what transforms teens into well-adjusted adults.

Troubled teens, expressed in Tool's *Jimmy*, as in James Maynard Keenan, and his heart-wrenching "under a dead Ohio sky" as the epitome of contagious depression from living near Cleveland. A city with 320 cloudy days a year, providing ample reason why the students in the Cleveland Metropolitan Schools have the highest rates of suicide in the country. Cleveland, the Calcutta of America, an insult to India's most polluted city. Believeland, the city LeBron left twice. Cleveburg, the capital of rock n' roll and cock n' hole. The Mistake by the Lake, Aaron's favorite city because to survive Cleveland is to refute death herself.

The band Tool flowed into A Perfect Circle and Maynard's message in *The Outsider* to those who don't understand their friends suffering from depression and only want "suicidal imbeciles" to "do it somewhere far away from here." Advice followed by Martin Manley, a sports statistician from Missouri who posted on his website the longest suicide note in history. He understood the dilemma of leaving a mess and so in the early dawn of August 15th, 2013, on his 60th birthday, he found a secluded spot on the south edge of a police station parking lot and pulled the trigger. He had called the police station minutes before to report a suicide and left a note taped to his chest, "I am sorry for the inconvenience." Martin Manley presaged the final wisdom gained at the end of life, a truth greater than, "We all die alone," as reveled so eloquently by Grandma Death, played by Patience Cleveland,[20] in *Donny Darko*. For Martin exposed a necessary truth for those contemplating suicide: there is a two-year waiting period after purchasing life insurance before beneficiaries of a suicide victim can receive payment.

Near the end of the playlist, Aaron passed by the kitchen cautiously, careful not to disturb the pristine kitchen with a distinct Mr. Clean scent emanating from the polished oak-not-maple hardwood flooring, paid for by Eve because she wanted the best for her grandson, and a sparkling white, ceramic sink, paid for by Marilyn, although the Insinkerator garbage disposal had been broken for years. Aaron paused in his cleaning process to fetch the day's newspaper. *The Times* as in New York, although he had never lived in Manhattan, never visited his father's relative in any of the four boroughs nor even vacationed there to dine on Brooklyn bagels or Queens quiche or Staten Island spinach or Spanish Harlem helado or even Bronx borsch. He sat on the ground and spread the paper on the floor, his back against the yellow couch. He scanned the Society pages for the obituaries, relishing how people's entire lives, as well as the trauma of their passing, could be compressed into a few lines. Aaron also looked for suicides disguised as accidental or natural death, because he knew the line, "Succumbing after a long bout with cancer," was not what it seemed but rather meant,

> "The man, probably a dentist, swallowed a handful of Dilaudid after suffering from interminable pain for years. Despite his family's pleas to continue on and his doctor's reluctance to help him die, the man tongued thirty pills, one per day for over a month until he had a secreted a stash beneath the mattress and finally swallowed en masse with milk to make them go down easier."

Aaron also knew that when the cause of death was listed as "hunting accident", it probably meant a suicide because every hunter knows when his gun is loaded.

After scanning the Obits, he stood up to examine the bottoms of his socks for loose particulate matter, such as dirt, specks of food and fuzz balls. Items which had to be removed by hand, leaning against the counter with the other hand, one leg crossed at the knee resting on the other bent knee, risking personal safety by standing like a flamingo in a sock upon a slippery, thrice daily waxed oak-not-green-ash hardwood flooring. Finally, Aaron walked into the kitchen and considered reaching for the Sacred Relic of Martin de Porres, Saint of the Broom, and fantasized about the repetitive joy of sweeping the oak-not-hickory-pecan hardwood flooring.

Aaron examined his socked soles once again in the morning light and crept on tippy-toes directly to the sacred altar, a circular glass beverage coaster with the emblem of a red cross. He had obtained the disk at the 10th annual Suicide Prevention Conference at the National Cathedral in D.C. where he heard Desmond Tutu speak, but he'd been more interested in the gift shop with its Helen Keller paraphernalia and seeing that her braille/sign teacher, Anne Sullivan, was entombed in marble beside Helen. At the end of the sermon, Aaron learned that the little South African's grand sentiment of Compassion was on display, side by side, in the catacombs below the church.

From this glass-crossed pedestal, Aaron lifted a clear plastic bottle with bold, red lettering and matching red handle and nozzle. The Holiest of Holies, the noble embodiment of cleanliness that is not only next to but supersedes godliness. For Aaron could not live without the Holy Trinity of household cleaning products, specifically Mr. Clean as the bald, Black, gold ear-ringed approving Father, and Comet as the Celestial Holy Ghost of scrubbing powders, and Windex as the Son incarnate in bluish liquid form.

Aaron's favorite religious[21] tool was Windex, a combination of Isopropanol, rubbing alcohol to the layman, mixed with the inky scented, organic solvent 2-Butoxyethanol, and ethylene glycol, a weak acid of pH six. The last ingredient is water although its marine coloring is a highly guarded trade secret, albeit the leading conspiracy theory circulating OCD chatrooms is that the blue coloring is not the harmless dye Blue #1, *brilliant blue*, or the non-toxic dye *indigotine* Blue #2 but rather the covert dye Blue #3, which Aaron named *Lapis Windexate*, the same carcinogen found in blue M&M's used to sterilize children of low-income families. The real question presented to Aaron during his ruminations was why the creators of Windex even bothered to add blue dye.

The reason was explained by Moises, the only other male colleague at the Suicide Prevention & Crisis Hotline Center. Moises Montoya didn't man the phones since the lines were manned by women but instead worked as a janitor four-nights a week because five nights would have made him a full-time employee requiring health benefits and the bosses restricted non-essential paid personnel to 29 hours per week. Moises had explained this to him one Saturday night during a lull in calls, and Aaron clearly remembered the day because Saturday tends to receive the least amount of calls because nobody wants to kill themselves on Saturday when they can just wait until Monday.

In the late evening/early morning, Moises had explained to Aaron in hushed tones that blue cleaning liquids always designated glass cleaners. Green colored bottles meant disinfectant, or as Moises said, "Yous know, like fer da shitter." Red and purple dyed liquids meant heavy duty cleaning agents, "De kind yous betta wear da gloves for."

In this concise delivery, the inherent blue nature of Windex was revealed to Aaron. To return the favor, Aaron explained to Moises that the *-ex* suffix of Windex was Latin for "beyond". As in beyond that which can be seen, beyond the divine, beyond the crystal-clear ontological revelation that Windex is indeed the one household product which enables humankind to shine the window of one's very soul with tidy circular ablutions.

To which Moises had shaken his head and said, "Crazy white boy, itz just glass cleaner."

Entering the kitchen after checking his socks one last time, Aaron raised the Holy Blue Water from its permanent spot on the counter atop the cross-inscribed coaster. He administered the first spray of mist upon his two fingertips before a brief pause with religious gesticulations and a slight private genuflection. He looked over his shoulder out the window to make sure no walked in on him, then exhaled slowly with great pleasure, switching the nozzle to stream. He repeated this act of adjusting the nozzle three times to make certain, back and forth from the off position through mist and ending at stream. He readied himself with great anticipation, seductively stroking up the bottle to the tip of the nozzle with thumb and forefinger until, at last, he was ready to pump the handle. With the first pull, he slowly built pressure, and each subsequent yank the tension swelled until an airy drizzle emerged. The final stroke released intense pleasure,

"Ahhhhh!"

Long arches of aqua-tinted fluid majestically splattered on the pale-hued Formica countertop, reaching every corner of the kitchen, his grip furiously pumping the red handle in a frantic motion. Aaron leapt around the room wide-eyed and panting, one squirt behind the faucet then another stream splashing upon the glass-faced cabinetry and also across the white refrigerator door. Soon, the stove top was heavily coated with fluid pooling in the drip pans, drops falling upon the white-flesh-toned oak hardwood flooring. After ninety seconds of furious pumping, his right hand became numb and flaccid, the fluid barely eeking onto the receptive counter. The next twelve minutes were spent lackadaisically cleaning up his mess, an embarrassed afterthought. Exhausted, he feinted into the velvet couch wearing socks moist from excess glass cleaner.

Sufficiently relieved, Aaron was prepared for the party. A spotless house ready for his grandmother and mother and aunt and ex-wife and daughter and best friend from work.

Suddenly, his mother's words sank in.

"I'd be okay with it."

He felt unmade. The shock reverberated and her indifference bothered him, because deep within the conflicted expanse of his childhood he'd always known. Since Aaron first displayed unstable behavior after his encounter with Norton the Breathing Forest at the age of six, Marilyn had developed a coping mechanism common with mothers of depressed sons. She had mentally prepared to bury her son.

Instead of waiting for his guests to arrive, he wandered down the hill and found a large granite boulder on the river bottom. He sat on the grey rock by himself for a few hours, shivering in the wind and holding his knees against his chest to keep warm until the pain in his stomach subsided. He went back only when he was certain everyone would be gone because, for Aaron, the best part of having a birthday party was not being there.

Chapter 6

Telephonic Introverted Masturbators
and the Brenda Approach

Aaron strolled home after dark and found an empty house. Jocelyn and Marilyn had thrown a party despite his absence. The mess left behind proved they had a great time. Crumbles of cake lay on the floor, and the trash can was filled with empty cans of soda and paper plates. Aaron was sweeping the floor for the tenth time that day when the landline phone rang, a call transferred from work. He had forgotten to remove his number from the back-up list to receive emergency calls.

Caller, labored breathing, frustrated affect, eager tone: "Is there a woman I can talk to?"

Aaron, as Franco, responding professionally but sensing the Caller's purpose: "You sure I can't help you?"

"No, I need a woman. I gotta relieve some stress."

Aaron remembered the first time he had received a call from a pervert. During Year One at the Crisis Center, the call had frightened him because he could hear the man masturbating in the background. At the time, he wasn't sure of what to do. In between strokes, the man insisted on talking to a woman for therapeutic purposes. Luckily, a Brenda was on duty that night.

Brenda wasn't a particular woman, per se, but a type. Aaron loved it when a Brenda worked the phones during his shift. A Brenda almost always had the same qualities: a Psychology degree with a special interest in gender and human sexuality; also, she's a brunette suburban white girl who even if blonde then consciously lowlights her hair with black tints; also, she carries the ubiquitous Starbuck's vanilla spice latte and wears an eccentric scarf indicating worldly travel; also, knee-high light brown leather boots with mascara serving as the only make-up; also, a Target knock-off brand push-up bra, usually black; also, she possesses a conversational ease with certain emotional verbs like *transcend* and *pro-cess* and other complex concepts like *Lacto-Fecal Fantasy*;[22] also, she has the ability to flirt with guys while faking an easy smile and is unashamed when a total pervert (i.e., grabby Mexicans, groping Italians, cigarette-flicking Turks, and any guy over forty) whistles at them because the Brenda won't hesitate to yell back something like "Fûck off creep!" or "Eat my twat!" or any other appropriate retort an Italian or Puerto Rican woman would employ without hesitation but when it's offered by a Midwestern white chick who hails from, say, Duluth, it's really surprising and she'll probably claim she's half Romana or at least a quarter Latina; also, the Brenda comes from divorced parents and most definitely has Daddy-issues. For which, after one particular encounter in the broom closet, no longer did Aaron use the term Daddy-issues lightly.

During the first year, Aaron was irritated by the Brendas' peppy attitude. "I just wanna help," they'd say with a smile and irregular seasonal attendance. Aaron noticed an increased influx of Brendas during the spring and fall season since they usually went home Back East or Up North or Out West or Down South for winter and summer breaks. Since every psychology/sociology major needed approximately 100 hours of contact time with patients, the Crisis Hotline offered a variety of clients with multiple personality disorders and a slew of schizophrenia. Some of the Brendas would flake out and disappear after a few weeks, preferring to change majors after releasing childhood, deep-seeded psychological trauma. Quickly, Aaron discovered working alongside a Brenda in the trenches was always a real treat because they enjoyed doing something no other Listener was prepared to do. The Brendas liked working with perverts.

Their personal life experience with high school rape and the ensuing serious drug abuse and indiscriminate wanton sexual activity for years after until the sudden realization in the fifth month of therapy or at 3 a.m. while writing their midterm essay for Psych 302, Abnormal Psychology, in which the Brenda figures out she's completely normal and her self-destructive grieving process is completely normal, too, and right then and there the Brenda makes a decision to stop snorting coke—despite hating her father for Not Being There.

As a man, Aaron has had little experience with taking the pervert-calls but he has no problem calling them that, even wrote *Pervert called twice today* as the title of several reports, much to the angst of Boss Lady who offered other terms such as sexual-deviants or the sexually-depraved or sexually-repressed-individuals but always a gender-neutral term even though ten out of ten times it's a dude. After considerable harassment from Boss Lady, Aaron eventually employed the acronym TiM for the Center's reports. TiM indicated a pervert as in a

Telephonic-introverted Masturbator, not to be confused with Titanium Manganese (TiMn), even though both were hard as rocks.

Aaron noted that the TiM has a propensity to call at night, usually drunk to boost his confidence, is single and between the ages of 18 and 29; but, he can also be from 30 to 50-years-old, married and sneaks home early from work while his wife and kids are gone; however, TiM also might be a grumpy 80-year-old man in wheelchair who has been a bachelor his entire life and got laid only three times while stationed with the Navy in Guam by the same olive-skinned prostitute and is so frustrated and ashamed when looking at porn that he can only get off by listening to a woman's voice that reminds the midshipman of his Micronesian lover. Essentially, the standard profile of a TiM eluded Aaron but he respected the Brendas for taking the call. He imagined dealing with TiM must be tough at first, and it sickened him to think about some pathetic jerk wacking-off while the Brenda was trying to Empathize and Process. Quickly, the Brendas learned to handle the perv by gathering after work and comparing stories over a six-pack of PBR.

Traditionally, meaning back in the 1950s with Chad Varah's Samaritans who started the world's first crisis hotline, the uptight British female Listeners were trained to immediately hang up on the pervert and code the offending phone numbers, which meant blocking the perv's future calls. During training, Aaron listened to an old example from Britain's NHS hotline.

Listener, proper woman raised on Victorian values: "Good day, you've reached the Center for the Prevention of…"

Caller, from one of London's neighborhoods like SoHo or Camden or Vauxhall or Hackney or Clapham: "Yes, uuum, I know, sweetie. But you cannot prevent this diiiick!"

"Excuse me?"

"How grand are your tits?"

"Sir, that is inappropriate."

"I'm prone to kill myself if you don't inform me as to the massive size of your baps."

"Sir, I refuse to take your threat of suicide seriously."

"But it's utterly killing me. I'm likely to explode! I'm dying here!!"

"I'm hanging up now. Good day, sir."

And that would be the end of it. The calls never lasted more than a minute after the *zzzzip* was herd in the background followed by labored breathing. After a few of these unseemly interactions, the Samaritans hired a few local prostitutes and named them all *the Brendas* who had an entirely different approach.

"Allo mate, this is the crisis hotline…"

"Ay sweatheart, do your tities bounce when you run?"

"Naturally. Same as your bawls."

"Darling, bet you've got big, juicy tities."

"Big as your mum's"

"What color is your brassiere?"

"Whatever's your favorite color."

TiM, pause: "…Come on now, sugar, work with me a little."

"Why? Are you feeling frustrated?"

TiM, longer pause: "…Ummm."

"Don't be embarrassed," the Brenda would say. "I won't hang up. Tell me about yourself. Do you work?"

"Yes."

"Interesting, right?"

"No, it's absolute rubbish."

And the Brenda had him hooked. He'd open up, first talking about his awfully boring job, then his lackluster marriage or crippling loneliness and eventually the shame of beating off to the helpful, soothing female voice of a caring, crisis worker for free instead of paying for a 1-900 or a 0871 premium rate number. Aaron knew he could never follow the Brenda Approach and acknowledged utter relief from their ability to take those calls, although sometimes he grew a little jealous because pretty, young Brendas were chatting up pervy, old guys with semi-soft chubs.

In Year Six, Aaron was nearly fired after he convinced a Brenda to put the sexually aberrant Caller on speaker so he could listen. He persuaded the Brenda to encourage the TiM with enticing lingo instead of offering soothing therapeutic advice. This was before incoming calls were recorded which only started in Year Eight when N.I.M.H. arrived with federal grants to update the national hotline. The Brenda in question was fresh out of college, and both self-loathing and cruel enough to go along with Aaron's little joke, permanently scarring the TiM on the other end of the line for the rest of his orgasmic life. The Caller, a mid-twenties Southern man, was busy wanking away on his lil' Jefferson Davis as the Brenda encouraged him with, "That's it, baby, that's what I like, give it to me," which in retrospect was a tad bit unprofessional, and right as the guy was on the verge of coming with his expected, "oh ooh oooh ooooh," and right at the last, "oooooooooh," Aaron busted in on their call with his deepest, fatherly bass-alto voice and demanded, "Son, what's going on here?!"

The Brenda's giggle didn't make it any better and poor ol' Bama was stricken with a life-long homophobic psychotic disorder which probably prevented any type of real intimacy for at least a decade. Aw hell, Aaron had thought, the sicko deserved it. Yet, he felt remorseful not from the call but because the Brenda quit working at the Center soon after from a sense of overwhelming guilt.

During Year Two at the Crisis Center, exactly a year and six months after his divorce, which has always led Aaron to suspect the immediate and damaging toll the job had upon his marriage despite the fact Lena was also a raging alcoholic but he didn't like to blame her for their break-up since he had been completely stoned for their entire marriage and certainly wasn't supportive or empathetic back in those days, and so after the divorce in his second year on the job he hooked up with a Brenda.

Two Brendas in fact, but the first was only a make-out session in the hallway after she had received an upset Caller and had empathized a little too much about the death of the Caller's dog, inexplicably stirring up emotions of second-hand grief regarding the Brenda's long deceased grandfather when she realized, ten minutes into the call, that she had loved her Golden Retriever named Maximillian a whole lot more than she'd ever cared for her very own grandfather.

Aaron had heard her tiny sobs in the hallway and innocently asked, "Are you okay?"

The first Brenda responded by kissing Aaron deeply with a sloppy amount of tongue, immature but not wholly un-erotic as evidenced by Aaron's sudden hard-on, a kiss which only lasted a few seconds. The Brenda apologized immediately after breaking the kiss and said it meant nothing.

"Most likely a life-affirming act necessitated by the psychic trauma induced by the Caller's pain," she explained.

"It's alright, I understand," he said to both Validate and Normalize the Brenda. Aaron didn't offer a clinical response and instead gave her a supportive hug, twisting his hips discreetly out of the way so as not to accidently poke her. Afterwards, Aaron never mentioned the kiss again nor tried to pressure a follow-up tryst. After all, he was nearly twice the girl's age and pursuing her would have made him feel like a TiM.

As for the second Brenda, she helped Aaron relive a fantasy conjured during middle school when he accidentally caught Ms. Middleton bending over in the broom closet as she retrieved a dust pan, revealing the lace undergarment beneath her black and ivory striped dress[23] which aroused Aaron's prepubescent mind for the remainder of the 8th grade.

The Brenda had arrived early to cover a two-hour morning shift before her 8 a.m. Pilates class and 9 a.m. graduate level Melancholia seminar at the university. Aaron couldn't help but notice the way she gave him the up & down glace when he stood to offer her a cup of coffee. He'd seen her twice and he couldn't be sure if she was checking him out, but on that particular morning, Aaron recorded two mental images. Firstly, she bit her lip unconsciously when their hands touched as he handed her the paper cup. Secondly, she was wearing an *Others Follow Destiny* striped, halter top, skater dress that reminded Aaron of his middle school crush. But he couldn't blurt out, "Waddup Brenda?" because that wasn't her name and he couldn't remember her real name since everyone used pseudonyms on the phone to protect their real identities. Also, "Hey Brenda, you remind me of my middle school teacher," was a poor opening line. However, his intention was apparently received by the Brenda and they stared at each other speechlessly for the required 3.5 seconds, which as any two sex-starved individuals know, is half a second longer than necessary. The Brenda dropped her purse on the chair and looked in the other room to make sure no one was around before grabbing Aaron's hand for a brief second. She let go and confidently strode down the hall to the broom closet and closed the door behind her. She didn't bother with an inviting look over her shoulder back at Aaron. The message was clear.

The broom closet, as Aaron soon discovered, was more of a large storage room for the cleaning supplies used by the janitor Moises. Aaron waited the obligatory twenty-eight seconds and then followed the Brenda. He opened the door and found her wringing her hands expectantly. He began to console her, his training automatic before remembering why he'd pursued the dark-haired, brooding Brenda into the broom closet. He closed the door and leaned back against the wall, giving her the space to approach him. Even now, locked in a closet with hopefully more than Seven Seconds in Heaven, Aaron didn't want to misinterpret the signs. Maybe she had been looking for some Windex and would later accuse him of sexual harassment, so he had to be sure.

Her trembling lips closed on his, not sloppy like the first Brenda's but more refined and practiced, tongue searching instead of dominating, mouth eager instead of hollow. The Brenda pinned him against the metal rack as she unbuckled his belt and lifted one leg to wrap around his waist while he lifted her dress and moved aside her white panties. He tried to enter her awkwardly from a side angle but failed with several thrusts as they kissed rapidly, and when he finally slid into her, she arched and threw her head back, whacking it on a shelf as she let out a suppressed moan of pleasure mixed with pain. The impact forced a plastic 28 oz. bottle of purple cleaning fluid to fall off the rack and roll onto the ground, causing Aaron to wonder what type of cleaning agent sloshed around in the bottle. Aaron recalled Moises telling him the purple detergent was for deep stains. Deep. Aaron's desire swelled.

They humped ferociously for almost ninety seconds until Aaron's legs began to tire. Thankfully, the Brenda demanded, "Do me from behind."

Aaron turned the Brenda around as she bent at the waist, laying her arms across the shelf. She inadvertently knocked off several more bottles of green and blue cleaning fluids, each one falling like ocean waves which excited Aaron even more. When he accidentally kicked a bottle of what he secretly hoped was Windex while plunging into the Brenda, the top of the bottle came loose and fluid spilled over the cement floor. Aaron slipped out of his shoes very carefully so as not to disturb their rhythm. He stood in socks soaked with Windex, the inky perfume driving him wild and the Brenda sensed his frantic humping was a little more frenetic than usual and she responded by bucking hard against him. Aaron lost control and spanked her with his left hand at first, then with his right, alternating back and forth with both hands, firing at will, with the Brenda whimpering little, muffled moans that almost made Aaron climax.

In the excitement, he started saying ridiculous things. "Your pussy's so clean. Now grab that bottle of SoftScrub. Yes, that's the one. Grab the shaft below the nozzle, that's right. Stroke it, up and down, baby!" while she cried out the typical, "Fûck me haaaarder!" but when he yelled out, "Who's yo daddy?!" the Brenda stopped bucking and placed her hand on his stomach to stop him.

Aaron stood behind the Brenda, his shoes off, white socks tinted blue, stiffly inside her as she brushed her hair aside and turned back to look at him. "Listen, could you not say that?"

"Oh, I'm sorry," Aaron said panting. "You don't like SoftScrub?"

"No, the whole 'who's your daddy' thing. I was raped by my step-dad from the time I was eight until I ran away at fourteen."

Aaron tried to pull himself out of her, but she pushed back with her hips. "No, really, it's ok. Don't stop. Really, I've processed it. Tons of therapy. It's just a trigger for me, OK?"

"You sure?" Aaron asked, instantly feeling himself get soft.

"Yeah, it's fine," the Brenda assured him. "Really, I'm over it."

Aaron seriously doubted she would ever be *over it*, but she clenched her pelvic floor muscles and Kegeled him back to life. And Aaron had no choice but to dismiss the terrible image of her abuse as a young girl and kept on humping. The Brenda got right back into it, the moaning, the pleading and in thirty-four seconds Aaron was right back on the edge of emission, switching his gaze from the curve of her waist to the three opened Ajax canisters, side by side, that left him wondering why the janitorial service didn't finish one can before opening another, and then switching his gaze back to her round breasts bouncing out from the side of her halter top dress with each thrust and the Brenda reached down to rub herself as he was about to come and he didn't have time to pull out of her because he was completely lost in the delusion of his middle school teacher bent over who had psychically transformed into the grad student Brenda surrounded by the toxic fumes of spilt window cleaner which was why he cried out the worst possible phrase for this poor Brenda right as he exploded,

"Who's yo daddy!!"

Chapter 7

A Classic Case of Victim-Blaming
Towards Medusa and Zombies

On the Monday after Aaron's failed birthday party, another Brenda started working at the Crisis Hotline Center, this one a recent college graduate majoring in both Psych and Sociology and Aaron was instantly smitten. Debz, leaning back in her chair, scoped out the new recruit as well.

Aaron spoke so Debz could hear him in the next stall. "Niiiice, she's totally my type."

Debz leaned over the pre-fab cubicle wall. "And what's that? Fast n' loose, wet n' perky, or young n' easy?"

"Wait, you trying to score this early? I'm barely awake. Fine, I'll give you a point."

Aaron and Debz played a brutal game at work to keep things interesting during the inevitable lull in phone calls. The game was a verbal contest of who could be funny or insightful or better yet, who could insult or out-gross the other. The only rule was that the other person had to say *POINT* when an exceptionally witty remark, personal jab, vicious cut or poignant diss[24] was delivered.

"Besides," Aaron continued, "I only like those brown haired, big-hipped Midwestern girls."

"Oh, you mean sad n' vulnerable. By the way, she's dirty blonde."

"Whatevs, close enough. Definitely Ohio or Indiana, right?"

"I was thinking Massachusetts. Looks like a poet-type from an all-girl's liberal arts college. Kinda reminds me of Emily Dickinson."

"You wanna put your dick-in-my-son?"

"Dude," Debz said glaring at him, "that doesn't even make sense. I'm a chick and you've got a daughter. No point for you."

"Sorry, haven't had my coffee yet."

Debz looked back at the new girl. "Why you think she's from the mid-West?"

"She's too nice. Apologized three times already. And she's got that doe-eyed smile like she's just happy to be here."

"Who the hell would be happy to be here?" Debz asked rhetorically. "She's must be sick in the head or somethin."

"Exactly. Think I'm in love. I claim dibs, you got the last one."

"What, that cold fish intern from Alaska? She was 60/40, missed your chance."

"Sixty percent into girls, and a forty percent preference for guys. You had a better chance," Aaron complained.

"Whatevs, turns out I don't like rotten Alaskan Salmon."

"Point," Aaron gagged. "Gross image, made me throw up in my mouth."

"You taste sperm?"

"Only when I suck your dad off."

"He's been dead for two years."

"That didn't stop me." Aaron wasn't sure if Debz's father had died recently, but necrophilia was always a quick way to score.

"Point. Fine, new girl is yours. Ya'know I like my ladies the way I like my coffee."

"Black n' sweet or cold n' bitter?"

"Nah," she said. "Ground up and stashed in the freezer."

"Nice one, point. But you nasty, guuuurl."

"Ya'know it, boeeeey."

Boss Lady circled around to each of the cubicles and introduced the new Brenda to the staff. Aaron stood up from the orange, plastic chair and read her name tag. Kellie. Of course, it ended with an *IE* and not a *Y*. Aaron suspected she would be high-maintenance and a burden, but figured she might be worth it. Her soft handshake matched her gentle smile and the comfort of her light hazel eyes. Aaron's attention was diverted when Debz pretended to grab at Kellie from behind. With a contorted expression on Debz's face and tongue hanging out, she mouthed words that Aaron guessed were *look-at-dat-ass!*

Luckily, Boos-lady didn't see and certainly would have written Debz up for yet another case of workplace harassment. Debz had proudly flirted with, more like awkwardly hit on, nearly every female co-worker in the building. Aaron knew she was overcompensating and doubted if she was a lesbian because he'd never seen Debz with a girlfriend but he knew for certain that she didn't like men. Debz told him that she'd tried it with a man once and found the encounter to be, "like a splinter sliding under my fingernail, repeatedly." Maybe, he thought, Debz was exaggerating her workplace sexualized behavior because she was in fact a non-binary misanthrope.

After Kellie finished her tour of the cubicles with Boss Lady,

Aaron averted his gaze and heard Debz harassing him.

"Got her in the spank-bank now?"

"Me? What about you? You were basically grabbing her ass, jee-zeus."

"I'll be rubbing one out later," Debz confessed. She reached down, pretending to grab her crotch. "Wait, maybe I'll do it right now, only takes a second."

"No, don't!" Aaron sat back down in his chair and covered his ears with both hands.

"Here I go, baby. Spreading my lips." Debz rocked her chair back, banging into the cubicle's flimsy particle board.

"Stop it! Seriously Debz, I can hear you."

"Can't stop, feels so gooood!"

Some of the other female co-workers looked in their direction, but most of the staff was familiar with Debz's antics and ignored her.

"Um gaaaawd, right there…yes…yaassss…and I'm done." Debz peeked over the edge of the wall. "Told you it wouldn't take long."

"Faker," Aaron said. "Fine, point. Think I've got a chance with Kellie?"

Debz smirked, "Doubt it, she's too innocent. Bet that turns you on."

Aaron's face beamed as he reached for the phone to follow up on a call. "Damn right! She's a Medusa. Girl got me hard as a rock, she's turned me to stone!"

"Point!" Debz exclaimed. "That girl is poiii-zahnnn," she hummed, singing a few bars from Bell Biv Devoe's *Poison* before getting back to work at her desk.

Aaron dialed the number and quickly reviewed the notes from a call taken over a week ago. He'd been meaning to get back to the family of a high school girl that had Attempted after being allegedly raped by her boyfriend, but he'd simply forgotten about them because the girl's mother was such a bitch. At least that's what the notes conveyed.

Aaron grabbed a yellow pad of paper to doodle on while chatting with the family. Perhaps because of the residual tingling in his penis caused by the recession of blood flow, he thought of Kellie and wrote *MEDUSA* on the top of the yellow pad. He grew disgusted about having a half-chub erection while returning a rape-then-attempted suicide call.

Hell, Aaron thought as a way of self-consolation, if Margaret Atwood could get away with a little story called *Rape-Fantasies*, then maybe I shouldn't blame myself for fantasizing about my co-worker while taking a rape call. Even though he continued to doodle about Kellie, the sharp pain in his gut reminded him that he was wrong.

The mother of the high school girl answered on the second ring.

Mother, irritated affect: "About time you called back."

Aaron, as Felipe, apologetic: "I'm sorry for the delay, we had to wait for the police report," which was an outright lie, yet both believable and a reliable method of deflecting anger.

Mother, testy, pitch raising: "What about my daughter? She was raped!"

"Ma'am, this is the Suicide Prevention Center. I've called to talk about your daughter's recent suicide Attempt."

"But she was raped by her boyfriend."

"I'm not doubting your version of the story."

"My version? What the heck do you mean by that?"

"Well, according to my notes," Aaron said, "your daughter reported consensual intercourse."

"No!" the mother cried. "That's not correct. You need to change that right now!"

"Ma'am, I cannot alter an official document. Apparently, she tried to hang herself in the shower but the curtain rod broke, is that right?"

"I don't know anything about a suicide."

"Well, that's what your daughter reported. Aren't you more worried about her life than her sex life?"

"Excuse me? Who the heck do you think you are?"

Debz came around and put her ear to the receiver. With an audience, Aaron told the mother, "Your daughter's vagina is none of your business. It's her body, her choice."

Debz snickered and quietly mouthed, "That's right, you tell her."

"Who's your supervisor? I'm a proper woman, I won't be talked to this way."

Debz took the receiver from Aaron and said in the blandest voice she could muster, "Hellooooo Ma'aaaam, yaaaas I aaaaaaam the superrrrvisorrrr. Whaaaat caaaan I dooo ferrrr yoooooou?"

The mother hesitated. "You sound like a zombie. Are you on drugs?"

"I wiiiish." Debz covered her mouth as she busted out laughing and handed the phone back to Aaron.

"You can see what I'm dealing with here," Aaron said to the mother. "I'm the only one here to help you today. Please bear with me, alright?"

"Fine," the mother sighed with resignation. "But my daughter made a promise. She wears a purity ring. There's no way she could have had..." whispering the next three letters, "s-e-x."

"You ever wonder why boys never wear purity rings?" Aaron asked. "I bet Brett Kavanaugh never wore a purity ring."

"That's not the point. My daughter was a virgin and that boy raped her! He stole what's intended for her future husband."

Aaron hardly listened as the mother ranted about how her underage daughter's boyfriend was three years older and could be prosecuted for statutory rape. The mother blamed her own daughter for wearing too much make-up and tight clothing, and leading the boy on with flirtatious texts which she, the nosey-mother, had read late one night when the daughter left her unlocked phone on the kitchen table.

"So embarrassing," the mother said, "some of the things she texted him, downright shocking. What exactly is a donkey-punch and buck-cake?"

Aaron figured she meant *bukkake*. "It's like cake frosting. Lots of it."

"Well, it's her own fault this happened."

An occasional "Uh-huh," and "Nuh-uh," from Aaron kept the mother talking for another fourteen minutes. Debz went back to her desk halfway through the mother's seamless and breathless sanctimonious tirade.

Aaron was preoccupied with his notes about Medusa and circled K-E-L-L-I-E with heart-shaped bubbles around her name. Listening to the mother victim-blame her own daughter was not surprising. Aaron had heard it many times. Parents, feeling guilty for failing to protect, ultimately shifted blame onto their children.

Aaron interrupted the mother. "Hold on, I'll tell you what I can do. This reminds me of a call I took last week."

"Really?" the mother asked, desperate for advice.

"Sure," Aaron lied, "reminds me of this woman named Medusa, I mean Matilda. Now, some parts of this story are hard to believe but it happened in a church."

"A church? You mean this woman was raped in a church?"

"Yes."

"That's terrible. I'm a Christian. I can't imagine such a thing would happen in the house of the Lord."

"You ever hear about Catholic priests and little boys?"

"That's different," the woman explained. "Those boys weren't raped, they were just molested."

"Oh, really?"

"Yes, men can't be raped. Everyone knows that," she said with finality.

Aaron cleared his throat and stammered, "I don't know what…to say…about that." Several rebuttals sprung such as, *Do you have any idea what happens to men in jail or the army?* He continued with the Greek legend of Medusa.

"Anyway, this Matilda woman was visiting the temple on Athena Boulevard."

"She was Jewish?"

"Did I say temple? I meant church."

"Good," the woman said, "because if she was Jewish, then she probably deserved what happened to her. You know how those people are."

Aaron swallowed the most obvious response of, *Jesus deserved it?* He continued, "There she knelt praying, minding her own business in the church. Soon after, in walks Poseidon," Aaron said mumbling the name.

"Poor Sid?"

"Yes, his name is Sydney," Aaron improvised. "But he's homeless so they call him Poor Sid."

"That's nice."

"Poor Sid sees this Matilda sitting by herself in the pews. He grabs her by the hair, drags her into a confessional stall and rapes her."

"She shouldn't have been alone. I mean, who goes to church by themselves?"

"As it turns out Poor Sid is the brother of the bishop of Athena's church. Later, the bishop finds the disheveled woman weeping in the stall and grows quite upset. However, when the woman identifies the rapist as the bishop's brother, Poor Sid, the bishop blames her for what happened."

"That's right, she can only blame herself. She's at fault. She was probably wearing a skirt. Or worse, pants."

"The bishop of Athena's church knew he had to protect his brother. Poor Sid was a known rapist, and the bishop didn't want his brother to go back to jail in Mount J'Olympus."

"Is that a federal penitentiary?"

"Basically. Suddenly, in a divine rage, the bishop cursed Matilda."

"He cursed at her?" the woman asked incredulously. "I don't believe it, priests can't take the Lord's name in vain."

"No, he didn't *curse at* her. The priest actually *cursed* her. Like an Old Testament kind of curse. Frogs, lice, boils, plague of locusts."

"I believe it!"

"The curses were numerous. The bishop decided to punish Matilda for her feminine beauty."

"I don't use Satan's little finger," the mother commented. "Says so in the Bible. Isaiah 64:6, 'All of us have become like one who is unclean, and all our righteous acts are like spoiled rags'. Using them is the same as having pre-marital sex. It's a sin."

Aaron motioned for Debz to come back over. He put his hand over the receiver and asked her, "What the hell is Satan's little finger?"

Debz looked bewildered. "Is she talking about tampons?"

Aaron said, "Oh, that makes sense."

He uncovered the receiver and said to the mother, "No, I didn't say anything about feminine hygiene products. I said the bishop cursed her feminine beauty for attracting the attention of Poor Sid. The bishop turned Matilda's flowing brown hair into snakes."

"Hair should be covered."

"Her painted fingernails became claws."

"Make-up promotes sin."

"Her voluptuous body changed into a snake. Her silky legs became chicken legs."

"Her legs were probably shaved and exposed. A man can't resist such temptation."

"Her creamy skin became cracked and aged."

"She had soft skin, too? You can't blame Poor Sid for being lured by her looks."

"And worst of all, everyone she looked upon was turned to stone."

"She smoked marijuana, too? Serves her right for getting raped."

"No, she wasn't stoned. Matilda's gaze with the power to melt hearts would now petrify bodies."

Debz silently mouthed *Point*. Aaron gave her a victorious fist-pump.

The mother was confused. "What are saying exactly?"

"You daughter sounds like Medusa, I mean Matilda. She turns men's cocks into rocks!"

Debz exploded in laughter. Aaron promptly hung-up the phone and received a solid high-five from Debz.

"Well," she said, "if that doesn't get you fired, I don't know what will."

After the call, Aaron looked at the doodles he'd made on the yellow pad of paper. Kellie's name, written on the top, was circled twice with an arrow pointing to Medusa. Down below, he'd written *Just World Hypothesis* on the side when the mother had mentioned the word ZOMBIE. Aaron was convinced that after a zombie invasion, the terrible mother would probably think that anyone turned into a zombie probably deserved it.

After Aaron finished the call, he disconnected the cord running to the land line. He leaned back into his chair, placed the yellow pad of paper onto his lap and decided to spend the remainder of the day sketching a screenplay for a Zombie film, a genre with the obvious metaphor for rape because the actors were usually attacked by a menacing, slobbering, growling, moaning, sex-starved, slightly rotting male figure.

Aaron spent the first few minutes of his hiatus from work explaining over the cubicle wall to Debz that zombie horror films were in fact misogynistic Romantic Comedies because the male lead was a complete asshole pursuing the innocent female actress. At the end, the zombies/assholes were killed/forgiven by the survivors/love interest. As though the infectious zombie bite/infectious feelings of love could be redeemed by a single act of kindness at the end of the film. Aaron knew this was complete nonsense because if zombies were indeed eating the living, then no one would be left to become a zombie. Like bachelors in a romantic comedy, everyone would either be eaten or married by the end. Aaron wasn't sure which was worse.

Aaron expected to hear some kind of retort from Debz but when he peeked over the wall, she'd snuck out midway through his rant. Bored and lonely without his verbal-sparring partner, Aaron spent the next few hours scribbling down a rough outline of a screenplay entitled:

LEAD GEORGE

Scene opens with George, metal worker at Tyson's Foundry, at the onset of a zombie invasion.[25]

George, running through industrial factory, gets bitten by an infected zombie and falls into a vat of liquid metal. His body is wedged above the vat in such a way that only his penis is dipped into the molten lead (TA#1).[26]

Close-up on George with Look of Pleasure (*L.O.P.*): "Aaaahhhhhh!"

George, wedged in vat above molten lead. George's friend, in an act of self-sacrifice, pulls lever which drains the molten lead. His friend is devoured by zombies.

George falls into empty lead pit. Whacking his mouth on the edge, spits out broken teeth. He also has a lead patch burned atop his head (TA#2).[27]

George stumbles through the automobile junk yard located next to Tyson's Foundry.

George, foot trapped in rubble of auto junk yard. Slowly becoming a zombie.

Cue sad music. George as zombie alone in junk yard. Camera pans up the hill to a long shot of prestigious all-women's college (TA#3).[28]

Dusk. Camera zooms in on a campus quad filled with female students tossing Frisbees and slurping shots of tequila off each other's smooth bellies while smoking phallic-looking bongs as several in the foreground are combing one another's luscious hair or intensely painting fingernails while dressed in tight fitting red or black lingerie, and others in the background are engaged in a slow-motion pillow fight wearing white tank tops and flower-print panties (TA#4).[29] Students are oblivious to zombie invasion.

Close-up on female lead. Kellie doing keg stand, slightly intoxicated, surrounded by other drunk friends who are talking about their boyfriends.

Kellie, disgusted by friends and looking especially smokin hot in reading glasses, because the smart, innocent girl is always the Last Survivor: "Boys, boys, boys. That's all you talk about. Y'all seriously failing the Bechtel Test."

Drunk Blonde Friend, hot but not sexier than Kellie: "Is that like a breast exam?"

Drunk Brunette Friend, classically proportioned meaning plus-sized and big-chested: "Think I failed that test in Government class last week. Something about the Civil War?"

Token DUFF, the Designated Ugly, Fat Friend who is way smarter than anyone else in the group and will probably end up marrying a very successful accountant and after years of working in real estate, she will home-school her three wonderful children: "No, idiots. It's a test designed to see if we, as the actresses of a zombie/horror film, can talk about anything else besides men and marriage" (TA#5).[30]

Kellie: "For real, there are no boys here on campus and you're still talking about them!"

Kellie, stomping off in disgust, leaves campus. Staggers down the hill into junk yard. She notices the silhouette of George in the darkness.

Kellie, drunk but cautious: "Hi there."

George: "Aaarrrghhh."

Kellie: "Oh good, you're the strong, silent type."

George, his foot stuck in the door of a rusted, classic car (TA#6).[31]

Kellie, sits down on rear bench car seat that is cinematically arranged in an open space, fabric slightly torn, her back to George. She lights a cigarette: "Want a drag?"

George: "Naaaaaaaarghh."

Kellie: "That's good you don't smoke. Terrible habit."

Kellie, sways drunkenly. Talks about her life, her hopes, her feelings and dreams.

George, behind her in the dark, occasionally lunging into the light cast by the moon, trying to eat her brains. Unable to reach her because of trapped foot.

Kellie, after twelve minutes: "You're a good listener."

George, his hands reaching out, brushes against her neck.

Kellie, leaning back: "I like it when you play with my hair."

George, his hands around her neck.

Kellie: "I like it when you rub my shoulders."

George, tires to choke her.

Kellie, moving away: "Too rough!"

George, can't pursue because his foot is trapped.

Kellie, turns around to look at George. His face is covered in darkness, but a spot of light illuminates the stenciled name on his workman's t-shirt.

Kellie: "George, that's a nice name. A strong name. Are you strong, George?"

George: "Yeeeeaaaaargh"

Kellie: "I bet you are."

Kellie, taking off her shirt in the moonlight: "Ok, you've been so patient. Now give me a kiss already" (TA#7).[32]

George, struggling madly, breaks loose from the car by pushing off from a control box with a switch, accidentally activating a large magnet overhead designed to pick up automobiles. The magnet slowly begins to descend.

George, free from car, attacks Kelly but he trips on a muffler and falls into her arms. They tumble to the ground, Kellie ends up on top.

Kellie: "Oh, you like a strong woman? That's so sexy! But I want you on top."

George, trying to eat her flesh, mounts and bites her neck. However, since he knocked out his teeth falling into the empty lead vat, George only succeeds in nuzzling her neck.

Kellie (L.O.P): "Yes, George! That feels soooo good!!"

Camera focuses on the large magnet lowering into position above them. When it gets close to the couple, George stops trying to eat her neck and looks down at his crotch in utter panic.

Close up on George's lead-zombie-penis tugged out of his pants by the magnet.

George, L.O.P. at lead-zombie-penis which is stiff, rigid, divine. Every young man's dream and every old man's memory.

Kellie: "Oh my Gawd! It's so .... shiny. Alright then, I'm ready. Give it to me, baby! Give it to me hard!" (TA#8).[33]

The magnet, hovering above them, smacks against a metal pylon which sends the magnet rocking gently back and forth. George's hips match the swaying of the magnet.

Kellie, frustrated: "No, that's not it...not there...definitely not there ... nope ... close ... closer ... yes ... yeeees ...oh Gawd, yeeeeeeees!"

George, hips gyrating in synchronicity with the swaying magnet as she moans from the thrusts of his lead-zombie-penis.

Simultaneously, George L.O.P. and Kelly L.O.P.

Clouds pass over the moon. Dogs howl in the wind. Birds soars overhead. Hours pass.

Kellie: "Whoa, you really can go for a long time. Give a girl a break."

Kellie, shoves George off her. She stands up, puts on clothes.

George, without her body to keep him on the ground, is hilariously flung up in the air and remains stuck to the bottom of the magnet!

Kellie, doesn't notice and while adjusting the strap on her sandal, accidentally leans against the same switch that de-activates the magnet.

George, falls to the ground, holding lead-zombie-penis in his hand. L.O.P. on his face.

George, leg grotesquely twisted underneath his body, reaches up at Kellie but is unable to stand.

Kellie, giving him a high-five: "Good for you, too?"

George: "Yaaargh."

Kellie, kisses George on his lead patch forehead: "You've got a little bump here."

George: "Yaaargh?"

Kellie: "I bet it hurts. Here, hand me your phone. I'll give you my number."

George: "Naaargh,"

Kellie: "Don't have your phone?"

She reaches into her purse, lights a cigarette, writes her dorm room number on a piece of paper and sticks it inside his shirt pocket. She points to the dorm on top of the hill.

George, notices where she is pointing.

Kellie: "Come visit me. I'll take care of that bump."

George: "Yaaargh."

Kellie, looking down his lead-zombie-penis: "And that bump, too."

Exit Kellie. She walks uphill to campus.

George, painful expression of longing on his zombie-face. A tiny piece of the lead on his forehead flakes off (TA#9).[34]

George, straightens leg with sickening cruuuuuuuunch, and shambles uphill to the college campus.

Cut to Kellie returning to her dorm room, finds Blonde Drunk Friends eating the face of Drunk Brunette Friend. Hilarious moment of confusion when Kellie thinks they are making out, then surprise...Zombies!

Kellie, running, screaming, in midst of zombie invasion.

Kellie, teams up with DUFF and several others armed with field hockey sticks, aluminum softball bats and a metal nail file. They are dressed in skimpy clothes ineffective in preventing blood-borne diseases such as the zombie-inducing viral strain and other STDs (TA#10).[35]

Kellie & Company, fighting, running, screaming, etc.

Cut to split-screen. Montage of George, slowly shambling uphill with piece of paper clutched in his hand, contrasted by Kellie fleeing from zombies.

Kellie & Co., fighting off frat-boy-zombies in Amherst College rugby t-shirts who are chasing girls (TA#11).[36]

George, on campus. He is shambling from room to room, every time comparing the piece of paper to each room number. B-4, B-5, B-6...

Kellie & Co. end up running in a complete circle back to her dorm room where their adventures started. DUFF killed by bookshelf falling on her.

DUFF, final words, exclaimed: "Always knew books would be the death of me!"

Kellie, last survivor, struggling with frat-boy-zombie in rugby t-shirt.

George peeks his head around corner, checks the numbers on the front of the door. Checks the paper. Re-checks the room number.

Kellie, struggling in the background.

George, in the foreground, checks the paper, re-checks the room number.

Hilarity ensures. Kellie fighting for her survival while George tries to determine if this is the correct room (TA#12).[37]

Finally, they look up from their personal struggles and make eye contact. She is unaware that he is a zombie (TA#13).[38]

In slow-motion, simultaneous L.O.P. on both of their faces.

Kellie, screaming in slow-motion: "HHHEEELLLPPP!"

George, with a love-sick moaning-face, staggers with arms outstretched: "Aaaaarrrrrgh!!!"

George accidentally bumps his lead-zombie-penis into frat-zombie-guy and pushes him out the window (TA#14).[39]

Slow-motion finalé with Kellie and George swirling in each other's arms.

George nuzzles her neck.

Kellie: "You're such a sloppy kisser!"

Fade to black.

—Roll Credits—

*

The five o'clock alarm on his desk clock alerted Aaron that his shift was over. As he put away manila folders filled with case files into the desk drawer, he gave one last thought to the mother of the daughter who had engaged in consensual sex with her high school boyfriend on the living room sofa, possibly after watching *Night of the Living Dead* while wearing a promise ring. Aaron was convinced that if this terrible mother were ever to view the film adaptation of LEAD GEORGE, she would certainly experience three versions of victim-blaming expressed as, 1) blaming the leading actress Kellie for getting raped in the junkyard by an ugly looking man with a shiny penis because she shouldn't have wandered out alone at night; and, 2) thinking the girls on campus deserved to get eaten by zombies because skimpy clothing explicitly conveyed their wanton morals; and, 3) happy the leading actress Kellie was devoured by a zombie at the end of the film because of her promiscuous activities, even though that's not even remotely how the film ended. Because, Aaron reasoned, the mother could tank a movie without having watched it, ban a book without having read it, and condemn her own daughter without having listened to her.

Aaron drove straight home, racing past the Alibi Lounge without even the slightest temptation to stop for a drink. Although he enjoyed Cape Cods with a lime wedge, at this point the red cranberry juice would only remind him of zombie blood.

Instead, he went home and found Zoë grilling veggie-burgers in the toaster.

Aaron approached his daughter and swallowed her in a big hug that conveyed, *I've had a rough day and I missed you and I need a hug to reaffirm that the world is not full of cruel mothers and evil men*. When she gazed up at him with a bewildered look, he told Zoë, "Your body, your choice."

Aaron left without another word and decided he absolutely needed to shower to wash away the residual grime left by the last caller's ill-conceived notions of motherhood. Over the years, Aaron had begun to understand why teenage girls frequently fought with their mothers. Mothers were a girl's worst enemy not because they were competition for a father's attention. Rather, a mother's animosity served to protect her daughter when she went off to college and was accosted by a horde of drunken frat-boy-zombies. Given the power, every mother would curse her own daughter like Athena had cursed Medusa. Maybe the spell was a blessing. Maybe Athena was only keeping Medusa safe so she wouldn't get raped again.

Chapter 8

Convincing a Caller-in-Crisis That the Listener-in-Despair
Is Way More Suicidal

Unable to sleep, Aaron spent hours on the stained yellow couch watching his favorite Star Trek episode on repeat.[40] When the phone rang at 1:23 a.m. on Monday night/Tuesday morning, he should have picked up the landline and regurgitated with requisite calmness the standard intro, "Hello, I'm the crisis worker for the National Suicide Hotline and Prevention Center. How you doin tonight?"

Sometimes, Aaron accidently emphasized the *you* and he ended up sounding like Joey from *Friends*, a rather creepy way to initiate a crisis call. On this particular evening, Aaron answered the phone in a personal style which only confused the Caller-in-Crisis.

"Sorry, but you're in for a bit of a ride tonight," Aaron explained. "I'm not really feeling like my usual self. Had a rough weekend."

Caller, male, mid-twenties, confused affect: "What?"

"I don't feel like listening," Aaron explained. "Got my own problems."

"Wait, is this the, I mean, I'm trying to reach the..."

"Perhaps I should have been clear in the beginning. Please don't hang up on me. Promise me that at least, can you do that?"

"Um, sure, I guess," the Caller said meekly. "Is anyone else there?"

"I need to hear you say it. Promise me that you won't hang up. One time, this guy called and shot himself over the phone. Not like he put a gun into the receiver and pulled the trigger and then picked up another phone and the bullet came out. Not like that at all. More like we were talking and *click-boom*. I still have nightmares."

"Ok, but I'm not sure what to say."

"Say it, say you'll promise not to hang up on me. I don't think I could take it. Not tonight. Because of that shooting."

"The one at Denny's?"

"Happened a couple of days ago but now kinda freakin out about it," Aaron confessed. "And if you hang up on me, I'll be devastated."

"Um, maybe there's some else I could talk to?"

"SAY IT!"

"Fine, jeez. I promise not to hang up on you."

Aaron exhaled slowly. "See, that wasn't so difficult, was it now? Now you've made a contract. You've signed your name in blood, written it in stone, crossed your heart. You can't go back on a promise, we're stuck together."

"Great, now what?"

"I'd like to get off the couch, maybe even go outside. I've been inside for hours, hiding. And one second can seem like hour, and a minute becomes a day and so an hour is nearly a year, and I've been trapped in my living room, my dying room, since 9 p.m. and that's about half a decade of sleep without dreams. Only fear. Panic. Pain. Sobbing agony."

Aaron used to have pleasant dreams. But that was before Norton the Breathing Forest appeared when he was six years old. Since then he's only dreamed of the one true power anyone has in life. The power over one's death. Every night while bored in bed and unable to quell the worries, he manifested methods of killing himself also known as SFs, suicidal fantasies. These fantasies were not sad or sexy or sadistic or surreal but straight up self-murder, sui-cide. Hundreds of ways, each one unique and beautiful.

The Caller in his mid-twenties repeated, "Sobbing agony?"

"When it hurts so bad you can't catch your breath."

"Dude, get a grip."

"That'd be nice. I'm tryin to go outside but that's where the people are. And I can't deal with people right now. They'll see how off-kilter I am and they'll look at me in the eyes, don't think I could endure the scrutiny."

"But it's two in the morning, nobody's outside. And it's dark."

"You've got a good point. The rain has stopped, cool air might help me," Aaron said, lifting the window as the petrichor wafted into the house. "Pretty tempting to go out, can't be that hard, right? But the sky is heavy, oppressive. I can sense the weight."

"I get like that, too," the Caller agreed. "My shrink called it agri-somethin. Like a phobia."

"Fear of agriculture? Corn and farm animals?"

"I don't think so."

"Oh, agoraphobia."

"That's it. I know how you feel. Sometimes I get scared, too."

"You know how I feel?" Aaron asked. "Tell me, how exactly does empathy work? Sympathy sure, that's easy. I stub my toe and you feel bad for me. But empathy? I stub my toe and you kick the wall to feel my pain. Ugh, I hate that word. Feel. The word smells like tar and wet hay and a dead jellyfish and three used condoms, like bric-a-brac baking in the hot sun."

"Bric-a-what?" the Caller asked, confused.

"Brick-a-oh-fuck[41] it, I'm talking about what it's like to feel someone else's pain. But here's the problem. I can't feel because my nerve endings are exposed and the world is sand paper."

"I can honestly say I'm feeling a little weird now. I didn't think the call would go this way."

"Feel, it's a ridiculous word," Aaron continued. "You ever have that feeling in the pit of your stomach caused by heartache? It's a gastrointestinal imbalance initiated by a chemical disturbance in the mind. The heart has nothing to do with it. That's the problem. We think, we don't feel."

Aaron wanted to explain to the Caller how most of his SFs, suicidal fantasies, were connected to his stomach. However, doing so would have required relating the entire historical context of how Ancient Romans emphasized the stomach in the same manner which contemporary society referred to the emotional capacity of the heart. The Romans believed the fluttering of one's heart was indigestion, symptoms easily cured by a large meal to soothe lovesickness. Perhaps they had it right, Aaron pondered, since he always binged on ice cream after getting dumped. He felt the same cramp while imagining what he'll say at Eve's funeral. She wasn't dead, not yet, but time stalked. His stomach, not his heart, held the ache of acidic bile swelled by tears on an empty belly. He was convinced the impending funeral stress will have him doubled over in pain, struggling to breathe. For Aaron, the anxiety of public speaking filled his legs with seawater and tightened his bowels, stomach heaving like a seasick sailor. He was less scared of dying than of speaking in front of an audience, meaning he'd rather be dead than give the eulogy, which is why he spoke to people over the phone.

Aaron continued, "I feel, you feel, we feel, they feel, it's like we're conjugating verbs in English class. But we don't feel and maybe we shouldn't even try. Our whole lives are a lie because we are trying to do the impossible. To feel normal. But we either feel too much or not enough, that's the problem. Hell, it even sounds slippery, like an eel. Say it with me. Feel, feeeel, feeeeeeeeels."

"…"

"SAY IT!"

"Fine, jeez. Feel. There, I said it."

"And what do you feel?"

"Me? Only confused."

"That's a good start," Aaron said, "knowing that you're lost. And being lost, you can't commit to a choice. It becomes impossible to stand up or leave the house. Stationary. Immobile. And what's wrong with that? Staying put means you can't make any mistakes. You can't *feel* anything. Maybe today's when I finally get around to making an honest Attempt because to be honest, you bastards are contagious, always calling me on this suicide hotline, slowly convincing me to do it. I'm not here to talk you down. You're here to talk me up. Up on the ledge. Ever think about that?"

Frequently, Aaron imagined leaping from the edge of a building but his favorite SF was utterly self-centered, pastoral, and romantically Oriental. He dreamt of relieving the stomach pain. The anxiety and fear could only be cut out, easing a lifetime of grief. In this particular SF, seppuku brought him relief since he knew the stomach, not his heart, held emotional suffering. Aaron envisioned himself as an old man in his seventies,[42] surrounded by family and friends. They have come to witness the final sunset of a man. Everyone sitting in white, folding lawn chairs arranged in a circle. Of course, he's at the center of the crowd because everyone is the star of their own dream. Dressed in white ceremonially death robes, he bows to the setting sun and reads his death poem. To everyone's relief, the poem is not a haiku. More lines than waka, less than Milton and ending with,

> *A sparrow flitters on cherry blossoms,*
> *waves crash beneath Sorrow's Cliff,*
> *soaring free.*

In this SF, he ends the poem with a laugh. Ultimately, the poem is like dodging rain drops by hiding under branches. Without meaning.

Aaron knew this dream would never be a reality. People only attend funerals of the dead, not the dying. Since death was inevitable, the result of a terminal condition called loneliness, he has made other plans. German plans. This SF begins in a white porcelain, claw-foot bathtub, warm water slowly dripping from the tap, keeping the water at a perfect 102 degrees with lavender scented bubbles. He swallows a handful of Nembutal, crushed up as a fine powder and poured into a bottle of Riesling. Taking his time, because he is finally *taking his time*, he slowly sips from a round crystal glass made more for brandy than for white wine. He listens to Wagner, perhaps the aria *Liebestod* from the final love-death scene in *Tristan und Isolde*. Certainly nothing from The Ring Cycle because in his last moments, he refuses to endure a screeching Brünhilde with her Valkyries or a swooning Siegfried on a fiery mountaintop. The window above the bathtub is open, letting in a slight breeze on a sunny, spring day in April, of course. The heated water slowly drips, the pitter-patter echoing in rhythm with the aria as a pair of twittering blue jays announce his terminal requiem. And when the time comes to *take his time*, as in the final weariness brought on by wine, Phenobarbitals and soothing lavender bathwater, only then does he reach over the edge of the tub, careful not to spill water on the tiled floor, and with his right-hand lifts the straight edge razor from a white towel, obviously a classic German blade like Boker or Dovo. He unfolds the razor from its wooden handle and rubs downwards on the inside of his left inner forearm to puff up the blue veins. In a fluid motion, he makes two vertical incisions, one at the top of his left wrist and the other at the crease of his inner elbow, the double cuts serving as suicidal insurance. Repeating his Attempt at fatal exsanguination, he switches the razor to his left hand although the blood from his left wrist has spread and caused the handle to become slippery, and he hates the idea of missing the veins of his right wrist and hitting an artery to make a mess of the situation.

The mess. In many of his SFs, the mess was a concern. He does not want someone to clean-up after him. His greatest fear was not the pain of dying or of Heaven or Hell or the sin of committing self-murder or the possibility that he might fail and end up a paraplegic vegetable. He feared making a mess, which provided a reason for the bath tub. The coroner merely had to pull the plug, allow the blood-tinted water to swirl down the drain and place his lifeless body in a black plastic bag to await cremation. Simple. *Däs Ende*.

None of his SFs included a final heroic act because Aaron knew death caused by depression was more common than sacrificial suicide. Like the devastated husband who lights himself on fire because his wife cheated on him is far different than the Buddhist monks who dies by self-immolation as a form of political protest. Suicide from a cause is far different than suicide for a reason.

After ten years of listening, Aaron had discovered that people don't ask about the causes but rather the how and why, as in, "How did she die?" followed by, "And what was the reason?" Aaron didn't know about causes either, but he had come to understand that most people don't just wake up one day and without provocation suddenly announce,

"I think I'll kill myself today," or,

"I can't take it any longer," or,

"There's no reason to go on," or,

"I have nothing to live for," or,

"I'd die for this cause," or,

"Today IS a good day to die."[43]

The road to suicide is long, traversing either depression or unimaginable pain or psychic trauma or martyrdom through self-sacrifice. People don't always need a reason to take their own life; however, everyone else left behind needs to know why they killed themselves. Aaron had speculated the reasons were similar to the 4-H but instead of head, heart, hands and health, the logic supporting suicide was one of the 3-Hs: hopeless, helpless or homeless. Any of the three would suffice. Maybe not right away, but certainly after a few years.

The 3-Hs were another of his SFs, not quite as glamorous as heroic death but certainly more common. He imagines himself living on the streets, completely alone, no family, no friends, long grey-peppered beard, matted hair, torn jeans, smoke-stained plaid shirt, dirt so far under his nails that even a Vietnamese manicure couldn't help, sleeping out in the cold on a flattened cardboard box lined with soiled newspapers, year after year.

Utterly hopeless; and,

fatalistically helpless; and,

chronically homeless.

Death in this SF is boring, stepping in front of a bus. Splat. When reflecting on the bus imagery to his 32nd therapist, she told him buses meant mobility, community, employment, and societal progress. She also said that he would stop fantasizing about bus related deaths when he started paying for his own therapy sessions instead of relying on his mother.

Although a great many of his SFs were about leaping to death, Aaron knew he would never throw himself from the edge of a cliff, despite his last name of Clifton, spiraling downward in slow-motion, the salty breeze on his face, bones cracking with sudden impact on the rocky shore. One of his SFs is to jump off the Bay Bridge, mainly because it's higher than the Golden Gate Bridge. Although 220 feet wasn't high enough for Kevin Hines who dove head first but then somehow twisted around to land feet first in the freezing water because he'd realized an important lesson the moment he let go of the railing: *I've made a mistake.*

Aaron certainly wouldn't jump in real life because it might look like an accident. And suicide has to be public. The dead want to show the world how much pain they've been in. More importantly, the dead want to make the living suffer.

"Hey, wait a sec," the Caller suddenly realized, "you're not gonna do anything stupid, are you?"

"Like what? You afraid to say the words?"

"No, I mean, you're not gonna, you know…"

Aaron pushed. "SAY IT!"

"Fine, jeez. Kill yourself. There. I said it."

"See, that wasn't so tough. No, I'm not," Aaron said calmly before asking, "Are you?"

"No. I guess not."

"Promise?"

"Fine, I promise," the Caller said without hesitation. "Thanks. I guess. Sure is a strange way to help people." Then he paused, "Can I hang up now?"

"Only if you *feel* like it. On that note, feeling suicidal is different than being suicidal. Feelings pass, remember that. G'nite."

Episode 8.5

The Wedding of Death and Despair

The next day, Aaron woke up early to prepare pancakes for Zoë before she went skiing with her high school Latin class for the entire weekend. A weekend in which Aaron prepared a long fall into depression. He planned these times alone to come apart using abandonment as an excuse. He enjoyed the solitude, inevitably triggering existential malaise, because only when alone did he question life's purpose,

> knowing the purpose of life
>> is to find one's purpose.

Yet, the New Age faux-wisdom didn't help him survive the long weekends without his daughter. More specifically, her fleeting departures foreshadowed the fear he was beginning to confront by asking himself, "What the hell am I going to do when Zoë leaves for college?" In order to cope with her weekend trips, Aaron also went away. He went to place called Crazy.

Zoë left immediately after gobbling down breakfast followed by a quick farewell hug. She yelled from the front door, "See ya in a few days."

Aaron inserted a heavily scratched CD into the player and pushed the repeat button, not for the whole album but rather one song. The repetition would help him descend into madness buffered by The Process. The musical torture recreated for Aaron the experience of the Panamanian dictator Manuel Noriega who was blasted with heavy metal music by the American military while holed up for ten days in the Vatican embassy. Noriega's descent into insanity had been gradual, but Aaron didn't have a lot of time to waste since Zoë would only be gone for the weekend. Without doing the dishes, Aaron retreated under the table, the one place he could safely unravel. He used well-practiced meditative techniques to protect himself while tweaking his mind with prescription drugs. Since becoming sober, the temptation to indulge in drugs was always a threat but today he gave himself permission to not only "fall off the water-wagon", but set it ablaze. He'd been planning for this intentional slip by collecting a stash of pills from Marilyn and Jocelyn for this occasion. Although he knew mixing the drugs was dangerous and could lead to an accidental overdose, Aaron convinced himself that he needed to fall apart in order to stay afloat.

To rapidly induce temporary euphoria mixed with despair, Aaron ingested six Ambien, five Sudafed, four shots of tequila mixed with a three-inch-long strip of crushed-up fentanyl, and squirted two mega-doses of Marilyn's prescription of Esketmaine up his nose before climbing under the table. The song echoed, "I take one, one, one cuz you left me."[44]

He was bored with the lyrics by the fifth round until the ketamine kicked in, and Aaron realized he was in trouble. He'd gone too far this time. Only The Process could protect him. As the pin-wheel of electro-translucent rainbows clouded his vision, he sensed a darkness in the corner of the room, lurking around the edge of the table. He refused to look at it directly, the insanity palpable. He repeated a protective mantra as an integral portion of The Process:

I'll be okay

    I'll be okay

        I'll be okay

            I'll be okay

                I'll be okay

                    I'll be okay

                        I'll be okay

                    I'll be okay

                      I'll be okay

The table rumbled like an engine and began to sway. Aaron told himself he'd be fine as long as he kept his hands inside the vehicle. Fortunately, the table idled but didn't travel. Motion without motion, a vehicle moved instead of moving. A vehicle in the same way that Buddhism is a vehicle.[45] Less a mode of transport, more a stationary condition. But as the table hovered, he worried about his hands. He looked down and watched his hands pulsate as blood inched through blue veins. He listened to his fingernails growing. He liked his hands.

To prevent his hands from becoming sucked towards the darkness-around-the-corner, Aaron tied his wrists together. He removed a jade pendant necklace from around his neck and looped the leather strap around his wrists. He tied the end to the base of the table's wooden leg, prohibiting the ability to extend his hands around the corner and into the unknown.

Aaron struggled to free himself for six more rotations of the song. He liked the rawness of leather cutting his flesh, made him focus on something besides the shapeless monstrosity lurking around the corner. Whenever he looked up, he saw it peeking out at him. He had lots of names for it: the Fear, the Darkness, the Sadness, the Horror, the Blackness. Always capitalized, simultaneously a tangible force and a formidable entity stalking him as he lay prone, exposed and tied up beneath the table. "I've gone too far," Aaron told himself, actually himself communicating with his other self, but not the Self, that uppercase capital S-self of the atman/Brahman duality but rather the lowercase s-self, and a little voice asked, "What is happening?"

Aaron, as both Listener and Caller, initiated The Process and continued the inner dialogue, one self conversing with the other self. "If I'm not myself but rather someone else trying to give me advice, should I trust him?"

The Process allowed Aaron to create an image across the room, a doppelgänger tied beneath a similar wooden table. Upon seeing this clone of the mind, Aaron seized upon one desire: to beat the living shit out of him! As in beat on the imposter until bowels loosened. No man could deal with such a primal challenge to his autonomous authority when confronted by an exact replica of himself.

Aaron Uno spoke to his duplicate, "I bet I could beat you up."

Aaron Dos responded, "How's that? I'm you."

Aaron Uno employed logic. "I'd kick your ass because I know your every weakness. I've spent so much time analyzing you, I mean me, that the fight would be over before the first punch."

Aaron Dos sneered, "You can't hurt me."

Aaron Uno lowered his voice and unleashed a deadly truth. "I know your greatest flaw. It's what every boy fears, a fear that plagues him through manhood."

"Oh, and what's that?"

"You're not brave enough."

Aaron Dos transformed into a little boy and lay sobbing on the floor. As the image dissipated, Aaron sensed The Process was successful. Regrettably, without circulation Aaron's hands began to darken, swell and throb. Consumed by a sudden panic, he hyperventilated and heard a voice spouting the truth of his self-induced predicament,

I am NOT okay.

Aaron slipped into a coma from a lack of oxygen and the mix of pills. Beneath the table, he miraculously manifested a vivaciously, vivid vision quest of attending an ostentatious and ornate wedding reception party along the South Carolina coast in springtime . . .

The bride is Death, the groom Despair.

Atop a white marble dais, the bride and groom are both dressed in black. Death wears a lace ball gown with long sleeves, and Despair in a silk tuxedo with dark grey ruffles. Above the dais is a steel-arched arbor lined with black roses and emerald vines. Behind the lovely couple is a large outdoor white brick patio with hundreds of circular tables covered by cream-colored silk tablecloths and decorated by china plates, crystal wine glasses and precisely placed silverware. Centered on each table is a white porcelain, casket-shaped vase filled with a dozen black roses. Inscribed in gold, cursive letters on each vase is a hopeful sentiment, *Marriage - the death of despair.*

Standing between Death and Despair, Aaron greets the well-wishes who have formed a long line of famous yet deceased people. As he shakes hands with or bows to each person, they in turn recite their **'dying last words'**.[46]

As Death waves to her numerous friends standing in line, Aaron apologizes to Despair for missing the wedding ceremony.

Despair whispers in Aaron's ear, "I was excited when the priest said 'til death do us part."

"Why?" asks Aaron.

"Because I'm marrying Death. Now we can part!"

Aaron clasps him around the shoulder. "Buddy, don't worry so much. Let's get some drinks." He motions to a tuxedoed waiter and orders bourbon for Despair and champagne for Death.

Four men at the front of the receiving line approach Death and Despair. The first man, dressed in a tattered Greek toga, is followed by a slender Indian prince and two Chinese men arguing loudly.

Rudely pushing his way past the others is a bearded, homeless man wrapped in a sheet. Socrates(†)[47] greets Aaron with an ancient forearm grip and announces, "Cock."

Socrates' wrinkled face breaks out in uproarious laughter at Death and Despair's shocked expressions. Aaron demands an explanation to which, in typical Socratic form, the ill-groomed Athenian recites his final words. "Let those bastards choke on a cock."

Thinking perhaps this is a poor translation, Aaron asks what he meant and Socrates utters with purple stained lips, **"'I owe a cock to Asclepius, the god of healing; will you remember to pay my debt?'"**

Aaron, tickled that the philosopher ended his life with a question, laughs and says to Despair, "That's so…Socratic. So-Crates until the very end."

Next is Confucius in a tall black hat, not to be confused with Abe Lincoln further down the line. Confucius is arguing with a severely inebriated Zhūangzǐ who seems to be ignoring Confucius and instead staring at a butterfly perched on Death's shoulder. Confucius turns from the drunken man and says, **"'I have taught men how to live'."**

Zhūangzǐ scoffs, "Eh, whatever old man." He then gently scoops up the butterfly and smiles at Death. **"'Above ground, I shall be food for birds; below I shall be food for mole-crickets and ants. Why rob one to feed the other?'"**

Despair is speechless but nods in agreement. Death elbows him in the ribs like a good wife and says, "Don't agree with those crazy, old fools."

Last in the holy gang is Siddhartha Gautama, dressed in a luscious, curry-yellow robe befitting an Indian prince. Aaron whispers discreetly to Despair, "I thought the Buddha would be fatter."

A waiter passes by with a tray of bruschetta topped with mozzarella cheese cubes soaked in olive oil. Zhūangzǐ and Socrates eat most of the appetizer but Siddhartha declines with a wave of his hand. "I'm on a fast." There is a long pause as everyone waits expectantly to hear what the Buddha will say.

The Buddha is silent.[48]

Aaron coughs twice and motions the line forward but the prince protests.

"Why in such a rush?" Siddhartha asks. "Life will be over soon enough." He clears his throat. "At the conclusion of my life, I turned to my lovely wife…"

Zhūangzǐ blurts out, "You mean the wife you abandoned to live in the woods?"

Confucius silences him with a wave. "Show some courtesy. Let the man speak."

Siddhartha continues, "And I told her, **'Beloved, that which causes life also causes decay and death'."**

The bride bounces on her toes excitedly. "Honey, he's talking about me!"

Despair sighs. "Ugh, you always get the attention. Everyone ignores me."

Death hugs him tightly. "Sweetie, what would you be without me?"

"Happy," says Despair.

The three philosophers and the prince wander off to the edge of the party. A few minutes later, Aaron spies them sneaking into the surrounding forest, convinced they are taking turns smoking a joint because he hears Confucius complain, "Hey Buddha, don't hog all the buddha. Remember the First Noble Truth—puff, puff, pass!"

The next coterie to approach the bride and groom are the French. They press forward together through the line, much too civilized to be surrounded by anyone else. Because, Aaron thinks to himself, those who don't speak French are barely human.

Nostradamus extends his hand to Death but she does the fake-shake and slides her hand through her straight, black hair.

Nostradamus says to Death, "I knew you'd do that." He then turns to Aaron with a look of recognition. "I know you."

"You do?"

"Well, not really, but I know how you die."

Aaron pleads, "Oh, tell me!"

Death shakes her finger. "No cheating. Let him find out for himself."

Nostradamus shrugs his shoulder, "Ok, but he's not gonna like it. Anyway, when I was 62, I gave my most accurate prediction. **'Tomorrow, at sunrise, I shall no longer be here'."**

Aaron is not impressed with his prognostication. "Big deal. Every man and woman can predict their own demise. Death is the only power we have in life."

"Sure, dying is easy," Nostradamus says. "Because we die exactly how we lived."

While they are talking, François Rabelais suddenly climbs up on the shoulders of Nostradamus and declares, **"Draw the curtain, the farce is ended. I go to seek the Great Perhaps'."**

And René Descartes climbs up on the shoulders of François and is about to speak but Aaron interrupts him. "I think, therefore I'm going to bed!"

René is not amused and says, "No, that's ridiculous. When my turn came, I said, **'So my soul a time for parting'**."

Marquis de Lafayette climbs even higher, up onto Rene's shoulders, waves like an excited boy at a parade to General Washington (who waits farther down the line) and says, "**What do you expect? Life is like the flame of a lamp; when there is no more oil—zest! It goes out, and it is all over'**."

Mata Hari, although Dutch, sashays over and with a seductive hip swivel, knocks down the towering pillar of Frenchmen. "Before they executed me," she purrs, "a French firing squad handed me a gaudy blindfold, and I told them, **'Must I wear *that*?'**"

Following the French in line are the Americans, creating a ruckus as they always do. They rush the dais, approaching all at once, before being intercepted by two of the greatest boxers ever to have thrown their hat into the ring. The two impressive men, hired as bouncers for the wedding of Death and Despair, are dressed sharply in 1940's vintage zoot suits. One bouncer is scowling and light-skinned whereas the other bouncer is dark-skinned and constantly smiling. Despite their achievements, these two World champions and professional boxers are working for minimum wage as part-time wedding bouncers.

The first bouncer is the somber Joe Louis in a cream-colored zoot suit with lime green wide lapels. The other is gregarious Jack Johnson dressed in a bright crimson zoot suit with purple accents. A grape fedora with a white feather sits atop his bald head, tilted to the side. They raise their mighty fists and yell, "Get in line! Get in line!!"

The rowdy pack of Americans swell around the bouncers and converge on Death and Despair, as they always do. Exasperated, the bouncers forcibly pick up each person and place them in a line because Americans never think the rules apply to them.

W.C. Fields, with his clip-on mustache and black top hat, pushes people aside and is the first to speak. "As I was lying in a hospital bed in Pasadena, I looked out the window to view kids below playing stick ball in the street. I took pity on them and said, **'Poor little urchins, no doubt ill-clad and improperly nourished. Something's got to be done'**. I coughed twice for the last time before looking out the window again. **'On second thought, screw 'em!'**"

Mark Twain giggles. "Not too shabby, ol' W.C., but I left the world a splendid cliff-hanger upon my deathbed. In my final moments,

I looked up at my daughter Clara and whispered, **'Good bye. If we meet . . .'"**

Elvis Aaron Presley butts in with a pained expression on his face and says in a Tennessee drawl, **"'I mah goin to da can'."**

Twain points over his shoulder. "The bathroom's right over there. You don't need our permission, son."

Presley shakes his karate hips even better than Mata Hari. "Nah, d'ose were mah faymous lass worrrds! I had to use da toilet." The Americans erupt in laughter at the potty humor, as they always do.

O. Henry is next and says in a solemn voice, **"'Turn up the lights. I don't want to go home in the dark'."**

Truman Capote, discretely checking out O. Henry from a distance, approaches with a lit European cigarette and says, "I died uttering what thousands of soldiers cry out, seeped in their own cold blood."

"And what's that?" asks O. Henry. "Don't leave us in suspense."

"Sweetheart, you're one to talk. What I said is, **'Mama— Mama—Mama'."**

"So much better, I wasn't as clever," rhymes Edgar Allan Poe. "They found me unconscious in a B'more gutter, at the age of 40 not even wearing my own sweater. I woke up in a hospital without a letter, and screamed out, **'Reynolds'.**"

Robert Frost diverges around the mob of Americas and sneaks up behind Death and Despair. **"'I feel as though I were in my last hours'."** He is joined arm-in-arm by Emily Dickinson who nods in agreement and whispers, **"'I must go in, for the fog is rising'."**

Aaron can't help but snicker at how *last hour* and *rising fog* most likely provided countless ammo for the fodder of undergrad Lit & Language term papers on the temporary mist of life evaporating with the rising sun in one's final hour.

Thomas Paine says, with utter common sense, "I was heckled by a priest on my deathbed. Monsignor asked if I believed Jesus is the Son of God to which I replied, **'I have no wish to believe on that subject'.**"

Herman Melville loudly interrupts, **"'God Bless Captain Vere!'"**

Everyone stares at Melville dressed in a drab overcoat and impressive black beard. Death and Despair look awkwardly at each other during the lull and Aaron imagines the author, essentially unknown at the time of his death, was most likely quoting himself in an unpublished manuscript with the title of something like *Billy and the*

Bud, a fine tale of a young seaman venturing out into the wet world to chase the elusive strain of marijuana called the White Widow. Melville's words also remind Aaron of Timothy McVeigh who, before he was given a lethal injection during his stay at a prison in western Indiana, quoted from the poem *Invictus*, "I am the master of my fate. I am the captain of my soul."

The same powerful lines recited by Q-dawgs in Omega Psi Phi frat houses residing predominately at Historically Black Universities and Colleges while getting branded, an odd rite of initiation given the history of treating slaves as property. And Aaron thinks of Frantz Fanon, Black n' proud until the end, who complained that the nurses were trying to turn him white by giving him blood transfusions for his leukemia, red blood from white donors, the same white imperial blood that spilt Black colonial blood for a thousand years, refusing to be white-washed by this white blood he managed a final protesting jest, **'They put me in the washing machine again last night'.** The same white nurses two years later and a thousand miles away in Mississippi who turned away Medgar Evers, assassinated in front of his daughter in their driveway, when he arrived at the door of a white hospital and told the attendant, **'Sit me up...turn me loose'**, for the ever proud Evers refused to die on his back.

Melville is standing in front of the bride and groom when Death tells him, "Sorry I came for you a little early. Should have let you finished that story about the sailor. What was his name again?"

Aarons answers, "Billy Budd, I think."

A sonorous, deep voice rings out. "Who callin my name?!"

Billie Holiday swoons up to the wedding dais and pushes Death aside to take center stage. The bouncers Jack and Joe converge, but a stern look from Billie freezes them in place.

Ms. Holiday, born Eleanora Fagan, addresses the crowd in a sensual voice. "I was only forty-fo years of age, layin myself down in East Harlem's Metro General cuz not even me, Lady Day, could die in a white hospital. Died with only seventy cents to my name and a body lay wasted by a thousand shots of jazz-fueled whiskey to drown my memory of chargin five bucks a lay when I was a mere thirteen, thirteen years old, I say! When booze wasn't enough, I tried smack, whack, uppers and downers. Enough drugs to issue one of those warrants and call in a raid on me at that white hospital, a raid from New York's Finest Blue to arrest this Lady Who Sings the Blues."

Bouncers Joe and Jack bow their heads in honor. Death and Despair have no choice but to let Billie Holliday finish her tale of woe.

"They handcuffed me to a metal bed post, like I was gonna make a run for it or maybe they was tryin to save me from slippin away, who knows? I sang out one last time to those coppers and nurses, cuffed like a criminal and dyin like a saint. I told em, **'Don't be in such a hurry'.**"

Glenn Miller takes Billie's hand and gently escorts her to the edge of the stage. He takes his turn in the center and blows out a few notes on his shiny brass trombone.

"We were flying to a gig somewhere over in France," Miller explains. "During the war, such an exciting time. As the plane plummeted into the English Channel, I asked the pilot, 'Where the hell are the parachutes?' and the pilot told me, 'What's the matter, Miller, you wanna live forever?' I looked at him through the smoky cockpit and said, **'Well, at least until I'm old would be nice'.**"

Sammy Davis, Jr. slides across the marble dais right in between Death and Despair. "**Don't cry for me. I'll be dancing in Heaven'.**" He grabs Billie's hand and slides off the edge as they twirl away together.

Glenn chases after them and cries out, "Hey, that's my girl!"

Aaron can barely hear Sammy's reply from the edge of the crowd, "Too bad, sucka!"

Unexpectedly, Frank Sinatra busts in and bellows out a serenade to the bride and groom, beginning with his final words, "**'I'm losing it'.**"

He sings while snapping his fingers, "Ooooh, baby, I'm losin' it, really losin' it, looooosin my mind over you. Oooh-ver youuuuuu."

Despair clutches his ears and begs Sinatra to leave.

When he refuses, the bouncer Joe Louis grabs ol' Blue eyes by the arm.

Frankie pleads with the Brown Bomber, "Hey Champ, go easy on me. Remember, I'm the one who got you a job as a door greeter at Caesar's Palace when Blacks weren't even allowed in!"

Joe holds out his hands helplessly. "Sorry pal, just doin' what I'm told."

Jack Johnson laughs. "Joe, you always were their dog. Layin down like a good dog. That's why I was the real champ and you were just a chump."

Joe turns around with that famous cold, dead look in his eyes. The two bouncers begin shadow-boxing each other, more playing around than engaged in fisticuffs. Ernest Hemingway, Jack London, F. Scott Fitzgerald and Hunter S. Thompson appear from the crowd and throw out wads of cash, placing bets on the fighters.

"I got ten bucks on the dark one," cries London.

Hemingway counters, "Fifteen on the lighter one."

F. Scott looks around and asks, "Would you tell one of those negroes to get me a gin and tonic? With a lime, please."

Hunter S. points at the two boxers with a long, ivory cigarette holder. "Aaaah, I see, another pair of dark-skinned men fighting for the entertainment of pale-skinned men. I love America!"

Death looks desperately at her husband. "What are we paying these bouncers for? They're supposed to keep order. Can't you do anything?"

Despair shrugs his shoulders. "Me? You expect *me* to stop them?"

Aaron steps up to the bride and groom and says, "I got this." He turns to the rowdy crowd gathered around the boxers and shouts, "OPEN BAR!"

Immediately, the fighters and betting men disperse as Aaron laughs. "See, that wasn't hard. Now, where were we?"

As the line reforms after the chaos, two stately dressed gentlemen wearing black bow-ties approach the wedding platform. One of the men is slightly balding and the other sports a wild, white-as-snow afro. Aaron is giddy with excitement to hear them argue.

W.E.B. Du Bois and Frederick Douglass stand apart and address the bride and groom.

Du Bois speaks first. "**As you live, believe in life. The only possible death'**," to which Death turns to her husband and mouths the words *Who, me?* before Du Bois continues, "'**is to lose belief in this simple truth because the great end comes slowly, because time is long'.**"

Despair frowns at his wife and whispers to Aaron, "Time is long when you're married to her!"

Aaron suppresses a small chuckle and waits for Frederick Douglass to speak. The noble man, a fighter each day of his 77 years, holds the crowd's attention without saying a word.

Suddenly, the Lion of Anacostia clenches his fists and yells, "'**Agitate! Agitate! Agitate!'**"

Frederick completely ignores Ottilie Assing(†), his intellectual consort, as she waves to him from the lawn holding a bottle of potassium cyanide. Down the line of greeters, voices rise up in chorus:

"Preach!!"

"Say it!"

"Aww Lawd!"

"That's a hard act to follow," comments Cecil B. De Mille, director of *The Birth of a Nation*. "And maybe I was wrong to make that film about the Klansmen."

Douglass and Du Bois surround him. "Ya think?" they say in union.

"Maybe. Maybe not. A real commercial success. White America never fails to applaud when they hang a Black man for sleepin with a white woman. Yet, at the end, did I not ask rhetorically, **'How much evil have I spread?'**"

"On that," Douglass and Du Bois say while shaking hands, "we can both agree."

"Step ah-siiide, gentle-men!"

A space clears around Malcolm X as Douglass and Du Bois hoist him up onto their shoulders.

Malcolm Little, also known as el-Hajj Malik el-Shabazz and a pimp named Red, clears his throat. "I knew, I said *I knew* they were comin for ME, yes, I knew it! They wanted ME dead. The chickens had come home to roost. I looked those men, those assassins!, straight in their eyes as they rushed ME with loaded shotguns. And I told em, **'Let's be cool, brothers'.**"

After Malcolm is lowered to the ground, Martin Luther King, Jr. strolls up with a glass of Tennessee Tea and places an arm around Malcolm's shoulders. "I must saaay, my fellow brotha, for a man bred of sooo much vi-o-lence, your final moments were certainly -- certainly an act of peace!"

"Well, what about YOU Martin? What were YOU thinking about?"

MLK sighs, "I was thinkin bout music, sweeeet music, standin on that balcony in Memphis. You see, I had just turned to my good friend Ben and said, **'Ben, play *Precious Lord, Take My Hand*. Play it real purdy for me'.** Well, I guess the good Lord was listenin that day, takin my hand right then and there."

The crowd is deeply moved by Martin's words and when JFK shyly creeps forward, no one seems to notice. He stands awkwardly for a bit trying to get people's attention until Jackie Kennedy grabs his hand and does a cute little cough.

A few people turn. "Look, it's thaaaat guy. Didn't he get shot?"

Jackie O. approaches Death and says, "I told him not to go to Dallas. But when we got there, everyone was so lovely. I told Jack, 'You can't say Dallas doesn't love you.'"

Ol' Jack looks over at his wife, "**'That's very obvious'** is what I said, right before the shot echoed through generations."

With a black gloved right hand, Jackie O. dabs a black silk handkerchief across her left eye. "And many years later, I gathered my children around me and told them, **'Don't cry for me. I'm going to be with your father now'.**"

The Presidential Couple bow their heads and move down the line. Suddenly cutting in line is Harvey Lee Oswald who refused to wear a bullet proof vest because, "**'There ain't nobody gonna shoot me!'**"

Death smiles. "We'll see about that."

The bouncers, Joe and Jack, having returned from the bar with more champagne and bourbon for the bride and groom, usher Oswald away.

A twelve-piece string orchestra with violins, violas, two cellos and a double bass begins to softly play *Precious Lord, Take My Hand* before switching over to a pop rendition of Phile's *The President's March*.

A somber league of older white men in powdered wigs approach, waiting their turn. To no one's surprise, a statuesque George Washington emerges first to face Death and Despair.

"Such a momentous fear did I possess of being buried alive," the general proclaims, "that the good Doctor promised to leave my corpse outside the vault for an entire three days. Only after his promise was secured did I venture forth with a hearty **'Tis Well'.**"

Or, Aaron ponders, perhaps ol' Cincinnatus hoped he might rise again after the third day.

The crowd formally applauds the 6'2" god-among-men, and then is interrupted by the pervert-among-men Mr. Grumpy Benjamin Franklin who pinches Death's tight fanny and whispers in her ear, "**'A dying man can do nothing easy'.**"

The First American then winks and says, "Doth thou knows't what I mean?! If he does nothing easy, then he does it hard. And if a dead man is anything, he's certainly hard."

Death is appalled but not for long because if Death is anything, she's always certain.

With a noose around his neck, a twenty-one year old Nathan Hale cries out dramatically, "**I only regret that I have but one life to lose for my country'**," which as everyone in the crowd knows is a line from the stage play *Cato* performed for Washington at Valley Forge during that cold winter in 1777, enflaming the new American Revolutionary spirit, leading many to resist British tyranny like Patrick Henry who also borrowed from the Roman Cato to say, **'Give me liberty or give me death'.** Same as when old man Nathaniel Hawthorne a few decades later said, **'What a boon it would be, if when life draws to a close, one could pass away without a struggle,'** fermenting the notion that perhaps only the young wish to die fighting while old men pray for an easy death.

An oddly appareled interloper paces among the Founding Fathers. In a racoon-skin cap, flip-flops and a tourist t-shirt that reads *I ♥ Alamo*, Davy Crockett marches forward.

"Surrounded by Santa Ana's troops, I killed sixteen men."

Jack Johnson pokes Aaron in the ribs and says, "Sixteen? Ha! My boy Benny, a cook down at the Alamo, says Davy surrendered. Like a chump."

The King of the Wild Frontier ignores the bouncer. "And I yelled out, **'I'm warning you boys, I'm a screamer!'**"

Death chuckles, "In bed."

Despair adds, "With chickens."

Two more Americans stand silently in front of the bride and groom. The men's calm demeanor is unsettling. The herd of other Americans back away from them and for the first time, quiet themselves to hear the two majestic men dressed in deer buckskins and feathered war bonnets.

Crazy Horse, called Tȟašúŋke Witkó in Lakota Sioux which means His-Horse-is-Crazy, finally speaks with tight lips. "I surrendered after years of fighting against the white man. Threw me in prison. They said I was reaching for a knife while Little Big Man grabbed my arms as some white boy stabbed me in the back. I cried out, **'Cousin you killed me! You are with the white people'.**"

Chief Poundmaker of the Plains Cree nation, known as Pîhtokahanapiwiyin, waits patiently until Crazy Horse is finished. The Chief of the Cree then utters clearly, "**"It would be so much easier to fold our hands and say 'I, one man, can do nothing'. We all know the story about the man who sat beside the trail too long, and then it grew over and he could not find his way again. We cannot go back nor can we just sit beside the trail'.**"

Crazy Horse stands proudly. "I killed the white man."

Poundmaker adds, "And I tried to make the peace."

Crazy Horse acknowledges Poundmaker. "Sadly, both our ways failed."

Poundmaker finishes with a bowed head. "Even though we were different in life, we are the same in death."

Angrily, Andrew Jackson pushes aside the two original, indigenous Americans. "Get outta the way, red skins! It's my turn. My famous last words were, **'I have only two regrets—that I have not shot Henry Clay or hanged John C. Calhoun'.**"

Harriet Tubman cries out, "Infamous words, you mean!"

Ol' Moses-who-never-lost-a-passenger busts through the crowd and throws at Jackson's feet a crumpled up twenty-dollar bill. In her other hand, she holds a crisp, new bill with her face on it instead of Jackson's visage. Tubman sings in a menacing tone,

"Swiiing looow, sweeeet chaaa-reeeot. Surprise, muĬhafŭcka!"[49]

John Brown, wearing a noose around his neck, gives Harriet a high-five. "Nice seeing you again, sista."

JB addresses the newly-married couple in a raspy voice. "After my raid on Harpers Ferry two years before the Civil War, I declared, **'I'm quite certain that the crimes of this guilty land will never be purged away but with blood.'** And yet my freed companion, John Anthony Copeland, expressed his sentiment even better than I by saying, **'If I am dying for freedom, I could not die for a better cause—I had rather die than live be a slave'.**"

"Woooord up!" says a familiar voice. The crowd parts upon the entrance of the long-legged Abraham Lincoln who strides confidently into the center. From his back pocket dangles a love-sick poem titled 'The Suicide's Soliloquoy' with melancholy intent, *This heart I'll rush a dagger through.*

"I tried," says ol' Abe, "to hold my wife's hand inside Ford's Theater, and of course my Sweet Mary protested, expressing that our neighbor Miss Harris would object to our public display of affection. I coyly responded, **'She won't think anything of it'**, before hearing the report of a pistol shot from behind me."

Mary Todd Lincoln gracefully floats up to him in a long Victorian ball gown darker than Death's and takes his hand. Mary leads him away, head nestled upon his arm. The crowd respectfully watches in silence as the noble couple wanders off to their assigned table where they sit by themselves.

Patient and quiet at the end of the American line is Thomas Jefferson. "Through the third night in July, best was my effort to persist despite illness, for upon the morn I asked, **'This is the Fourth? Ah, just as I wished'.**"

Aaron knows from grade school that ol' TJ stayed up all night coughing up blood to witness his country's 50th anniversary, and without doubt America was *his* country, his own country crafted by a life of service, uttering in respect at the end as well, 'I resign my spirit to God, and my daughter to my country,' his most beloved little girl, sweet Martha known as Patsy, the daughter for whom Thomas brought along Sally Hemmings when they dwelled in Paris and afterwards Thomas had to bend his democratic wicked knee to his young mistress, begging young Sally to return to America with him because Sally and her brother were free in France. But why did she go back with TJ, only to be enslaved once again? For love perhaps, the Romantics liked to believe, or maybe his promise to release their children from bondage upon his death, a promise which he held himself to, the only FIVE of one hundred and thirty-seven slaves to be freed. Unable to free the slaves himself because of tricky Southern manumission laws, he left the task to Patsy. After his death, she honored him like a good daughter and made her papa proud, the only approval a daughter ever craves from her father. And so, on the same day, the 50th anniversary of America, John Adams also passed away, his final breath loaded with ironic relief, **'At least Jefferson still lives.'**

Following the mass of unruly Americans are the proper Europeans, patiently waiting their turn. A slight woman is the first to emerge surrounded by four wild-haired men dressed in Victorian suede vests and cotton breeches.

George Sand smiles at Death and ignores Despair. Chopin, Liszt, Balzac, and Flaubert gather around merrily clapping in unison as she stands proudly before Death and Despair. The crowd of well-wishers is eager for her insightful words. Even Shakespeare leans in. She pauses dramatically and then enunciates with precision, "**Leave the greenery**'."

The crowd goes berserk! Aaron is not sure of her meaning and asks for an explanation.

Flaubert speaks first. "Our dear friend, Amantine Aurore Lucie Dupin, known to you as George, wished to have her burial plot remain unblemished and natural sans tombstone."

Balzac interrupts, "She wanted only shrubbery above her grave, nothing else. And you're wrong, my dear fellow, her meaning is encapsulated in my final words of, "**There is only one happiness in life, to love and be loved**'."

Liszt begins by saying, "What a brave man *she* was."

Her lover Frédérick Chopin concludes with, "And what a good woman *he* was."

And the crowd goes wild again!

William Shakespeare, with a hip-thrust and a spear-shake, causes a commotion at the front of the line. He asks for Death's hand and she offers it to him. He turns her hand over, proudly takes out a long quill and writes on Death's palm,

> *Good friend, for Jesus' sake forbear,*
> *To dig the dust enclosed here.*
> *Blest be the man that spares these stones.*
> *And curst be he that moves my bones.*

Death closes her own hand and the words disappear.

Next in the wedding receiving line, much to Aaron's delight, is Cosima Wagner.

"**Glorious Sorrow**'," she announces as Despair nods in agreement. For forty-seven years, she lived without the great composer and even greater anti-Semite, Rikard Wagner, who put the fat lady on stage and the *Vaag-near* in Wagnerian, the master of Bayreuth, who died right after exclaiming, **'My watch!'** as Cosima helped him to the sofa after a coughing spasm and his watch fell out of his pocket. Which are the same two words uttered by Toussaint L'Ouverture while imprisoned in a dungeon in the French Alps after surrendering to Napoleon upon leading Haiti's slave revolt, the only successful slave revolution in history. **'My watch!'** Toussaint cried out from his frozen cell, confirming for Aaron people's fascination with their watches, eternally suspicious of time.

Next is Oscar Wilde, who ran out of time in a small Paris hotel room at the age of 46.

"**It's the wallpaper or me—one of us has to go'.**" But when he kisses Despair's hand in a flirtatious gesture, he clarifies what he really said. "'**I am dying as I have lived, beyond my means'.**"

Suddenly, Spain's greatest author Miquel de Cervantes rides through the crowd on the back of a fat-bellied man under the delusion that he's riding a horse. He smacks the man a few times on the rump with a riding crop and announces, "**Already my foot is in the stirrup'.**"

Spain's greatest poet Lope de Vega pushes Cervantes off his make-believe mount and charges forward with a slew of young mistresses trailing behind, cooing themselves with ornate fans. From his velvet-lined waist coat pocket, he produces a long scroll of poetry scribed in elaborate calligraphy. "This I composed for the lovely bride on her wedding day," he says winking at Death. "When the flames of his passion smolder—remember,

Pues tales los hombres son:
Cuando nos han menester,
somos su vida,
su ser,
su alma,
su corazón!"[50]

Suddenly, Lopa de Vega stops reading, drops the scroll to the ground and admits, "**All right, then. I'll say it, Dante makes me sick'.**"

Oscar Wilde feigns an expression of shock. "My heavens, I hate to agree but you do have a marvelous point."

Aaron looks down the line for Dante to make sure his feelings aren't burnt but Death laughs and says, "Oh, he'll be around later for the dancing. Dante loves the Polka, because everyone knows Hell is filled with Polka music!"

Van Gogh(†) approaches next, the self-mutilating artist who died a miserable two days after failing to perish from a pistol shot to the heart while painting in a wheat field outside of Auvers-sur-Oise at 37, mainly because he didn't bring a second bullet and was terribly embarrassed walking back through town with a hole in his chest.

"**La tristesse durera toujours'**," Vincent says directly to Despair.

Aaron asks for a translation because of all the languages, he is certain Death and Despair both speak French.

Despair says, "There is no end to sorrow."

"No, that's not quite right." Death counters, "The sadness will last forever."

A smiling Raphael, also at the age of 37, leans over Van Gogh's shoulder to say, "**Happy'.**" They continue to argue, one morose and the other elated, with Van Gogh cupping his ear and repeating, "What?" as the line moves on.

The war hero Pancho Villa approaches and points to nine bullet holes in his chest. "**Don't let it end like this. Tell them I said something'.**"

Aaron gives him a high-five. "Something!" and waves him on.

Frederick Turner Jackson appears with a Harvard degree and a large manuscript tucked under his arm. "I was busy writing when Death approached," he says winking at the bride. "And before you took me away, I said, '**I am sorry that I haven't finished my book'.**"

Aaron asks, "Well, is it done now?"

Frederick sighs with slouched shoulders, pointing to the book under his arm. "Not yet."

Aaron slaps him on the back. "I totally understand."

Hunter S. Thompson(†), coming back from the bar with a lowball glass of Chivas and a white-powered nose, elbows Turner in the back. "Outta the way, old fart."

Hunter sways on unsteady legs, completely wasted, an un-lit cigarette dangling from his mouth. He slurs, "I typed a note, *Football Season is Over*. Nothing else to look forward to, you understand? Couldn't write, couldn't think straight, and no football? Got my wife on the phone, told her, '**...this won't hurt'** and pulled the trigger. She hung up on me, I ain't jokin! Why? Cuz she thought the gun sounded like the clack of my typewriter."

Aaron leans forward, their foreheads touching. "Well, did it? Did it hurt?"

"Not any more than life did." Hunter leans back and shouts towards the bar, "Francis Scott! Jack! Papa!! You drunk bastards, set me up another shot!"

As Hunter staggers away, two young punks approach. The first one, a smooth-talkin white boy, hits up Hunter for a cigarette. When Hunter tells him to get lost, River Phoenix looks like he's about to cry. **"I'm gonna die, dude'."**

The other one is wearing a blue bandana tied in the front on his forehead and holding a 40 oz. glass bottle of Colt .45 malt liquor. Aaron instantly recognizes the 25-year-old Tupac Shakur and is tempted to beg him for an autograph.

Tupac slides up and pimps Death by placing a big, wet kiss on her luscious lips because as Aaron knows, Tupac Amaru never once feared death. He only hoped that when he died, he wouldn't come back reincarnated because there could never be 2Pacs. Holding Death in his arms, he gives Aaron the up n' down look of mad respect and chimes out in that ghetto-angel voice, **"I'm dyin. I'm dyin'**," while pointing to a hole in his chest.

Tupac lets go of Death and she ashamedly looks at her husband-to-be. She exclaims, "Whaaat? He's Tupac! What am I gonna do, NOT kiss him?"

Tupac juts his chin at Despair. "Yo D, if you can't find somethin ta live for, best find somethin ta die for."

Patrick Henry calls out from his table, "You right, son! Come sit by us."

Tupac pimp-limps across the brick patio and takes a seat at the table of Founding Fathers.

Next in the slowly decreasing reception line is Gertrude Stein.

"What is the answer?" she asks. When no one, not even Despair is able to come up with a witty retort, Stein speaks again. **"In that case, what is the question?"**

Alice B. Toklas approaches from behind to take Gertrude's arm before saying, **"Yes'."**

Aaron is a little bewildered by her short reply and Alice is kind enough to explain. "You see, I died twenty years after my Gerty, offering plenty of time to think about what I should have said to her. A simple *Yes* would have sufficed."

"Yes?" Aaron asks. "That's it?"

"Yes is what I wanted to say to you," Alice turns and stares directly into Gertrude's eyes. "Yes, whatever you want me to do for you, my tender buttons. Anything for the love of my life on your deathbed. Anything to put you at ease, to give you rest, to assure you in your final moments that I love you deeply, beyond words. Yes, my dear, that is the answer to any question and all your requests. Yes."

They shed private tears and slowly walked away together, arms intertwined.

The tender scene influences a bubbly Christina Rossetti, who is jumping up and down in line, impatiently waiting her turn. "**I love everybody!**"

"Even us?" say two men in crisp Nazi uniforms from behind her. Christina frowns and moves on, her dark mood pursing even in the afterlife. The first man is Erwin Rommel(†), the Desert Fox. Holding an empty cyanide canister, he whispers to his son, "**The poison takes but three seconds and none of the usual steps will be taken against my family, that is, against you**'."

"The things we do for our children," Aaron says while standing between Death and Despair. The fear of losing Zoë has haunted him since the moment of her birth, resolving to live exactly four minutes were she to die tragically. Four minutes, the amount of time a brain can survive without a heart pumping oxygenated blood. He wouldn't even resort to self-harm because his heart would simply stop beating without her.

The other uniformed man is ol' Adolf who died in April, the suicide month, who stands alone humming the Mel Brooks tune *Springtime For Hitler in Germany*. Since tyrants always need a scapegoat, Mein Herr swallowed poison and blamed, "**the universal poisoners of all people—International Jewry**'."

Pushing Adolf out of the way with a hard shove is John Reed, founder of the American Communist Labor Party, who declares, "**You know how it is when you go to Venice. You ask people, 'Is this Venice?' just for the pleasure of hearing the reply**'."

All the Italians in line raise their glasses of red Veneto wine in agreement and laugh in that boisterous Latin manner.

Several Japanese men, an iconic Chinese man in a green army outfit and a few bearded European gentlemen stand rigidly in line, waiting their turn to greet Death and Despair.

The first is Yukio Mishima(†), who approaches Death slowly and bows deeply.

"Sitting in my hotel room," Mishima explain, "I finally made up my mind to commit *seppuku* and prepared the tanto blade with paper wrapped around the handle to catch my blood. I didn't want to make a mess. Then I stormed out onto the balcony and shouted to the gathering crowd below, 'Long live His Imperial Majesty'".

Aaron nods respectfully, wanting to utter noble and heroic words to the Japanese writer, but can only muster a simple, "Very patriotic of you."

Mishima then turns to Despair, "Eh, I walked back into my room, pointed at the crowd and told my friend, **'I don't think they even heard me'**."

Aaron smothers a sad chuckle as Mishima bows again and leaves quietly.

Hokusai is next and Aaron blurts out, "Hey, you're the guy who painted the big wave…"

"Great Wave."

"Yep, that's the one. The only Asian painting I studied in Art History 101."

"Sadly, because European art pales in comparison to ours. **'And if Heaven had only granted me five more years, I could have become a real painter!'**"

When out of nowhere, Pierre-Auguste Renoir pops up his head and grumbles, "*Oui*, I understand. I died an old man with brushes strapped to my arthritic hands and said, **'I am still progressing'**."

Hokusai hands his cup of saki to Renoir who in return offers his glass of white wine, and neither liking the taste of the other's drink, trade back and together stare at the lilies floating in the fountain.

Another Japanese man, Kusakabe, recites a Chinese poem, **"'It is better to be a crystal and be broken, than to remain perfect like a tile upon a housetop'**."

"That sounds familiar," declares a famous Chinese fellow in a star-emblemed cap. Mao Zedong pushes the masses aside as he addresses Death. "My dear, you look lovely, for a capitalist oppressor and mistress of the Imperialist regime."

Death sighs, she's heard this sentiment before. And glancing down the line, she spies Lenin and Marx, and knows she's in for a long afternoon.

Mao continues, "I was asked by a journalist in my final hours if I thought the report was true that the Chinese people despised Communism. And I told that pawn of the oppressor, **'Really? No one? I don't believe it'**."

Fidel Castro hobbles past Mao and Zhou on a wooden cane and declares in a powerful voice, "**I'm thinking of cutting my beard!**"

Standing next to him is Karl Marx. "Heaven forbid it! Without your beard, how will they know you're a Communist?"

Castro points at Marx, "How can they NOT recognize me? They might condemn me, but history will absolve me!"

Karl shrugs and sighs, "Good luck, comrade."

Curious, Aaron jumps off the dais and grabs Karl Marx by the coat. "But what did you say before dying?"

"What do you think I said?" Marx asks rhetorically. "I told them to **'Go on, get out! Last words are for fools who haven't said enough.'**"

Aaron retreats and accidentally steps on the shiny, black leather shoe of a short, balding man. V.I. Lenin says, "And do you want to know what I said?"

"Well, if you insist."

Lenin stands proudly and places an arm behind his back. Marx, Castro, Mao and Zhou lean forward intently to hear the little man's words. Vladimir twirls his mustache and announces, "**Good dog'.**"

"What, that's it?" Castro says grumpily.

Mao is not impressed. "Russians. Pathetic example of the true Communist state."

Karl clutches his own stomach and doubles over in deep laughter. "Don't you get it? 'Good dog' was the punch line for a joke about Trotsky's mom because yo momma jokes are the best way to go out."

Castro cries out, "Yo momma is such a communist…"

"She gives it away for free!"

Marxist laughter fills the air as the Communists move on.

There is a lull in the receiving line as Death and Despair make idle chat, and like most newly married couples, try to imagine what they'll say to each other for the next fifty years. Finally, a soggy woman with long, stringy grey hair approaches in a drenched overcoat.

Virginia Woolf(†) is silent before Death and Despair for several moments. She looks around uncomfortably while fumbling with the rocks in her pocket.

She utters quietly, "I drowned myself in the Ouse River as I reached 60 years. Left a note on the mantel for my husband. **'Dearest, I feel certain I am going mad again…You see I can't even write** this properly. I can't read. I owe all the happiness in my life to you'."

Suddenly, Woolf yells, "I'll be right in!" She breaks from the crowd and jumps into the fountain where Renoir and Hokusai are bathing, the two men having fallen in after close inspection of the floating lilies. They play together like mermaids in the cool water until the bouncers Joe and Jack call for towels and assist the three swimmers out of the fountain.

After the commotion fades, a few bespectacled and scholarly men approach. The first is wearing the ubiquitous Irish leather vest.

Death sighs, "Uh oh, the writers. I should have known they'd be following Virginia."

Despair smiles, "Hey, I know these guys! They're good friends of mine."

James Joyce is first and holds up a glass pint half filled with absinthe. "I died because I got lost and couldn't find a pub."

"Lost in Dublin?" Aaron asks. "Impossible, because there's a pub on every corner."

"An inside joke," Joyce explains. "Like when I died of a whiskey-ulcer and was referring to *Finnegan's Wake* when I said, **'Does nobody understand?'**"

Aaron responds, "No, we really didn't. Not even a little bit. Riverrun, my ass."

Vladimir Nabokov clasps Joyce around the shoulder. **"'A certain butterfly is already on the wing'."**

Joyce nods, "Nicely said, brother."

William Saroyan joins them by encircling his arms around Nabokov. **"'Everybody has to die, but I have always believed an exception would be made in my case. Now what?'"**

Death points a long finger at the fine mustachioed gentleman and smiles. "You'll see."

Franz Kafka follows and drapes his lanky arm around Saroyan. "I died of consumption."

A voice interrupts from the crowd, "Consumption?"

Kafka sighs, "Ask Keats about it."

"Tuberculosis!" the writers cry out in unison.

Kafka continues. "I begged my friend to burn all my papers and said, **'So there will be no proof that I was ever a writer'.**"

Aldous Huxley leans on Kafka and says, "Poor Franz, you should have gone out like I did. See here, old chap, I had The Cancer and decided to go out trippin balls."

Kafka asks, "Tripping?"

"Balls?" inquires Nabokov.

Huxley nods. "I took two injections, not one but two doses, of LSD before passing through life's hallucinatory veil because like Cheech & Chong taught me—you never get off on one!"

Robert E. Howard(†) sturdily embraces Huxley's arm. Several of the writers ask him, "Bob, what are you doing here?"

Howard looks down at the ground and mumbles in a Texas accent, "Well, ah created Conan. Duh Barbarian."

The distinguished writers cast doubt. "An amateur writer of Cimmerian pulp? Maybe you should wait at the back of the line."

Howard sighs, "Ah shot myself in da temple whens I was only thirty. Found out momma wasn't gonna wake from her coma and ah said, **'All fled—all done, so lift me on the funeral pyre. The feast is over and the lamps expire'.**"

The writers pause. "Not bad, Bobby. Not bad at all." They encircle him with pride.

Stephen Townley Crane, also thin from the effects of TB, announces, "When I was near the end, I told those around me, **'When you come to the hedge that we must all go over, it isn't so bad, and you don't care. Just a little dreamy anxiety, which world you're really in, that's all'.**"

Hart Crane(†), clinging drunkenly to the other Crane, says, "We're not related. He wrote *Red Badge*, but my courage came while cruising for gay men under the Brooklyn Bridge. While aboard the steamer *Orizaba*, I made a pass at a sailor and got punched in the face. And since no one understood my homoerotic poetry, including the jealous T.S. Eliot, I jumped off that ship at the age of 32, cried out, **'Good-bye, good-bye everyone!'**"

Aaron ponders what would motivate a man to take the time to say goodbye before jumping. Perhaps because suicide is a public act, even when done privately because the body is often discovered. Even drowning in the great ocean leaves a corpse upon the beach.

William Burroughs, jotted in his diary the day he died of a heart attack at the age of 83, **"Love? What is it? Most natural painkiller. What there is—LOVE'.**"

"How romantic," Death says, eyelashes fluttering.

Despair sighs. "Love is only a pain killer if infatuation is the pain."

Aaron slugs him playfully on the shoulder, "Why always so glum, my man? Today's your wedding day."

"Guess what weddings and funerals have in common?" riddles Despair.

"What?"

"The death of freedom."

Death laughs and turns to Aaron, "Don't mind him. He's always like that."

Goethe is the last to join the line of writers who stand together, literally brothers-in-arms.

Death leans over to Despair, "Goethe, he's my favorite."

Despair glares jealously at the handsome German. "Of course, he is."

Johann, who died in a darkened room, looks to the sky and yells out, "**Open the shutters so that more light can come in. More light!**"

Reluctantly, the long Joycean-Nabokovian-Saroyan-Kafkian-Huxleyan-Howardian-Goethean line of novelists slowly disperses. Aaron notices they gather together at one table, ordering whiskey and borrowing numerous chairs from nearby tables. They steal several other vases and remove black magic markers from their pockets to draw over the inscription. They cross out the original *Marriage—the death of despair*, the message too cheery for temperamental authors. Since the end of sadness implies happiness, the writers are compelled to compose wittier verses:

Marriage—the breath of prayer ; or,

Marriage—the deaRth of this pair; or,

Cribbage—the math of dós peers; or,

Remarriage—the mess of an affair.

Tentatively, staunch bearded men approach Death and Despair. They stand disjointed and solitary, but gain confidence as their numbers swell, each encouraging the other.

Immanuel Kant adjusts the powdered wig atop his head and announces, "**It is enough'.**"

Death doesn't understand. "What's enough?"

Kant strains for an answer. "It, the indescribable it. The thing-in-itself or the world-as-it-is. It's enough. Get it? Got it? Good."

"Oh, no," Aaron frowns, "the philosophers are here."

Death reaches for Despair's hand and breathes out sharply, "We can do this, honey."

Despair worries because, after all, she's Death. Everyone is afraid of her. Death's not afraid of anyone, he thinks. Until now.

Søren Kierkegaard, shoulders sunken, dejectedly mutters, "I have no advice, for either of you, since I remained unmarried when I died at the age of 42."

Despair sighs. "Lucky you."

"When they asked me whether my life had turned out the way I expected, I told them, **'Yes, that is why I am very happy and very sad that I cannot share this happiness with anyone'**."

Death lets out an excited chirp. "Are you saying marriage solves the dilemma of one's existential crisis?"

Søren shrugs. "Perhaps I should've gone through with the engagement to Regine Olsen. But instead I got scared and broke it off. Told her, 'I'm too sad most days, I'll only bring you down. It's me, baby, not you. Please believe me, my lil' Danish muffin, I'm no good for you'."

Aaron covers his mouth and whispers aside to Despair, "Wow, thought the ol' Fork would have better advice."

David Hume pushes people aside with his big belly. "In my dying hand, I wrote a letter to my good friend Adam Smith and told him, **'I am dying as fast as my enemies could wish and as easily as my friends could desire'**."

G.W.F. Hegel thrusts his arm forward. "Move over, fat boy. When I died, I said, **'Only one man ever understood me. And he didn't understand me'**."

Heinrich Heine laughs, "Everyone one of us could've said that. I was bedridden for the last eight years of my life and yelled out at the end, **'Write—Write! Paper—Pencil!'**"

Carl Jung, holding a crystal wine glass, says to the bride and groom, "At the end of a long life, I understood what's important."

"And that is?" Aaron asks.

"I had just turned to my friends and said, **'Let's have a really good red wine tonight'**."

"Cin-cin!" the Italians cry out with raised glasses from their table, never ones to miss out on a toast.

"Well," Sigmund Freud says, "not sure I can top that because I died of jaw cancer."

Death smirks at him. "Guess a cigar was more than just a cigar."

Freud laughs, "You got me there. And I begged for morphine in my final hours and said, **'Now it's nothing but torture and makes no sense anymore'.**"

"Hey Siggie," Despair says, "the same could be said of your book *Ego and the Id*."

"Touché."

Three white-wily-haired men, squinting near-sighted from calculating figures and yet divinely far-sighted, emerge from the line. They stand awkwardly until motioned forward by the bouncers Joe and Jack.

Sir Isaac Newton announces, "At 84, I was unsatisfied with the answers I'd discovered. I said, **'I have been only like a boy playing on the seashore and diverting myself now and then in finding a smoother pebble or a prettier shell than the ordinary, whilst the great ocean of truth lay all undiscovered before me'.**"

Next is Galilei Galileo. "At 77, I defied the courts until the ends, saying, **'Yet it moves'.**"

Isaac nods, "You were referring to the Earth?"

Galileo shakes his head. "Given my age, I was rejoicing about my bowels. It moves!"

Albert Einstein shuffles in, looking lost. "Hey Isaac, or should I zay Itzak. Didn't zhey call you Big Nose? Son of Isaac and Hannah, had a lil Jewish in you, eh?"

Newton shrugs, "So what? The real question is why time and space are so different. Aren't they interchangeable?"

Einstein scratches his head, "And after ze Big Bang, vhere did all ze antimatter go?"

"Doesn't matter," Sir Isaac says, smiling at their private joke. "What did you say at the end?"

Albert shrugs, "I can't remember. At 76, I revealed ze secrets of ze Universe in simple terms and how mankind might achieve sub-atomic light speed by converting matter into energy and back to matter again by laterally traversing through trans-dimensional portals spontaneously created when solar quasar pulses interact with captured neutrino bursts."

"But?" Isaac asks.

"I muttered my revelation in German and sadly, my nurse vas an American. And Americans barely speak English."

The three scientists quickly find a table and borrowing a pen from the writers, scratch out long mathematical equations on the white tablecloth.

Aaron motions over a waiter with a tray of bruschetta and chopped olive tapenade for the bride and groom. Death, looking a little pale, is starving and devours several appetizers as the next guests arrive. Despair orders another bourbon on the rocks.

Over the next two hours, the line progresses as Aaron tries to stay awake by stamping his feet to keep the blood flowing. Despair is halfway through a bottle of Jack Daniels. Death's smile is locked upon her face and yet she remains hauntingly beautiful, greeting guests with graceful ease.

Aaron notices a trend in the final words of the well-wishers. He figures the three most common expressions announced by the nearly dead and the quickly dying are,

"Into thy hands, oh Lord, I commend my spirt;" or,

"Tell my wife I love her;" or,

"Water."

Aaron knows these sentiments are equally ineffective to alleviate the fear of dying, until he hears one man by the name of Mark Hanna, a senator from Ohio, who says, "When they asked me if I wanted a handkerchief to wipe my sweaty brow, I told them, **'Yes, I would like one, but my wife takes them all'**."

Maybe laughter, Aaron thinks, is the only pain reliever.

The line dissipates down to none, the well-wishers having moved past the bride and groom to their respective seats at the numerous circular dining tables. The last remaining man is the bouncer Joe Louis, alone because the other bouncer, Jack Johnson, is leaning against the bar chatting up Fitzgerald's flirtatious wife Zelda. The same Jack Johnson who most likely said as his final words, 'Look out for that tree' after storming out of a Jim Crow's Southern Fried Chicken Diner because he'd been refused service by a racist restaurant owner for being himself, always too Black, too strong, too big, too proud, and most dangerous of all, gettin down with too many white women.

Joe Louis turns to Death and Despair, **"I'm ready'.**"

Aaron steps off the marble dais and watches as Death and Despair make their way to the head table, an elaborately decorated rectangular table covered by a white silk tablecloth, burnished silver candelabras, and dozens of black roses in white vases. But instead of taking a seat, they amble hand-in-hand past the table to a portable, wooden mini-crib that Aaron has failed to notice.

Death and Despair, oblivious to their guests, peer into the crib and smile with loving affection. The parents make ridiculous cooing sounds and occasionally smile at each other, whispering in each other's ear.

Aaron, curious to see the progeny of Death and Despair, peeks into the crib.

"What *is* that?" Aaron asks horrified.

Death smiles. "She was born like this."

Despair adds, "And we're so proud."

Aaron forces himself to look again. The horribly grotesque form of a baby's corpse lays rotting in the bottom of the crib. The head is elongated and misshapen, the eyes missing, the hands curled into deformed claws, the skin blackened with veiny cobwebs, and the mouth agape in utter agony.

Aaron looks back to the doting parents, mystified by their attention. His shock turns to anger. "How can you love such a creature? Why are you keeping it?!"

Death smiles, "We'll love her forever."

Despair adds, "And she's not dead."

Aaron jumps in surprise as the baby turns on its side and whimpers a pathetic cry. "It's still alive?" he asks incredulously.

"Of course," Death says calmly. "She's our baby. What choice did we have?"

"You could have smothered her," Aaron says. "With a pillow."

"Why would we do that?" Despair asks.

"Because it would have been merciful! You could have let her slip away in the bathtub. Or left her outside for the wolves. You could have, no, you *should* have smothered her! Anything but this wretched life. Why did you keep her?"

Death smiles, "Of course we kept her."

Despair adds, "Because life is sacred."

. . . and Aaron awoke from his long coma as the meds wore off. He wasn't sure how many hours had passed but he was exhausted and had pissed himself several times. Puke oozed from the side of his mouth and he thought how fortunate he'd been to fall asleep on his stomach.

The image of the horribly deformed infant lingered eerily in his memory. From beneath the table, Aaron stretched his muscles and was grateful to be alive, grateful for his limbs, grateful for his eyes. More than anything else, he was grateful his precious Zoë had not been born deformed, misshapen, impaired. "What would I have done?" he asked aloud, and then repeated, "What would I have done?"

Aaron slowly recovered from his semi-lucid, drug-induced dream reeking of sweat, urine and bile. A shower might help, Aaron thought. He wanted to crawl out from under the table, but bathing seemed such an arduous endeavor. He'd have to find a washcloth and use soap on his armpits, his feet, his crotch, and next use shampoo and conditioner, but then his long hair would be wet. The commitment seemed daunting. He flopped back onto the floor.

From his vantage point beneath the table, he glanced at the microwave clock and noticed many hours had passed. Tomorrow was now today.

Aaron panicked. A thousand tasks flooded Aaron's mind because Zoë would be coming home in a few hours from her skiing trip. He needed to clean up the piss and puke stains on the carpet, then do the dishes, scrub the tub and toilet, mop the kitchen floor, dust the bookshelves, change the sheets, fill the fridge with food but first he had to go shopping. Wait, no, he told himself, first I have to stand up.

But Aaron knew that errands weren't enough of a motivator to get him moving. What really did the trick, every single time, was that he didn't want his daughter to see him

overdosed,

immobilized,

weak and cowering,

emotionally-crippled,

spiritually-deformed,

lying on the floor.

He needed to be strong, if not for himself then for Zoë. And he needed to visit Eve at the nursing home before lunch. She was expecting him, or so he hoped.

Aaron used his teeth to untie the leather bands and crawled out from underneath the table. He got to his knees and stayed there for a while. Finally, he stood up and became dizzy while adjusting to the altitude. While holding onto the back of a chair for support, the hundred faces of the dead from his dream flashed as a real memory. Death and Despair standing on the marble dais. The rowdy Americans. The sophisticated French. The ancient philosophers and the drunken writers. The bassinet with a rotting baby.

Overwhelmed by the final haunting image, Aaron suddenly mumbled what his dying last words would be. "Did I help anyone?"

Sadness and lethargy offered temptation to hide from the world again but others needed him.

And that was enough.

Chapter 9

Twelve Hearts on Valentine's Day
and Why Nobody Should Begin Dating in February

Failing to expel the wedding dream from his mind, Aaron took a shower and went straight to bed. He didn't hear Zoë return as he slept soundly through the night. He dreamt of Eve handing him a lilac-colored, handwritten note inscribed with grass-script cursive words,

Be Here Now.

The paper slipped between his fingers and before he could grasp it from the air, he was awoken by the beeping of a fire alarm, not from smoke but instead a failed nine-volt back-up battery. Awake with a throbbing headache and surprised Zoë had slept through the alarm, Aaron threw the breaker switch to silence the hard-wired smoke detector and waited until 6:30 a.m. when he knew she'd be getting up for school. Sitting in the kitchen, he ate a bowl of cold oatmeal and read the paper until he heard footsteps on the stairway.

"Good morning."

"Mrnin," she mumbled, and Aaron judged her flat affect as nothing more than sleepiness but worried she might be suffering from seasonal affective disorder or the onset of a depressive phase induced by a monthly hormonal surge. Despite his concerns, Aaron remained silent until they reached the front entrance of North High School. The battery on her car had died two days earlier and neither one of them had bothered to search for the jumper cables. Aaron didn't mind toting her around town because the parental task reminded him of when she was younger and he suspected Zoë wanted a break from the whole independent, teenager act. They didn't speak on the way because he knew better than to press a teenage girl for words until at least noon, and besides, she looked a little pale.

When he tried to touch her forehead to check for a temperature, she peeled away and said, "Ugh, I'm fine. Basically. Bye."

She bailed out of the car at the edge of the parking lot and Aaron drove home to take a nap, the meds he'd taken over the weekend sapping his willpower. He texted Boss Lady to say he'd be coming in late, again, and was dosing off when the phone rang.

"Why'd you send your daughter to school sick?" the school nurse asked. "She's here in the infirmary. The rules are clear. Don't send a contagious child to school. She might infect everyone else. What kind of father are you?"

"The kind that lets his daughter make her own choices," he said and hung up.

Aaron drove back across town. Zoë, once again without a coat and wearing fuchsia tights under a paisley skirt and a t-shirt with *Black Jesus* stenciled above the silhouette of a cross, waited for him on the curb where he had left her thirty minutes earlier. She remained silent on the way home and ran up the stairs before he could ask any questions.

Aaron gently rapped on her door.

"I'm OK," Zoë responded. "Just gonna sleep for a while. Love you."

Speaking through the door, Aaron told her about a training session in Denver that he needed to attend for the next few days. She grunted a response, and he made the rash decision to sneak in a quick round of golf. Golfing in Colorado was a year-round sport because as everyone said, "If you don't like the weather, wait five minutes." The high elevation meant that during a blizzard, the sun could melt the snow even before it hit the ground. Aaron searched under the Christmas decorations and Hanukkah candelabra in the basement and found his old set of clubs he'd scored at a thrift shop for twelve dollars. He tossed the dusty bag into the trunk of his car and drove to the public golf course. Aaron swallowed three painkillers to ease the lingering pain of his vasectomy, even though his sack had not hurt in a few days, and walked quickly to the tenth tee without paying. They rarely checked the back nine and he often snuck onto the course during the off season.

He set up a stolen, yellow range ball atop a plastic tee and prepared to slice it right into the woods. He took two practice swings just as his phone rang. He immediately answered the call from the Poinsettia Nursing Home because Eve could be in trouble.

"What?" That's how Aaron tended to answer his personal phone. No name, no brief greeting, no elaborate salutation. After all, the person had called him and probably needed something.

"Is this…?" The voice belonged to the senior LPN, senior as in head nurse and not senior in terms of age.

"Yes." Aaron interrupted her. "How's my grandmother?"

The senior LPN recited verbatim from a script Aaron had heard on numerous occasions. "Your grandmother, Ms. Eve, she is not well." Aaron hated how they reduced the women in the nursing home with diminutives. They called the women *Miss* followed by their first name, like Miss Helen or Miss Fern but never Mister John or Mister Sam. Men were always referred to by their last name. The nurse continued, "Well, sir, she is experiencing painfully uresis possibly due to a urinary tract infection which could lead to a pelvic inflammatory disease which would require surgery to remove her infected ovaries."

"But she had a hysterectomy back in the Fifties."

"Sir, I don't think you understand. She needs to have a urinary test done as soon as possible. We cannot take her to the doctor's office, it's not part of our contract. Service providers only respond to imminent danger. Can you have her at the doctor's office by ten? We've already made the appointment. Thank you, have a nice day."

Aaron canceled the call and picked up his stolen range golf ball that, like a priest, had never made it even into one hole. He waved on the group behind him before leaving the tee box and silently debated whether to run a scam and collect money from the golf pro. The old man who operated the desk was forgetful and sometimes Aaron could play a round of golf for free and then ask for a rain check and get his money back that he had never paid. Aaron often fabricated a tale about a pregnant wife in labor to explain his reason for the sudden departure off the course, but sometimes the guilt bothered him. Aaron tried to lie only on the course when he would jot down a five instead of an eight, but he knew the truth about golf—how one plays the game imitates life, a game described by Mark Twain as, "A good walk ruined." Deciding against his plan to score a little cash, Aaron placed his golf clubs back into the trunk.

Sitting in his car and feeling anxious about visiting Eve, he thought about sniffing a puff of the Esketamine nasal spray that he carried in the glovebox, but resolved in the moment to remain sober. His recent stumble from sobriety had nearly killed him. Also, Aaron didn't want to be hallucinating and drowsy on his trip to the nursing home, driving slow as a sloth on a turtle's back.

He idled in the parking lot and listened to a few songs from the Nineties Classic station. Upon hearing Nirvana for the second time in ten minutes, he wondered when Nineties grunge became classic rock. Probably about the same time, he realized, that the automobile industry began using those same Nineties tunes to focus on Aaron's age group as the targeted demographic for car commercials which was precisely the same moment he officially became old and could no longer wear his favorite pair of shoes, the black and white checkered slip-on Vans.

Finally, he left the parking lot and arrived fifteen minutes later at the Poinsettia. He decided that after visiting Eve, he would drive to Denver in the afternoon for a SAFE-T training session. He feared the Suicide Assessment Five-step Evaluation and Triage seminar might prove to be terribly boring but the brochure posted above Debz's desk at the office had intrigued him because it featured a Black woman on the cover. Aaron hoped to find out why Black women completed suicide far less often than any other group. On the slim chance a Black woman attended the conference, Aaron suspected her answer might be something like,

"It's a white thing;" and,

"I'm too busy taking care of my damn relatives;" and,

"No need to kill myself when y'all trying to murder me!"

Aaron entered the Poinsettia, a retirement community of merriment and good tidings with a color scheme of green, red and white to evoke a year-round Christmas spirit with greeting mats by the front door that read, *Ho, Ho, Ho, this is Living!*

Yet, with the abundance of drooling, shambling, zombified, upright corpses, Aaron wanted to grab a black magic marker and write, *Woe, Woe, Woe, this is Dying!*

Luckily, he'd resisted the temptation to deface a nursing home. He searched for Eve in the usual spots: the front hallway with two new and exquisite leather couches in front of a wide television screen permanently tuned to either cartoons or the infomercial channel; or, in the Fifties era soda-shop next to the cozy reading room with a large selection of un-creased classic books which is why Aaron at times referred to the Poinsettia as the Historic Hotel; or, in the cafeteria with its constant supply of spearmint tea and cafeteria-style trays with divided portions.

"I've never had a bad meal," Eve would say on occasion.

And Aaron couldn't but help respond, "Sure, but you've never had a good one either," which was the main reason why he took her out for lunch when he visited before noon.

The scent of lavender guided Aaron into a grand library where he found her playing the piano. Performing the same song, over and over, for the first time. The blessing of dementia or Alzheimer's or whatever it's called these days, Aaron thought, was a wide-eyed wonderment of the world. Eve would light up with joy every time Aaron entered the room, even if he had only stepped out to use the restroom. In that memory-erasing moment, Eve would celebrate his return as though he had circumnavigated the globe. The cruelty of dementia was a vacant stare, eyes dim and cloudy grey. She no longer resembled the strong woman who had traveled to a hundred countries.

When Aaron was a little boy, Eve revelled him with fantastic stories, like the cannibals of Papua New Guinea who portered her Mendel, cedar lined touring trunk overland to remote villages while Eve and her husband failed to convert the natives despite Christianity's appeal to cannibalism by eating the body of Christ. She also told of touring southern India before Western-funded Ashrams popped up like marigolds, and she visited Rhodesia before white farmers stole Zimbabwe to build a crappy hotel on the good side of Vic Falls. She had spent a lovely day wandering through the Hermitage Museum when the country was called the Soviet Union. She had napped on Pig's Bay, Bahía de Cochinas, before bearded Cubaños stormed down from the Sierra Maestra mountains. While vacationing in Buenos Aires, she heard Evita speak at a tear-gassed rally begging Argentina not to cry for her while the crowd wept chemical tears. And before that, she had camped in the hills above Dien Bien Phu before artillery fell from the Viet Minh, which Aaron as a little boy had confused with the *Rats of NIMH*. Her tales had shown him the world.

Sadly, time had stolen these stories from her. She was now the unbelieving child when Aaron recounted her adventures back to her. "My heavens," she would say, "who would go to so many places?" which crushed Aaron's heart, more like a punch in the stomach since the Romans were convinced the center of their emotions resided not in the heart but rather in the lining of their intestinal tract.

Eve pounded the keys to *Claire de Lune*, firm notes flowing into the next with only a slight hesitation from her arthritic fingers. The same song again for the first time, over and over, Eve instantly forgetting that she had played it when the final, elongated C rang out before starting again, a musical Ouroboros with no end or beginning like the first/last sentence of *Finnegan's Wake* but she wasn't awake or asleep, merely a cloud of minutes clumped together to construct a day no different than yesterday. *Fin* as in "the end", Finnagain and again and again until death, that's what Aaron thought of Eve's life and why he was determined to get her out of the nursing home whenever he could, to help her escape the monotony of aging routine.

Eve played on the piano as Aaron found a chair in the corner behind her. He silently wept when she struggled with a chord but today was a good day because she turned and recognized him.

Her face lit up as she smiled. "Oh, honey, are we going somewhere?"

"Let's do lunch. Are you hungry?"

After a long pause, Eve tilted her head. "I have no idea."

"Let's get you outta here," Aaron said, reaching for her purse and then remembered she didn't carry one. She would have lost the purse and besides, there was nothing that she needed to carry. She possessed no car keys since she didn't drive, no house keys because she no longer owned a home, no credit cards, no cell phone, none of the tangible manifestations of independence.

Walking to the car, Eve took his arm by gently placing her wrinkled hand inside the nook of his elbow. Aaron set her in the front seat, reaching across to click the seat belt, the scent of lavender filling the car. The public radio station played opera music and they were both pleased to hear Rossini's *The Barber of Seville*.

As Aaron pulled out of the parking lot, Eve pointed at the grey clouds in the distance and said, "The trees say thank you when it rains."

"That's nice."

Before they had reached the end of the street, she pulled on his sleeve. "Where do I live?"

"Back there."

She turned around and saw a woman walking her dog and suddenly asked, "Have you found a nice girl yet?"

"No, but I've found something better."

"Oh," Eve asked with arched eyebrows, "and what's better than a nice girl?"

"A bad girl."

She smacked his knee in delight and laughed. "Oh, thanks for making me laugh."

Her gratitude was not why Aaron made the frequent visits. He wanted to see her because she helped him into this world and he'd be damned if he didn't help her out of it.

Aaron dropped his grandmother at the doctor's office knowing they'd take good care of her, and he decided there was no reason for him to waste an hour sitting in the waiting room reading the kid's magazine *Circus*. Instead, he asked for them to call when Eve was finished with the exam, the third one this month, and he jotted his number upon a pad of paper for the preoccupied receptionist. He checked the time and noticed he could catch part of a weekly support group that he wanted to attend after his recent relapse. After all, sobriety required work.

Aaron strolled across the street to a red-bricked Presbyterian Church and up to the third floor for the 10 a.m. meeting of Al-Anon. He didn't attend Alcoholics Anonymous for himself but rather Al-Anon in order to cope with his ex-wife, because it's always easier to deal with someone else's problems.

He arrived after Group had finished reading the numerous Twelves, read aloud one at a time by each participant, first the twelve Noble Truths then the Twelve-fold Path to Enlightenment and next the Twelve Traditions and lastly the Twelve Concepts of Service. Aaron snuck in right after he heard, "Participation is the key to Harmony," but with Becky moderating, Aaron anticipated discord.

As the Treasurer of the local chapter of Al-Anon, a group of non-alcoholics dealing with the alcoholic in their life, Becky cleared her throat, glared at Aaron and said, "Okway, wet's get stwarted. Hi, I'ma Becky."

"Hi, Becky," Group replied although everyone knew Becky but Aaron had grown accustomed to the way people talk in Group. Becky, the once red-headed beauty now withered by three divorces, a buried son and two packs of smokes a day, informed Group that one hundred and twelves dollars were collected last month from donations and book purchases before she proceeded to read from a little textbook Aaron had seen but could not afford. After several months with Group, he still had not purchased a copy to support the Winer's Cult as members of Alcoholics Anonymous called Al-Anon, because Group was usually a room full of women whining about their drunk spouses. Aaron was a bit of an anomaly because he wasn't there for himself, despite his struggles with addiction, and not even for his drunk ex-wife because a decade had passed since his divorce. Rather, he was there to help Zoë figure out how to deal with her drunk mother. He had offered to take Zoë to Alateen after reading the pamphlets and seeing the photos of happy teens embraced by sober parents, but then he questioned how it could be anonymous if people were spreading their pictures around town on free brochures until he noticed the small print which stated the people in the photos were not members but actors. Which is about the exact moment Aaron figured out the duplicitous nature established by the fake-photos of supposedly anonymous persons indicting the weekly gatherings were rather a Gateway Drug for Support Groups and decided to spare his daughter the agony of Alateen.

Aaron couldn't tell if Becky was reading from *One Drink At A Time* or the insightful *Courage to Drink* or the instructive *Paths to the Bar* or the helpful *Wine for Today* or the supportive *Discovering Booze,* and Aaron was sure he was getting the titles wrong because it should have been *One Day At A Time* and more positive sounding advice.

"Hi-wah pow-wah," Becky announced and Aaron believed the women in Group were of Native American decent, possibly the local Pueblo Indians who were praying to Hiawatha of the Iroquois or Pocahontas of the Powhatan people, and that Hi-wah pow-wah was a concoction of Hiawatha and Pocahontas Powhatan, and Aaron was pleased to be included among such noble people. Sitting between two women who both reeked of cigarette smoke and cat piss, he laughed out loud when Becky spoke with a stroke-induced lisp, "Hi-wah pow-wah. Wet's hode hands and pway to our hi-wah pow-wah."

Aaron was spiritually disappointed when he realized Becky was slurring her pronunciation of Higher Power, a sneaky way for Christians to conjure the image of the divine without saying God. In this duplicitous manner of invoking the Higher Power, they pretended to include non-Christians or even open-minded Atheists who might believe in the penguin spirit animal from *Fight Club*. He wondered why they didn't go ahead and say, "God" since they were meeting in a church attic, closer to heaven than anyone else in the building. Despite his irreverence, he kept coming back to Group. Over the last few months, he'd settled on the idea that he enjoyed the meandering voices of the ladies in Group. While he waited for Eve who was being examined across the street at the doctor's office, Aaron jotted down twelve personal revelations he'd gained while attending Group, writing little notes in the margin of a booklet left behind from a previous meeting.

To Be Present, the first bit of wisdom, was rearranged in his memory as Ram Dass' *Be Here Now*, words which lingered from a slip of paper out of a dream Aaron had the previous night; and,

To Trust One Other Person was the second idea. Even a decade after his divorce, he struggled with trust issues but had no problem telling his problems to people begging for change outside a marijuana dispensary instead of opening up to express emotional vulnerability to women that he brought to bed although that number has been greatly reduced to zero since Zoë started spending more nights at his house rather than staying with Lena; and,

To Extrapolate Serenity, the third observation, was a phrase connected to the Serenity Prayer: "God grant me the serenity to accept the things I cannot change; courage to change the things I can; and wisdom to know the difference." Aaron associated this sermon with the canceled-too-early-and-he'd-never-get-over-it series of *Firefly* aboard the starship Serenity and pilot Washburne's final serene words, "I am a leaf on the wind, watch how I soar"; and,

Let Go & Detach was the fourth, a rather redundant saying, but he wrote it down in red pen inside the margins of the *One Day At A Time* booklet because he knew that to achieve the treasured Buddhist state of non-attachment after a lifetime consumed by a Western, capitalistic, greedy, physical human state of attachment, one must go through the daily and painful act of constantly detaching from perceived needs. For Aaron, detaching meant he must first be attached in order to become non-attached, and this paradox of attaining a temporary state of non-attachment was easily remedied by a cigarette and a glass of cabernet.

Respond but Don't React, the fifth discernment, was the same advice he gave Zoë during her first driving lesson when an eighteen-wheeled semi tractor-trailer roared by their tiny, wind-blown Honda as Zoë merged onto the highway having finally reached fourth gear and *reacted* by slamming on the brakes instead of properly *responding* by stepping on the gas pedal; and,

Project the Positive, the sixth insight, which momentarily reduced Aaron's dread of the endless midnight-through-dawn *What If's* that kept him awake; and,

Peace, the seventh perception, elusive because people often mistake pleasure for happiness until they realize the greatest teacher in life is suffering; and,

To Take Care of Myself 3X per Week, the eighth helpful pill of advice, which seemed selfish to Aaron since mothers in the 1950s like Eve never had something called *Me Time*, they just drank a lot until the arrival of Mommy's Little Helper, that little benzo drug Diazepam, marketed as Valium, and helped housewives relax with the unfortunate side effect of suicide; and,

Hand in Front of My Face, the ninth proverbial smack in the face, forcing Aaron to focus on what's directly in front of him and not be distracted by the chaos of life's traffic, but also had the unfortunate side effect of blinding him from approaching potholes; and,

Acceptance is a Revolving Door to Detachment, the tenth concept which Aaron disagreed with but wrote down anyway since he doesn't have to agree, he only has to show up; and,

To Find Joy in the Journey, the eleventh notion, utter Buddhist nonsense but this reminded Aaron that when he attempted to hide from the world by growing out his beard and letting his long hair fall across his face, people would ask him, "You look sad, do you suffer from depression?" and he'd laugh and say, "Suffer? It's the best part of my day!"

Show Up for the Job, the twelfth and final reflection, possibly the most important rule and finally some good advice that he related to because in regards to his daughter and grandma and mother and aunt and ex-wife, Aaron was certain he'd harmed them by spreading his darkness through an ill-tempered disposition, but he showed up for the job and maybe more, because the day after making nachos, he told Zoë, "I've tried to be a good dad," and she said, "No, you haven't tried. You've succeeded."

Right in the middle of invoking Group's invocation of Hi-wah pow-wah, Aaron forcefully embraced the first principle of *To Be Present* by suppressing the frustration of dealing with his alcoholic ex-wife as well as the incompetency of Eve's nursing home which created a temporal schism and sent Aaron hurling towards a present-orientated frenzy of events which forced him into the present . . .

with the ringing of his phone, disturbing everyone over forty, and he is surprised the doctor finished early until he reads the number on his cell and jolts for the door, heading out of the room with an ear pressed to his phone as a statement to the others in Group which expressed a *sorry-to-leave-the-room-but-this-call-is-really-important* type of hurried posture. He doesn't usually take a call during Group but coming from Lena, he fears the worst.

"What?"

"Why'd you keep her home from school today?"

"Because she's sick. I gotta go." He can hear the slur of words, the hesitation in her come-back. Not even noon, he thinks, and she's already plastered.

Lena carries on for six minutes, repeating herself four times as Aaron listens with Compassion and Empathy and then he realizes Group is messing with his head, turning Acceptance into Dependence and Enabling into Weakness so he thinks *fu°Ck*[51] *that* about Lena's rant and hangs up. Embarrassed to return to the Al-Anon meeting, he races back across the street to the Urinary Specialist to pick up Eve, but she's not ready for another ten minutes, and so he paces in the hallway and wishes he hadn't left Group early and is mad at Lena for pulling him out and also wishing for a cigarette although he doesn't smoke and trying not to check his phone to read the twelve angry texts from Lena that he has recently labeled as T-exTs because they come from his -ex and finally Eve emerges with negative test results on a carbon printed receipt. Of course it's negative, Aaron thinks. Same as last time and the time before but the Poinsettia needs proof to file an insurance claim. Aaron doesn't mind because he wants to make sure Eve is healthy.

Over a quick lunch of Ruben sandwiches at a café next to the Presbyterian church, Eve constantly asks for her purse and Aaron can't effectively explain that she no longer carries a purse and so instead of taking her to the bookstore and suffering another hour of, "Honey, where's my purse?" Aaron thinks *fuCk*[52] *that* and unceremoniously drops her off at the entrance to the nursing home and goes by himself to search for the DSM-5 at Farms & Shameless Booksellers but to his utter disgust he mentally exclaims *fu€k*[53] *that* when he sees the price tag of $146 whereas he knows the DSM-IV[54] goes for about six bucks on-line. He checks the time and decides to catch a movie before heading up to Denver for the SAFE-T training session. He sneaks into a matinee showing of another installment of the MCU by Marvel, Inc., now Disney, Inc., about masks and capes and wishing DC would get their act together and put out a really good movie about JLA and how Martian Manhunter lives in Denver whereas Batman hunts in Gotham and Superman writes opinion columns in Metropolis and Green Arrows shoots boxing-glove arrows in Star City and Green Lantern,

Black Canary and the Flash all live in fake towns but the only real city is Denver, and Aaron thinks maybe Denver is a fabricated comic-movie town like the others, and halfway through Aaron wants to skip out on yet another predictable foil where the villain is merely the opposite of the hero but since it costs him $9, he endures despite knowing that now he's resigned to pay TWICE for a bad film, once in cash and the second payment in time, until he remembers that he snuck in without paying.

During the climactic ending as the wise-cracking hero is about to save the girl trapped in a burning car/sinking ship/plummeting elevator/suburban household, Aaron's phone vibrates and Zoë's on the other end, crying about how she sliced her finger and maybe needs stitches because it won't stop bleeding.

"How'd you cut yourself?" Aaron asks. "I thought you were sleeping upstairs. Musta been one helluva nightmare."

"I couldn't sleep and felt better so I went back to school."

"Thought the car battery was dead."

"Neighbor gave me a jump. We really should buy jumper cables."

And thirty seconds later he's already in the car racing down the frontage road next to the highway and taking deep breaths, no need to rush, he tells himself, because it's probably a superficial wound but he's still panicking, and he calls Lena and she mentions the accident happened two hours ago so she thought Zoë was fine but he needs to see the injury for himself. And he tracks Zoë down at school, pulls her out of English class because it's pointless now-a-days since sentence diagramming is no longer taught, and Zoë explains how she lacerated her finger cutting an avocado during lunch, and he takes one long look and it is deep and bloody enough to cause the bile to collect in his mouth and the teacher says, "It's no big deal, just take her to EmergiCare," and he evokes the energy to eloquently elucidate his emotions by yelling a grammatically correct response, "FÜck that!"[55] and drives straight to the Emergency Room at the hospital because the EmergiCare clinic is always a complete waste of time, and it's only when the admitting nurse robotically announces, "Happy Valentine's Day," that Aaron is acutely reminded that he has no time for a girlfriend who certainly would have given him grief for canceling a date on this most capitalistic of romantic days and besides, Aaron thinks, no woman wants to go on a date to the hospital with an injured kid that isn't her own. For an hour, they sit in the waiting room until they're admitted and reviewed by two kids not much older than Zoë, probably trained last week as EMTs, and finally they see a doctor who's maybe thirty and he says, "She'll need a few stitches but no nerve damage. Good you brought her in to prevent infection because the hands are often dirty. The lacerations occurred on the dorsal aspect of the digitus secundus containing nerves and vascular vessels."

Aaron completely ignores the doctor because he's busy texting Lena and telling her to get down to the hospital but Aaron can deduce by her responses that she's too drunk to drive and so he responds with his usual *fuk*[56] *that* because Lena should be here for his daughter's sake but instead tells Zoë that her mom is busy at work but she'll come over to the house later. Aaron's anger surges digitally, composing a lengthy T-exT but halfway through decides to call Lena and then hangs up when it goes to voicemail. He hugs Zoë before going into the bathroom and washes his face with cold water and stares at the mirror and says to himself,

"I can't do this alone."

And he breaks down crying for forty-five seconds until someone barges in and Aaron pretends to be okay and silently yells in his mind *uck*[57] *that* and struggles to be strong for another hour until he can get his little-girl-who's-not-so-little-anymore safely home. Aaron is relieved he didn't go to Denver but is worried that he forgot to tell Boss Lady. Staring in the bathroom mirror, Aaron looks at his perpetual frown and the dark circles under his eyes while promising to clean up his act and stop doing drugs and keep it together and be present these last two years before Zoë leaves for college and not fade away because every time he even thinks about Fading Away, some minor tragedy happens and it turns out Zoë really needs him, or Eve or Lena or Marilyn or Jocelyn, and so he curses himself instead of blaming the world by feeling a very large *Fu☾k*[58] *Me* which forces him to remain present. Here, in the now.

Chapter 10

The Dating Scene as a Player in *Suicide: The Game*

Aaron brought Zoë home from the hospital in the early evening and within minutes, she was begging to visit her friend's house.

"I just need to hang out with Crow and Thyme," Zoë explained as she grabbed the car keys with her good hand. "Cutting my finger was so traumatic and I need a little moral support right now."

"You should rest. And moral support? You're not facing an ethical dilemma."

"Ugh, daaad," she said with a well-practiced eyeroll. "Fine, emotional. I don't need a lecture on semantics."

"Oh, you mean morale-support."

"That not even a word."

"Should be. Want some nachos?"

She grabbed him by the shoulder. "Don't try to trick me into staying. What do you always tell me?"

"Floss your teeth?"

"No…"

"Do your homework and argue with your teachers?"

"Nooo…"

"Kick every boy you meet right in the nuts?"

"Daaaaad…"

"Fine, what is it you think that I always say?"

Zoë looked at him and said, "My body, my choice."

With a silent hug, they parted and Aaron didn't argue. Her logic was sound and he had no intention of trying to control her. She wasn't purposefully mean or disrespectful, she always let him know where she was going, and she even texted back. She was a good kid, but he was hurt by her departure because only a few years ago, he'd been the salve to ease the bumps and bruises of the day. When she sliced her knee on the corner of a table, he smothered it with Vitamin E and a bandage. When she spilled boiling soup on her thighs, he had grabbed the ice packs. When her heart was broken for the first time in the seventh grade by Jean-Claude, the neighborhood bad boy who was a year older, smoked cigarettes and had a fake, French accent because his parents had flown him to Paris that summer, Aaron wiped away her tears because that's what fathers do. She was growing up quickly and wanted her friends. She didn't need her father anymore, but Aaron missed his little girl.

Anticipating her return, he set up one of their favorite board games. When she turned eight, they emigrated from *Candy Land* and *Monopoly* onto more complex games like *Settlers of Catan* and *Carcassonne*. He loved those days when the two of them spent hours playing together, laughing and trying to outwit each other. She'd been so busy lately with her friends and school that Aaron was beginning to think maybe she had outgrown silly games with her father.

Aaron dug into the recesses of the closet, and underneath *Dominion* and *Arkham Horror*, he discovered one of their favorites. *Suicide: The Game*, first edition, printed by Hasbro in 1999 after the Columbine shooting. A game for the whole family with two or more players, ages 8 and up. The rules allowed for a solo version, but *Suicide: The Game* was more fun when played with others.

He set up the board on the dining room table, a hex-based map of a mansion surrounded by geographic features. The game resembled *Clue* with rooms such as a bathroom, living room, back yard, porch, basement, and garage. The outside landmarks included a golden bridge, haunted forest, children's playground, fishing pond, and lover's leap atop a cliff. He carefully stacked the five piles of cards[59] and re-read the rules[60] since a few years had passed since they last played. He set up the character sheets, selecting Gothic Teen as the Suicidal Player, and the Housekeeper and Taxi Driver as the Prevention Players.[61] Aaron placed the cardboard character markers on the board and filled a small bowl with tokens resembling a pistol, rope, bottle of pills and straight razor.

Several hours later when Zoë returned from her friend's house, Aaron was finishing up a solo version of the game. She looked at the board and crushed Aaron's hope of re-connecting with his daughter when she said, "Can we play some other time? I'm kinda tired."

They warmed up a bowl of left-over spaghetti and since Aaron was feeling a little suicidal, an after-effect of winning the game, they turned on an episode of *The Bachelor*. The syndicated series was halfway through its 21st season with a guy named Nick. Aaron was keenly aware of its manipulative and malignant societal impact, reducing any viewer's

Emotional Stability rating by a few points, but he loved watching unscripted drama. Aaron understood that film/stage/television actors emoted a fake condition that came naturally to the players of *The Bachelor/Bachelorette* where real tears flowed.

Tears on screen proved to be cathartic for Aaron, regardless of his mental unhealth, crying at odd moments like during the cat food commercials or the opening credits of the show. The real reason Aaron loved the show was because of Rachel L., who would later be the first Black woman to star in *The Bachelorette*. As the name indicated, *The Bachelor* centered on a man who Aaron only tolerated to discover more about women. The star of the show, Nicholas V., that crafty ol' St. Nick, represented the perfect date, the Perfect Guy, despite the obvious fact that he's a player, as in a pimp-player and not a board game-player, because he's kissing, groping, and holding hands with other women directly in view of his main love interest. Nothing drives a woman crazier than being ignored by a man, or at least that's how modern television depicts its masculine heroes. Add alcohol, promoted liberally by producers, and it's like gas to a fire. Add interviews, demanded frequently during a menstrual cycle, and it's like napalm!

Aaron was flabbergasted that anyone would desire and sign up for such a horrid and uncertain experience. The attention and self-promotion probably served as the only ontological validation of people's existence in this age of social media. And the money was decent.

Aaron secretly resented the star of *The Bachelor* and he often wondered how any other guy in Bachelor Nation could ever compete with The Guy. The Guy is always super romantic with detailed and planned dates of helicopter rides, boat trips, scuba dives, dancing in the street, and shopping around the historic district because apparently women love a man who arranges detailed plans. Yet, the best quality is that he Listens. The Guy keenly Listens with intense, soul-penetrating-heart-felt-eye-contact, the most romantic action a man can do for a woman. With keen hearing and held gazes, the women are helpless and fall dramatically in love on camera, in front of millions of national viewers. Sadly, the Guy is so distracted by the attention of 29 other women that he doesn't have time to reciprocate her pronouncement of love, maybe a gentle gesture or a held hand would suffice, but it's that Listening-with-eye-contact that crushes every time. Of course, the major flaw is that they never fight. Not even when he dumps her. He simply looks away at a perfectly timed moment, captured in a hi-definition close-up, with his still-Listening-but-averted-eye-contact, and the world discovers she's not the One when he says,

"I care so much for you, but ___;" or,

"You are the sweetest, kindest person, but___;" or,

"I've had so much fun with you, but___;" or,

"You're perfect, but___;" or,

"You deserve to be happy

(just not with me)."

And soon the viewer realizes The Guy is a master Dumper. Taking one big dump on America. And we can't turn away. Without a single fight, the drama is not between the Guy and his date, instead the tension exists between the women who are competing for his attention, which ultimately plummets them over the emotional edge. The elimination process is also unfair to the Guy because the poor bastard has to break up repeatedly with 29 women in similar fashion saying,

"I just don't feel this in my heart;" or,

"I just don't see a long-term commitment with you;" or,

"My heart is just leading me somewhere else;" or,

"This just isn't, like, going anywhere;" or,

"I just have to be true to myself

and I just don't feel that with you;" or,

"You deserve better;" or,

"It's not you, it's me

(but obviously it's you)."

It's the "but" at the end or the "just" at the beginning that signals uncertainty and the inevitable downfall which always occurs a few minutes after the woman reveals her affection for The Guy by saying the words the entire *Bachelor* franchise centers around: "I love you" or more importantly "I don't love you". His courteous response is to dump her quickly as the camera rushes up to seize the hi-def close-up of her big-teary-eyed-emotional-breakdown and Aaron wants to reach through the screen and strangle the Guy for being an asshole for the 29th time. But that's why viewers keep watching, not because anyone wants the Guy to ultimately find happiness, but instead for the terribly cruel emotional journey to find true love. Viewers only want a happy ending when the trip was a nightmare.

For weeks, Aaron watched it alone, every Monday night after locking the door and turning off the phone. He even disconnected the

Christmas lights still decorating the window frame still up in February to prevent any side glare on the screen of his weekly dose of emotional dumpage. When Zoë came home from her friend's house, he offered to re-watch Episode One but she was in one of her anti-gender, anti-normative, feminist phases.

Instead of sitting next to him on the sagging yellow couch, she stormed out of the room and screamed, "If I got a rose, I'd throw it down at his stupid feet, look right at the camera and yell, 'Fŭck the Patriarchy!'"

As Zoë stomped up the stairs to her bedroom, Aaron couldn't have been prouder of his daughter. One of his many fears of the future was the impending crisis of college, and he hoped she'd be fine. Her revulsion of the Patriarchy meant she wouldn't be partying with entitled football quarterbacks or popular basketball centers or handsome soccer forwards which meant she wouldn't be raped while drunk at a freshman party. Instead, she'd probably end up getting arrested for protesting Trump's immigration policy.

After Zoë went to bed, Aaron clutched the blanket and engaged in an hour-long cry session. Following the conclusion of the latest episode of *The Bachelor*, Aaron turned off the television. Alone in the silence, a creeping fear kept him awake. Zoë would soon be leaving for college.

College. Despite his earlier confidence in her well-being, the thought suddenly terrified him. She would be so vulnerable, so exposed, and he wouldn't be there to rescue her. He dreaded the thought of her struggling with classes and dorm roommates and ill-tempered professors and drunken frat-boy-zombies and even worse, the long-haired, gorgeous Philosophy grad-student filling her head with Marxist ideology. He often joked, "Where we going to school?" with an emphasis on the *we*. Yet, he knew she'd leave and he'd stay. Of course, he would help her pick out the schools to visit, make the grand college tour, assist with the application process to her top choices, worry through the Christmas break of senior year about getting accepted into her number one school, and rejoice around Spring Break when she finally decided on which college to attend. He'd help pack the car with her collection of classic vinyl records and a dozen pillows because that's what fathers do. Then she'd be off and he'd be alone which always brought him back to the dreadful prospect of trying to find someone to spend his life with after Zoë went to college. Yet, in order to find someone, Aaron would first have to go on a date.

Dating. The idea had seemed preposterous to Aaron once he struck forty years of age, because he no longer felt the desire. Felt, as in the urge to pursue a woman even though his libido had finally diminished from Overpowering Biological Imperative to Moderately Time-Consuming and he began to wonder what he actually liked about women. Forty, the year he could focus on an objective besides getting laid.

Aaron suspected dating was much easier for a single man than for a single woman even though men like to think it's easy for a single woman to pick up a guy. She only has to wander into the nearest bar, point to the first guy and whisper, "Come here fella."

Done and done.

From personal experience, Aaron knew that picking up strangers in a bar was not the best way to meet someone. The point-and-whisper technique might work for the select few but was an extreme example of a linear thought exercise akin to caveman ideology limited by a biologically masculine perspective which, for Aaron-as-single-guy, cumulated in a simplistic interrogative mood: Do I Wanna Get Laid Tonight?

When the answer to DIWGLT lay in the affirmative, generally most of the time except when the Cavaliers are down by a point near the end of the fourth quarter, then Aaron-as-single-guy would proceed to go out on the town. Traversing the scene as a single man merely required him to scrounge up a little cash, rinse with mouthwash, and locate a clean shirt. Within a minute, he'd be good to go.

Aaron speculated that for the single female, the mechanism of dating was much more complex, supposing the lady in question doesn't point-and-whisper considering the amount of creeps out there in this fictional watering hole that is loaded with guys waiting for her to saunter in and point-and-whisper directly at them. Certainly, women who are inclined to point-and-whisper have mastered the art of sauntering, most likely in Devious Scream 6" stilettoed heels, Passion Red lipstick and a Betty Grable strapless party dress. In actuality, the point-and-whisper technique is a rare occurrence because, honestly, what if he (the man she randomly selects) is heavily-infected with numerous STDs; or, has a pocketful of GHB and plans to date-rape her; or, is a stalker with PTSD who served in the first Persian Gulf; or, a man with ED and can't get it up; or, a man suffering from ED, as in emotional-dysfunction, and won't cuddle after the guaranteed all-too-rapid-bunny-rabbit-humping-one-night-stand encounter; or, a man who is currently UNEMP and doesn't have a job, forced to live in his parents' basement; or, drives a rusted Hyundai made in SKR or worse, a Chevy from DT as in Detroit; or, suffers from a profound case of MAS, Male Answering Syndrome, and is always right even when he's not; or, the worse yet, is inclined to wear a man-bun to family functions while also a card-carrying member of MRA, Men's Rights Activist, and counters any argument about sexual assault with the slogan NAMALT, Not All Men Are Like That, and secretly doesn't call his mother on Sundays? Thus, the point-and-whisper approach is too risky as a viable way of finding a man. Finding a hard man, yes, but certainly not for securing a good man, a date, a boyfriend, a potential husband, or a bachelor named Nick.

Aaron-as-single-guy had but one question to answer (DIWGLT). This rigorous self-inquiry was followed by a very short list of activities (brush teeth, find clean shirt), mere suggestions that probably did not include doing the dishes. The single female, in Aaron's imagination, is forced to compile a much longer list tilted BGOD, as in Before Going On a Date. Among the top details may include recalling whether or not she's on her period. She knows the bloody condition is a deal breaker, not for him but for her, because if things go according to plan, then they might end up back at her place. Aaron continued the monologue of this imaginary single lady by understanding that she wants to take her date back to her place because the guy's place is invariably filthy, stinky, sticky, and packed with his roommates playing a car-crashing—bad-guy-shooting—touchdown-scoring video game.

Come to think of it, Aaron's fictionalized woman realizes as she looks around her imaginary apartment that Aaron has concocted for this thought-experiment, she'd better clean up around here because there's no way she can make-out with some guy in this dirty apartment. She spends the next thirty minutes doing the dishes, picking up a week's worth of dirty-maybe-clean-not-sure clothes and taking out the trash before scolding herself for being too presumptuous that she might succeed and find a man tonight worth bringing back home but at least her apartment is clean. The night proceeds as usual, enduring harassment on the way to the club and groping inside the club, and when she does decide to bring him back after three shots of tequila and two raspberry wine coolers, she's completely forgotten that she is menstruating until they start making out with her bra undone while he's working his way down south as in kissing her belly and struggling with the top button on her jeans, and when she suddenly remembers Aunt Flo is in town, she grabs his head quickly, yanking it to her eye level and says,

"Um, let's slow it down, OK."

Not framed as a question and the guy thinks, "Hey, what the hell? Thought she was a sure thing after the third shot of Cuervo."

Or, if he's a little insecure, "Wait, does she still like me?"

Or, if he's selfish, "That's cool, I don't eat pussy."

Or, if he's a real basturd, "She better give me head."

And that's why a certain time of the month is not the best time to start dating, or so Aaron thought, not really knowing what it's like to endure an appendicitis every single month, but he understood a little better now that he's seen his daughter suffer.

As for the other points contemplated by Aaron's imaginary lady on her list of things to do BGOD are requirements numerous in complexity and always mandatory which can be categorized under the title of Hair Maintenance.

First, leg hair. How long has it been since I shaved, Aaron's imaginary woman asks herself, gently petting her calves? Two days. Should be good enough. Checks again, little stubblies poke her hand. Ugh, better shave again. Into the tub/shower for a major overhaul. Starts at her ankles, works upwards, takes a total of five minutes. Afterwards, she inspects her arm pits in the foggy mirror attached to the shower wall. Three days growth? A few swipes with the pink razor, then a few more to make sure, two more strokes, got it, wait, once more, ok, good. Looks in the mirror again, sees the faint line of hair on her upper lip and makes a mental note to take care of that later with the tweezers. Next, she checks *down there* and Holy Mother of God, has it been that long? Tarzan would need a machete to get through that bush. Back to the hair on her head and she is ready to begin. Shampoo, lather and rinse. Applies conditioner, lets it sink in for three minutes, grows impatient after twenty-three seconds, rinse. Washcloth, soap and wait, is the oven on? No, haven't cooked today. Ahhh, soap in the eyes. Wash bottoms of feet, back of the knees, legs, stomach, one breast, then the other. They look uneven, even more so than usual. Hmmm, she thinks, ol' Lefty seem a whole cup size bigger. That's ridiculous, wait, will he notice? Hold on, is that my phone ringing? Turns the shower off. Listens. Nope, it's the dog barking next door. Shower back on. Wait, did I do my hair already? Shampoo, lather and rinse to make sure. Conditioner for twenty seconds … finally done. Towel dry, hair wrapped up. Tweezer-time. The mustache goes first, then plucking of the eyebrows, and lastly a few nose hairs. What the heck Bilbo Baggins, she tells herself, those are some hairy toes! Dry razor, no problem. Now for the make-up. Ok, nothing fancy, a dab of blush and eye-liner with light mascara. No eye-shadow, she decides, I'm not from Jersey. Lipstick? Calls her sister for advice. No answer. Texts her BFF#1, and she replies NEVER, implying one should not wear lipstick when out looking for a guy but maybe when in a vacation spot with lots of tourists and cruising for a quick hook-up. So, she needs a second opinion. Hits up BFF#3 (since #2 is in Thailand with her boyfriend, that lucky bitch!), and she says, "No, are you insane?!" Ok, no lipstick. Decides to put Revlon's Russian Red in her purse, just in case. Sends a group text to BBF#1, 3, 4, 5, 7 (6 is not on the list anymore) to make sure they are going out tonight. Deliberates before inviting her bleach-blonde work colleague who is really nice but a little too pretty. Writes text, checks for spelling (they do work together, after all). Sends. Instantly regrets.

Time to do her hair. Grabs blow-dryer, curling iron and straightener (she hasn't decided whether to go curly, wavy or straight) and waaaait an unholy second and stop the bus at Grandma's house because, hold on, is that a freakin grey hair?! Plucks it out, convinces herself the grey was only a blonde strand. Curl, blow, brush, and thirty minutes later, she's ready. Not ready like a guy who wakes up, throws water on his face, brushes his teeth and says, "I'm ready". She's not ready-ready, but she is ready to get dressed.

Aaron suspected women start composing an outfit with the shoes. As for men, shoes are something they place on their feet on the way out the door. And so, Aaron's fictional lady getting ready for a date questions whether to wear the Jeffery Campbell black flats with ankle strap or the Steve Madden red low heel pumps. Ugh, she ponders, everyone's wearing Maddens, so maybe the aqua Vans? Too old school. She resists the comfortable Doc Martens because they make her look like a folk-punk, thrash-grass rock star. The brown leather thigh highs from Nordstrom's? It's not Han Solo season. She commits to the heels. Decides on a matching purse and the hard part is done. Changes her mind back to the black flats but likes the red purse better. Decisions, decisions. Hell with it, she thinks, and goes with the Cole

Haan loafers because they match nearly everything, even her straight leg 505 Levi's, which she is determined to wear, but she'd have to lose five pounds to fit in comfortably and instead selects the beige slacks. She hesitates when she sees a flowery summer dress and grins widely because it hasn't fit since high school but she'd never toss it because she wore the dress to an amusement park on the last day of summer when she kissed her first boy, his mouth tasting of grape popsicle. Next, she ponders a low-cut T under a plaid, long-sleeved shirt with sleeves rolled up to the elbows. She tries on her Eminem baseball-style cap, backwards, and laughs out loud while starting over. Push-up bra, obviously not the new Victoria's Secret Dream Angels, that's more of a third date bra, but the JC Penny light brown push-up, and matching panties. Shoot, those are both in the hamper. Going with the black panties, she tells herself, but they don't match the bra. Screw it. Looks in mirror. Big mistake, she realizes too late because she's seen the flab. Performs ten standing crunches, vows to swear off pumpkin-spice lattes for the next week, and puts her pants back on. Jeans it is, and a cotton T-shirt with an ironically-iconic, Eighties hair-metal band logo like Def Leppard or Poison or Twisted Sister. Completes outfit with a slightly worn, tan leather jacket and twirls twice in front of the mirror. Hair ok, butt looks good, shoes…ugh, shoes! Seriously, loafers with a leather jacket? Ugh! Her phone beeps twice, and she races out the door since BFF #1 is waiting on the sidewalk out front.

Aaron wondered if a burka might not be a whole lot easier. And they say Western women are free.

The prospect of dating overwhelmed Aaron as he reclined on the wobblily couch after Zoë's return from her friend's house. The thought of her imminent departure to college and his impending solitary status depleted his hormonal reserves and left him unbalanced before bedtime. He was anxious about falling asleep because of the inevitable battle between cortisol versus oxytocin in which the outcome was always the same. Aaron would awake crying.

Morning tears, his only bedtime companion. Aaron's sixteenth therapist had explained how the excess cortisol was like the connective tissue between vivid dreams and depression, and the numerous reasons why Aaron woke up in tears, from

    too much cortisol, from

        adrenal glands panicking, from

            excess anxieties, from

> over-reacting to eustress/distress all day, from
> dream-time expanding seconds into years
> and waking up exhausted, from
> > excavating the geological layers
> > of the psyche.

Tears greeted him most mornings because his brain was slowly flooded overnight by the stress hormone cortisol. The overactive adrenal glands produced a fight-or-fuck response within Aaron as he slept and his mind would panic in an overworked REM state. Anxieties would be replayed in his dreams, stressful situations magnified in the temporally distorted realm of dreams, stretched from momentary seconds in real time into fantastical years. Thus, every morning he would wake up tired, nay exhausted, and anxiously sad, nay devastated.

Excavating the geological layers of his psyche through the night left him with two types of stress, one called eustress, a good type of stress, and the other called distress, the not-so-good-are-you-kiddin-me-this-isn't-normal type of stress. Both stresses were endured throughout his day, yet again producing too much cortisol, thus repeating the cycle. This repetition triggered a release of more stress hormones which caused Aaron as the host to respond with either fight or flight;[62] but pitifully, he could not physically exert himself by fleeing or through combat to expel the cortisol from his blood stream since he was asleep and thus the hormone flooded his brain, causing vivid, awe-inspiring, poetical-lyrical-spiritual inspiring dreams that were the envy of cheery folks who slept peacefully.

His twenty-fifth therapist, after a particularly difficult session about parental abandonment, gave Aaron a pamphlet which announced in bold red, white and blue letters, "Cortisol is public health enemy #1."

Underneath the patriotic message, the pamphlet's author recommended five ways to lower cortisol levels without medication.

The first Ah—to wake up and hit something. Hit it hard, with a stick to create a solid *thwack*. The adrenaline produced by this fight response combats the corruptive cortisol. Aaron destroyed two lazy-boy chairs before he found a slightly torn heavy-bag made of canvas in the alley behind a boxing gym.

The second Ahh—to take ten deep breaths while in the shower. Aaron started the day by showering before work which usually ended with him lying in the tub without the drain plug and letting the water rain upon him for many minutes and when he stood up too quickly, he'd get dizzy and so the flush of oxygen helped clean the cortisol and the pressure in his diaphragm helped stabilize his blood pressure, yet this daily procedure also made him chronically late for work.

The third Ahhh—to have friends and sex. Not to have sex with friends, a sure way to sour a friendship, but rather to make friends or to make love. Oxytocin, which Aaron mispronounced as oxy-toxin because it sounded toxic instead of the correct oxy-toe-sin, is known as the cuddle hormone produced after an orgasm. It can also be created in small doses when forming deep, personal bonds with friends such as via phone calls on the suicide hotline. Aaron suspected he acted selfishly by working for the Crisis Hotline Center as a way to produce his own source of oxytocin while providing the same hormone for the depressed, anxious, nervous, over-whelmed and suicidal.

And women, too.

The fourth Ahhhh—to scream until his vocal cords burned, to laugh loudly when he cried, and to physically excise through exercise his daily bleak outlook upon waking. Which is why, Aaron figured, people went jogging in the morning, but never personally an option for him because that would entail getting his ass out of bed.

The fifth and final Ahhhhh—to verb, the masculine remedy for depression. All the points listed on the pamphlet could be summarized as To Do Something, requiring action like orgasmically squirting a Windex bottle. However, the only movement Aaron could muster was to turn on the radio when he woke up, hoping the melody would both elevate and motivate but seeing how music often molds to the mood instead of changing it, Aaron never tuned to the Country station and preferred Heavy Metal as his morning coffee.

Aaron, having depleted his emotional reserve by watching *The Bachelor* and wallowing in single-status self-pity, checked on Zoë one last time. As a parent, universal calmness only occurred when his daughter was either eating or asleep. Retaining a local semblance of fleeting contentment, Aaron headed to bed without any intention of ever finding a girlfriend. Because listening to heavy metal and screaming loudly and talking on the phone with friends and breathing in the shower and hitting a bag with a stick seemed a whole lot easier than   going   on   a   first   date.

Chapter 11

Seducing with Divine Goddess, Set II,
Despite Hesitations for the Last Time

The morning greeted him with a brief session of uncontrollable sobbing. Aaron heard Metallica on the radio, crawled out of bed, took a long shower/bath, hit the punching bag with a walking stick fifty-six times and drove up to Denver so he wouldn't miss the second day of the seminar since he'd been a little busy the day earlier. And that's where he met Janice D.

Aaron parked in the vast garage of the downtown Marriott Courtyard hosting the Suicide Assessment Five-step Evaluation and Triage annual seminar. The highlight of the second day was a Death & Dying Workshop, a class designed to guide professionals as well as family members through the Five Stages of Grief. After such an arduous week, he was excited about the topic mainly because he wanted to learn more about those professionals with the highest rates of suicide, like white male dentists because of the exposure to lead fillings and easy access to prescription meds which inevitably leads to addiction, both reasons taking a toll on their sanity; and, white female therapists because listening to people bitch all day would certainly drive anyone over the edge; and, Black male cops because of the real possibility of shooting a Black boy who looks like their own son weighs heavily on their conscience; and Black saleswomen because dealing with rude, entitled, angry, old white women every day is definitely the worst job, ever.

Sitting in his car, Aaron reached into the glovebox for a blue lanyard, proof that he was a crisis worker attending the conference. Nurses wore yellow lanyards, the color black for doctors, white for the clergy, green for school counselors, and pink for cancer patients. While staring in the rearview mirror and adjusting a striped purple tie he'd found last week at the Arc Thrift Store, Aaron admitted to himself that he was not attending the conference for professional reasons. He'd signed up to cope with Eve's imminent demise. Thinking of his grandmother's death caused him to remember the personification of Death from his wedding dream. The same dream from merely two days ago that seemed years ago, time flowing neither backwards nor forwards but in mutable directions. Dreams linger, and so Death and Despair stalked him.

Before heading into the lobby of the hotel, Aaron leaned back against the driver's seat. He closed his eyes as the image of Death in a wedding veil blended over his grandmother's face. He suddenly recalled yesterday's lunch with Eve. He had sat across from his grandmother at the diner across the street from the Presbyterian Church while she repeatedly smoothed the red and white checkered, plastic tablecloth.

After ordering a Ruben sandwich, Eve began with her usual opening. "Darling, how's the world treating you?"

"Worse each day."

Eve countered. "Not as bad as it is for me. You try being ninety-six."

"You don't look a day over ninety."

"Raise your hand if I've already told you this one," she said before reciting her favorite poem. With Alzheimer's, Eve knew there was a chance of repetition. Anytime she told a story, she'd ask Aaron if he'd heard it before but of course he would never raise his hand. He loved her too much to interrupt.

"Grow old with meeee.

The best is yet to beeee.

That's a bunch of S-H-I-Teeee."

Aaron laughed and as they waited for sandwiches, Eve asked, "How's Helena?"

Eve had always called Lena by her full name, Helena. "Grandma, we got divorced years ago."

"I'm sorry, I forgot. Do you at least have a girlfriend?"

"Rarely."

"Dear, you have such a good heart, any woman would be lucky to have you."

"But I've got a bad soul."

"Have you found a girl you could spend the rest of your life with?"

"No," Aaron teased her, "but I've found one I could spend the rest of the night with!"

Once, Aaron had introduced Eve to a girlfriend. While appraising the woman, his grandmother had said, "She's nice but which one is your *favorite* girlfriend?" Aaron spent the remainder of the evening explaining to his girlfriend that Eve suffered from Alzheimer's. However, Eve suspected the truth because Aaron was indeed dating three women, an excursion he found to be like simultaneously riding a bronco and conducting an orchestra while performing open-heart surgery.[63]

As Aaron took a sip of water over lunch, Aaron knew Eve was pressing him about girlfriends because she hoped he would someday give marriage a second chance. "You'll get re-married someday."

"Why make the same mistake twice?" He wanted to explain to Eve that marriage was an antiquated institution that turned people into property, like the institution of slavery. Marriage kept people confined like the federal institution of prison. Marriage taught people to conform like the institution of higher education. Marriage beat people down like the institution of law enforcement. Marriage drove people crazy like the mental health institution.

She dismissed his joke. "You'll fall in love again."

"Only if I fall in line."

Despite their jokes, or maybe because of them, Aaron felt Eve was the only one who understood his anguish. Maybe that's why she paid for everything, he thought, to lessen his burden. When the check arrived after lunch, Eve magically produced two lavender-scented twenty-dollar bills from her jacket and handed them to Aaron. As they left the restaurant, she said,

"I'm ready to go to the other side."

"It's time for me to go Upstairs, dear."

"Help me get there?"

With a sigh, Aaron held her hand. "Not yet."

*

At the Death & Dying Workshop, Aaron entered the dimly lit conference room with a projector illuminating a pull-down, white screen. Even without the lights on, Aaron sat next to the most beautiful woman in the room, a natural instinct he wasn't even aware of until a few years ago. An unconscious act for Aaron, and it didn't matter if the woman was married or single. He always situated himself near a handsome woman not because of a delusional desire to sleep with her, but rather because ugliness is drawn to beauty. Also, he sat next to a superficially beautiful woman because he wanted to display confidence such as, "Listen here, I know you think you're hot and every other guy will be scared to make eye-contact or sit near you, but hell, I'm gonna saunter over nonchalantly and sit my ass down and introduce myself," which Aaron hoped would be the best approach to meet Janice D.

Janice D. was not her real name but instead the *nom de plume* written on the name tag above her right breast upon a mauve blazer matched with beige dress slacks. She was toying with a brochure that had been handed out at the door by a pair of elderly volunteers that were possibly the speaker's parents because what parent doesn't love hearing their child speak in public. The brochure announced the self-help title in bold 26-point font, *Death & Dying: What It Means and What You Can Do About It by Dr. Simon Trowel* followed by a slew of initials B.S., M.D., Ph.D., and that he minored in biochemistry at Gonzaga and double majored in psychology and forensics before attending Med school at blah blah and post-Doc work in dementia and osteoporosis, and a sport climber on weekends who mounted the dome of El Capitan in under six hours and Aaron knew this guy was full of S-H-I-Tee and said so to Janice D. the moment they shook hands, her honest little laugh and a slight touch on his forearm alerting Aaron to the possibility that she was a) single and b) yes, interested.

After his spontaneous introduction, Aaron placed one hand on the chair next to her without asking *is this chair is taken?* because it obviously wasn't, thereby shooing off the other middle aged, slightly balding and paunchy divorced psychotherapists and clinicians that were circling Janice D. but lacked cojones like stag boys at prom.

They continued shaking hands, he standing above her, and he asked what the D stood for, trying not to stare down her cleavage but the well-placed name-tag and height advantage certainly gave him ample opportunity.

"The D stands for Death," she purred and he laughed without letting go of her curved and properly limp hand.

"Then Janice is for the Greek god," he said, "like Janus," purposely drawing out the *oous* syllable and she nodded, not letting go of his hand until long after Aaron had sat down.

"And your name, Mr. No-name tag?"

"You got me there, I tend to avoid badges," Aaron explained. "I'd rather introduce myself the old fashion way. When people simply shook hands and asked each other their names." He examined the brochure with feigned interest.

"You're not going to tell me your name?"

"Not yet."

She laughed a pretty little laugh that Aaron though might be charming for about the first three weeks of a relationship but then became utterly disparaging once the recipient discovered she only laughed like that when faking it.

"Fine," Aaron continued, "but I'll show you mine only if you show me yours."

Her eyes widened in mock horror and fanned herself with the brochure. "Why, how presumptuous of you, good sir, isn't that a bit too soon? For heaven's sake, we've just met!"

Aaron's pulse jumped. She's got a quick wit and a sharp mind, he thought while observing her bright green eyes and dyed reddish-brown hair to hide the grey. He noticed lines around her eyes that made her look both wise and sad at the same time.

"Right then, name's Aaron."

"Susan, but you can call me Janice D." They shook hands again, basically a convenient excuse to touch each other.

"Great, we're going steady now?" Aaron asked. "Wanna wear my letter jacket?"

She chuckled at his lame joke, and an adorable smile emerged that Aaron believed this time was real. She coughed lightly into a handkerchief.

Aaron read aloud from the brochure which asked rhetorically, "Is someone in your family dying?" Aaron nudged Janice D., imitating a clinical demeanor. "Are you sad? Remember, Depression is not a normal part of the Grieving Process. Sadness, yes, but not Depression. Because the sad, albeit normal, grieving person does not have a low self-worth."

Aaron looked up and winked at Janice, "Normal, right. Since when is sadness the new normal?"

"Since Trump."

Aaron smiled and knew they'd have lots to talk about. The brochure continued with a quick outline of the Five Stages of how to deal with a dying loved one. Each line was short enough to fit on the page without spilling over for the purpose of saving space. This Dr. Trowel, among his many accomplishments, was a connoisseur of efficiency:

Denial—The first coping mechanism. Don't abandon them.
Anger—Discover the source of their anger. Death is scary.
Bargaining—Begging for time to resolve issues. Issues = tissues!
Anticipatory Grief—Be present and listen. Sadness is normal.
Acceptance—Enjoy every day. Today is a good day to die.

In the margins of the white paper, he made little notes about the Five Stages of Grieving in relation to suicide, since everything Aaron read, including Gibbons' *Decline and Fall of the Roman Empire* as well as *The Wizard of Oz*[64] seemed relevant to suicide. Aaron's fascination with suicide was career-driven, and like every other professionally-minded man, he was caught in the intellectual undertow of his work, like a physicist who sees Uranium 238 neutrons IN the dots of his 1st grade daughters connect-the-dots homework when she says, "Look Daddy, it's a clown;" and, the Pakistani radiologist, after staring at x-rays for hours, can only see broken femurs IN the tree limbs while walking through the park with his Indian intern boyfriend who smokes unfiltered Camels; and, the civil engineer who sees only a sine/cosine wave function necessary for the stability of a cantilevered bridge IN the frosting of a chocolate cake at his son's birthday party.

Aaron scribbled in the margins of the brochure while joking with Janice. "Tell me, what's the difference between dying and death?"

"The first you can have sex with, the other won't put up much of a fight."

"I like the way you think, but no. And dear God," he said, drawing his hand to his chest in surprise, "that's terrible!"

"I know. Thank you," as she took a little bow in her seat. Aaron received another glimpse at her name tag/cleavage/red bra with underwire, not a generic push-up but Victoria Secrets' very own Dream Angel Lace. Memory flashed of his grade school teacher.

"All I know," Aaron said with a smile, "is that dying is like dating. Way more fun with a partner."

"With that," she said, "I most certainly agree," her hand brushing against his knee, more flirty than slutty that for Aaron silently declared her intentions, which he summarized in a succinct mental list:

> Hi, my name is Janice and a) yes, you should ask me out for coffee after this stupid lecture is over; and b) yes, please open the door for me like women in the 1940s who were flattered

by the simple act of kindness and also, I'm a little needy and will lean into you when we walk to the coffee shop but I'm not overly-dependent or completely helpless so don't offer to carry my hand bag; and c) yes, I've made up my mind to have sex with you, so please don't talk about your ex-wife or ex-girlfriend or ex-boyfriend or pretend to be a walrus by putting straws up your nose.

Aaron allowed her hand to linger on his knee and with a nod he silently responded:

Hi, my name is Aaron and a) yes, I get it that you're in charge here and I'm man enough to be okay with that; and b) yes, I'll buy dinner after coffee and don't worry, it'll be a classy seafood restaurant that is both informal so you won't feel insecure about appearing underdressed and yet also expensive enough to show that I care; and c) I'll pick up the check after dessert while you're in the restroom and when you get back, I'll have your coat in one hand and the to-go box in the other as we head for the exit.

The last point was a neat little trick Aaron was convinced every woman knew because he'd been on a few dates when his partner would run off to powder her nose, with cocaine or blush, at the exact moment after dessert but before the bill had arrived, allowing him to pay without a fuss or pretending to reach for the check or the awkwardness of going Dutch on a first date, universally considered a boner-killer/vag-closer, a situation which required an absurd amount of alcohol to remedy.

Meanwhile, the lights dimmed further and Dr. Trowel began the lecture by troweling up a joke. "What's the difference between mostly dead and all dead?"

Aaron jumped up and spoiled the punch line by yelling, "Loose change!"

Aaron knew the doctor had stolen the bit from the classic film *The Princess Bride* and his interruption got a good laugh from Janice D. but only a scowl from Dr. Trowel. Aaron decided not to interrupt the next introductory joke.

"Not long ago," Dr. Trowel began, "I was working as a mortician in the Dade County Coroner's Office. I performed an autopsy on Mister Sam, a thirty-five-year-old African-American male who had died suddenly of cardiac arrhythmia. Upon removing the man's clothes, I made an amazing discovery. This Mister Sam had the longest penis I'd ever seen. I thought long and hard, no pun intended," Dr. Trowel said with self-induced canned laughter. "I realized there was no way I could send him off to be cremated. This was truly the biggest penis I had ever seen and had to save it for the sake of posterity. Sparing the gross details, I summoned my professional knowledge and carefully removed this tremendous member, my interest purely medical." Laughter from the crowd. Janice D. coughed again into a red handkerchief.

The doctor continued. "I placed the penis in a jar of formaldehyde and took it home to show my wife. 'I have something to show you', I told her, 'you won't believe what it is. It's the most amazing thing I've ever seen'. You should have seen the surprise on her face. 'Oh, my Gawd', my wife screamed, 'Sam is dead!'"

Laughter ensued and Aaron wondered why people laughed at jokes. Did social expectations demand compliance? Or did the anticipatory build-up throughout the story demand release, like an orgasm, upon the last line? Aaron could only summon three points as to the possible source of humor for this particular gag. First, comedians are convinced that audiences love dick jokes. Secondly, the joke was sociologically humorous because the Black man died stereotypically of congestive heart failure, the most common cause of death within the African-American community, caused mainly by a poor diet due to low income compounded with cigarettes, drug abuse and alcohol consumption. Thirdly, by combining two elements, dick and Black, thereby creating a big, Black dick joke which was important to the Caucasian audience because the obviously white doctor was castrating a Black male, reminiscent of the punishment elicited by a slave-owner, thereby eliminating the threat from his slaves of raping his very own wife and daughters. Or possibly this joke was funny because the wife had been banging a Black dude unbeknownst to the doctor, conjuring the even more frightening realization faced by every slave-owner of the distinct possibility that his wife was sneaking down to the slave shacks willingly, looking for that Mandingo-dick, a lustful craving on his wife's part utterly terrifying for the slave-owner despite the fact that he himself was raping Aunt Jemima in the kitchen and Sally H. in the upstairs bathroom. Aaron thought that perhaps the doctor could have ended—and received honest, social commentary laughter instead of trite, socially cliché laughter—with the observation that Public

Enemy's 1990 platinum selling album should not have been entitled *Fear of a Black Planet* but instead *Fear of a Big, Black Dick*.

He considered sharing these thoughts with Janice D. but instead said, "Great, another big, Black dick joke."

Janice laughed. "And what red-blooded, American girl doesn't like that?"

The lecture turned mundane and soon Aaron and Janice were overcome with compiled statistical data and percentages. After eighteen minutes of listening to Dr. Trowel, Aaron came to the conclusion that of the Five Stages of Grief in terms of suicide, the first step was the most dangerous.

Denial, the first step. The suicidal person[65] is DENYING life itself, utterly in denial of their mutable emotional state while denying past psychic pain.[66]

Anger, the second step. The suicidal person is ANGRY at their current life, uncaring parents, distant siblings, poor genetics, lack of children, ex-spouse, ineffective doctor, stupid dog, lazy cat, and they are utterly powerless to outwardly express that anger, turning the rage inward until it becomes depression.

Bargaining, the third step. The suicidal person BARGAINS with themselves by hoping that *It*, meaning the current crisis triggering their particular suicidal episode, will change. *It* will be better in the future if only they can change the behaviors of others, because it's so much easier to change someone else than it is to change yourself.

Anticipatory Grieving, the fourth step. The suicidal person experiences PITY, but only self-absorbed, selfish pity. They grieve for the loss of what their life could have been, and maybe a tinge of pity for those left behind, but that's doubtful since suicide is a selfish act because those with ideation are incapable of thinking of others. They can only focus on their own pain and the desire to end emotional/mental/physical suffering. Essentially, they are grieving for themselves.

Acceptance, the fifth and final step. The suicidal person has ACCEPTED their condition and is able to act by killing themselves, and their sense of relief is utterly glorious! The fear washes away and they are left with what can only be described as Calm Ocean.

Aaron knew from the many calls at the Crisis Center that acceptance is tricky because it's temporary. Sometimes, the suicidal person has merely accepted the idea of delaying the act for an hour or a week. And other times, maybe after their first or fifth or fifteenth failed Attempt, they are temporarily restrained from repeating the act of suicide because failure reinforces despair. Aaron wrote the difference between the two concepts at the bottom of brochure and circled it three times,

DEPRESSION IS INACTION / SUICIDE IS ACTION.

Suddenly, the thought made Aaron very horny. This was a predictable reaction, according to his fifth therapist, because thoughts of death often instilled a zest for life within the clinically ill. He remembered his therapist saying, "Sex is the affirmation of life, and sometimes you can even screw your way out of despair." Emboldened by this therapeutic motivation, Aaron quickly stood up and grabbed Janice D.'s hand. Together, they fled through the darkness of the conference room for the rear exit door. On the way, Aaron tossed the brochure into a wastebasket because he craved life instead death. Janice didn't resist possibly because she was bored by the lecture but Aaron wanted to believe she left with him because he was more interesting than Dr. Trowel. Sex, after all, was the greatest form of competition.

They skipped the coffee house, and the seafood restaurant, too, since Aaron had no money to pay, and drove straight back to her place. She leaned on his shoulder as they rushed along the sidewalk to her two-story brownstone. She didn't verbally invite him in and he didn't ask. He simply followed her inside after she opened the door.

They kissed and partially undressed at the entrance. Aaron didn't bother to look around at her choice of home décor as he struggled with her red lace bra, the rear clasp always a male-prone obstacle. She leaned away from him with her back against the wall.

"I should be honest with you," Janice D. said as she coughed again.

"Doesn't that talk usually happen afterwards?"

"I guess, but I want you to know why I attended the conference."

"Fine," he said, hands falling away from her exposed back. "Why, Susan?"

"Janice, please. Let's keep the illusion. You'll see why."

"Alright. Why were you there? Professional interest? A parent dying?"

"No, me."

"Me what?"

"I'm the one who is dying." She pointed to the handkerchief covered in blood.

"Oh… I see. Ooooh." Aaron eased away from her.

"Don't worry, it's not contagious."

He laughed and hugged her close for that's what he did when he was scared. "No, that's not what I was thinking. So, what is it?"

"Cancer."

"Breast?"

"Nah, already beat that. Ovarian."

"I'm sorry."

"Please don't. It's rare, really rare. A bilateral Krukenberg tumor. It's spread to my lungs now. Be dead in a few weeks, maybe even days. I'm lucky, I guess. Whatever."

"Ah, great. Denial. I see you learned a lot at the conference today."

"I've passed through that already. I've accepted my fate. That's why you're here."

"Why is that exactly?"

"For your big, Black dick!"

Aaron couldn't help but laugh. "This is a little weird."

"Then you'll love the next part. I've decided I want to die in bed. Having sex."

"Can you? I mean, can you do it with ovarian cancer? Doesn't it hurt?"

"Don't be ridiculous. You're not that endowed, the cervix basically stops you from going into my uterus. And if you're hitting my ovaries, then we're doing it wrong."

Aaron sulked. "Fine, whatever."

"Don't get bent out of shape," she laughed. "There's nothing more fragile than the male ego."

Aaron laughed. She was right even if he hated to admit it.

"You're right, sex did hurt," she admitted. "But then they took out my ovaries last year when I hit Stage Three. Then a hysterotomy and most of my liver and pancreas. Got a mastectomy just in case. See," she said jiggling her breasts, "these are fake."

"Losing your tits may have saved your life?"[67]

"I wasn't using them anyway. And my gall bladder and spleen came out when I hit Stage Four, then it moved into my lymph nodes and bones. My lungs are basically bloody, Swiss cheese."

While talking, they had sat down half-clothed on the wooden step that led from the hallway to the living room. Aaron's mind receded from seduction to the academic. "Why is it that cancer usually attacks the sex organs, right? Prostrate, breast, cervical, ovarian, anal…"

"Don't get any ideas, Buster. I don't play that game."

"No, I mean, oh, forget it." His face reddened, surprised that he was suddenly embarrassed. An essential source of his power when talking to women was that he waited for them to breech the topic of sex. He continued with only slight stammering, "What I mean is, well, maybe it's God's way of saying, 'I gave you a toy to play with and now it's gonna kill ya.'"

"Let's leave God out of this, OK? But you're cute, despite a morbid sense of humor."

"You're the one who wants to be fucked[68] to death."

"That not what I said! Don't make it sound like I want to be brutally raped by a horde of Vikings until dead."

"Vikings? Interesting fetish."

"No, I said I want to die while having sex, otherwise known as D.A.S."

"D.A.S.?" Aaron asked.

"Yes. Dick Assisted Suicide."

"Not sure I wanna be a part of this," Aaron said, backing away. "Sounds illegal."

"Not in Colorado. All I want to do is die in bed," Janice D. said, pulling him closer.

"In bed? You mean like a sixty-year-old business man who has a heart attack while cheating on his wife with his twenty-year-old mistress?"

"Exactly."

"Then who am I in this scenario?" Aaron asked.

"The pretty little secretary, obviously," she said with a smile. The finality of her request was undeniable and Aaron was aroused by her acceptance of death. Nothing was sexier than a woman taking control of her destiny.

"Fine," Aaron said with resignation since he was more than a little curious to test-drive his updated anatomy after the vasectomy. He hoped his Lincoln had not become a Lada. "So, we gonna do this or what?"

Her bedroom was elegant in that fifty-year-old-woman-sort-of-way who has been living alone for several years, either widowed or divorced or without a roommate, and has mastered the art of comfort. Beyond Bed decorations with titles like Home Elegance or Moonlight Dreamscape and a ridiculous amount of plush down-pillows, a silky comforter sewn with cloud mist, one thousand thread count Egyptian cotton sheets, a velvet sham to match the window dressings, everything in passion pink and Roman purple with streaks of heavenly aqua with no compromises for a masculine mate. Again, Aaron ignored the décor and scooped her up, realizing she was much lighter than she should be, an indication of her terminal illness. He gently placed her on the double-dutch red comforter, although more of a dark pink hue. They played for a while, clothes in various states of coming off and going back on in a pretend struggle of power, for the loser would be naked first, and they both knew this and took their time getting undressed. Finally, they reached a compromise and in between long kisses, disrobed each other simultaneously. She pulled his plaid boxers below his knees, while he lifted her hips and peeled away her Dream Angel red panties and together, they kicked off their own underwear in one fluid motion of flip-bend-twist-heel-lift-kick which wasn't as elegant as they imagined, more like engorged seals rolling on the beach.

Susan as Janice D. paused and as she spread herself for him, Aaron asked, "So, if you die while we have sex, would you mind terribly if I finish before calling for an ambulance?"

They laughed together, breaking the spell of forced romantic interest that precedes any act of discourse or intercourse. Easing the tension was important to him because he wanted something else from her besides her body. They laughed for a moment until she began crying, not sobbing but a subtle one-tear-and-chuckle-kind-of-cry that means, *I give up*.

Aaron was caught in the push-up position above her, but not inside-her yet and she not around-him yet. Aaron, observing her sadness as though from a great height, completely unattached and without empathy, thought at this point before his-entry and before her-reception, he didn't want to dominate her, or dance her around the room in various positions or show her a new-thing-or-two, or make her cum or explode on her or in her or with her, but instead he was getting exactly what he wanted. To see her completely exposed and naked and afraid and truly scared of dying alone. Only then did he make love to her.

Her little sobs intertwined with panting moans, and Aaron hovered uncertainly whether he should stop, but her long fingers with red-polished nails grasped his hips tightly as she begged him to continue. At first, she lay there like most gorgeous women tend to do. In such a woman's experience, the man has always done all the work, thrusting and busting and licking and bending and lifting and Working It until done, with minimal effort on her part. And Aaron wondered if he would even notice when she died. After the sobbing ceased and the moaning completely took over, she pulled him down onto the sheets and mounted him, fully surrounding him with each hip thrust and he was helpless under her intensity, rubbing her clit against his stomach muscles until she reached a thundering crescendo and then slowly eased the tempo, her petite feet resting on his calves, greeting each other mutually with hips, chest, eyes, lips, mouth, tongue in each motion, not like waves crashing into a boat but instead waves on a beach, the first receding from the shore and the other coming in with the tide and so he was no longer screwing her nor she squeezing him, but taking their time in unison.

Aaron worried about his performance after the vasectomy, but Dr. Capon had assured him everything would work normally. Two days after the surgery while taking a shower, Aaron had experimented with his equipment and found that he could maintain an erection. Yet, as he reached the point of orgasm, he felt like a leaky dam refusing to burst. The pressure built as usual but wouldn't release. After a longer period of manual encouragement and finally, to his relief, the levee broke with the same amount of seminal fluid as before the operation. Sadly, he didn't shoot as far although his man-sauce looked and smelled the same just without microscopic sperm in the fluid. He figured the sperm was being absorbed back into his body, like it always had done. For Aaron, the biggest change was mental because now he couldn't get a woman pregnant and he feared this new sterility would effect his virility.

Afraid of his orgasmic congestion, Aaron fabricated a lie by telling Janice D. that he had difficulty reaching an orgasm because of emotional blockage. He'd found that people didn't follow up with questions about psychic damage whereas they might be curious about physical blockage. Aaron was relieved when she neither questioned him nor cared about his emotional and physical condition. After she climaxed for the second time, because she was an experienced woman who knew how to guide-a-man-to-help-herself-get-off, Susan as Janice D. and Aaron as himself fell asleep in each other's arms and his final thoughts before lust-expired unconsciousness were whether or not he could screw this woman to death and if he did, could he finish?

When Aaron woke later, the sky had darkened. Aaron slid his arm out from under her neck without waking her and snuck out of bed to search for his phone. He texted Zoë to let her know the conference was running late and that he'd be back tomorrow. He didn't expect to hear back from her but figured letting her know was the parental thing to do. She'd probably take the opportunity to have friends over and he wasn't too worried they'd get drunk and invite boys over. He didn't worry because anxiety required uncertainty and he knew for a fact they would be partying. He only hoped they did the dishes.

Aaron returned to bed as Janice fluttered awake. They chatted about the conference and a few random details of their lives but nothing personal. Aaron didn't mention his daughter or his ex-wife or his dying grandmother and after three minutes, Janice shushed him with a finger and brought him to life with her hand.

Janice did all the things that Aaron pretended to like. She looked back over her shoulder while he was behind her and asked in a husky voice, "You like that?" Later, when he pinned her down, she said with determined opportunity, "Do anything you want to me." Next, she cried out the obvious, "I'm so wet!" and the desperate, "Take me!" and the hilarious, "Give it to me, big boy!" and the pseudo-feminist, "Make me feel like a woman!" but he paused when she looked at him with a smirk and said, "My turn to tie you up."

Aaron was curious and didn't resist the idea. "Why?"

"Because I gotta see if you can take it."

"Oh," Aaron said with confidence, "I can take it like a man."

"That's right, stud," she teased him. "You'll take it like a man…in prison!"

Aaron pretended through most of the night, focusing instead on her pleasure. When she asked him what he wanted, he confessed that nothing excited him more than when a lover whispered in his ear two magic words.

"And what's that?" she asked.

"Nothing gets me harder than when a woman says, 'I'm ovulating.'"

"You're so weird. Most men would run for the door."

"Maybe that's why I like it," Aaron admitted. "Those two words mean that my partner is a ticking time-bomb and I'm lighting the fuse. It's the risk that's exciting."

"Sorry, no kids today. They took out my uterus. What else gets you excited?"

"Men are easy,"[69] Aaron said, "but the really difficult goal for us is how to make a woman reach the big O."

"I'm so tired of that. It's like our orgasm is a project. I'm tired of men working on me. I'm tired of being a project."

"Let me guess, they'd bend you over the side of the bed and pound away?"

"Yeah," she said, "and I'd be screaming because unlubricated friction burns like Cleopatra's hot, sandy pussy."

He laughed when she called it her pussy. Such a non-threatening term, cute like a kitten. Had she said vagina, a word more akin to a man-eating lion, he might have been tempted to leave early.

"Alright," he offered, "here's what might[70] work." And since Aaron's erection made him a terrible listener, despite taking crisis calls for a decade, he said, "Let's have this project be about you, alright? Relax, we'll give it a try."

He leaned in and whispered in her ear because he knew anticipation is more erotic than the deed. "You lay in my arms and I'll caress your hair by running my short nails gently along your scalp while you vibrate your clit with that battery-powered, mini-massager I noticed atop your nightstand."

To her credit, Janice wasn't ashamed. She reached for massager and got to work. Aaron did as he'd promised, and the key for him was not to look bored. He didn't put a finger inside her because he might have accidentally bumped her right arm and moved her off the Spot that she'd been searching for over the last few minutes. When she looked up and asked if he was okay, he reflected the placid visage of a man who wanted to be there, cared about her, deeply loved and respected her. And he did not say, "Cum for me!" because that added unnecessary pressure and he knew Janice was a sexually-mature woman who had no intention of being rushed.

When she was done, Aaron took his turn and stashed any illusions of love & respect. He let the animal out and hid his face on her shoulder, refusing to make eye contact. The volcano built slowly inside his surgically altered testicles, but the plumbing felt clogged. The usual pressure seemed greatly reduced, the lava of his passion had been extinguished. Vesuvius had become a creek. From now on, his eruption would be a trickle.

Together, they reached a false summit. He could tell that Janice D. faked her orgasm because she was sore and wanted a nap, whereas Aaron faked a moan because he feared a painful and tepid explosion. After she fell asleep again, Aaron grabbed the remote and watched the game on television but he wasn't a sports guy and couldn't tell if the competitive engagement was NFL American Football, MLS Fōōtball, NHL Hockey, IBA or WBA Boxing, RFL Rugby, NASCAR, WWF, MMA, however he was fairly certain the game being played was not the NBA because he had studied basketball. Even though bored with the game, he didn't try to screw Janice D. while she slept because *Sleeping Beauty*[71] fantasies, besides being creepy and morally deviant, are considered rape in the second degree, a class C felony punishable of up to forty years in a glass-and-steel confined prison.

Aaron watched her sleep and concluded that she was the perfect woman. He could be totally honest with her only because she'd be dead soon. He'd always held back a bit of himself when with a woman, but with her he could let go and tell her everything. The dark secret of self-harm he'd endured as a teenager—the drugs and the cutting in a slow escalation of pain. Instead, he woke her up and said, "Let's travel."

"Where?" she slurred sleepily.

"Let's take a cruise. How about the Mediterranean? Italy. We'll get off the boat and drive through Tuscany while singing Puccini."

"I don't like opera."

"We could lay in each other's arms adrift a Venetian gondola."

"I get sea-sick."

"We could visit the isle of Capri and take the tram to the upper most vista and witness the emerald sea."

"I'm afraid of heights."

"Woulda been fun," he muttered.

"And I hate Italian food."

Maybe she wasn't perfect, he thought, but that was the problem. Aaron wanted every relationship to be perfect and gave up at the first sign of reality. But that didn't stop him from dreaming.

Aaron, in his quest to create a perfect night together, presented Janice D. with Divine-Goddess, Set II, the penultimate, 244th position of the Kama Sutra. Whereas Set I was far too subtle and could take up to a week to perform correctly, and certainly not Set III, much too rigorous for her fragile condition. The three sets required strength on the man's part and flexibility of all a woman's parts. He began by first washing his hands with mild hand soap like Caress instead of Dove which left a pasty residue. He approached Janice quietly and massaged her feet with rose water, but since she seemed to be out of rose water—difficult to secure outside of a Turkish *hammam*—he instead applied scented massage oil that he had discovered behind the mirror of the bathroom cabinet. Then, Aaron moved his hands up her legs to the back of her knees and then to her thighs and the entire time whispering to Janice D. his intentions in the third person, like, "Then he rubbed his thumb against her wet pussy," and said *pussy* like he was ordering a poussey-fouissey at a fancy French restaurant.

With Janice D. laying comfortably on her back surrounded by feather pillows and her body covered by a silk white sheet to keep her warm, he came up onto his knees and sat perpendicular on the left side of her slightly oiled body and kissed her deeply on the mouth, then lightly on her neck, tongue teasing around the ear lobes but not directly in the eardrum, then back to her mouth and sucking her lower lip, retreating when she pressed into his mouth, the whole time with his left hand slowly rubbing his way up her thigh in small circular motions and then onto her pubis by tracing the edge of her trimmed pubic hair. When she was ready, he quickly washed the oil from his hands and switched to a water-based lubricant before gently spreading her lips apart with two fingers and placing them barely inside her, curved gently upwards, then plunging a little deeper inside, inch at a time, without rapid or jerking motions, toying with her G-spot[72] in tiny circles then pulling out to gently press on her sensitive U-spot,[73] then plunging deep and hard to her hidden A-spot[74] and lastly retreating completely and settling with his thumb upon her swollen clitoris.[75]

Janice D. was finally prepared for an introduction to Kama Sutra position #244, otherwise known as Divine-Goddess, Set II. Aaron slowly placed his index and middle finger inside her to caress the raised patch of her G-spot, using his thumb in an alternating lateral and circular motion atop her erect clitoris, while the fore portion of his left ring finger he placed pressure against her anus and left it there for the remainder so as not to contaminate her urethra, leaving his pinky finger with nothing to do but stick out at a weird angle and occasionally catch on the bed sheet. While his left hand was completely occupied, Aaron slid his right arm under her neck so she was supported by the inside of his elbow as he reached down to caress her right breast and occasionally lightly pinch her nipple. Every so often, he would squeeze his right arm, compressing his bicep against her carotid artery and his forearm against her jugular vein, restricting blood flow and causing her to swoon, a word Aaron especially appreciated from the days of Lord Byron or Charlotte Perkins Gilman and her yellow wallpaper, when feinting couches were especially made for "hysterical" women. Aaron preferred this technique to outright choking with a clenched grip which would have only focused on her windpipe to produce a slower swooning effect as well as completely restrict his right hand to that one constrictive act, whereas the beauty of the Divine-Goddess, Set II, was the maximum utilization of *his* entire body to please *her* entire body, which he admitted was a bit selfish since he gained so much pleasure from her helplessness. Meanwhile, he managed to stiffly rub the soles of her feet with the instep of his foot which had to be firm because any light tickling would have been counterproductive at this point. He kissed her on the mouth and moved his right hand from her breast to her head and gently raked the scalp with his fingernails, then collected a handful of her hair and pulled hard, causing her neck to arch backwards and involuntarily open her mouth while compressing her neck with his right elbow. With her mouth open, he sucked on her tongue before rotating his entire body to suck on her clitoris then up to her nipples and switching back and forth every few minutes between her swollen lower lips and her mouth. Aaron resisted the temptation to keep her on the edge for hours but since she could die at any time, he allowed her orgasms to crash frequently. The Divine Goddess was pleased.

Before dawn, Janice D. passed out again. Aaron grabbed a terry cloth robe from behind the bathroom door and stepped out onto the chilly balcony and looked over the city. Her house was located in a fantastic spot near Cheeseman Park. She must have done well in her career, although Aaron had no idea what she did for work. He figured she might be a nurse or psychologist because he'd spied a pack of cigarettes and an ashtray upon a small iron-wrought table. He lit a cigarette and enjoyed the frosty view.

When he came back inside, she was dead. He knew right away, didn't even have to search for a pulse. Her eyes were wide open, staring up at the ceiling. He pocketed an empty prescription bottle found in her left hand because he knew that's why she had selected him. He hadn't picked her up at the conference, the choice had been hers all along.

He called for an ambulance and the EMTs removed her body on a stretcher. While responding to the questions from professionals who deal with daily death, Aaron never once thought about how he didn't get a chance to finish, or if she had been happy with him, or why she hadn't left a note to those people in the family photos scattered around the room that she had refused to mention, or if she had died satisfied, or how he would deal with this type of sudden grief and how many depressed hours under the table this would take to process, or if this would limit his ability to quickly erect a protective shield through The Process, or if he would see her face in the next woman he made love to and how long it would take him to get an erection next time, or if he might from this point on develop necrophiliac compulsions. None of this bothered him because Janice D. was gone and maybe he'd finally done something nice for someone else. He'd been a real man, he'd fucked a woman to death.

Episode 11.5

A Table Built from Trees
within Norton the Breathing Forest

Aaron skipped the third and final day of the conference and left Denver before dawn, driving at a very slow pace and refusing to pass anyone. The world moved too quickly and he needed to breathe. He needed control. Halfway up snowy Monument Pass, he got stuck behind a grandmother crawling along at 45 mph and Aaron smiled. The world raced except for the elderly because they knew the finish line was a grave. The grandmother, and he knew she had grandkids because of the baby seat in the back, finally pulled off for gas at the Piñon truck stop. Aaron listened to the entire first album of the British band Bush and decided to put *Glycerine* on repeat when he got home and spend a little time under the table.

Turning a one-hour trip into three, he arrived safely at home around 8 a.m. and found the house in disarray. Hurricane Zoë had struck, or what Aaron called El Torñádo. The kids had probably partied through the night, Aaron guessed, and since he wasn't supposed to be home until later, Zoë most likely was planning to clean after school. Aaron wasn't upset by the mess, in fact it gave him something to focus on. Something other than Janice D.'s dead body sliding into the coroner's blue body bag.

Aaron figured he had a few hours to sneak in a little mental breakdown and immediately began stripping away his calm by worrying about,

getting kicked out of the PTA meetings; and,

checking on Zoë's sliced finger for infection; and,

cleaning the fridge for Jocelyn's weekly delivery; and,

hoping Marilyn had taken her medication; and,

remembering to take Eve out to lunch; and, trying to forget Janice D.

He waited to clean the house as a way to dig himself out from under the table. He played an overly scratched compact disc by the band Bush but when the lyrics skipped at, "Must be your skin that I'm sinking in," he altered his selection by putting on *My Skin* by Natalie Merchant. He could listen to the first twenty seconds of her haunting voice on repeat for hours. Dear ol' Natalie was the modern version of

Mary Shelly because she exposed monstrous loneliness with her hypnotic words,

> *As if I'm becoming untouchable*
> *the slow dying flower*
> *in the frost killing hour.*

Natalie's voice reminded him of the time Sylvia Plath was pulled from the cellar, a limp bag of bones after she tried to kill herself the first time, retold in her poem *Daddy*. To set himself in the proper mood, Aaron crushed three tablets of OxyContin and four Ketamines, snorting them to quicken the effects. Then, he crawled under the table and remembered the first time he met Norton . . .

Little Aaron is seven years old. He and his mother Marilyn receive news that Eve might be dead. A Carnival cruise ship specifically designed for the elderly, a luxury liner named *Memory*, has caught on fire and is sinking. The uncertainly of Eve's whereabouts causes a flurry of panic. Marilyn calls the corporate office, but they know nothing and suspect Eve is lost in *Memory*. Aaron worries about his grandmother and he suddenly develops a mild fever and cough. His mother decides to let him stay home sick from school. She tucks him into bed and gives him 40 ml of Children's Tylenol with acetaminophen. In her rush, she accidentally gives him twice the recommend dosage of Extra Strength Tylenol with codeine instead of the medicine for kids. Marilyn believes that prayer will save Eve and so she leaves for church. Twelve minutes later, Lil' Aaron begins his first journey on a synthetic opiate. His pupils constrict, his breathing becomes shallow, his pulse races. A *feng shui* crystal ball hangs in the corner and splinters rainbowed light on the wallpaper. The wall becomes a forest, long strips of bark lined together to create an alpine scene in early fall, golden tips of quaking aspen, vibrant emerald pine needles, straight paper birch trees shedding white skin. The ceiling throbs with forest fauna, flexing outward and sucking him into a land where ravens squeak, mice caw, leopards gurgle and fish roar. Lil' Aaron wonders if this is how the world really looks, maybe he's seeing clearly for the first time. He confuses the effect of the medicine for a spiritual revelation when he hears a voice. The voice is the sound of the neighbor's motorcycle revving. Lil' Aaron has seen the motorcycle many times. The motorcycle has the name *Norton* printed on the side of the gas tank. Aaron thinks the name is funny. The voice and the scenery blend to form one supreme entity.

"Are you ready?" asks Norton the Breathing Forest.

Lil' Aaron squirms in bed and struggles to speak, his tongue stuck to the top of his mouth. "Ready for what?"

"Are you ready to kill yourself?"

A new voice announces, "Not yet."

The response is not Lil' Aaron's but rather another voice coming from under the table. Aaron is forced to choose between two battling entities, Norton the Breathing Forest or The Friend Under the Table. Lil' Aaron throws the blanket off his sweating body and constructs a fort under the table with pillows and sheets. Within the warm colored cloth hanging down around him, he is safe. He is home.[76]

. . . while Aaron listened to *My Skin* on repeat, effectively urging him forward to a place he couldn't achieve merely with pills. Laying on the floor underneath the table with only a few hours until Zoë returned home, childish fears arose accompanied by a ringing in his ears and a darkening of his vision. His stomach cramped and every muscle began to ache, his woes psychosomatically driven.

The troubles arrived in waves, not as a tsunami but rather small ripples with a calm interval in between each cold shock. The Process allowed him to be an outside observer, and he preferred water symbolism. When forced by a therapist to convey more terrestrial images, he would relate himself to the epicenter of an anxious earthquake with trembling shockwaves. When forced to emit fire imagery, he'd say his flaming thoughts occasionally subsided into dull embers.

Lying immobilized on the carpet, he felt compelled to run. To run so fast his thoughts couldn't keep up, running right out his house and down the street and out of town, escaping the psychic, psyche-ache pain, self-loathing hatred, inwardly-directed anger, and guilt of disappointing Eve and Lena and Marilyn and Jocelyn and ultimately Zoë, the last thought keeping him glued to the floor because immobility was better than running away.

Burning a small Calm Ocean candle beside him under the table, the scent eased him as the waves of uncertainty prepared to crash again. He worried about so many little details, but in that momentary respite between the tidal wave or earthquake or raging fire, he would focus on the carpet underneath his fingertips. His face inches away, he could see the lint and dirt in the space between the weave of the beige tight knit Berber carpeting stretched tight to the corners and he wondered how the installers managed to pull it so tight, imagining a time years ago when three men in overalls yanked on the ends. Aaron petted the carpet over and over again, the repetitive act distracting him as the waves passed, slowly releasing his breath until the panic subsided. Aaron turned over and laid on his back, staring at the underside of the oak table. He read an engraved seal that proved the table was constructed in a furniture factory outside of Burlington. A dark, walnut Vermont Farm Table set upon four 30" legs, and long enough to seat six guests or hide one prone guest, with round edges instead of a square-edge apron. The wood was covered with a plant-based, non-polluting standard oil finish instead of a dark stain. The natural wood always reminded Aaron of his first trip into Norton the Breathing Forest.

Aaron spent his time inspecting the underside of the table, laying on his back and gazing up at the irregularities within the wood grain which offered more detail than a starry night. The view also meant he didn't have to go outside. The grain told a long story of a tree abducted from Norton the Breathing Forest, a tree that had witnessed many years, from a seed punching its way through the ground to a flimsy stalk to finally towering above the other trees with birds singing in its branches until lumberjacks wearing plaid arrived with axes. The grain felt smooth as Aaron traced a finger along the circular patterns left by 100 grit sandpaper. The dull finish on the wood offered no reflection, preventing Aaron from any sort of introspection, letting him dwell upon the pristine nature of the underside as opposed to the topside. The damaged surface above had numerous scratches from keys and dishes and glasses and bongs and pens and screwdrivers and the clutter of life. The underside was a fresh start. Clean. And that's why his mind dwelled under the table, even when out in the world.

While under the table, he viewed the mortise and tenon joinery fastened tightly with wooden pegs. The inter-connectedness and simplicity of wood provided a safe haven. An isolated island that limited his decisions and simplified life because the greatest dilemma was whether to lie on his back and stare at the walnut grain or turn onto his left hip until it ached forcing him to roll over onto his right side or lie completely on his stomach atop the soft, tight fibers of the

Berber carpet. Four simple body positions inside a four-walled room without walls, the space between the table legs creating an illusory barrier, with a slab of wood above to shield from the overhead light bulb.

Time passed without moving, a version of stationary time as in time-within-confinement. Then another wave broke the détente. Aaron feared Zoë was in danger, at this moment, falling down stairs or getting bullied at school. Sadly, he knew she was safer at school than at home in sight of his episode. He only had a few hours left, and so Aaron tried to explore the trigger for his trip beneath the table. He ignored his physical senses melting to a focused point and instead reflected on the moments leading up to the present. Shuddering from the overwhelming details of Janice D.'s demise, he realized she had nothing to do with his pause from sanity. He had rendered himself utterly helpless in a selfish act of mental instability.

He reached past the self-loathing blame and discovered a darker secret. To confront this obstacle, he would need help, professional help. Aaron grabbed the phone and called his twenty-ninth therapist who always reminded him that he was only acting crazy, very different from being crazy, although she began every session with, "You know you're crazy, right? Now, let's get started." He made an appointment for the next morning, about seventeen hours away and he took a pad of sticky notes and began to count down the 1,020 minutes, and marked off the minutes as they passed for about half an hour until he grew bored scratching on paper and threw the pad across the room and called to cancel the appointment. He reminded himself that he'd been down frequently, and if he could only stop crying, he might survive.

His grandmother Eve would whisper in his ear in rough times, "This too shall pass," but Aaron's twenty-third therapist assigned to him during a brief stay at the psychiatric ward had informed Aaron that his mental condition could progressively worsen over the years. Each episode would degrade the sheathe covering the cerebral synapses. He'd decided that the shrink was lying in an attempt to convince Aaron to take the pills. Anti-psychotics and anti-depressants and anti-emotion drugs that dimmed the brain and dulled the pain. That particularly grueling visit to the psych ward with a seventy-two mandatory internment was when he developed an overriding fear of doctors for taking away parts of his peace. They took his blood and temperature and pulse but they never gave it back. When they tried to take his insanity, he fought back by burying it. Over the years, he let it out in small ripples instead of one big splash.

Aaron also learned to bury his depression by hitting the re-set button of his brain. First, he'd rub the mastoid process behind his ear then work his way up the temporal bone to the base of his skull at the first cervical vertebra called the atlas and press with both thumbs into the external occipital protuberance. The cranial sacral massage released magical powers, or at least Aaron thought since he didn't understand the dynamics of SomatoEmotional Release, but the technique induced a twenty-second pause like hitting the on-off switch of a glitchy computer, and Aaron called this massage trick *My Little Death*.[77] This was not an Elizabethan euphemism for orgasms,[78] but instead a respite from the cycle of unhealthy and racing thoughts. *My Little Death* was his way to avoid taking the mood-stabilizers and anti-psychotics that he'd resisted at the psych ward because they made him ill, and Aaron wondered what sick person in their right mind would ingest poison? However, Aaron argued with himself, had he been in his right mind, then he would have remembered that when he had the flu, he went to the doctor's office for medicine. When he'd contracted pneumonia three years ago after smoking twelve dabs of shatter from a gravity bong in a moldy bath tub, he'd taken antibiotics to cure the infection. If he so readily accepted aid for his physical health, then why did he resist help for his mental health?

During every minor depressive episode, Aaron managed to convince himself that he only needed *My Little Death* and a little time to relax after exhausting the mind through self-examination and exhausting the body through exercise and exhausting the spirit until it crashed against the wall of consciousness. Sometimes, the deception worked.

Suddenly, after performing *My Little Death* while under the table listening to *My Skin* for the 87th time,[79] Aaron recalled the elusive trigger that had led him into an emotional break down. He'd blocked it out since returning home.

He had been driving back from Denver, stuck behind the grandma for miles, jamming to Bush when his cell phone rang with a call from the Denver County Coroner's Office. The young coroner who had placed Janice D. in a blue body bag wanted to report to Aaron that he'd done a preliminary autopsy on her body.

"That was quick," Aaron responded.

"Well, I'm calling out of a sense of professional courtesy. After all, we work in the same field."

"You mean," Aaron said, "my office supplies dead bodies for your office?"

"Precisely. I thought you'd like to know that I've found no signs of foul play. She was taking so many medications, would be hard to determine morbidity. I've signed her death certificate as dying of natural causes."

"Thanks," Aaron mumbled as he removed Janice D.'s empty prescription bottle from his pocket and lobbed it across the room into the trash can.

"But," the coroner added, "standard protocol demands we test the urine of all females for the human chorionic gonadotropin hormone."

"Meaning what?"

"She was pregnant."

Aaron threw his phone into the couch. My little death, he thought. The death of his unborn child.

At 3:55 p.m., five minutes before Aaron guessed that Zoë would be home from school, Aaron buried the grisly revelation. He screamed from deep within his diaphragm, so loud his vocal cords would be raw later, and he pounded his fists on the ground until his sliced knuckle split open again, and pushed himself off the floor and crawled out from under the table. Realizing he hadn't eaten since yesterday, he searched the fridge for meat, slices of cheese and a loaf of oat bread. When Zoë barged in a few minutes later with some friends to help her clean the house, she apologized for making such a mess and took a bite of his turkey sandwich.

Aaron hid his unstable, mental condition and escaped for a walk while they cleaned the house. He thought about Janice D., the pregnancy and wondered if she had lied about her hysterectomy. Had any of her stories been true? When he returned, a note left by Zoë explained a Friday night sleep over at her friend Cāste's house. Relieved, Aaron instantly fell apart and climbed back under the table. *My Little Death* awaited him.

*

Months passed in a flash and Aaron spent more and more time under the table. He grew a scruffy beard with flecks of grey and even though already skinny, he lost weight. Marilyn and Jocelyn tried to fatten him up, but he ate only cereal and ramen noodles. Zoë started sleeping most nights over at Crow and Thyme's house so Aaron had plenty of time to do absolutely nothing. In late spring, he received a message from the Poinsettia that Eve had fallen on her way into the dining hall and fractured her hip. Aaron let Jocelyn and Marilyn deal with her recovery, but he believed their efforts were useless because he knew Eve's lack of mobility meant death was imminent. His visits became less frequent as she quickly deteriorated. He ignored Lena's calls and sparsely responded to his daughter's text messages. He stopped answering the door for his mother and aunt. He rarely left the house. He missed many days of work and had a voice mailbox full of threatening messages from Boss Lady and bill collectors. Spring slid into summer and still Aaron could not forget Janice D. until Zoë surprised him one morning in search of a rainbow.

Chapter 12, part I

Seeking Rainbow

With a plea, the adventure began.

As the summer sky brightened, Aaron heard Zoe's car pull into the driveway. He crawled out from under the table and pretended to be sleeping on the lumpy yellow chaise lounge. He couldn't bear the idea of Zoë finding him curled up in a ball on the floor. Zoë woke him like she did when six years old, tiptoeing into the room and jumping on his belly. The impact was manageable when she weighed a mere twenty pounds but hurt considerably now that she was sixteen, although he'd never let on because one of his greatest joy was that they hugged afterwards. Given the conflicting nature of boundaries experienced by teenage girls in high school, he'd be lucky in a few months if Zoë would even let him touch her. Soon their contact would be relegated to pats on the shoulder and high fives. He missed the days when he rocked his newborn daughter in his loving arms.

"Come on Dad, we have to go have to have to have to, we just have to go!"

Aaron rubbed his sleepy eyes. "Go where exactly?"

"Utah! The Rainbow Gathering, in a national park, on top of the highest mountain in the whole state, with rainbows and naked, pot-smoking hippies and drum circles, don't worry, you know I don't do drugs, and we just need a tent, maybe some food, and one parent to go as a chaperone, and the other dads were like, 'What the heck is a rainbow?' and they're so much older than you and they've got real jobs, like lawyers or doctors, and besides, you don't have a real job…"

"A real job?"

"You know what I mean. Answering phones isn't a career." Like most children, Zoë had a dim understanding of her parent's employment. Besides, Aaron was a protective father and never shared the troubles and trauma of working at a Crisis Center. She had problems of her own, a place harder to navigate than the realm of dealing with suicidal, chronically-depressed, anxiety-driven, maniacal psychopaths. A place called high school.

Zoë continued. "Besides, I told Thyme and her sister Crow and they got reeeeally excited and Crow's girlfriend wants to come along, you remember Alanis, right? And of course my best friend Cāste."

"Wait, what?" Aaron rubbed sleep-dried crust from his eyes and wiped away the image of Janice D. that still haunted him every night.

"And we can leave right now since we don't have any pets!"

"What about the goldfish in that little aquarium by your bed?"

"Died last week."

"And the turtle?

"Dead."

"And the hamster?"

"Dead."

"And the snake?"

"Choked on the hamster. Dead."

"Wait," Aaron asked, "what about the dog and cat?"

Zoë smacked him on the shoulder. "Blind cat and bad dog? Wake up already! Mom got them both in the divorce."

"Oh, right." He missed those stupid animals.[80]

"Come on," she begged. "Get up! Thyme has a big tent and we'll chip in for gas money and pack in a bunch of food and Cāste said she went last year with a busload of homeless guys and they didn't even need food cuz it's like freakin paradise up there, so can we can we can we go? Come on, get up already!"

Aaron sat up. "Hold on, what did you say about pot?" Zoë smiled, knowing her father was kidding because she was the reason for his sobriety. She'd caught him smoking weed out of a three-foot glass bong when she was twelve, coming home early from the movies to a skunky odor lingering in the living room. Zoë's friends thought it was cool that her dad got high, but Aaron promised himself right then and there that he would try to live a sober life. For years, he'd hidden his drug addictions from his daughter but when she asked him, "Do you smoke weed?" he couldn't lie to her and they spent the rest of the evening talking about drugs. Told her the difference between LSD and XTC, between PCP and GHB, and that the difference between coke and crack is probation for a white man versus ten years in jail for a Black man. Told her that he would stop smoking marijuana because dope made life harder, made him stupid, soft, slow and worst of all, not present. Told her how accepting troublesome emotions is much easier when sober instead of numbing with alcohol and weed. He hoped his honesty would prevent Zoë from becoming a stoner. Of course, Aaron admitted, he'd be the last one to know.

Aaron continued, "And we'll need a bigger car if we're taking...wait, how many girls are going?"

"Ugh, details!" Zoë screamed in delight as she ran upstairs to grab her backpack. "Come on, daddy, get up. We gotta pack the car! It'll be fun, I promise!"

When she came downstairs fifteen minutes later, she was wearing a purple t-shirt with *Feminist as Fuck* on the front side and denim capri pants. Aaron didn't make a conscious decision to leave, he simply put on a pair of black jeans, black boots, and a grey t-shirt. He found an old hammock in the basement and stuffed it with a ripped flannel jacket and a blanket. Zoë pushed him out of the house and together they drove to her friend's house.

Outside of a ramshackled farm house, several teenagers were loading up an old, white Ford Taurus station wagon with a dented front grill and rusted body. The automobile was owned by the mother of Thyme and Crow, whose name escaped Aaron but was something like Saturn or Jupiter. They would have left sooner but the tags were expired and they had to wait for the mother to head down to the court house and wait in line on a Friday morning—with everyone else who took off Friday morning to stand in line at the court house—for expired tags near the end of the month. While he waited, Aaron explored the car and lifted the hood, checking the engine like a dependable parent, one who is responsible for a car load of teenagers driving across the Great American Desert. However, he immediately closed the hood after the hoses reminded him of Medusa. Everything looked fine until he read 314,781 on the odometer and turned the ignition to hear the grinding of the automobile's six cylinders, casting doubt on the success of traversing mountain passes and smoldering deserts. Searching for the proof of insurance only revealed a roach in a glass jar, not the kitchen scurrying-out-of-the-light variety of roach but instead a half burnt, poorly hand-rolled, stinky-wacky-tobacky kind of roach that Aaron instantly recognized.

Aaron confronted the mother about the weed when she returned from the court house with an updated registration card. She wore flip-flops and a bathrobe decorated with pink flamingos and palm trees, and Aaron imagined the clerk's laughter at seeing her waiting in line.

"Listen here, Saturn ..."

"Planetary Illumination."

"What?"

"I've changed my name."

"Again?"

"Yes, and please don't dead name me."

"Ok, what is it now?"

"Planetary Illumination of the Mysterious Plane."

"P.I.M.P.?"

"Well," she said with a frown, "I hadn't thought of that. Now I'm gonna have to change it again."

Frustrated, Aaron asked, "Whatever, are there any more drugs in the car? We're traveling to Utah and weed is illegal over there."

Her eyes grew big as she exclaimed, "Headed into hostile territory!"

"Also, the car has only three working seat belts. And the inside smell like a swamp."

"I don't think there's anything else in there," P.I.M.P. said unconvincingly. "Besides, I don't smoke weed anymore. Ever since it became legal a few years ago."

Aaron pointed to three large cannabis plants growing next to the tomatoes. "What are THOOOSE?!"

P.I.M.P. shrugged her shoulders. "I eat it now. Smoking is bad for your lungs."

"Ugh!" Aaron threw up his arms and went back to helping the girls load the car. When he stuck his head inside, he wrinkled his nose and asked, "What's that swamp smell?"

"Herbert was caught in a flood," Thyme replied.

"Sorry your dog got swept away. Did he die?" Aaron thought perhaps they had brought home their drowned mutt in the back of the car and never vacuumed out the wet dog hair.

"No," Crow answered for her sister, "Herbert the car."

"Nice to meet you, Herbert," Aaron said, shaking hands with the steering wheel. He turned to the girls and said, "There are lots of famous Herberts. My favorite is the name of the sea-lion that saved Kevin Hines after he jumped off the Golden Gate Bridge."

"He survived?" Crow asked with amazement.

"Barely. He doesn't recommend it."

"Well, we named the car Herbert after the author of *Dune*," Thyme explained. "It's my favorite book."

Apparently, Frank Herbert[81] had history. He was part of the family, like a withered uncle with decrepit knees. The car wobbled while idling with mysterious wiring patterns and the radio crackled static from a broken antenna and the cassette player had been jammed with bubble gum. Aaron sighed when he realized there'd be no music on this road trip. The receptacle for the cigarette lighter sparked occasionally, the bulb was burned out in the dome light, and the headlights flickered when Aaron pulled the knob. Aaron wondered how poor ol' Herbert was supposed to carry six vagabonds on his aching back across the state line and home again. Reminiscent of the Ancient Chinese proverb, Aaron said to himself, "We'll see."[82]

With the tags renewed and the insurance located, Aaron tossed the roach and kicked the tires. He tried to check the oil, but couldn't find the dipstick. He looked under the car and saw thick, black oil dripping out, which reassured him that the car did indeed have oil. Zoë and the other girls gathered supplies from the house and filled the car with food and ready-to-go backpacks, because Colorado teenagers always have a pack/sleeping bag/hiking boots stashed in their bedroom corner, ready to head out at the first mention of a campfire. Aaron was convinced that six backpacks and six people would never fit in the same vehicle, already jammed with two bass ukuleles, a six-string Martin acoustic guitar, a steel five-string banjo, a pair of matching tambourines and a wooden djembe drum that P.I.M.P. said she'd picked up in Brazil but looked more like an order from Amazon. Also, thrown into the car were various homework assignments and pre-calculus books that Aaron was certain would go unread. Thyme brought a collection of mismatched rubber flip-flops and Crow gathered her neon-hued leather sandals. Aaron insisted on a huge bag of Wild Habanero Cheetos whereas Cāste wanted granola with raisins and Alanis pleaded for granola without raisins. Zoë packed a folding knife and two colors of hair dye, raspberry blue and royal magenta. They found a four-person tent to sleep five girls, as well as gallons of fresh water, six wooden bowls and utensils, fifty feet of hemp rope, a box of graham crackers, three bars of dark organic chocolate, one 100oz bag of over-sized marshmallows, and a sack of ripe avocados for something Aaron had seen the girls devour in mass quantity called *Guac on Toast*.

Working as a cohesive unit, the girls threw the backpacks on top of the car and strapped down the luggage in an elaborate system using two forty-foot, self-tightened black nylon straps. First, the straps were crisscrossed beneath the roof luggage rack then around the first pack, tightened and held firm by a double hitch and onto the second pack and interlaced to the next and so forth until the gear was conglomerated into a compact pile and firmly secured atop the buckled roof of poor ol' Herbert.

After Thyme and Crow hugged their mother goodbye, the Rainbow Warriors were ready for an adventure. Pulling out of the driveway, P.I.M.P. yelled to Aaron over the busted muffler, "Have fun, and bring everyone back!"

As Aaron waved goodbye, she reached in through the window and latched onto his arm like an overly-protective, sandal-wearing, vegan lamprey. "Promise me."

"Sure, whatever," Aaron said, yanking away his arm. "I promise."

Around noon, Aaron's little Rainbow Family departed amidst loud celebrations of glee with only one U-turn a few miles out for a wallet accidently dropped in the driveway. Over the first few miles, Aaron initial suspicion of a road-trip without music proved wrong. A broken radio did not equate to silence. Crow and Thyme, each with matching nose rings and gothic black hair, banged on the tambourines. Alanis, with a headful of dreads, played a ukulele. Cāste, in overalls and a stripe of magenta dye across her moon face, plucked on the banjo while Zoë jammed on the guitar. The girls sang an acoustic version of Badflower's *Ghost*, strumming off-key instruments all the way out of town. The lyrics of the song, "I tried it once before but I didn't get too far," gave him an idea for a game they could play later. When the power-windows buzzed at mile ten of their journey and refused to lower, Aaron foolishly believed the air-conditioning might work. Adding to his horror, he discovered today's teenagers continue to smoke cigarettes despite the warning labels and the older generation's vast research and litigation to prove harm—completely ignored by their kids. The girls had no problem chain-smoking unfiltered cigarettes in one hundred plus degree weather where the high desert plains meet the Eastern slope of the Rockies in a car without A/C. The car door windows were operated by a goofy electrical system, leaving a window halfway up or down until hitting a bump in the road and slightly jarring the correct wires half an hour later at which point the glass continued its downward or upward journey, convincing Aaron that ol' Herbie Hancock danced to his own tempo. Incessant cigarette smoke drafted from the front of the vehicle and out the hatchback window wedged slightly ajar by a tie-dyed handkerchief while exhaust fumes wafted into the vehicle. Aaron wasn't sure what would kill him first, instantaneous lung cancer or carbon monoxide poisoning.

For his own sanity, he quickly gave up control and let Zoë drive. He had no intention of driving the whole way. After all, this was their trip and he was lucky to be invited. Aaron sat in the back and taught the girls a few classic riffs on the guitar. Zeppelin, Marley, the Stones, Steppenwolf, Bowie, the Doors, even a little AC/DC.

"Ay-cee what cee?" asked Cāste.

"Holy crap, what are they teaching in school these days? Goes like this," Aaron said, strumming the first cord of *Hells Bells* but accidentally flowing into *Smoke on the Water*.

"Hey, that's Deep Purple," Alanis shouted. "My grandpa loves their stuff!"

Great, Aaron thought, another reminder that I'm old. As if being surrounded by teenagers singing acoustic, emo rock wasn't bad enough.

The enthusiasm of a new journey quickly evaporated. The girls grew quiet, putting away their instruments and taking out hair brushes and books. Suddenly, he heard music coming from the second row of back seats. Alanis had brought her cell phone and a portable speaker.

Fearing he'd be subjected to hours of America's Top Forty hits, Aaron presented a distraction inspired by their knowledge of Badflower's suicidal lyrics. "Hey, let's play a game."

"Like what?" Thyme and Crow asked together.

"Let's only listen to the music of rock stars who have completed suicide. We'll take turns naming a band and someone else gets to choose the song."

Alanis laughed. "That's weird, but I like it. Ohh, I could make a playlist called Dead Man's Chest."

Zoë shrieked from the driver's seat. "Ugh, Dad, not this again. What's with you and suicide? Remember last winter when you sent out suicide notes from famous actors instead of Christmas cards? Grandma Marilyn didn't like that."

"Let's do it," Thyme shouted. "Let's play Dead Man's Chest!"

"That sounds cool!"

The other girls overruled Zoë, and Cāste spoke up first. "Obviously, we start with Nirvana."

"Good one. Kurt Cobain was twenty-seven. Blew his own head off with a shotgun. Nobody was surprised. Shocked, yeah, but not surprised."

Alanis played the beginning of *Negative Creep*. Quickly, the girls became bored and started shouting out band names to test Aaron's knowledge.

"Soundgarden."

"Yah, that one hurt. Chris Cornell strangled himself, not much older than me, with exercise bands in a hotel bathroom."

"How could you not see that coming?" Cāste said peering at the phone over Alanis's shoulder. "They've got a song here called *Like Suicide*."

"True, but *I Awake* is the best. Best first line in all of rock n' roll."

"What's that?" Crow asked.

Aaron sung in a deep voice, unable to match Cornell's lyrical majesty, "Woooke up de-preeeessed."

Crow laughed, "I can relate. Oh, what about Linkin Park?"

Aaron sighed. "Chester hung himself right after Chris. Two of the best, gone forever."

The girls couldn't think of anyone else. Aaron took her phone and flipped through Spotify. He played the first twenty seconds of a song, told them the name of the musician and how they had died before moving on to the next song. He knew their attention span couldn't endure an entire song.

"Nick Drake died of a drug overdose at twenty-six...oh, this one is Joy Division. I think you'll like it. Ian Curtis was twenty-four when he hung himself in his Manchester kitchen...both guys in Badfinger hung themselves...the lead singer of Boston...the guitarist in Fleetwood Mac...the keyboardist for the Grateful Dead slashed his own throat...then there's Bored Nothing. They had this song named *I Wish You Were Dead*, guess it came true...Oddly, the glam-punk band named Suicide never lost any of its members. How about some jazz? Anyone like jazz?"

The girls looked around the car like he'd spoken Latin. They were familiar with the word but had no idea of the meaning. No one responded. Crow had nodded off, her head crooked at an uncomfortable angle but the other girls were awake and listening.

"Check out this incredible jazz artist named Donny Edward Hathaway. Right before dying, he said that some white people were trying to kill him and had connected his brain to a machine in order to steal his music."

"Sounds paranoid."

Zoë chimed in. "Sounds like something The Man would do."

Aaron continued. "What about Wendy O. Williams? She was the lead singer of a punk band called The Plasmatics. Wendy was a radical female singer back in the Eighties. You should check her out."

"Sounds like a freakin role model."

"I don't know about that. She tried to kill herself back in '93 by hammering a knife into her chest."

"Ouch!"

"But when the knife got jammed in her sternum, she changed her mind."

"Ya'think?"

"She tried again a few years later with an overdose of ephedrine. The blade and the pills weren't working, so she eventually shot herself."

"That's sad."

Cāste opened a bag of granola, the one with raisins, and asked, "What about Led Zeppelin?"

"Well," Aaron said, "now it gets complicated."

"What do you mean?"

"Is an accidental drug overdose the same as suicide?"

"Of course not. It's just an accident."

"But," Aaron pushed, "what if all they wanted to do was live hard, do a ton of drugs and leave behind a pretty corpse?"

Zoë laughed. "I'd call that being young."

"I see," Thyme said. "Like self-destructive behavior, right?"

"Exactly. Sometimes these rock gods kill themselves slowly."

"Like who?"

"I don't know," Aaron said. "All of em!"

"So, what about Led Zeppelin?" Cāste asked again.

"Fine," Aaron relented. "Ask anyone my age or older who's the greatest drummer ever and they'll say John Bonham. Even the magazine *Rolling Stone* agreed. He had tremendous endurance, a lightning fast right foot, and a grasp of the groove. But ol' Johnny was a mighty alcoholic. The day he died, he'd downed forty shots of vodka."

"So, how'd he die?"

"Choked on his own puke."

"Gross."

"And as for the best guitarist, Jimi Hendrix, please tell me you've heard of him."

"Yeah?" the girls said uncertainly.

"He didn't play music, he created sound. Heavenly riffs and futuristic solos with unmatched flare and charisma. He died at the age of twenty-seven."

"27 Club!"

"What?" Aaron asked, acting confused. He wanted to hear their version.

"You don't know about 27 Club?" Zoë asked.

"They were all twenty-seven years old," Thyme said.

"Yeah," Cāste added, "Jim Morrison and Janis Joplin and Kurt Cobain."

"And the trippy part," Alanis said, "is that they had white Bic lighters in their pockets when they died."

"Curse of the white lighter!" the girls screamed.

"Hate to break it to you ladies," Aaron said, "but I don't think Bic was making disposable white lighters back in 1970."

"Oh."

"And Brian Jones died at twenty-seven, too."

"Who?"

"Started the Rolling Stones. He and Jim Morrison both died on July 3rd, about two years apart. One in a pool, the other in a bath tub."

"That's weird."

"Dad, you're such a downer," Zoë said, smiling at him in the rearview mirror.

"Don't you mean *drowner*?" Aaron said, laughing at his own joke.

"How'd Hendrix die?"

"Well," Aaron finished, "his friend Monika gave him nine barbiturates to help him sleep, which was like eighteen times the prescribed amount. And he was drunk."

"Let me guess," Alanis said. "He choked on his own puke."

Aaron figured he had dominated the conversation enough and stared silently out the window as the girls talked among themselves. Since they wouldn't make it to Rainbow before nightfall, they decided to stop and camp overlooking the confluence of the Green and Colorado Rivers. While the girls set up their tent, laughing in the dying light, Aaron played the djembe under a piñon pine tree and silently watched the flowing waters of the two mighty rivers. The sounds of the drum reminded him of when he had traveled after college, a trip paid for by Eve, when he stood on the tip of Africa and watched two oceans slam into each other, one calmer than the other, while penguins played upon the beach. He had cut his trip short after only a week because after traveling to the edge of the world, he had found himself still hopelessly alone. Now years later, far from the Cape of Good Hope after too many nights under the table, Aaron watched from atop his perch along the canyon wall as the lazy Green River joined the turbulent Colorado in its journey to Mexico. He'd read recently that the river was sucked dry before reaching the border, transmuted into Los Angeles/Las Vegas illumination. By the time he went back to camp, the girls were giggling in their tent. Aaron slept outside on the ground atop a colored Mexican blanket, like a loyal guard dog.

In the morning, a coughing and sputtering Herbert Hoover[83] delivered the six campers high up and above the clouds, along dusty roads, sliding on unmarked gravel twisting through the national park to a vast dirt parking lot filled with 70s era VW buses that were still running, not just the engine but also running from the law, and also banged-up Ford pick-ups loaded with long-haired hitchhikers, paint-chipped Toyotas with bald-tires scrapping their low carriages along the dusty path, 80s hatchback Hondas with bumper stickers announcing "I Brake For Hallucinations" or "I Want To Believe" from the X-Files or "What a Long Strange Trip It's Been" from the Grateful Dead, and even a few Hyundais that must have strained four cylinders to *think I can, think I can* up to the top of the peak. Aaron parked the struggling Herbert West[84] along the tree line, choosing a tall pine hopefully indicating some type of orientation to be found again days later amongst the thousands of abandoned vehicles decorating the hillside.

Crow and Thyme unburdened the roof of luggage while Zoë, Alanis and Cāste divided thirty granola bars, twenty pounds of rice, ten pounds of lentils as well as gallons of clean water, the tent bag, various footwear, and stringed instruments. Aaron grabbed his meager gear of a checkered flannel jacket, blanket and hammock. The girls packed and repacked their already stuffed duffels, occasionally stopping to braid each other's hair. Aaron took two naps until they were ready.

With Zoë in the lead, followed by Cāste, Alanis, Thyme, Crow and Aaron bringing up the rear, they hiked out of the improvised parking lot and into the mountains for five torturous uphill miles. Following a wide dirt path lined with floral delights which were ignored by Aaron who instead was shocked by the variety of human fauna littering the road to the mountain top: college kids on summer break, ravers jittery from EDC in nearby Vegas, New Age gurus in ripped jeans, yoga moms, aging hippies with knee braces, hordes of unsupervised filthy-faced brats, cash-deprived Burning Man rejects, the bearded homeless with Army rucksacks mixing with the clean-shaven, wealthy weekend warriors in Adidas track suits and hauling REI topline, exterior frame backpacks. Also hiking up the hill to Rainbow were ascetics handing out pamphlets discussing the benefits of veganism as well as bald disciples of Hare Krishna in orange robes.

With thousands converging on federal land, the National Park Service hired a slew of employees to monitor the swelling masses. Aaron overheard two park rangers on his way up.

"Look at these bums. Didn't think there be so many!"

"Damn hippies."

Aaron laughed. The annual income for most of these visitors to Rainbow probably surpassed the combined salary of the two state employed park rangers.

Aaron briefly worried that the girls wouldn't make it to the top as he found himself struggling under the hot summer sun, the high elevation squeezing down on his lungs. And yet, the girls didn't complain once. No bitching, no fighting, no excuses. Tougher than a platoon of Marines, without pause, right to the top without even a water break. For this was their adventure, not some parent-derived expedition to drag them into nature and away from their iPhones, where every teenager asked, "What are we supposed to do, exactly?" Those Family Weekends always failed because parents were dragging the girls away from their boyfriends and gal pals to spend quality time together—to do what, exactly? To cook hormonal hot dogs on a propane stove since climate change had forever pushed the fire warning into the red and campfires were no longer allowed. To sit around in the dark smacking away mosquitoes. To be bored, lonely and isolated with over-protective parents who didn't understand them—to do that, exactly.

Aaron understood this was the girls' adventure and at Rainbow, they knew exactly what to do once they heard the greeting announced by every member of their new family of ten thousand, "WELCOME HOME."

Not a simple "Hello," or "Hey wassup girl," or "Hiya cutie," or even a nod but a heart-felt, "Welcome home." At first, Aaron was put off by the greeting, seemingly forced and uttered by a bunch of perverts using it as an excuse to talk to and check out and give the up n' down stare to his crew of young ladies he'd sworn to protect and bring back neither dead nor pregnant. Yet, he was starting to understand that they weren't *his* group of girls because they could protect themselves. Perhaps the exhaustion of the hike wore down his fear, but Aaron felt something new, as in some new Thing inside him as they emerged from the forest path and into the great expanse of Rainbow's peak, ten thousand smiles linked with laughter, smoke curling from rock-lined campfires, and a thousand congas, Navajo war drums and goat-skinned goblet drums pounding in unison Rainbow's collective heart. The pure contagious joy steadily beat into him and the girls acknowledged the greeting and responded in kind by dropping their packs and racing through the tall grass and Aaron found himself dropping to his knees as though in prayer, grasping the dirt with tears in his eyes and saying aloud, "Welcome home."

Not merely words, but a real, soul-embracing pronouncement of the truth that at long last, after searching his whole life, he had finally made it. Destiny had brought him here to dwell amongst his real family. Welcome home. Welcome to the earth and the sky. Welcome to a field of Blazing Star flowers and Blue Bells beneath tall Cottonwoods and wide-eyed trippers sucking on long strands of Mormon Tea, thousands and thousands of glorious souls celebrating life together, and growing each day. Thousands of his sisters and brothers hugging and kissing and dancing naked and walking barefoot in the dirt, safer than he'd ever imagined possible, more freedom than offered by booze or weed or pills or television or any other distraction. Everyone singing,

"Welcome home Sister,

Welcome home Brother,"

and he believed the words. Aaron witnessed the change in the girls—in their posture, in their eyes, in their hearts, for they were all learning how to love again.

Zoë and her four friends searched for a flat spot to camp as Aaron watched where they pitched their tent, placing his hammock in a tree that was neither too close to impeded their freedom nor too far to prevent their security. Although he trusted them to look after each other, he stayed close by. Just in case danger appeared in the form of hungry grizzly bears or a pack of wolves or a horde of horny, frat-zombie-guys or cult leaders or creepy pervs or creeping rapists or meteors and earthquakes and flash floods or even the rare Polynesian cultist who sacrificed young virgins to Pele, the Volcano Goddess. Aaron remained alert because he knew that at Rainbow, anything can happen. Since the girls craved independence, he feigned absence to give the illusion of space. Space, the desperate plea of every teenager and so he gave the girls some space—he became the watchful sun, a satellite, an eye in the sky, an orbiting asteroid that could intervene at any moment.

Aaron experienced the first night without pills, hallucinogens, booze or weed. He was offered White Widow, Golden Goat, OG Kush, Sour Diesel and many other strains of marijuana, but responsibility and sobriety were more important than getting high. He felt that here, of all places, he didn't need any drugs. He was also surprised to find Rainbow in a state of prohibition. Alcohol was the White Man's Curse that made every college stud rage instead of chill, and the lack of beer allowed Aaron to worry a little less about his daughter's troop.

He hadn't seen the girls in hours until Zoë ran back up the hill and told him they were hanging with new friends down at Lovin Ovens or Rainbow Crystal Kitchen or some such place and not to worry, and so he began to relax, trusting his neighbors, starting to forget the fear-mongering instilled by the media. He was able to breathe again. He fell asleep in his hammock, drums beating and crowds howling in the distance. Embraced by a magnificent dream, Aaron viewed himself over-the-shoulder, moving and talking as a third person character . . .

Aaron sees himself sitting alone in a dilapidated train station, cold and cracked cement floors, dark alleys stretching out from the platform. An empty train arrives and he boards alone. At each stop, a few people join him. Each new station offers decaying décor, but the painted walls turn from drab to colorful the further he travels. The wallpaper becomes more elaborate and the platforms brighten as the number of travelers swell at each stop. An unseen presence leads the crowd from station to station. At first, it is a formless essence, yet as the miles race by, SHE begins to manifest from a voice of bliss to a dancing, swaying loveliness, waiting at each stop. SHE is guiding him from the Insane World of Civilization to the Rainbow Gathering of Light & Love. After a long journey, the train-travelers arrive at their destination with people from around the globe, a million in total. And SHE who has led them with such grace and beauty of movement disappears before he can see her face. The masses disembark and climb high into the mountains, some people mounted on hairy neon mules, others riding upon the backs of friends. At the peak, Aaron discovers a glorious meadow a thousand miles wide, full of waist high blossoming blue milkweed. SHE, the elusive unseen force, appears again and is waiting, beckoning him closer with arms outstretched, naked and free. Her smile is bright as the sun, a smile that Lifts Up Your Spirits. She is Mother Gaia, a combination of every woman he's ever loved.

. . . and Aaron woke in tears because he missed every single woman he'd ever known as he muttered to himself, "What have I done to drive them away?"

He stretched and stood up from the hammock, the moon nearly full and high above him. He had to take a piss and thought about relieving himself in the trees, but bodies were littered everywhere. Tents had been erected every few feet and people slept on the ground in between. He walked quietly to the make-shift bathroom which was a latrine pit about five hundred yards from the main gathering of a thousand tents. Drowsy and using only the moonlight to guide him, Aaron accidentally bumped against an old man coming around a large tapestry hung to give the latrine a bit of privacy.

"Hay, wadch whar ya goin," the old man cried out.

"Sorry, didn't see you," Aaron apologized. "I've never been here."

"T'aint whar ya been buts whar ya goin."

The ol' Coot's mumbled words lingered as Aaron wandered back to his hammock. He stopped at a campfire on the way and told some wide-eyed nearby trippers around their campfire, "A wise man once said to me, 'Life's not about where you've been or even where you are going, but instead where you are now'." The acid-addled hipsters howled in joy and wrote down the words in their journals of hand-made, Tibetan, acid-free paper. Aaron promptly forgot the entire event and went back to sleep.

The waking dawn revealed a sleeping Roman army encampment. Aaron strolled barefoot around tents pitched merely feet apart and wondered why humanity tended to clump together. There were always the exceptional cases of those lingering on the outskirts, hidden among the trees, but most people huddled near one another for protection and convenience. Thousands of people living on top of one another created several health concerns, mainly clean water, hot food and proper sanitation. Examining the overview, Aaron witnessed the nature of how a Roman army must have sustained itself but instead of shield-and-sword soldiers, Rainbow nurtured peace-and-love warriors.

The main concern of any large number of people traveling in unison has always been fresh water. Rainbow achieved this by tapping into a pristine river and channeling the water via hundreds of meters of temporary PVC piping. Several weeks before the event, Rainbow engineers had arrived and ran the piping from a clean water source to a dozen man-made taps where attendees could draw fresh water. These taps where the basis for each individual kitchen later constructed by the next cluster of pre-Rainbow engineers. These kitchens varied in theme, such as the abundance of Lovin Ovens, the joy of Bliss, the lassitude of Fat Kids, the nakedness of Jah Love, and the Christian loaves at Bread of Life.

Aaron returned to his hammock and heard the girls stirring in their tent. He decided to leave them alone and ate breakfast nearby at the kosher kitchen of Home Shalom. He sat with four New York City Hassidic Jews who welcomed him with a jubilant, "Shalom!" Aaron ate an onion bagel but refused their kosher, organic, psychedelic-mushroom-omelet. Flashbacks of his near overdose that resulted in the Wedding dream prevented him from partaking, but he was amazed at the copious amounts of powerful hallucinogens consumed by the Hasidics. By the end of breakfast, Aaron was overcome by Talmudic knowledge and managed to slip in a single question. "Do you guys trip like this every day?"

The long-bearded men whispered in confidence before addressing him. "Except on the Sabbath, because even Elohim took the day off."

Aaron spent the day wandering adrift the vast spectacle of Rainbow, disrobing and joining a naked parade which ended at a game of baseball in a thousand-yard meadow, and as the day unfurled, Aaron discovered he was a master of many talents, such as spinning a fire-staff without burning his hair; and, hand-drumming in rhythm with one hundred pounding hearts; and, braiding the long, dirty hair of strangers; and, chanting holy prayers in Sanskrit; and; capturing fish with his bare hands; and, immediately guilty about watching the fish struggle for life out of the river, drowning in the air.

As Aaron grasped a flopping salmon, the ol' Coot he'd met earlier snuck up behind Aaron and asked, "You again?"

Aaron looked at the old man and begged, "Why does it struggle?"

"Why do you?"

"Because life is hard," Aaron moaned.

"Only because you make it so."

"I don't understand."

The ol' Coot smiled. "Look at the fish. It's easier to kill than to capture."

"Why?"

"Because like you said, life is hard. But death is easy."

Aaron released the fish into the river. He looked at his fingers swimming in the mountain stream and noticed the knuckle he had scrapped with a cheese grater many months ago was finally beginning to heal. He relaxed on a flat rock partly submerged by mossy water and breathed in new life. He dozed dreamlessly, one of the first times in many years.

After several hours, he meandered through Hobo Alley on his way to Tea Time. But he got lost and found some new colorful friends at Rainbow. With each new connection, his arc widened, expanding his consciousness. As the stars emerged, Aaron stumbled across Thyme and Crow spinning fire, Alanis bouncing across a slackline, Cāste teaching a yogi the real meaning of love, and Zoë playing a ukulele on stage at Granola-Funk Theater in front of a crowd of thousands. These scenes were the highlights for Aaron because as he was soon to discover, at the end of every rainbow is a pot filled with fool's gold.

The following day after the silent prayer session of July 4th, a contrast to the raucous of celebratory fireworks, Aaron rallied Zoë and her friends to make the long hike down the mountain to Gary Herbert[85] and drive back to Colorado in time for holiday with family. Although devastated at leaving the light & love of Rainbow, they craved the one thing missing from their rustic setting: a hot shower.

The girls stashed their gear atop Herbert Mullin[86] and said goodbye to the dozen boys who had followed them from the camp because as Aaron had learned, no matter how many girls are in a group, there will always be twice as many boys. Near dusk after many long-faced farewells, Aaron got behind the wheel as the girls played songs of universal love they'd learned around the campfire at Rainbow. A rare happiness washed over Aaron, but suddenly evaporated when he saw flashing lights in the rearview mirror.

Herbert Elliot[87] was pulled over by the police around midnight on Utah State Route 58 a mere fifty-eight miles from the border for a busted tail light. Of course, this was an obvious ruse for the State Troopers because they had several reasons to suspect Herbert Flam[88] was carrying contraband. For one, the car was leaving Rainbow and reeked of campfire, dirt, patchouli and body odor. More importantly, Herbert Williams[89] bore license plates from Colorado, a state that had legalized marijuana whereas the religiously-intolerant Utah had yet to be persuaded by dope's financial incentive.

Two Mormon cops moseyed up to the window and addressed the only man in the car. The officers were pale skinned doppelgängers with sharp features, greased-back hair and mirrored sunglasses, even at nighttime. To Aaron, they both looked like Agent Smith from *The Matrix*[90] and the illusion of his Rainbow-inspired happiness suddenly unplugged.

Agent Joseph Smith 1, grinning: "Well, well, well, what do we have here?"

Agent Joseph Smith 2, wrinkling his nose: "I think I smell some of that mar-ee-jew-wanna."

Aaron, the anti-Semitic hairs raising on his neck: "You wanna marry a Jew?"

AJS1: "What? No! He's already got four wives."

AJS2: "Besides, we don't marry outside the faith."

Aaron knew they didn't smell pot in the car. He would never be so stupid as to carry drugs in a carload of teenagers through Utah. He'd asked everyone to either smoke or leave behind any excess dope at Rainbow. Aaron knew the cops were merely stating a reason to search the car. He began to protest, but knew he was powerless because there's nothing a cop hates more than a hippie with an education.

In the light of a full moon, the two officers asked Aaron and the girls to get out of the car and sit by the side of the road as a K9 unit was released from the back seat of the patrol car and began to sniff the insides of Herbert from New Zealand.[91] Within seconds, the dog pawed at several different backpacks.

With powerful flashlights, the officers got to work opening the Rainbow luggage. In Cāste's bag they found two grams of Golden

Goat, Alanis had a fist-sized nugget of Sour Grapes in her sock, Thyme had tucked away a pipe filled with Danny Zuko, and Crow had a love letter from one of the dirty boys from Kid Village with a joint of Red-Headed Stranger. To Aaron's great relief, Zoë's backpack came up clean. At least his daughter had listened to his request to travel free of pot's potent portable paraphernalia.

Aaron wasn't upset with the revelation of the numerous discoveries. Each time the cops located a new source, they exclaimed like children at Easter opening plastic eggs to reveal candy. However, this venture revealed pot, pot, pot and more pot.

AJS1: "Got some pot here!"

AJS2: "Found more pot."

AJS1: "Wait a second..." He looked up at his partner with a serious gaze.

Aaron swallowed hard because he knew this was the look men give each other when a righteous hammer needed an anvil. When displayed on the faces of two pious, law-abiding, upstanding Mormon men of the community, the look meant somebody had fuckeÐ[92] up.

The cops withdrew a small, black case from a backpack and marched Aaron over to the front of the cruiser. With the girls seated on the ground and out of hearing range, the two officers placed the diary-sized leather case on the hood of the car and put hard questions to Aaron.

AJS1: "What's in the case?"

Aaron, innocently: "No idea."

AJS2: "How old are these girls?"

AJS1: "Who is responsible for them?"

Aaron, proudly: "I am."

AJS2: "Where are their parents?"

AJS1: "Where you coming from? Where you headed?"

Aaron sensed danger. The angle of flashlights cast long shadows on their faces and words emerged in slow-motion from the mouths of the two uniformed men. Over the next twenty-four seconds, a life changing series of events took place. Aaron knew the time span was exactly twenty-four seconds because he had watched plenty of basketball and the shot clock[93] was ticking.

AJS2 (*24 seconds and counting*): "What are you planning to do with these girls?"

AJS1, pivoting angrily: "Are you some kind of pimp?"

AJS2, assisting disapprovingly: "He looks like a pimp."

Aaron gazed down at his purple and red horizontally-striped Guatemalan pants, and an orange and yellow vertically-lined Moroccan hoodie. He wasn't sure where he'd gotten the funky outfit but dimly remembered trading clothes after the naked parade. He looked more like a jester than a pimp.

AJS1 (*18 seconds and counting*): "Maybe he's the leader of a cult."

AJS2: "You in a cult, mister?"

AJS1: "We don't like cults around here."

Aaron, blocking defensively: "I'm not in cult." He was tempted to expound on the rationale that the Church of Jesus Christ of Latter-day Saints was basically a non-Pepsi-drinking, big-underpants-wearing cult, but he decided such a tactic would not have improved his situation.

AJS1 (*9 seconds and counting*): "Listen, we don't mind the pot."

AJS2, passing kindly: "We see it all the time."

AJS1, posting up merrily: "Really, it's not a big deal."

AJS2, charging coyly: "I mean, who didn't smoke a little in college, right?"

Aaron, shooting hopefully: "That's great, so we're free to go?"

Agent Joseph Smith 1 (*3 seconds and counting*): "You would be, but…"

Agent Joseph Smith 2, dunking harshly: "Except for this."

The game buzzer expired in Aaron's mind as the first officer undid the latch on the small case and as the contents spilled out, time slowed even further as a hypodermic needle rolled slowly across the hood of the police cruiser. Then the concept of time had its way with Aaron, as in totally gang-banged him, and time stopped completely as one word filled his mind in large neon-buzzing letters: HEROIN.

Aaron's heart dropped like a three-pointer in overtime. The light of the full moon illuminated a spotlight on the hood of the cruiser as the rolling needle made a clunky sound with the plunger half out and black tar swishing inside the barrel. There was no denying the obvious, the needle meant Aaron had royally fucked up.

Chapter 12, part II

... with Herbert and Seven Hundred Bucks

Aaron was looking at eight-to-ten years in prison. The cops made sure he understood this. They demanded to know where he'd gotten the heroin, how long the girls had been strung out, and the location of the cult's headquarters.

"There's no way out of this," they told him.

Aaron also understood that since heroin was traditionally a Black man's drug, white privilege would not help him out of this predicament. He imagined himself being placed in handcuffs in front of his daughter, booked into the county jail, hiring a lawyer over the phone, sitting in jail for weeks before getting a hearing when he'd be sentenced to many years of hard-labor in the Utah State Prison. He worried about relying on Lena and asking her to come and get the girls while begging her not to tell Jocelyn and Marilyn that he'd been busted and certainly to keep the news from Eve, maybe make up a story of how he'd landed a new job in Australia for the next decade. Aaron thought how he'd miss taking Zoë to college and hearing about her new friends and the awful cafeteria food, and how he'd miss her wedding and the birth of her own kids. Aaron suddenly couldn't breathe because Eve would die while he was in prison.

They began to cuff him when Crow jumped up and ran over to the patrolmen.

"It's mine," she confessed.

The cops refused to believe Crow, knowing that an adult was more prosecutable than an under-aged first-time offender. After describing the details of the leather case, the police had no choice but to throw her in the back of the cruiser. The cops confiscated the pot but decided not to arrest Cāste, Alanis and Thyme because they had a real bust on their hands. They knew the marijuana charges would probably be dropped by a forgiving judge, but there was no way a proper Mormon official could look the other way when heroin was involved.

Zoë, Cāste, Alanis, and Thyme sobbed uncontrollably as Crow was arrested, and the adrenaline fleeing Aaron's body left his knees and hands shaking. Crow was oddly calm because she wasn't alone in the cruiser. After all, the cops were fathers themselves and they put her in the back seat with the dog. As the police drove back to the station, Aaron and the girls watched Crow smile as she hugged a happy German Shepherd.

Aaron turned Herbert York[94] around and followed the cruiser back to the station. On the way, Aaron noticed a few hotels and he decided they weren't leaving town without all of Zoë's friends. He knew Crow was scared and there was no way, as a man and a father and a human being, that he would leave anyone behind. After all, he'd made a promise directly to P.I.M.P, Crow's mother. He had promised to bring everyone back. He figured it might take more than a few hours to bail out Crow, and he needed a place to rest and come up with a plan. He had to first call P.I.M.P and explain how her daughter was in jail, then he had to figure out how much cash he would need to bail Crow out of jail. They found the cheapest motel near the station and in a bit of outstanding wisdom, Aaron booked two rooms. The first for Zoë and her friends, and the other was for himself, because no one wants to be stuck in a hotel room with a bunch of crying teenaged girls.

Around 2 a.m. as the girls settled into the motel room and took showers, Aaron tried to call the police station from his own room. He had decided not to bring a cell phone to Rainbow because he'd wanted to experience the wilderness without technological interruptions. Truly, he had basked in the bliss of a peaceful weekend without hearing the buzzing ring tones of texts and calls. Unfortunately, the phone in his room was broken.

Aaron went back to the lobby, saw a red landline phone hanging on the wall and asked the night clerk for the Yellow Pages.

"What's a Yellow Pages?" asked the pimple-faced, college student behind the desk.

"Forget it. What's the number for the cop-shop?"

"Huh?"

"Jail. Know the number?"

The desk clerk pointed to a piece of paper taped against the wall that listed the police station, the fire house, the maintenance man and a plumber.

Aaron dialed the top number and a sleepy, British-accented voice answered after a few rings.

"Good evening, have you any idea what time it is?"

Aaron thought this was a strange way for a deputy to answer the phone.

"Is this the county jail?"

"Heavens no, my good man," the man said pleasantly. "This is room 204."

Aaron looked down at the lobby phone. He had forgotten to dial 9 to reach an outside line.

"Sorry," Aaron said before hanging up.

He dialed the number correctly this time and after a few rings, the same British gentleman answered the phone.

"Good evening, sir, I do think you've misdialed once again."

Aaron apologized, hung up and asked the clerk why he couldn't get an outside line. The boy simply shrugged his shoulders. "I didn't even know we had a phone up here."

Aaron tired the number again, dialing both 9 and the local area code.

"Good evening, sir, we thought it might be you again," the gentleman said calmly. "I think you've misdialed again. We'd appreciate it greatly if you'd stop ringing our room."

"If you know it's me," Aaron exploded, "then don't pick up!"

"Would be far too rude not to answer."

"That's so very British!"

"Good night, sir."

Aaron slammed the phone down and cursed himself for not bringing a cell phone. The digital clock above the desk blinked at 2:31 a.m. Aaron walked down the hall and banged on the girls' door. They were chatting quietly, eyes red from the emotional outburst of witnessing their friend's arrest. Boxes of tissues and empty wrappers of candy bars from the vending machine surrounded the bed. Aaron knew Alanis had a cell phone because they had researched suicidal bands a few days earlier. Unfortunately, her phone had a meager 1% charge remaining. She said her charger was somewhere under the back seat of the car.

Aaron returned to the car, but the overhead light inside Herbert Kenwith[95] was broken, making it difficult to search through the various debris under the seats. He walked to the lobby and asked the boy behind the desk for a flashlight who searched beneath the cabinet but came up empty handed. Next, the desk clerk searched the back closet for six minutes before emerging with a massive aluminum flashlight. When he handed it to Aaron, the flashlight seemed underweight.

Aaron tried the switch with no effect. "Got any batteries?"

As the boy took out two AAA batteries from the television remote, Aaron asked incredulously, "Seriously?" He unscrewed the bottom of the flashlight and pointed. "I'll need four D batteries."

The boy motioned outside. "There's a 7-Eleven about two blocks away."

Aaron snatched the flashlight and marched down the street. The lonely stretch of downtown Vernal, Utah, was quiet in the early hours before dawn with three blinking stoplights. Not a soul stirred on the empty street.

The sleepy 7-Eleven clerk was roused by the bell on the door when Aaron entered. He used a credit card to purchase a huge bag of Spicy Habanero Cheetos and a pack of eight batteries since they were out of the four pack. Aaron returned to the motel and checked in on the girls. The door cracked open and a hand swiped the bag of unopened Cheetos. He figured they probably needed it more than he did. Aaron returned to the car with the operational flashlight and located the cord under the backseat. Unfortunately, the phone charger was for an automobile's 12-volt outlet and did not have the wall adapter. Aaron turned the car's battery on and was completely surprised when the cell phone worked because he had suspected the cigarette lighter outlet might be broken. He sat in the car while dialing the police station.

At 3 a.m., the officer on duty at the jail searched the records for Crow's offense. "Ah, here it is. Class one felony. Bail has been set at seven thousand dollars."

Aaron coughed hard. "Did you say seven THOUSAND?"

"Yes, sir," the officer said. "She'll be processed by six in the morning. And you'd better hurry."

"Why?"

"Today is July 4th. Federal holiday, we close at seven. And since this is Friday, you'll have to wait until Monday to post her bail." The officer hung up.

Aaron had no idea how to raise seven thousand dollars at 3 a.m. in Vernal, Utah. But he'd made a promise.

The cell phone's wifi was broken so he couldn't use Google to find a local bail bondsman. He left the keys in the ignition to charge the phone and returned to the 7-Eleven hoping they had a Yellow Pages. After searching in the back office, the sleepy-eyed clerk found a copy printed three years earlier.

Aaron promised to return the telephone directory and walked back to the car and unplugged the cell phone. Unfortunately, the cigarette lighter outlet in Herbert Henry Dow[96] had failed to sufficiently charge the cell phone since it blinked at 1%. Aaron stayed in the car and reconnected the phone into the outlet since at least the cell phone was operational as long as it remained plugged in. Sitting in the front seat with the Yellow Pages on his lap and holding a flashlight since the overhead light was broken, Aaron searched for a bondsman in Vernal, Utah.

The first three phone numbers in the outdated directory had been disconnected and so expanded his search to include the towns of Naples, Jensen and Fort Duchesne. The next two did not answer since the time was now 3:30 a.m. The next five bondsmen hung up immediately when they discovered Aaron was not only from out of town, but from out of state. They feared he might be a flight risk and they'd lose their money. Aaron couldn't argue with their logic but kept dialing. Aaron called offices in Provo and Salt Lake City but was rejected by twelve bail bondsmen.

At 4:30am, Aaron made a thirteenth call because he refused to give up. He'd break Crow out of jail if that's what it took. He was not leaving town without her. He didn't care if she was shooting smack, in his mind she was too young to know better. Besides, she'd confessed to the heroin and saved his ass even though he wouldn't have been facing 8-to-10 years in prison if she had simply left the needle at Rainbow.

On the thirteenth call, Aaron heard a friendly voice. His hopes lifted. He'd spent a decade at the Crisis Center listening to voices and instantly knew he might have a chance because of one difference from the previous twelve men he'd talked to earlier. This bondsman was a woman.

Keeping his own voice calm and parental, Aaron explained how he was a father traveling from Colorado with a car load of teenagers. Someone had planted the drugs on this poor, innocent girl while on a religious retreat. He did not mention the Rainbow Gathering. He did not mention the marijuana. He did not mention a lot of things.

"Listen here," the woman said. "Your story sounds…"

"Yes?" Aaron asked hopefully.

"...like a bunch of crap."

Defeated, Aaron began to hang up but then spouted, "Fine, you're right, the girl is a dope-fiend. They smoke weed and party hard and hang out with bad boys. But that doesn't mean we won't come back for her court date. And I can't let her rot in jail, I made a promise."

"And how do I know your word is any good?"

Despondently, Aaron said, "I'm trying, aren't I?"

"Hold on a second," the woman said. "What's your name again? Where you from?" She spent the next few minutes Googling him. After confirming that Aaron owned his home outright, she discovered his name in a newspaper article.

"You work at a crisis center?" she asked.

"That's right."

"You take suicide calls?"

"That's right."

"My niece killed herself."

"I'm sorry." Aaron remained silent afterwards because the bondswomen was deliberating and he didn't want to dissuade her from a beneficial decision.

"I wish someone had talked to her before she died. Maybe tried to help her, you know?"

"I do."

"Well," the woman said with a deep breath, "we'd better get you back to work."

The bondswoman in Salt Lake held a contract with a man in Myton who could be there by 6 a.m. but Aaron needed to come up with ten percent of the bail.

Aaron exclaimed, "That's seven hundred dollars!"

"That's our cut. Give us seven hundred and we put up the seven thousand. We get our money back when she shows up for court. That's the way it works."

"Do you take a credit card?"

The bondswoman laughed. "Cash only. Can you get it by six in the morning?"

"I'll figure it out." Before hanging up, he expressed his gratitude in the simplest of terms. "Thank you."

Returning to his room, Aaron grabbed his wallet and spied a twenty-dollar bill surrounded by a few loose singles. He headed off to the 7-Eleven again where he'd seen an ATM and returned the Yellow Pages to the clerk. He reviewed his checking account, found it empty, then checked his savings account and discovered he had eight hundred dollars to his name. They were in luck.

Unfortunately, automated teller machines inside convenience stores in Utah dispense a maximum of four hundred dollars. He withdrew the cash and needed to come up with another three hundred bucks in the next hour. Aaron raced back to the motel and banged on the girls' door. No one answered. Thinking they were asleep, he banged louder until a man emerged from the neighboring room.

"A wee bit early for such a racket, wouldn't you say?" the man said with a British accent.

Aaron apologized and asked, "You don't happen to have three hundred dollars, do you?"

"How many English pounds is that?"

"Oh, about two hundred."

"In that case, certainly not. How about a fiver to keep it down?" the man said as he threw a bill on the floor and shut the door.

Aaron quickly scooped up the money and while racing to his room, he heard giggling and splashing from the pool area. He looked over and saw Zoë doing a cannonball off the diving board. Unable to sleep, the girls had decided to go swimming.

Aaron ran over and nearly slipped into the pool. "Hey, who's got an ATM card? We need three hundo to bail out Crow."

"Yippeeee! Good job, Dad!"

"We're getting her out today?"

"If we can get the cash in the next hour," Aaron explained.

"Right on!

"Cool!"

Zoë, Alanis, Cāste and Thyme climbed out of the pool, grabbed towels and raced back to the room. Digging through their backpacks, they came up with twenty-three dollars and forty-two cents. As for ATM cards, Zoë had left it at home, Thyme had lost her card several months ago and Alanis didn't have a bank account. Cāste said her card was somewhere in the car.

"Doesn't anyone have more cash?" Aaron pleaded.

"Money's not accepted at Rainbow," Alanis explained. "We only brought enough for gas."

"Communism, man. We shared everything," Thyme said. "Remember how we never paid for anything at Rainbow?"

"Except with love and kindness," said Cāste.

Damn hippies, Aaron thought. Maybe that park ranger had been right about us.

"Welcome to the real world," Aaron said, stressed and fatherly. "We need money now or we'll never see Crow again!"

The girls panicked and ran to the car to search for Cāste's wallet. Eight minutes later, after discovering another six dollars and eighty-five cents in loose change, they found her card in an empty box of macaroni.

"So that's where I put it," Cāste said.

"Why there?" Aaron asked.

"Duh!" Zoë explained. "Because mac and cheese can always be trusted!"

In the early light before dawn, the four girls and Aaron ran to the 7-Eleven and tried to access Cāste's bank account. Unfortunately, she couldn't remember her PIN code.

At 5:56 a.m., Zoë and her friends sat in a circle on the linoleum floor and held hands. They chanted a helpful mantra to assist Cāste's memory. They burned incense until the clerk yelled at them. They even played duck-duck-goose to distract Cāste until they knocked over a stand of Twinkies.

Exactly seven minutes later, Zoë grabbed Cāste by the shoulders and shouted, "Remember when we were at that DIY last month and we needed some cash to get into the show but we didn't have any and when we went to the ATM, I asked how you remembered the PIN and you said, 'My mom's birthday'."

Cāste exclaimed, "You're right! But which one of my moms?"

"How many do you have?" Aaron asked.

"Well, there's my biological mother. And my step-mom and her wife, who is like a mom to me, too. Then there's my dad's third wife."

"Your step-mom is gay? I didn't know that," Thyme said. "I thought that other woman was your aunt."

"Step-mom said my dad cured her of men forever."

"Focus!" Aaron screamed. "We're running out of time."

"That's four moms," Zoë explained.

"Fine," Aaron said calming down, "ATM's allow three guesses before locking you out. You've got four birthdays codes." He pointed at the keypad. "Good luck, kid."

"You've got a seventy-five percent chance," Alanis said. "Three out of four, right?"

Zoë and Thyme cheered, "You can do it!"

Cāste punched in the first code. Wrong. Then the second code. Error. She had two choices remaining with one more chance. Cāste looked at Zoë. "Which one do I pick?"

"What are the choices?"

"My step-mom was born on October 25, 1969, and the first four digits would be 1025."

"God, she's old!" Aaron exclaimed before realizing he was only born a few years afterwards.

"Her wife's birthday is July 19, 1993. That would be 0719."

"Wait," Aaron said, "your step-mom is twice as old as her wife? That's cool."

Zoë pushed Cāste aside and stared at the keypad. "My dad's right, twice as old. That's the answer."

"What?" they said in unison, leaning over her shoulder.

"Look," she said, pointing to the letters above the numbers on the buttons. "If we take the letters C-R-O-W, it becomes…"

"2769," Aaron contributed. "But what does Crow have to do with the access code?"

Zoë rolled her eyes. "We're getting the money for her, right? The universe is telling us something."

"That the numbers and Crow are somehow connected," finished Cāste.

"That's it!" Zoë and Cāste shouted together. "It's step-mom's b-day! That's the code!"

The girls danced around the broken Twinkie stand in celebration as Aaron scratched his head in bewilderment.

As Cāste typed in the code, Zoë explained to her confused father. "It's easy, her step-mom was born in October which is the tenth month and twice ten is twenty, since she is twice her wife's age. Then add seven because July is the seventh month and what do you get?"

"27."

"Right, 2 and 7 are the first two numbers of CROW on the keypad."

"That's a weird coincidence."

"And her step-mom was born on the 25th, and twice of twenty-five is fifty. Add fifty to the day of her wife's birthday which is 19 and what do you get?"

"69."

"See," Zoë explained, "like I said, 2769. The numbers for CROW."

"That's just…" Aaron was again about to say *a coincidence*, but he'd found that two coincidences usually equaled a providence.

Unfortunately, Cãste looked up from the screen and said, "We've got a problem."

"Wrong code?" Aaron asked crestfallen.

"No, Zoë was right," she said.

"So, what's the problem?"

"We need three hundred dollars, right?" Cãste asked pointing at the screen.

They careened over her shoulder and stared at her account balance: $239.

"That'll have to do," he said, looking up at the clock above the desk at the convenience store. The time was 6:09 a.m. The bondswoman's agent was probably waiting at the jail. Aaron had fifty-one minutes to get there in order to post bail before the jail closed for the long holiday weekend.

Cãste managed to withdraw $220 because ATM's only dispense twenty-dollar bills. While running back to the motel, Aaron mentally calculated their money. Aaron's $400 combined with Cãste's $220, added to the $24 from Aaron's wallet, and $5 from the British guy, and $23.42 from the girls' backpacks, and $6.85 in loose change from the carpeted floor of Herbert Grönemeyer[97] totaled an amount equaling $679.27, leaving them about twenty bucks short.

The girls and Aaron ran into the lobby and begged from the desk boy. They were certain he had a little cash they could borrow. After a little encouragement from Thyme's sweet smile, the desk clerk mentioned that he didn't carry cash but he did have about twenty bucks in his bank account.

"Well," Aaron pleaded, "let's run back to the 7-Eleven and get it."

"Why don't I just use the ATM over there?" he said, walking to the rear of the lobby.

Aaron managed to control his anger and didn't strangle the kid. In his frantic rush through the early morning hours, Aaron had failed to see the cash machine in the lobby. He could only blame himself. He stomped his feet in repressed anger.

"How much money do we have?" Zoë asked to distract her father, watching his cheeks redden.

Aaron spilled out the bills and change he been collecting onto the floor. They helped him count out $679.27. He had been correct in his estimation.

"With twenty bucks from the kid, we'll be close. We need seventy-three cents more," Aaron said. He checked the time and at 6:22 a.m., realized he had only 38 minutes remaining. "Alright, we're cutting it kinda close. I hope they don't close up early. I'll head back to the car and use the phone to call the jail."

The kid handed over his twenty bucks and said, "Why don't you just use my phone?"

Aaron reached out to throttle the boy. He couldn't believe the kid had a cell phone this whole time. Zoë saw her father's eyes twitching with controlled madness and stepped between them to grab the money from the desk clerk.

"Thanks!" she said before handing the money to Aaron. "Go Dad, hurry!"

Aaron sprinted for the car. He jumped in the driver's seat and searched his pockets for the car keys. He found them in the ignition because earlier he had needed the car's battery to charge Alanis's cell phone. Unfortunately, he knew what would happen next. He tried twice but the engine didn't turn over. The battery was dead.

Aaron jumped out and looked around the parking lot. A proper-looking couple was loading their car a few spots away. Aaron ran over and breathlessly asked for a jump.

"Good morning once again," the British gentleman said. "What do you mean by jump?"

"Ugh!"

"Oh, jump-start?"

"Yes!"

"Your vehicle's bah-tree has gone flat, has it?"

"Yes!"

"Do you by chance possess jumper cables?"

"Let me check!" Aaron raced back to Herbert Spencer[98] and

quickly searched through the social debris of travelers that littered the interior of the car. He cried out, "They're in here somewhere!"

"You've nothing to fear," the gentleman said. "If you'll fetch the cables from the boot of my automobile ..."

"Boot?"

"The rear. I think you Yanks call it the trunk. Which is funny because the trunk of an elephant is in the front."

"Argh!"

"You seem to be in a hurry."

"What's the time?"

The man checked his watch. "About zero seven thirty."

"Whaaaat?!" He grabbed the man's wrist. The time read 7:32 a.m. The energy from Aaron's spirit drained away. He slumped on the ground of the parking lot and stared at the ground. He was too late. The jail was closed and they would have to leave town without Crow. There was no way he could afford to spend the weekend in Vernal, Utah, and still have enough to bail her out. The four hundred from his account was the majority of his life's savings. He noticed three cigarette butts on the ground and grabbed one with the most tobacco. He placed the tiny vatch in his mouth as he patted his pockets for a lighter that had not been there in years.

"How unsanitary!" the gentleman cried in horror. "That's quite possibly the most disgusting thing I've ever seen." The gentleman smacked the filthy butt from Aaron's mouth.

Aaron reached under the car to re-claim his prize. As he pulled his hand away, the rusted and jagged tail pipe ripped open the scab on his knuckle. He watched the blood trickle down his arm and suddenly saw three shiny quarters near the rear tire. He wiped his knuckle on his shirt and picked up the loose change, accounting for the remaining seventy-five cents needed to make an even $700. As hope swelled, the man spoke which further encouraged Aaron to believe the adventure wasn't over. Not yet.

The gentleman tapped his watch and said, "My mistake, I forgot to adjust for the time change. Your country is quite large. We were in Nebraska yesterday."

"That means..." Aaron snapped up his head and grinned widely.

"Yes, it's only six thirty-five."

"Funny how life changes so quickly. I've still got a chance!" Aaron exclaimed. He connected the live cables and re-ignited the ancient heart of Herbert Spencer[99]. Unfortunately, the surge of power played havoc with Herbert's inner electrical guts.

Ten blocks from the police station, the dashboard lights burned out. At nine blocks, the turn signals failed. At eight blocks, the headlights went dark. At seven blocks, Aaron didn't see the tree limb in the middle of the road because his headlights had gone out. The wooden limb bounced against the under carriage and dislodged the muffler. At six blocks, Aaron reached for the radio to block out the noise of Herbert von Karajan's[100] dragging muffler, then remembered the radio had not worked this trip, and so he was amazed to discover upon touching the ON button that the surge of power from the British gentleman's battery caused the radio to blast at full volume. Unable to turn the radio down or off, Aaron proceeded onward to uncomfortably loud country music. When the song recited a lyric about the singer's broken-down Chevy, Aaron empathized. At five blocks, a light rain sprinkled the windshield. At four blocks, Aaron utilized the wipers until the fuse blew, leaving the wiper blades directly in Aaron's line of vision. At three blocks, the heater came on and fogged up the windows. At two blocks, Aaron unrolled the window to let the cool, morning air dissipate the fog, but the window stopped a few inches down. At one block remaining until he reached the jail house, Aaron stuck his head out the window to see the road because,

heat blasted out the vents, fogging up the windshield; and,

rain poured in through the cracked window; and,

wipers blocked his view; and,

radio roared melancholy music; and,

headlights were busted; but,

Aaron smiled because life is a struggle.

He pulled into the parking lot, muffler screeching on the ground. Despite the adversity, Aaron had finally arrived. As he stepped out from the dilapidated vehicle, he focused solely on the cool sprinkle of rain that offered a blessing upon his face.

At 6:47 a.m., with thirteen minutes to spare, Aaron grabbed a book from the back seat and jolted into the police station. The agent sent by the bondswoman was sitting in the waiting room. The man held a large manila envelope stuffed with papers.

"We don't have much time," the agent said. "Sign these papers. I'll let the duty officer know we are ready. You bring the seven hundred?"

"It's all here," Aaron said, pulling loose bills and spare change from his pockets onto a plastic chair.

The man looked incredulously at the ever-growing pile. "You're paying with quarters, and dimes and … pennies?"

Aaron counted out the money and ignored the agent's disdain. When Aaron reached seven hundred, the bondwoman's agent asked, "Rough time putting this together?"

"You have no idea," Aaron said, exhaustion overwhelming him as he fell into a chair next to the agent.

"Well, the young lady should be out soon. I'll get everything ready. Sign here to sign over your house as collateral. You knew that, right?"

Aaron sighed. "I do now."

As the man busied himself with paperwork, Aaron opened the book he'd brought from the car. He always brought a book to a waiting room because the very nature of a waiting room indicated that one never knew how long they would have to wait. Hence the name. And Aaron hated waiting.

To his pleasant surprise, the book he had blindly grabbed was a copy of Hagakure's 17th century classic, *Book of the Samurai*. Opening to a random page, Aaron worried that he didn't have enough cash to spring Crow from jail. He worried that perhaps the agent from the bondswoman would raise the price seeing that Aaron had exactly $700.02. Secondly, he worried that maybe he'd be thrown in jail when Crow pleaded not guilty to possession of heroin and instead blamed it on the only adult which happened to be Aaron. In this flash of despondency, and surprisingly the first time this evening, Aaron contemplated suicide because he knew there is no way in Hell he could survive 8-to-10 years in the Utah State Penitentiary. To subside the flooding panic, he read a random passage from Hagakure's masterpiece:

A samurai who came up with a cash shortage
when closing out an account book
sent a letter to his daimyo saying,
"It is regrettable to have to commit seppuku over a matter of funds.
Please send money."
It is said that even wrongdoings can be managed without detection.

Aaron closed the book and breathed easier because he knew this was simply a matter of money, and money could always save white people in this country.

The jailer brought Crow out at 6:59 a.m. Without a word, she looked down at the floor. The bondswoman's agent and Aaron shook hands. As they left the station, an officer turned the sign around at the front door to read *Closed*. Ashamed, Crow climbed in the back seat and curled into a ball.

Aaron, afraid to ask her if anything had happened during her overnight stay in jail, hesitated before saying, "They treat you alright?"

She looked up, age and tears filling her eyes. "Yeah, I just wanna go home." No longer a girl, jail had transformed her into a young woman.

Aaron nodded and drove to the motel. Fortunately, Herbie the Love Bug[101] was functioning properly, all his electrical aches and mechanical pains had magically vanished. Opening the door of the room, Zoë, Thyme, Cāste and Alanis flew off the bed, straight past Aaron and embraced Crow in an enormous eight-armed hug of joy and relief. Aaron left them and celebrated on his own with a quiet cup of tea in the lobby. The time was half past seven.

As Aaron relaxed on the lobby's fake-pleather couch and relished the notion of capturing a few hours of well-deserved rest in a room he had purchased but rarely visited, he noticed the desk clerk absent from his station. Instead, the kid was out in the parking lot erecting wooden barricades.

Aaron strolled outside to breathe in the morning's fresh air. He had fulfilled his promise. They were all coming home. He felt proud of himself. Unfortunately, the journey wasn't over. Not yet.

Aaron noticed the other hotel guests were packing up and leaving. The parking lot was much emptier than it had been an hour ago. He tapped the kid on the shoulder and asked, "Where's everyone going?"

"Didn't I tell you at check-in? They're blocking the street at eight this morning for the parade."

"What parade?"

"The Fourth of July!"

His momentarily relief evaporated like fog on a windshield. Aaron dropped his paper tea cup on the ground and raced back to the girls' room where he hollered that they had thirty, no twenty-six minutes, to pack up and check-out.

"Why?" the girls demanded.

"Because Vernal sounds like venereal. It's a disease that we can't get rid of!"

"What?"

"They're closing the town for some stupid parade. We'll be stuck here forever if we don't leave right now!"

While the young women collected their gear and strapped their backpacks on top of the car, Aaron grabbed a metal coat hanger from his room, tied the hanging muffler to a metal strut and hoped that it would hold for the rest of the journey. In the few remaining minutes, he laid down on the hotel bed for the first time. He had aged a decade overnight but the light of Rainbow buoyed him. Despite the exhaustion, he felt young and rejuvenated, even hopeful. He found an electric razor under the sink left behind by a previous guest. He trimmed his beard to a rough shadow and shaved off a few years.

They escaped with two minutes to spare, barricades falling down behind them like a railroad crossing. Aaron didn't let anyone else drive until they had safely made it across the Colorado border. Singing songs of liberation, they reclaimed their vibrancy and Aaron figured the moral of the Rainbow adventure and the ensuing drug-infused calamity was a lesson he wouldn't forget: Don't drive a Ford Taurus.

They traversed safely across the state of Colorado without incident and Aaron returned all the young women home in time for the traditional festivity of watching fireworks on the Fourth with family. As Zoë and Aaron curled up on the porch and witnessed the fiery explosions above the city, he knew there was more to be learned than simply the necessity of taking a reliable vehicle on a road trip. The real lesson had been revealed in the middle of their journey home when he read a bumper sticker on the rear of an orange Volkswagen Bug. The VW had passed them on the highway doing a mere 65 mph, but Aaron had been creeping along slower because he refused to risk getting pulled over again. The futuristically-optimistic bumper sticker featured the dancing Grateful Dead bears and announced in bright blue letters: "It's Not Where You've Been, But Where You're Going."

As he recalled the face of the ol' Coot who had relayed the same message many, many hours ago, Aaron with his crew of ashen teenagers reeking of four-day-old patchouli and mountain sweat had learned a different lesson.

It's not where you've been, but where you'll never go again!

Chapter 13

All White People Must Evacuate the Earth

Aaron and Zoë sat dozing on the porch around midnight, relieved to be home after their long journey. They idly chatted about how the distant pop of fireworks signaled the death of the American Empire as they craved a by-product of the American Dream—junk food. Zoë cracked open her piggy bank, gathered a handful of change, and together they strolled to the corner Loaf n' Jug for a cherry Slurpee and a dozen donuts. Outside the store, Aaron smiled at a homeless woman who might have been thirty but looked sixty. The dark circles under her eyes lacked the deep furrows of time and her hands, nails bitten down to the cuticles, were absent of wrinkles. The woman smiled back a toothless grin. Meth, Aaron thought, it's a hell of a drug.

Aaron gave her a few coins and automatically said, "Welcome home."

The woman titled her head at his greeting, reached into her pocket and silently handed Aaron a scrap of paper. Perhaps the lack of sleep for many hours distorted his mental faculties and he took the dirty piece of paper without thinking and nodded in gratitude before walking into the store. Aaron found it strange that he had received something in return from the woman since most beggars usually take but don't give.

While Zoë hunted around the convenience store for various incarnations of high-fructose corn syrup, Aaron inspected the piece of paper, expecting Mormon literature or an uplifting passage from the Jehovah's Witness. The list contained handwritten words in cursive, mostly unreadable because the paper had been smudged with water and dirt. The heading was barely legible in faded ink: *45-Fists of DàHú GōngFú.*[102]

Below were several titles, such as *Idle Iguana, Pathetic Python, Sleeping Sloth,* and *Flaming Flamingo.* Poorly sketched diagrams in pencil lined the margins, resembling old drawings of dance partners with highlighted footprints connected by dotted lines. Aaron was unable to decipher the confusion.

The easiest to read was *Cursed Crane*, the seventeenth entry. Standing in the middle of the candy aisle, he imitated the dance maneuver and knocked over several boxes of Butterfingers.

Zoë looked up from the Slurpee machine. "What are you doing?"

"Nothing, oh, never mind."

"Don't get any of that junk," she said, pointing to the candy bars on the floor. "Where are the donuts?"

"I'll get some. Jelly?"

"Get me a glazed."

"If you'll hook me up with a half n' half Slurpee."

She titled her head. "Half what?"

"Doesn't matter, surprise me."

Aaron picked out four glazed donuts, two Boston Creams, three chocolate dipped and three old fashioned, the last choice Eve's favorite that he wanted to bring on his visit to see her in the morning. He sat down at a small table in the corner while waiting for Zoë. He turned back to the mysterious scrap of paper and tried to read it again. He brushed his thumb over the seventeenth entry and the ink and dirt seeped into his skin.

Suddenly, a vision struck. Aaron leaned back against the plastic bench, mind reeling from the powerful image. An invisible attacker reached out to grab him, and he witnessed himself flowing through the dance routine, his hands responding in a flurry of strikes. Incomprehensibly fast at first, then slower each time as the image replayed in his mind for what seemed hours. Finally, his body moved so slowly that Aaron could see the precise movement of his wrist, the angle of his elbow, and the way his heel came slightly off the floor as he pivoted. He could even see the slight crook of each finger. Watching himself move in the flash hallucination was like watching a hummingbird in slow-motion.

He looked up and noticed Zoë was filling a second Slurpee cup. The entire image had occurred in a matter of seconds, but he knew with certainly that he could perform the routine flawlessly. The movement felt comfortable, like a childhood memory of climbing a tree.

Aaron looked at the paper and *Cursed Crane* had become unreadable from his exposure through direct osmosis. He turned the paper over and found numerous other smudged entries on the other side but the forty-third entry, *Bhutanese Barking Dog*, remained intact.

When Aaron rubbed his thumb over the dirty ink, a similar seizure struck him. He could see himself moving again. At first, the dance occurred too quickly for him to comprehend until the scene slowed considerably and he could make sense of the routine. This one took longer for there were more pieces to fit together, such as stepping away from an attacker. Aaron, caught in a time-loop, was utterly exhausted by the end. His muscles ached and he had a throbbing headache.

When the image passed and Aaron looked up from the fragment of paper, Zoë stood in front of him with two frozen drinks. Once again, mere seconds had passed. Also, he noticed the words were now completely illegible.

Zoë looked down at him. "You look tired. Feelin OK?"

Aaron stood and headed for the check-out line. "Been a long day."

"And night. Thanks again for bailing my friend out of jail. Here," she said, handing him a Slurpee mix of cherry and grape. "This will pick you up. Tons of sugar."

"Thanks."

After paying the clerk, he looked for the homeless woman who had given him an incredible gift for a few coins, but she had vanished. I was wrong, Aaron thought. Sometimes a beggar will give more than they take.

Aaron doubted that she existed and the only proof was a crumbled-up piece of paper. He looked at it once more and then threw it on the ground. He didn't need the paper anymore since he had memorized the routine but he wondered what to do with this new knowledge. They made it home without further incident and the sugar provided a steep crash. They were asleep within minutes, donut crumbs littering the table and half-consumed Slurpees melting on the counter.

Aaron slept for ten hours and woke energized, an unfamiliar circumstance for him. The camping trip had obviously lifted his spirits. Rainbow had instilled in him a love of the universe, and since he knew life was not a Love Story[103] but rather a death story, he decided to check in at the office. Saturday was typically a slow day at the Suicide Prevention & Crisis Hotline Center and he hoped to catch up on a little work while Zoë slept. Since they'd been gone for a few days, Aaron naturally worried about his grandmother and decided to take Zoë in the afternoon for a visit to the Poinsettia Nursing Home.

Strolling into the Crisis Center, Aaron contemplated leaving his job. His conscious effort to get fired over his contentious interaction with Boss Lady was clearly evidence of unhappiness with his career choice. Yet, social work was hard no matter where he worked because the over-sized, emotionally exhausting and ever-increasing caseloads would follow him. He dreamed of someday ridding himself of the contagious, psychic garbage that Callers dumped on a Listener. Essentially, he made people feel better by momentarily lightening their burdens.

Hearing Debz's mezzo-soprano voice engaged in a phone call, Aaron thought about how each counselor differed in their approach. Only a few of the counselors imitated his emotional avenue to reach the desperate. Most refused to personally care about their clients whereas Debz flatly resented them.

"What are you doing here?" she asked Aaron.

The Caller mistakenly thought Debz's inquiry was directed at them and Aaron could hear the Caller asking, "What do you mean here? What am I doing on this planet? That's a good question."

"Not you!" Debz yelled at the Caller before placing the phone down on the desk. She didn't have the audacity to hang up on people like Aaron did, but she did leave them hanging.

"Great trip," Aaron said, answering Debz. "We made it home alive. Back to life…"

"Back to reality," she finished with a melodious tone.

"Back from a fantasy," he hummed, continuing the lyrics from the band Soul II Soul.

When Debz couldn't recall the next line, she said, "How is it that you remember more old school R&B than me?"

He scowled at her with upturned lips. "Point!"

Aaron looked through the pile of manila folders on his desk and instantly regretted coming in over the weekend. Debz, still ignoring the Caller as they droned on, opened a brown paper lunch sack when Aaron abruptly asked, "Why do you yell at the Callers?"

"People want to be told what to do," Debz told him while biting into an egg-salad sandwich.

Aaron leaned on the cubicle wall separating their work space. "I can barely get out of bed before noon on the weekends. How can I advise anyone else?"

"We're not supposed to give advice, remember?"

"You do."

"When?" Debz asked defensively.

"Remember that one girl you told to get an abortion?"

"She was fourteen!"

"And last week, there was that woman you told to leave her husband."

"That abused, dumb-ass housewife? She needed to divorce that bastard," Debz said. "He nearly choked her to death."

"Well, she was trying to hang herself."

"Hey, just because you're trying to strangle yourself doesn't give someone the right to choke you!"

Titling his head to the side, Aaron said, "I guess. And what about the kid you told to run away from his parents?"

"They were his foster parents," Debz explained. "And they were molesting him!"

"I'm not saying you're wrong. I'm trying to prove a point."

"Which is?"

"That you give more than advice. You straight up tell people what to do."

"Well," Debz said with a shrug of her shoulders, "it's not like I'm telling them something new. I'm reflecting back what they are thinking. I give their inner thoughts a voice."

"And what about the other day? That one teenager, what did you say again?"

"Told him to jump on the gay-bus and head outta town."

"Well, what about that? How's that not advice?"

"Dude," Debz said and put down her sandwich as she loaded a rubber band around her finger to shoot at Aaron. "That kid is gay as hell. He's nineteen, works for minimum wage at some awful fast-food joint and still lives at home with his oppressive, conservative, Evangelical parents. He needs to get his tight buns outta the closet and outta this town. I told him what he wanted to hear. Gave him a lil motivation."

"Wait, gay as hell?"

"Apparently that's what his own mother said, not me."

"Maybe, but did you know his mother called back later?"

"She did?" Debz asked doubtfully.

"I took the call. Mrs. C., right? Her son is Josh, calls him Joshua."

Debz lowered the rubber-band finger gun and looked at Aaron. "What did she say?"

"Mrs. C told me her sweet Joshua stole the change from the family swear jar and bought a bus ticket to California."

"Really?"

"And Mrs C. told me that if her gay son killed himself, then she'd be okay with it."

"Seriously?"

"Nah, messin with you."

Debz aimed her finger gun and shot Aaron in the face. "Bastard, I knew you were lying. She didn't call, did she?"

"Nope, I read the details from your notes."

"No points for you today, lyin-ass honkey!" Debz said with fake anger. She picked up the phone off the desk and uttered, "Uh huh," before resuming her lunch.

Aaron didn't inform Debz that she had guessed correctly, Mrs. C. had not called the Suicide Hotline. Rather, Aaron had called Mrs. C. last week after reading Debz's notes and perceiving the need to contact the family for two reasons. First, to cover for Debz in case the boy ran away from home. Debz would certainly lose her job if word ever got back that she'd told the boy to run away. More importantly, Aaron had been curious about the mother.

The mother had answered on the third ring in the middle of the day. Housewife, Aaron suspected, which nowadays meant she worked from home.

Mrs. C., conservative, Evangelical, homophobic, oppressed housewife: "Hello?"

Aaron, as Fredrickson: "I'm calling in reference to a call made by your son Joshua earlier. He gave his permission that we could speak with anyone at this number." Aaron knew the boy had not given his explicit permission, but the box on the form had been left unmarked.

Mrs. C., slightly Conservative, Evangelical, homophobic, not-so-oppressed housewife: "Yes, I know my son called. We talked about it. And I'm talking to my husband when he gets home tonight. We've been very worried."

"What are you planning to do?"

"I don't care if my husband won't listen, we are getting our son some help."

Aaron, inquisitive affect: "Help because your son is suicidal or help because he's gay? You knew that, right?"

Mrs. C., politically middle-of-the-road, Christian, gay-friendly, not-so-oppressed housewife: "Of course I know my son is gay. And I love him."

"And your husband?"

Mrs. C., liberal-leaning, Episcopalian, gay-friendly, not-so-oppressed housewife: "He's learning. We're in a church group at St. Mark's. We talk about it with other parents. The pastor is a lesbian."

"And how do you feel about your son's suicidal thoughts?"

"It's not a sin or anything. I mean, we all get a little down sometimes."

"Has he ever Attempted to kill himself?"

"My sweet Joshua? I hope not, but then again, a mother is always the last to know."

"I'm sorry, I wanted to state the obvious. He did call us after all."

Mrs. C., liberal, Episcopalian, gay-friendly, liberated housewife: "Listen, I'm a nice person. I give money to the soup kitchen and the homeless shelter on 4th street. ACLU and the Southern Poverty Law Center. And Greenpeace. And UNICEF. And D.A.R.E. And M.A.D.D. And …"

Aaron, pushing too far: "That's great. Good for you. By the way, your husband is gay, too."

The call had ended abruptly and Aaron was fairly certain he'd done more damage than good. Aaron knew his slightly offensive demeanor was merely a way of buffering the damage. He took their pain only on the condition that he gave a little back.

Back in the office, Debz continued ignoring the Caller while she ate a sandwich as Aaron perused papers on his desk. He didn't know how many more days and months and years he could continue this Sisyphean task. For every

troubled mood; or,

tormented mind; or,

tortured mentality; or,

tainted morale; or,

turbulent mental-masonry

that Aaron rolled up to the sanguine mountain top, there always lurked another boulder to trample him down to the valley floor. Many times, he had thought about switching jobs until he realized the only place that would hire someone with his experience was the local Rape Crisis Center. Aaron promised himself never to work there. With Zoë living under his roof, he'd be a basket-case, nut-job, loose-screw, total mess on the floor constantly worrying about her. He also did not want to work there when he found that, a) the letter "a" stood for alone, because he'd be the only male on staff, and more importantly, b) the letter "b" stood for Bundy, because Ted Bundy had volunteered at the Seattle Rape Crisis Center.

The latter twisted and disturbing fact prevented Aaron from leaving his current place of employment. He worried that the women working at the Rape Crisis Center would suspect him of being a sick pervert who gained pleasure from seeing the aftermath of horrific sexual assaults. He couldn't stand that kind of scrutiny. He would be second guessing himself and possessed no strategies on how to console a girl who'd been raped by a man whom she knew and trusted. Like an uncle.

Aaron also knew that one in ten rape victims were men and he would have no idea what to say to a guy with that kind of socially-tabooed trauma. Aaron might be inclined to say,

"Guys can't be raped!" or,

"Why didn't you stop him?" or,

"Why didn't you bite it off?!"

Aaron struggled with the fact that men use the word *rape* differently than women. When women say "rape", they mean a physical violation that leads to mental/emotional trauma. Rape is rape because, "No means No!" Like with a dog, *sit* means sit. Sit doesn't mean Fido can run off and chew on a bone or chase a cat or scratch some fleas on his ass. Once taught, the dog knows exactly the meaning of *Sit!* Like dogs, boys needed to be taught that "No means No!" from their fathers & uncles, straight coaches & gay pastors, kind neighbors & mean landlord, friends & enemies. Any man that comes into a boy's life has a duty to convey this simple message of respect. And why don't little boys learn this cornerstone of ethics from their mothers & aunts, sisters & girlfriends? Because men only listen to other men.

On the other hand, men tend to use the word *rape* to signify a financial loss. Generally, when a man says "rape" he is referring to the notion that he's been robbed, such as, "Dude, I was raped by the government last tax season," or, "U-Haul totally raped me on mileage. 99 cents a mile, seriously?" or, "My ex-wife's Jewish lawyer raped me. Bitch got the house AND my car!"

For men, when the word *rape* is used to actually convey sexual assault by a man onto another man, then a modifier is placed before the word such as Prison/Army Rape or Male Rape, implying that this type of violation is far worse than Female Rape. Men place the same value on money that women place on their bodies, their emotional stability, their mental health, their privacy and their very sense of safety. The problem is that money can be replaced, personal safety not so easily. In fact, a guy will be pissed at his homeboy for not paying a $2 bet made when the Browns raped[104] the Steelers by a score of 51-0. And yet, he'll believe that his friend will pay up far quicker than he'll believe the woman who claimed she was raped by Ben Roethlisberger in the bathroom of a nightclub in Georgia while the sheriff watched because, after all, ol' Ben wins Super Bowls with the Pittsburg Steelers whereas the college girl was probably drunk and flirtatious.

Zoë presence in the house and the fears of a father overriding his career choice, he decided to stay right where he was at the Suicide Prevention & Crisis Hotline Center. Somehow, dealing with suicide seemed easier than rape. Rape haunts whereas suicide relinquishes.

Aaron settled into the paperwork piled on the desk but couldn't focus. There was one folder that had been plaguing him for quite some time. He couldn't believe six months had passed since the shooting at the local Denny's. The city had been pestering Boss Lady for the official report on the incident, and she in turn had threatened him with a salary cut. Aaron didn't see much point in worrying since there was little difference between 18k and 17k per year. Boss Lady should have threatened him with something far more ominous, like switching Debz to another office. Without Debz around to make work fun, he would have seriously considered leaving for the Rape Crisis Center.

Aaron needed a few more data points to finish the paperwork on the hostage situation he had failed to negotiate. He considered himself a failure but Boss Lady was pleased because no one had been killed.

"Except the shooter," Aaron had said.

"He doesn't count," she had said coldly.

Aaron looked through his notes on hostage situations and remembered one from around the time he was born. The case dated back to 1977 when Corey Moore stormed a police station in Warrensville Heights, Ohio, and issued two simple demands.

Corey first demanded to talk to President Carter about the way Blacks have been treated since 1619 when the first batch of African slaves were brought to the Americas at the new colony of Jamestown. Corey detailed to the President that twenty African men were unloaded from a Dutch trading ship and sold for food. Corey reminded the President that historians often forget that ninety English women[105] were deposited on these fertile shores, as well. The women's trans-Atlantic passage cost 120 pounds of tobacco each, paid for by the recipient of these indentured servants. *Recipient* implied a landowning white male who basically turned these women into slave-wives. Since a cigarette contains one gram of tobacco, each woman's life was valued at about 2,700 packs of cigarettes.

Corey's wife, Leah Moore, forced her way into the police station and issued her own demands. She wanted to speak with her husband. The hostage negotiator optimistically believed Leah might be able to talk some sense into Corey. The negotiator was woefully mistaken.

"Leah," Corey cried out with a gun pointed at the police chief's temple, "for Gawd's sake, get me a pack of smoke or I'm gonna kill this white man!"

"Get it yo'damn self, you crazy bastard!"

"Baby, tell em I'll put the gun down and go home with you for a carton of Parliaments."

"Ten packs of smoke? Back in the day, you woulda been worth at least 3,000 packs!"

Next, Corey coolly communicated his secondary stipulation by accentuating each separate syllable,

"All   white   people   must   evacuate   the   Earth."

In his Georgia drawl, President Carter answered Corey, "Aaah son, now listen here-ah, let me gat back to yah on thaaat one."

Click. End of presidential phone call.[106]

As Aaron sat back and reflected on the hostage scenario from forty years ago, he was surprised that Public Enemy had titled their third album *Fear of a Black Planet*. Chuck D and PE could have collaborated with Parliament/Funkadelic for a sure platinum-selling album titled *All White People Must Evacuate the Earth* with songs like, "Why Are Lando, Finn and Mace the Only Brothas in Star Wars?" and "L. Ron Hubbard Was a Black Man Named L. Ron Hoyabembe" and "Why are Black Actors Only Cast as Aliens on Star Trek?" and "Leave All the Honkeys on Mars with Matt Damon" and "Even Pale-skinned Aliens got White Privilege!"

As Aaron scanned the report, he struggled to find any connection between the two hostage situations. The intervening decades had brought about a change in the different methods employed by the police when dealing with hostage takers. At Denny's, the police had stormed in and shot the man without hesitation whereas in the 1970s, the police had literally called up the President of the United States. Aaron could only think that maybe the answer lay in the changing dynamic of suburban neighborhoods.

Aaron remembered that for a few years he had lived in a small suburb of Cleveland that bordered Corey Moore's town of Warrensville Heights, Ohio. The only detail of the house that Aaron clearly recalled was a large wooden fence in the backyard, a fence that ended up in the Supreme Court. As a kid, Aaron lived with his mother Marilyn in a house directly on the border between the two suburbs. Aaron's suburb was predominately white whereas on the other side of the fence in Corey Moore's suburb was 99% Black. Therefore, to prevent accidental integration through teen-dating, the mostly white suburb of Shaker Heights acted like China during the Mongols or East Germany during the Communists or the United States during Trump. They built long walls to keep out the unwanted. After many years of litigation in the state court, the Supreme Court finally dismissed the case and kept intact the legality of these wooden borders and bothersome traffic diverters which forced commuters to drive miles in the wrong direction. The fence soared as housing prices dropped and eventually white people fled further out to places like Beachwood and Pepper Pike. Corey Moore should have been more realistic. He should have said, "All white people must evacuate Cuyahoga County" since they were leaving anyway.

As for the current neighborhood in which Aaron resided, Southeastern Colorado was much different than Northeastern Ohio in one resounding fact. In 1977, the same year that Corey was holding up the police station, a serial killer named Ed Kemper was sneaking out of Santa Cruz, California. After murdering ten people including his own mother, the Co-Ed Killer drove east for days through the desert. He carefully listened to the car's radio, expecting to hear news of the horrific defilement of his mother's corpse—Ed had decapitated her, putting her vocal cords in the garbage disposal to eternally silence her. On April 23rd, 1977, Ed found himself in the dusty town of Pueblo, Colorado, where he surrendered to local police. With this knowledge, Aaron wrote a final note on his report regarding the Denny's crisis:

"The Caller/shooter/hostage-taker was psychologically distraught by the confines of his neighborhood and the limited opportunities provided, which forced him to express his pain outwards by hurting those that he perceived had hurt him—*because Pueblo breaks even serial killers.*"

He signed the papers and placed them back in a folder before sliding it under Boss Lady's office door. On Monday, she'd be relieved to discover he was finally finished but would scold him for sliding the papers under her door when the drop box would have sufficed. Aaron left without saying goodbye to Debz because the smell of egg-salad irritated his stomach, and he drove home to wake up Zoë.

They ate a few left-over donuts for breakfast and wrapped up the old-fashioned ones for Eve. On their way to the Poinsettia Nursing Home, they first stopped to buy gas at the corner Loaf n' Jug. Aaron looked for the homeless woman that had gifted him the scrap of paper with ancient knowledge, but she was nowhere to be found.

Zoë entered the store and paid twenty dollars in cash on the correct pumping station while Aaron filled up the gas tank. He clicked the latch and locked the handle in place, then looked around to view the parking lot. Aaron noticed one scary looking guy with ripped jeans and dirty long hair that he'd seen several times and recalled the man had hit him up once or twice for loose change. Aaron wasn't bothered by his persistent begging, often offering a buck or two because he figured the man probably needed it. Aaron guessed that living on the street was harder than most people could imagine. Neither the hot, hungry days nor the cold, lonely nights could match the hardship of boredom. Standing around for twelve hours waiting for the shelter to open would leave anyone feeling existentially empty.

The man dug through the trash while mumbling to himself. Aaron thought he looked much older than his actual age because of the grime. He looked like a coal miner with layers of dirt on his face, neck and hands. His fingernails were charred and toes poked through the holes in his shoes. Aaron thought the man looked very *street*, like someone he did not want to mess with because, essentially, the man had nothing to lose. For this man, rock-bottom was a comfortable place to sleep.

Aaron watched the man amble over to entrance of the store and dump out the ashtray container to search for cigarette butts. This didn't bother Aaron since the man was only looking for a smoke. However, the man left a huge mess right in the pathway of the customers coming out of the store.

Aaron could not contain his irritation. "Yo, my man! You gonna pick up after yourself?"

The man screamed without looking up. "Don't fúckin talk to me! Don't look at me!"

Aaron heard the click of the gas handle and noticed the meter at only $19.26 worth of gasoline. The store owned him seventy-four cents. Aaron carefully walked towards the entrance as the homeless man continued to curse at him. Aaron was tempted to return back to the car, but the store owed him some money and back in the day, three quarters could have bought him an hour on a *Galaga* arcade machine. Three quarters also had bailed out Zoë's friend.

The man screamed, mostly at the trash can, when Aaron approached. "Come on now," he said to the man, "you don't need to be like that."

Aaron hoped his calm voice and easy demeanor would set the man at ease. The man ignored Aaron and kept up his diatribe of filth, cursing Jesus and Mary and the many patron saints, as other patrons in the gas station lot stared at them. When Zoë came out of the store, the man suddenly lunged at her.

Aaron couldn't reach the man in time to intervene physically so instead he hollered, "Hey, I'm gonna fùck you up!" Aaron wasn't sure why he chose those exact words, but he hoped the gratuitous use of *fuck* with a hard, authoritative tone would garner the man's attention long enough to allow Zoë a chance to escape. He needed to protect his daughter.

The man stopped and turned on Aaron. He calmly said, "You can't hurt me." Then his voice peaked in a shrill, "Pleeeeease jack me up, I wish you would!"

A hidden part of Aaron, the part that usually hid under the table, sprang from the deep well of hatred. When turned inwards, his anger became self-loathing depression. When turned outwards at a homeless man threatening his daughter, his anger erupted as violent rage. An alto-pitched voice that did not sound like Aaron announced with eager intent, "You want me to hurt you? Right on!"

Aaron and the man took two steps towards each other but froze because,

crazy
    recognizes
      crazy

and suddenly they were like two dogs who don't know what to do when the fence is pulled away. Silently, Aaron and the man slowly backed away from each other.

Zoë came around the man and grabbed her father's hand. "Dad, what's wrong with you? Let's get out of here." She pulled him back towards the car.

Aaron didn't take his eyes off the man as he retreated. He conjured no plan of action if the man attacked because Aaron had not been in a fight since the second grade when Mean Mikey was pulling the hair of Silly Susy and Anxious Aaron decided to do something about it, which amounted to a lot of pushing and crying.

Suddenly, someone pulled on his right shoulder. The secrets of *Cursed Crane* soared within Aaron and he reacted as though he had practiced the movement ten thousand times. Without looking, he smacked the guy behind him right in the balls. As the poor guy bent forward, Aaron chopped him in the throat.

The guy, dressed in shorts and a white tank top, gasped for breath. "I … was … just … asking for the time."

The homeless man again lunged at Zoë with both hands and this time Aaron did not attack with words but rather lashed out with the ferocity of a *Bhutanese Barking Dog*. Aaron pushed the man's arm away, continuing in a circle to strike the man in the groin.[107] As the man doubled over in pain, Aaron elbowed him squarely on the jaw.

The homeless man fell to the ground dazed. People gathered and pulled out cell phones to record the fight for YouTube, but the action was over. Aaron stood over his enemy victoriously. He had successfully protected his daughter. And that's when Aaron got punched in the face.

He never saw it coming. The guy in a white tank top had delivered a sucker punch while Aaron was distracted and staring down at the homeless man. For the first time, Aaron personally witnessed the stars of bitter pain. He suspected the starry effect was produced by his soft brain tissue concussing against the inside of his hard skull bone. His mouth had been open, and the sudden blow caused him to bite down on his tongue. On his way to the ground, he tasted metallic blood as his right eye swelled and was surprised that his plan had not worked. He had flawlessly performed two superb techniques and incapacitated his opponents, and Aaron could hear Mike Tyson's famous words as the ground rushed up to meet him. "Everyone's got a plan until they get punched in the face."

As Aaron struggled to his feet, the homeless man and the guy in a white tank-top rushed him again. Zoë stepped in front of her father and held up her hand. Aaron couldn't see what she was holding because of the swelling, but the effect was instantaneous. The two men's aggression dissipated like fog in wind.

Backing away, the homeless man screamed at him. "What the hell?! Why'd you attack me?"

Aaron wiped blood from his mouth. "Because you were going after my daughter."

"The first time I was reaching for the door, you idiot. Tryin to be nice."

Aaron considered that maybe the man had been opening the door for Zoë. "What about the second time you grabbed at her?"

"Tryin to get her out of the way."

"Why?" Aaron asked confused.

"You were freakin out, man! Look what you did to him," he said, pointing to the guy in the white tank top.

Aaron didn't know what to say. He looked around at the gathering crowd, shame and guilt slowly flooding his gut. The certainty of his righteous action faded into doubt. He had only been trying to protect his daughter. He turned back and said the one thing that will always calm men down.

"I'm sorry."

The two men silently stared as Zoë and Aaron retreated. Sitting in the car, his hands shook from the evaporating adrenaline. Aaron realized he had nearly made a lifelong mistake. The error was not losing the fight, but rather allowing the altercation to become physical in the first place because he had a lot to lose these days. He was no longer a twenty-year-old carrying a helium-inflated ego and a plutonium load of hyper-masculinity. He was a father, a land-owning, tax-paying citizen with a daughter that needed him to be present, a grandmother that needed constant care, and a mother and an aunt that needed his help as they grew older. His purpose was clear, he was needed to help carry the burden of imminent death. And someday, he might even be able to pay the bills.

Aaron wondered what would have happened if the homeless man had pulled a knife. He could have been stabbed in the face over cigarette butts. The man hadn't been hurting anyone. Aaron discovered the hard way, like so many men before him, that he wasn't as tough as he imagined. The homeless man had very little to lose whereas Aaron had everything to lose. Like the samurai, toughness and victory were determined by what one is willing to lose. Unlike the samurai, Aaron was unwilling to sacrifice his life. Not yet. But he was beginning to understand that no outcome could have been beneficial for him because it had been a no-win situation. Every possible scenario ended in defeat. Zoë could have been injured. Or he could have been robbed. Or he could have been beaten soundly and ended up in traction. Or he could have cut his hand on the homeless man's teeth and contracted Hepatitis C. Or he could have accidently crippled the guy who had asked him for the time and been sent to prison for aggravated assault. Aaron was lucky to have escaped with only a minor bruise. For his family, if not for himself, he had to stay healthy. He had to stay alive. And for now, family was reason enough.

Zoë stayed quiet on the ride home, but he could tell she was upset. As they turned into the driveway, she looked at him. "Why did you have to get in a fight?"

"I was trying to protect you," Aaron protested meekly. He had been beaten and embarrassed in front of his daughter and needed to regain his authority.

Zoë sighed. "Dad, I had it under control."

"What are you talking about?"

Zoë held out her hand and revealed a small container. "When I heard you arguing with the man outside, I bought some pepper spray. Figured we might need it."

Aaron perceived a vision of the two men withdrawing at the end of the fight not because of Aaron's fearsome display of martial arts but rather because Zoë had threatened them with a blinding dose of chemical spray. Sitting in the car with a blackening eye, he swelled with confidence because he knew that Zoë would be fine in college.

The blissful sensation instantly evaporated when Zoë turned to him as she opened the car door. "You get in any more fights, and I'm moving back in with my mom."

She collected her school bag and left the car door ajar. Aaron waited until she was inside the house before sobbing, the door chime providing a tempo for his falling tears.

Chapter 14

A Contributing Editor at Vanity Fair UK,
Suffering from Aphasic Migraines,
Gets No Help Researching an Article about the
Teenage Suicide Epidemic

A week after returning from the Rainbow Gathering, Aaron was ordered to participate in an interview with Susie Stillwater, a contributing editor on the staff of *Vanity Fair* with an impressive résumé of gripping narratives and in-depth reporting. Boss Lady informed him the reporter would be calling to discuss the research he'd been compiling for a pamphlet the Center wanted to distribute to high school counselors. Aaron was tempted to ask Boss Lady, "What pamphlet?" but decided not to piss her off at nine in the morning. Instead, he huddled in his office and threw a few paper clips over the wall at Debz. A harsh grunt alerted him that she was in no mood to mess around since she was only on her first cup of coffee.

"Rough night?"

"Ugh," she muttered.

"With your mom. Point."

When he received no further response, he threw another paper clip and heard a satisfying splash.

"Bastard," Debz cried, "that landed in my coffee!"

"Two points."

Aaron settled into his chair and thought about what he might say to Susie Stillwater when she called. He wasn't good at chit-chat, and suicide lacked the flippancy of topics like the weather or last night's game. He decided to convey one of his earliest memories at the Crisis Center.

On Aaron's first day of work in Year One, a twelve-year-old boy hung himself. Self-inflicted asphyxia via mechanical compression to blood vessels in the neck, causing a reduction in oxygenation of the brain, leading to cerebral hypoxia, anaerobic metabolism, and acidosis caused by a brown leather leash. A thin leash from the animal shelter the boy had used every day after school when taking his puppy to the park. The puppy was an adorable, fluffy buttercup poodle the family had yet to give a name and still called Puppy even though they'd owned the dog for over five years. Aaron knew this because he had spoken with the boy earlier that same morning for twelve and a half minutes.

Aaron often mentioned this anecdote when asked about his profession while chatting at a dinner party or receiving funds from the United Way and Rotary Club or interviewing with a journalist for the local paper. He hoped this story would suffice for an interview with a such a prestigious outfit that had won numerous National Magazine Awards, although Aaron had stopped reading *Vanity Fair* after the cover of Caitlyn Jenner had made him feel both aroused and terribly disturbed. Leibovitz had managed to capture both masculine fantasy and fear in a single shot.

Usually, Aaron would begin by explaining how he'd spent a decade of his adult life at the Suicide Prevention & Crisis Hotline Center, an organization originally started as a for-profit business with four landlines reached at 1-900 Don't-Die with the motto, "Spending a dollar per minute may save your life." This business was absorbed by a nationally funded Prevention accreditation service and changed the number to 1-800 Talk-To-Me, but received so many calls about people's financial problems, divorce settlements, malfunctioning lazy-boy chair incidents, bed-wetting, embarrassing nocturnal emissions, etc., that the Feds were overwhelmed by calls and changed the phone number again to 1-800 Do-It-Now, with a late-night jingle on PBS to the tune of a radio hit from the rock band *Queen*, "Don't try Suicide, nobody's worth it. Don't do it!"

However, this sentiment was slightly confusing to those with reoccurring suicidal ideation, possibly giving them the subtle indication to go ahead and do *it*, as in kill themselves, and not do *it*, as in call the hotline. Aaron would complain during these conversations with people that his knowledge of *felo de se*[108] had increased whereas his salary of $18,000/year had not. He collected ill-humored bits of datum that were popular at dinner parties, such as the numerous euphemisms involving the act of *sui caedere*,[109] as though one is merely acting suicidal, like acting in a play but without an audience and alone in a theater for the final soliloquy. Euphemisms like "Taking One's Life", as if taking instead of giving was positive like,

taking a friend out to dinner; or,

taking out the trash; or,

taking a woman out on the town; or,

taking a wife.

Euphemisms like "Erasing One's Own Map". Demapping, as in deleting your map, the deep contours of a face. Euphemisms like the "Bojangle Dangle", suicide by hanging that also racially implied a lynching; or,

Lead Aspirin (suicide by pistol); or,

Blowin the Lights (by shotgun); or,

Bought the Fumes Farm (by carbon monoxide); or,

Slippin the Wire (by razor); or,Suckin Poppers (by pills); or,

One-Way Ticket on the Night Train (pills & booze); or,

ALL ABOARD! (pills, booze, dope, uppers, downers & powerful sleeping agents, as in totally pharmacologically committed).

Aaron's personal favorite, because of his last name Clifton, had always been the expression "Jumpin to Conclusions". Another euphemism for suicide was "Breakin the Law" since suicide was illegal in twenty of the fifty U.S. states up through the 1980s and two Southern states held fast through the 1990s with *Wackwitz v. Roy* in Virginia declaring *it*[10] a common law crime, like a common law wife, both ill-advised by attorneys. Also, to this day there remains an antiquated consensus that to aid or assist in a suicide is not only against the law but goes against God's law. This ethical debate has been cluttered by the opinion that the person killing themselves is in fact aiding and assisting themselves in the act of murder, thus prosecutable. Helping someone to do *it* remains a felony in most countries except Switzerland, Germany and the Netherlands and most states, except the liberated Western states of California, Washington, Oregon, Colorado, Hawaii, and Montana as well as the two Eastern havens of The People's Republic of Vermont and the Politician's Swamp of the District of Columbia.

Therefore, when Aaron was asked at dinner parties what he did for a living, he'd say, "It's not what I do for a living, but instead what I do for the dying." To lighten the mood, he'd offer bits of ill-humored information for comedic relief, to ease not his discomfort of talking about death but instead to disperse the tangible tension seen in the cringing shoulders of stay-at-home moms every time he said the word *suicide*.

Suicide. Worse than a curse word. Worse than whispering a yo' momma joke to a best friend at his mother's funeral. "Hey Slim, yo momma's so dead, but she still gives great head." Worse than saying at a West African UNICEF fundraiser, "I've got Ebola. Don't worry, it's not an airborne contagion." Worse than talking about the Three Taboos of Polite Conversation—sex, politics, and religion—summarized in three words: "Trump rapes nun."

A few days after the Rainbow Gathering while attending a Fourth of July Weekend neighborhood barbeque, Aaron eased their troubled suburban minds with odd statistics.

"Who," Aaron asked, "do you think kills themselves the least?"

"We have no idea," a clique of housewives said, stabbing at Monterrey Jack cubes with tiny plastic forks while hoping someone would change the topic.

"White men kill themselves the most. In America, I mean. With a gun, usually."

"Interesting," they said, without moving their lips.

"Of course, women try twice as often, but men succeed four times more. Than women. Maybe women just can't commit."

Polite laughter. Shifting in shoes. Gazing at cell phones.

"Alright, I'll tell you. The Jews. Jews kill themselves the least, as an ethnic group."

"Really?" Interest piqued. "Because everyone else is out to get them?"

"Maybe. They've done prolonged studies. Maybe it has to do with the tight-knit families in Jewish communities, they generally don't move far from home. Or maybe survivor's guilt from the Holocaust, or those strict laws forbidding suicide in the Torah."

A woman jumped into the conversation, breaking one of the three commandments of polite discourse. "But Protestants and Catholics have those same Biblical laws. Doesn't stop them, right?"

"Ok, here's the thing," Aaron continued. "We all know married people kill themselves a lot less than single people, right?" Nodding like they know. "You could say marriage extends your life. But among married Jewish couples, they complete suicide twice as often!"

Real laughter. Aaron followed up with an old man accent, "Bubbala's been driving me crazy for sixty years! I'll get back at her, *oy vey*, won't she be sorry!" More laughter. He segued by pointing out the lovely flower centerpiece on the dining room table, then into how deliciously the Prosecco wine complimented the prosciutto. Later, Aaron heard the housewives re-telling the same joke to friends around the fondue, saying the word *suicide* without cringing hesitation.

For interviews, Aaron tried an approach other than summarizing data. Instead, he gave anecdotal evidence by talking about the boy and his puppy. A child's death usually silenced people and prevented any follow up questions. Except for reporters, they always wanted the gritty details.

The woman from *Vanity Fair* called right after lunch. Sleepy from eating too many *Game of Thrones*-themed Oreo cookies, Aaron was in no mood to talk. He'd already passed on three callers but picked up when he noticed the international prefix.

He interrupted Susie Stillwater and asked, "You in London?"

Stillwater response was sharply proper, as though she'd dealt with this line of questioning on numerous occasions. "Ooob-vee-ous-lee. I'm with Vanity Fair UK."

"Then how can we meet in person?"

"You're precious," Stillwater answered with a laugh. "Nobody does that anymore."

"When do you wanna do this?" Aaron asked, hoping to postpone the interview.

"Right now. Over the phone. That'd be fan-taaaas-tic. Let's get started," she said with a crisp and sweet tone rising at the end of each sentence.

"Can we at least Skype?" he asked, "I'd like to see who I'm speaking with."

"Whom."

"What?

"Whom, not who," Stillwater schooled him. "And ending a sentence with a preposition, really? Who are you, Winston Churchill?"

"Wait, has the interview started?"

"No, I'm dispensing a few pointers. Americans and your atrocious grammar."

"Alright then, cuz I was about to say it's not going very well."

"Fine, let's FaceTime," Stillwater said. "Will that work for you?"

"For whom?"

"See, you're getting it."

"No, I mean whom are you calling back?"

"Who, not whom."

"But you said…"

"Not in this case. Only as the object, not the subject."

"Ok," Aaron said utterly confused, "who is calling whom?"

"You've got it."

"No, I'm asking."

"Hanging up now. I've got your cell number."

"Wait…" Aaron blurted before being disconnected.

A few moments later, Susie Stillwater appeared on Aaron's cell phone, a pasty woman in her late thirties with auburn hair drawn up in a ponytail. Dressed in a grey sweat top with the blue emblem of the University of St. Andrews, she reclined on an aqua twill couch with a small canister of Aleve and a BPE-free plastic bottle of water on her lap. Aaron deduced the seven-hour time difference probably meant she had recently returned home from the office.

"So," Stillwater asked, rubbing her forehead, "what can you tell me about the recent teenage suicide epidemic in the States? Why the increase this year?"

"This year? Teen suicides have been on the upswing since the seventies."

"Really?"

"Well, in the mid-seventies, eleven kids killed themselves in San Mateo. And twenty-eight kids on Chicago's North Shore. These cluster groups were scaring the hell out of parents. Over the next decade, many schools scrambled to implement suicide prevention programs but suicide rates kept creeping higher. I remember Nancy Reagan on the television in these Choose Life public service announcements, 'If you have suicide on the mind, wait a minute.'"

"Did it work?"

"'Just Say No' would have worked better, but Nancy used that one for drug awareness. Leave it to a woman to start a slogan with the word *just*, such a submissively feminine word, like apologizing while asking for permission."

"Hold up, are you saying suicide prevention programs actually made the problem worse? May I quote you?"

"Whatever, but you'd be wrong. Talking about it helps, that's proven. It's the type of prevention that's the problem."

"Such as?"

"People went way overboard with this cuddly and soft approach to suicide," Aaron explained. "Like puppet shows and silly skits and revisions of *Romeo and Juliet* where the teens live happily ever after."

"The Bard is rolling over in his grave."

"Exactly, he knew you can't treat em like kids. There was this one psychiatrist from Cleveland who obliterated the romantic notions of suicide during his lecture to high school students. He showed hospital videos of pumping pills from a girl's stomach, a boy with half his face blown off, some left paralyzed after slitting their wrists, and others left blind after drinking poison. Then he led the students through a guided meditation scene that involved swallowing pills, climbing into bed and holding their breath as the drugs took over."

"Did that work?"

"Who knows. Probably scared most of them. Which is good because a lot of these kids I talk to every night try killing themselves a little at a time. You know, practice. That's why cutting is so popular. Tiny slits, deeper each time."

"And?"

"What do you mean, 'and'? They should be scared, suicide ain't nothin to mess around with. By the way, there was actually a decrease in suicide rates a few years ago."

"Why?"

"When gay marriage became legal in the States, suicide rates dropped. Tells you a lot."

"Interesting, I'll look into that."

"But last year, the rates for teens surged."

"Because?" Stillwater asked.

"I could give you a thousand reasons. Lingering national economic stress or an increase in substance abuse or the effects of repressing sexual assault or maybe even the Werther effect."

"The what now?"

"Named after Goethe's hero, Werther. Fictional character shot himself at the end of the novel and teens across Europe started copying him. Goethe felt awful because, as he put it, kids were 'transforming poetry into reality'. Anyway, rates generally go up after a publicized suicide. Celebrity suicides can actually have a suggestive effect. I guess it's contagious."

"You think so?"

"The month after Robin William committed suicide, there was a ten percent increase. Remember in early June when Anthony Bourdain killed himself three days after Kate Spade?"

"Of course. You're saying they were connected?"

"They both hung themselves but no, Kate suffered under years of anxiety and depression. And Tony's blood sugar dropped after missing a meal. Well, that and seeing his ex-wife with another man."

"What?"

"I'm guessing hers was planned, his more spontaneous. For example, imagine suicide as the metaphor of stepping out in front of a bus. For years, Kate saw it barreling towards her but Tony suddenly found himself in the middle of the street and," Aaron slapped his hand on the desk for emphasis, "whack!"

"Sounds quite different to me," Stillwater said.

"Both made a personal choice. They weren't encouraged to die by some hypothetical, social contagion, an idea argued by Émile Durkheim a hundred years ago. He thought people with suicidal ideation would kill themselves sooner or later. A fatalistic view but hey, he *was* French."

Stillwater choked while sipping from a water bottle and spewed liquid on her phone. Laughing, Aaron said, "Hope your phone is water-proof."

She wiped her mouth on a throw pillow. "How can you be so glib about Kate and Anthony? I loved Kate, own two of her scarves. We were quite shocked over here. Traumatized even."

"I remember. We got a lot of publicity after those two. Social media exploded, newspapers and magazines ran stories all summer about increasing suicide rates. We even scored a little extra funding. You could say they helped the cause."

"Let me get this right, celebrity suicides are a good thing?"

"Reminds us that if a million bucks and adoring fans don't lead to contentment, then what ever could? Television personalities, fashion designers, even rock stars. Everyone running from pessimistic existential dissatisfaction. Celebrities simply have better drugs."

"Can I quote you on that?" Stillwater joked.

"Remember the lead singer of Soundgarden?" Aaron asked. "Doesn't matter if the celebrity was in a grunge band venting depression or on a cooking show dreading divorce. After the noise quieted down, Chris Cornell and Anthony Bourdain still found themselves alone in a hotel bathroom."

"You're saying sadness equals suicide?" Stillwater asked. "Can't be that simple. Depression can be cured with pills."

"Depression might come from the brain's pharmacy, but the world writ large is the doctor who ordered the prescription."

"Stealing that."

"Go right ahead," Aaron said. "Anyway, suicide is the second leading cause of death for teens."

"What's the first?"

"Boredom."

"Good one," she laughed. "I need some color for my article. Got any stories for me?"

"Straight to it, huh? Alright, my first day on the job, there was this kid and his puppy," he said, hoping the ensuing story would quickly end the interview.

"Teenager?"

"Does twelve count?"

"Sure. Go on."

Aaron hated how she constantly interrupted him. He'd never get through the story and decided to speed it up. "Kid was walking his dog and the leash broke. Dog ran out into the street and was hit by a car."

"Let me guess," Stillwater said. "Kid goes home and hangs himself. He's crackers. Big deal. Tell me something I don't know."

She's a tough one, Aaron thought. Might be hard to shake her.

"Fine," he said. "I spoke with the kid soon after the dog died."

"And?"

"He couldn't imagine living life without his best friend. I tried to tell him he was so young and that he'd get over it."

"Guess that didn't work out so well."

"I don't say that anymore," Aaron sighed. "I don't tell anyone to just get over it. There's that word again. Just. Besides, I really don't know how to talk to boys. Or to men."

"We'll get back to that," Stillwater said, jotting in a small notebook. "Your boss mentioned you're writing a pamphlet."

"Not really writing, more wronging."

"What?"

"I don't write, I wrong."

"Super," she said without a laugh. "It's a pamphlet for college, correct?"

"High school."

"Right. Yanks call it high school. Have you finished writing the pamphlet?"

"Not yet."

"Have you even started?"

"Not yet."

"Do you know what it's about?"

"Not yet."

"Are you even a writer?"

"Not yet"

"Sounds like a struggle." Stillwater pushed, "Let's be honest, you don't know how to help these kids, do you? Do you consider yourself a failure?"

"Not yet."

"Well," she said, looking him up and down on FaceTime, "this has been a complete waste of time. At least you look professional. Sweater vest and slacks, how quaint. Dressing for success even if you are a failure." Aaron was glad she couldn't see that his beige slacks were several sizes too big and torn at the cuff, and the sweater had moth holes on the back side.

Debz had been listening in on the call and leaned over the wall. "Give it to him, guuurl! But he's not a failure. He just sucks at his job."

"Hey," Aaron protested, "easy now."

"Point!"

Stillwater looked confused. "What was that about?"

"It's a game we play." Aaron, under siege by the two women, decided to offend their feminine sensibilities. He spoke loud enough for Debz to hear. "Yes, I try to dress up occasionally, because you can either dress for success or dress to suck less."

"Hmmm?"

"You know, dress up to suck less. You're what, about forty years old?"

"Don't be a twat."

"Well, I'm forty and I've found there are only two things a man needs to express on a first date. That he's free of STDs and has a vasectomy. A man like that is golden."

"Ace," she said indifferently.

"But for a woman, it's different. At your age when heading out on a fancy date, you're probably dressed up in an evening gown. But since the sexual debauchery of your twenties, you've acquired both a sense of fashion and self-respect. Dress up to suck less. I've always figured the older a woman gets the less head she'll give."

"Age has nothing to do with it," Stillwater said, unphased by Aaron's vulgarity. "It's called wisdom, you bloody wanker. Besides, I wouldn't know about any of that but go ahead and ask my girlfriend."

Debz laughed over Aaron's shoulder. "Ha, sucka! She's a dyke, she don't play the Game of Thrones, she plays the Game of Flats."

Stillwater laughed and took three blue pills with a gulp of water. "That's smashing, haven't heard that one in ages."

Aaron pushed Debz away. "Hey, this is my interview, get outta here!"

Stillwater leaned forward. "She's a sharp one, right? Maybe I should talk to her."

"She can't help you. She don't take teen calls," Aaron said, motioning with a thumb for Debz to get back in her cubicle.

Debz drooped her shoulders and meandered to her desk, muttering, "All I do is take teen calls…"

"Please don't be offended," Aaron said, focusing on the reporter. "I'm testing the waters, judging how you react. Always thought an interview should go both ways."

Debz landed a final parting shot. "Like your mom goes both ways! Point."

Stillwater rubbed the back of her neck with a free hand. "Listen, this is mildly entertaining, and I do emphasize mildly, but I'm completely knackered."

"So, how bout it? Are there behaviors you don't tolerate any longer on a first date?"

"As a lesbian? I think maybe it's different."

"Maybe, but I doubt it. In the beginning of any relationship, you gotta do things that aren't exactly fun, know what I mean? Like pretending to enjoy baseball. I've always suspected a young woman, say under twenty-five, is constantly trying to please her partner. She'll say things like, 'I just want to make you happy,' but then maybe over the next ten years…"

"You can stop, none of this can go in the article."

"…up until say thirty-five, they are finally figuring out their bodies and their own wants and needs, physically I mean, then say late thirties, it finally happens." He paused for effect.

"What happens, Mister Man? In your expert opinion," she said, feigning interest.

"She is able to finally separate her emotional needs from her physical desires. Something any eighteen-year-old boy can do without thinking, in fact thinking has nothing to do with it, merely a reaction to the idea of sex, a biological hard-on careening through the generations with the sole purpose of procreation for reasons beyond his control, certainly not mixing love into the equation. Yet mature ladies, say around forty, maybe after their first divorce, finally unburdening themselves of some asshole husband who only wanted one thing for the last two decades until his sex-drive finally kicked down into, say, third gear going about twenty miles per hour, kinda idling most of the time instead of revving in first gear at eight thousand RPMs, totally red-lining the dick-tachometer since the age of fourteen. Finally slowing down in his forties, he looks over at his wife one night and asks, 'What the hell are you good for?' and so she panics, convinced that her body no longer attracts his attention, because for two decades she's known the adage passed from every mother to daughter since Naomi to Ruth."

"And what Biblical knowledge is that?" Stillwater asked, putting her notepad down.

"Screw a man once a week, he'll love you. Twice a week, he'll do anything for you. And suck his dick once in a while, that poor slob will think you're his goddamned soul mate!"

Stillwater offered only silence, her face drawn tight.

"So," Aaron asked, "have you figured that out?"

"Not yet," she said with a wink. Stillwater closed her notebook and asked, "This is completely off topic, but earlier you mentioned an interesting point. You don't know how to talk to men? Explain."

"Do you?" he asked. "Know how to talk to men, I mean."

"Now that you mention it," she said, "not really. Don't have much use for them. I have a female boss and a girlfriend. I'm an only child who was raised by a single mom. I had a gay aunt who came over on the weekends and even she had a female dog."

"A real bitch, huh?"

"Stupid joke. Moving on. Wait," Stillwater announced, "I'm going to call you out on that."

"I thought this was an interview, not a lecture."

"Not when you start dropping gender-discriminatory language. I can handle the oral sex nonsense, but I'm going to reclaim the word *bitch*."

"Here we go," Aaron said, preparing himself for a feminist rant.

"This won't take long," Stillwater declared. "Bitch is a powerful word. Yes, I'm a bitch. I'm a strong woman. I'm a nasty woman. I'm a dirty girl. I'm a woman who gets the job done. I speak up in meetings and praise other women for their ideas and I do it in front of men. I'm a bitch because I don't need a man to open a jar of pickles. I'm a bitch because I have zero time for small talk. I'm a bitch because I point when I want something done. And I'm a bitch because I never say sorry, I just say 'Ta, cheers!'"

"Jeez, no need to be a biátch. Is that correct, did I say it right?"

"Almost, but more elongated like bee-aah-ch. Fine, back to the interview. Or should I say not-an-interview because I can't use any of this but now I'm intrigued. Curious, exactly how does one learn to talk to men?"

"You don't. Let them do the talking." They both laughed as Aaron continued. "Seriously, talk about work and you'll be fine. But here's the thing, no one wants to talk about suicide, or even worse, suicide prevention, and since I am a man, after all, I had to figure out how to hang out with guys, right?"

"I guess so. I never did but whatever. Seemed like a waste of time."

"Well," Aaron said, "I figured out two topics would help me. The first was sports."

"Ugh. I mean cricket is alright, but you're talking about American football, right?"

"Doesn't matter. I picked a team at random. Basketball because the season's longer. Thought it would be fun to root for an underdog team from the heart of America, so I picked the Cleveland Cavaliers. And I like maroon and gold."

"Isn't that the team with LeBron?"

"King James in da houuuze!" Aaron cried out. "Sorry, it's an automatic male reaction, can't help it. Yes, he was in Cleveland before taking a long vacation to Miami but then the Prodigal Son returned and even the mayor wanted to rename the Mistake by the Lake to Jamestown or LeBronville. Now he's playing ball in Hollywood."

"Sorry, didn't quite catch that. I did read how he donated a considerable amount of his own wealth to educate kids."

"Eighty-seven million dollars at first. He started a foundation to pay for the education of hundreds of children in Akron. And another eight million for the I Promise School."

"Rather impressive."

"Exactly. See, that's why I memorized those stats and figures. LeBron played every game last season and scored an average of twenty-seven points per game. And remember when Kyrie Irving won the Championship game by draining a three pointer against Golden State, right in Steph's face?!"

"Nope."

"Kyyyy-reeeee, baby! Sorry, comes right outta me. I have no idea why, but other men know these things too, or at least pretend to, and we have to be able to drop stats on Monday morning around the water cooler or at half-time down at the local bar. Yesterday, standing in line at the bank, wearing my favorite NBA hat and this guy behind me was like, 'Dude, the Cavs suck!' No way I'm gonna back down and lose face, so I told him how the King is on his way to breaking Kareem Abdul-Jabbar's all-time scoring record, and the guy said, 'Yeah, you right bro, LeBron is tight!' and with a solid brohug, we're now friends for life."

"Moving on. What's the second topic to help you connect with men?"

"I learned to play golf. And violà, conversation for years. It's a simple sport that men love because it's the same game, over and over and over again. Same course, same grass, same holes. Kinda like marriage."

"Seriously, you made a golf-sex joke? Is that all we are to you men? Three holes and a warm body?"

"No, of course not. You can also cook."

Stillwater chuckled. "That's both hilarious and quite perverse. I take it you're single?"

Debz cried out, "Ha, sucka, she got you again!"

Aaron ignored Debz and said, "Ok, seriously, let me try to give a straight answer. Yes, we talk about sports and golf and work and more about work, but we usually talk about ourselves."

"That's not true, I hear guys talking about women constantly. Degrading usually, but you do talk about us."

"Sure, we talk about women. We talk about the pieces, but not the whole puzzle. We focus on eyes or legs or hair color. T and A, basically."

"How boring."

"Pieces. We talk about the things we've done *with* her, like how we went hiking last weekend. Or what we've done *to* her, like bragging about how after the hike we nailed her on top of Pike's Peak. Or what we've done *for* her, like carrying her down the mountain after she sprained her ankle."

"Such little boys, never growing up."

"And do you know why most men remain boys?"

"Because you're childish and immature. And you only listen when spanked."

"That's probably true. It's because their mothers spoiled them. As a result, they're always testing a woman's limits."

"It's the mother's fault? That's downright cliché."

"We're curious to see what we can get away with. That's why boys with strict mother's end up marrying strong women. They never got away with misbehavin and grew up right. Oh, I almost forgot. We talk about cars a lot, too."

"Shocking," she said sarcastically. "I hadn't noticed."

"I always forget that one cuz I don't know much about cars. Tried to change my oil once, added antifreeze by accident. Car didn't run so well after that. That's why I own Hondas, they last forever. Where was I?"

"Describing your vast insight into the female tolerance for male incompetency. Hold on," Stillwater said. She placed the phone down and Aaron could hear a faucet running in the background.

During the break, Aaron opened a drawer and pulled out a canister of cashews. He figured she'd be hanging up soon and was surprised when she returned with a wet hand towel draped across her eyes and forehead. She leaned back into the stiff couch cushion and asked rhetorically, "You were saying?"

Aaron continued his diatribe with a mouthful of nuts. "We either brag or complain about women, but never really talk about you as a separate entity. More like the effect women have on us, yet another way to talk about ourselves. I met a guy at a barbeque last week, a dentist probably, I wasn't listening, and he talked about his wife for half an hour and I still knew nothing about her. Clueless as to her interests, her passions, where her family originated, the fears that keep her awake at night, religious views, her position on the Brett Kavanaugh scandal, any of her dreams and aspirations, if they had kids together, or even where she worked. The husband only complained about how miserable or happy she made him. When she finally came over to join us, I figured out in two minutes that she loved the poetry of Robert Browning, we had a mutual friend who volunteered at the East Side Soup Kitchen and she was passionate about some professional sports team named the Reds but I wasn't sure if she was talking about hockey or baseball. I also discovered she had an irrational fear of insects that kept her up at night because," and Aaron imitated her silky New Jersey accent, "'of da creepy-crawly bug-scene in *Indiana Jones and the Temple of Doom* where da female actrezz, I forgot her name, she gotta reach into dat awful hole n' pull some kinda lever, oh my Gaaawd, I ken feel dem bugs all ova my skin!'"

Aaron paused before switching back to his regular Colorado accent[111] and finished by saying, "The dentist's wife was the most interesting person in the room and so I flirted with her shamelessly right in front of her boring husband to show him how lucky he was to have such a brilliant woman in his life."

Stillwater leaned forward and removed the towel from her face. "You're such a tosser."

"Not yet," he said with a smile. "Alright, we're almost done but I wanted to give you something for your article."

"God praise the Queen!" she exclaimed, opening her notebook.

"Remember the boy and his puppy? The kid who hung himself with the dog's leash."

"I remember."

"Well, the dog wasn't dead after car ran it over. So, the kid picked up a rock and smashed the puppy's brains out."

"Bloody hell."

"Exactly. The kid was very specific. And his mother caught him. She had seen him through the window. His mother scolded him, said he was going to Hell for killing the puppy."

"And?"

"Well, he ran upstairs to his bedroom, called the suicide hotline and told me the whole story. Said he was going to kill himself."

"Why, because he'd executed his dog?"

"No, because his mom was a biaaaatch!"

"Really?"

"The boy wanted to get back at her. I mean, sure, he was upset about the dog but also angry because his mother had made him feel guilty. He only wanted to end the puppy's misery."

Sounding like an ol' granny, Stillwater said, "Cor blimey."

Aaron suspected she was making fun of him because he hadn't been exactly helpful for Stillwater's article, so he offered one final explanation. "I know why teens are committing suicide."

"Pray tell."

Before hanging up, he said, "The guilt mothers place on their kids. That's what killing them."

Corrupted by Christian Rock and the Falling Star

Once a year, Aaron suffered an unholy craving more potent than sugar or dope, starting around Halloween and lasting two weeks at most, during which he found himself scanning the radio stations for a particular genre easily identified by a single line: The upbeat chorus, the pseudo-rock guitar riffs sans ear-shattering solos, pounding bassline via drum machine, and the whiny, privileged, suburban, upper middle-class, white, adolescent voice, recently dropped an octave yet sometimes breaking on high notes, professing divine passion repeated in the chorus with an obvious message,

nail and kneel,

saved and sky,

passion and pain,

blood and Bethlehem.

Christian Rock. The theological predilection began after Aaron graduated from college when people teased him mercilessly until he learned to hide his embarrassing musical inclination. Aaron feared losing favor from his family and friends given the contrasting combination of his childhood connections. The ultra-reformed, vastly-assimilated Judaic heritage passed down from a distant father, the kind of lineage that allowed admittance to the Jewish Community Center but didn't demand a Bar Mitzvah, whereas his mother Marilyn offered a Catholic viewpoint but had only managed to drag him on a few annual church ski retreats. This experience was the extent of his Judeo-Christian conditioning. Listening to one type of religious music would have indicated parental preference, and Aaron wanted to please both his parents despite his father's absence, because even an unseen father demands obeisance. This conflict manifested itself by Aaron's annual holiday selection of both *Fiddler on the Roof* and *Jesus Christ Superstar.*

The fear of his parents discovering any overt religious musical interest forced him to hide Christian Rock CDs in his collection or on his computer under the comedian Chris Rock. He also barred himself from programming radio or satellite stations with names like The Message or K-Love, not to be confused with the power forward on the Cleveland Cavaliers. Even as an adult, his aberrant musical predilection only lasted a few weeks per year and he'd listen secretly in his car with the lights off, engine idling in the driveway to keep warm during the cool autumn nights, his fingers on the steering wheel drumming to the Jesus-inspired refrain. He loved the drastic struggle, the epic sadness, the iconic oppression, the heroic self-sacrifice, and the mythic obsession with blood and misery and sin. The thematic images intertwined with lyrics of idealistic courage and classic endurance inspired by electric passion and cosmic love. The passion softened him, snagged his soul and opened his heart.

Adrift, the only way Aaron described himself after graduating college. Since kindergarten, society had provided him a purpose. Awoken by an alarm to arrive at school by the first bell, he studied in class until the next tolling. Even recess and gym class had a buzzer, and he changed subjects every hour at the sound of yet another bell, only to rush home and repeat for sixteen years. Grade school, junior high, high school, college. Every institution preparing for the final exam— accepting a job at a place where another bell would urge him to clock-in and clock-out on time, never questioning this routine because he'd been programmed from inception.

For the first time, in those first few days after college, he found himself without an alarm. Unemployed, out of school, living in a new city and setting up a new apartment, cross-legged on freshly steam-cleaned beige carpet while eating Chinese take-out with warped chopsticks and wondering what to do with his life. On 92.9FM where "Jesus Rocks the Rockies," he absently listened to a few songs without knowing, tapping his foot, staring at the off-beat wobble of an overhead fan, his earthly possessions taped up in boxes scattered in the wrong rooms. Dishes in the bedroom, CDs spread out on the bathroom floor, and shampoo bottles on the porch. Finally, he was out on his own, out of his mother's house, out of his college dorm, and out into the wide world. Alone, out of his mind.

For several months before the end of college, the anxiety of impending solitude created an overwhelming numbness that could only be relieved by cutting himself. He had started with tiny cuts on his fingertips, the throbbing pulse familiar company. He progressed to his wrists, inside of his thighs, edge of his hip, anywhere easily covered up. The cuts were shallow and healed quickly with vitamin E oil. Adrift in a cycle of self-harm, Aaron hoped to anchor his nervousness by finding a new place to live.

On his first night alone, he decorated his new apartment, hanging M.C. Escher posters with scotch tape, setting up a desktop computer on the kitchen table, and throwing down a mattress on the floor. In those few hours until dawn while he unpacked, the radio covertly snuck praise-worthy songs into his vulnerable soul. He was humming along to the chorus before he even knew the words.

Regrettably, the blaring Evangelical radio waves repulsed Aaron's friends and prevented them from helping him unpack. For the first few days, alone in his new apartment, he witnessed the Holy Spirt in every song by every artist, completely contaminating his listening experience as he started to keep score for the Trinity.

Keeping a list of popular music, Aaron discovered the Son is sung about nearly 66% of the time, the Father garners 33% and the Holy Ghost isn't fairing so well. The Doors *Waiting for the Sun* scores one for Jesus, but Luther Vandross and his *Dance with my Father* gives a point to the Big Man, but back to the kid for The Beatles and their declarative *Here Comes the Sun*, and Cat Stevens's famous *Father & Son* gives an alley-oop double point for both, yet Beyoncé takes it back to G-d with *Daddy*, and The Velvet Underground's *Who Loves the Sun* scores another for the Jewish-carpenter. But where is the spectral spirit? Perhaps *Ghostbusters* because he ain't afraid of no ghost or even *Spirits in the Material World* by the Police but Aaron admitted to himself that would be really stretching it and gave up his tally, and after three days without explanation, Aaron rose from his delusions and returned to his collection of Grunge without another thought of religiously-deceptive lyrics, so that even songs like Soundgarden's *Jesus Christ Pose* and *Hand of God* and *Heretic* held no particular relevance for him. That is until about a year later, around Halloween, when he heard *Smells like Teen Spirit* and his obsession for Christian Rock returned for another week or two. Score one for the Holy Ghost.

One week after moving into his first apartment, baptized by a vulnerable, religiously addled emotional state, Aaron made a pilgrimage to a concert headlined by the band 10 Years. He thought they were a Christian Rock band because they had song titles like *The Wicked Ones* and *Cast It Out* and *Waking Up the Ghost* and *Chasing the Rapture* and *Halos* and *From Birth to Burial* and finally *Wasteland*, a name more T.S. Eliot than Biblical.

In the parking lot, Aaron scored a ticket for himself from some kids smoking ditch weed and huffing on colored balloons filled with nitrous oxide. Dancing in the middle of the group was a blue eyed, blonde haired girl in a tie-dyed skirt tripping on LSD. And that's how he met Lena.

"Hey."

"Hey."

This fascinating bit of unscripted dialogue led to kissing, and Aaron blamed the residual acid from her tongue as the culprit for his lack of memory and lack of control. The drugs also blurred his grammatical integrity and he found it remarkable that the dread-headed singer could race through first, second and third person pronouns in the very first stanza.

> *She, she is the love that you make and break.*
> *And he, he is the drug that you hate to crave.*
> *And I, I am the liar you made to praise.*
> *And you, you are the one we want and made.*
> *We are the loss of your innocence.*

Exploring the wide-open amphitheater with Lena, they found an abandoned blanket and watched the teeming mass of American adolescence. Aaron extemporized how the song meant there were three wicked people coming for an unspecified listener.

"The He, She and I of the song, they're coming for You."

Lena disagreed. "You're overthinking it. It's just a stupid song."

"But the We represents the collective consciousness of temptation."

"Stop talking and kiss me."

"Three people who have been corrupted by heartbreak, drugs and lies. And misery loves company."

"Check out the clouds…"

"Especially when the youth can be so easily corrupted."

She looked at him with dilated pupils. "Is that what you're trying to do? Steal my innocence?"

"You're the one who dosed me." The song continued and repeated a line that stuck in Aaron's head.

> *We are the loss of your innocence.*
> *Kill yourself to save yourself from yourself.*

"That doesn't make any sense," she said in between kisses.

"Sure, sometimes the pain is too much." Aaron showed her the scars on his left wrist. She traced a lone finger down his flesh inscription.

Impressively, she didn't flinch. She rolled up her tie-dyed sleeve and exposed her wrist to prove her own pain. Ten cross cuts, some fresh wounds and others healed by time.

Aaron instantly fell in love. Without a word, he grabbed her hand and raced towards the swarming bodies in front of the stage. A raucous mosh-pit had developed at the start of *Wasteland*, a video Aaron had seen on MTV and figured the song dealt with the atrocities of human trafficking but after listening to the lyrics figured out the lead singer was probably singing about heroin. Holding hands, they plunged into the wild mob. Aaron was elbowed in the back by a drunken skater punk and he lost hold of Lena's hand. The sky went red as the drugs kicked in. The song changed but the crowd didn't notice, they continued moshing during the silence. Bodies were

sweating

bruising

crushing

screaming.

Aaron loved being right in the center of the crowd, surrounded by bodies on all sides, his fist pumping wildly in the air and unable to breathe. Aaron pushed close to stage and looked up at Jesse, the lead singer. With impressive dreads flailing wildly, the man's voice exuded passion, his eyes shone sorrow and his cheekbones radiated honesty. Every girl wanted him, and every guy wanted to be him. Aaron developed a man-crush that would prognosticate future events, although he hated the term man-crush.

While earning bruises in the mosh-pit and building up his tolerance for self-harm, Aaron decided that "man-crush" is still a crush, and adding *man* as a prefix fails to prevent one's masculinity from being feminized because it sounds even more girlie. "Man-bun" sounds like a Danish pastry and when a guy with a man-bun grasps his penis like a two-handed sword, he mistakenly thinks he's a samurai like Toshiro Mifune. Additionally, a "man-purse" is made of coarse leather and presumedly holds large caliber guns and meat sandwiches, but it's just a handbag. "Man-flu" involves more moaning, but it's just a bad cold. A "mankini" shows off way more hair than a bikini, but it's just a swimsuit. "Manscara" and "manliner" are just cosmetic make-up tools for goths and drag queens. "Mansplaining" assumes women are stupid and is associated with assertiveness and leadership, but it's just the act of talking-without-listening. And a "man-whore" is just a slut.

Aaron looked for Lena in the crowd and hoped she wasn't hurt. He pushed off from the stage to search for her but was distracted when Jesse the lead singer climbed up on a piece of scaffolding and hung over the crowd. No one seemed to notice as people thrashed wildly to the pounding drums and echoing guitar riffs. Aaron was torn between finding Lena and making sure the lead singer wouldn't plummet to his death. The man dangled only about fifteen feet above the crowd, but a fall from that height could easily snap his neck, leaving the handsome rock star with a severed lumbar vertebra resulting in a future locked in a wheelchair and eating dinners through a straw.

The crowd wasn't looking up as the lead signer let go of the metal scaffolding and hung by his legs while miraculously clutching the microphone in both hands. Aaron appraised the crowd and discovered no one preparing to catch him. Aaron pointed up but everyone mistook it for the universal sign for Heavy Metal music with index and pinky finger extended as horns, and they imitated him by throwing their fists into the air. And that's when Jesse the Rock God fell from the sky.

Aaron rushed forward and caught the falling star squarely in his arms. Together they crashed to the ground, both unhurt. Talk about a man-crush, Aaron thought. Another body had cushioned their fall and lay under them. Someone else had seen the singer fall and sacrificed themselves to save him. As the singer stood up, lyrics unhalted through the whole performance, Aaron noticed the other person was none other than Lena.

The two of them seemed to be the only people who had noticed the singer's stunt. Aaron reached for her hand as the singer pushed through bodies back to the stage, unaware that his acrobatics had re-united two lost lovers. After surviving the mosh-pit, Aaron and Lena returned to their stolen blanket where she opened herself to him in the fading light. Their love was quick, furious, adrenaline-enhanced, and over before the next song ended.

Years later, Aaron wouldn't remember most of the details of that night but he would always blame that Jaṭā haired singer. Maybe Aaron would not have found Lena that night, searching the crowd for some girl tripping on acid that he'd made-out with earlier. If he hadn't found her again, then he wouldn't have gotten her pregnant and their marriage wouldn't have failed because of the pressures of a new born baby on a young couple, and she wouldn't have started drinking and he wouldn't have ended up taking the first job offered as a social worker because he heard a line at a rock show about killing yourself to save yourself.

Aaron blamed others for a lot of things that night but even over ten years later, he still blamed himself for the loss of Lena's innocence. He'd seduced a girl who only wanted to kiss. As the first song had prophesied, Aaron figured out that Lena was the broken love, he himself was the drug, and Zoë was the one they both wanted and made. In retrospect, Aaron was amazed that his whole life could have been determined in one night by going to a rock concert and taking acid for the first time to conceive a love child on the lawn of an amphitheater while seriously considering the positive attributes of suicide. And the saddest part for Aaron—they weren't even a Christian Rock band!

Chapter 15

Piercing the Veil of Mirage

Sitting at his desk in the Crisis Center after talking to the reporter from *Vanity Fair*, Aaron received a Xanax-inspired call. Many calls Aaron received were from teenage girls Attempting. Usually, they were not actively in the act of a suicidal Attempt but certainly on the edge of a nervous boyfriend. A large portion of those calls were not directly *from* the girl herself but rather *about* the teenage girl. The call was often made by the same get-on-again-now-get-off-me type of boyfriend who was on the receiving end of desperate texts indicating that she, the Attempting girlfriend, might be pregnant and threatening to down a bottle of Xanax.

"Xanax, really?" Aaron asked the nervous boyfriend. "How many bottles does she have?"

"I don't know, maybe half."

"It's a Benzo but she'll be fine. She's going to need a lot more than half a bottle, believe me." As long as she didn't mix it with alcohol, Aaron thought, but he didn't mention that in order to ease the kid's mind.

"She's not gonna die?"

"Give me her number and I'll find out."

"But won't they arrest her? It's a crime, right? Wait, never mind." The boyfriend, insecure and realizing he might be over-reacting, decided not to give Aaron the girl's number and hung up.

In case the boyfriend or the Xanax-girl called back, Aaron needed to persuade them that suicide was no longer viewed as a crime. The word *commit* sounded criminal which was why he tried to say *complete* suicide instead, even though Aaron knew that most people considered both homicides and suicides to be an act of murder. The fear of being killed is innate but the truth is scarier:

Across the globe,
> suicides occur more than twice as often as homicides
>> which proves we are a greater risk to ourselves
>>> than from anyone else.

The Xanax-threatening girl called a few minutes later after she found out her boyfriend had reported her intent to the suicide hotline.

She assured Aaron that she was fine, but of course she wasn't. Occasionally, a teenager would call who was exactly Zoë's age, same tonal voice inflections, same American accent with an emphasis on abbreviating words like *bee-tee-dubs* instead of the extended, and shorter to pronounce, *by the way*.

Aaron discovered she wasn't taking Xanax. In fact, she didn't have any pills. Rather, she was in the middle of cutting herself, holding a steak knife in her right hand, left wrist extended, phone cradled under her chin. Aaron knew this because the girl was very specific. Said she'd been in twenty-eight different foster care families over the course of her life. Said her twelve-year-old sister killed herself last year, and Xanax-girl was the one who found her bleeding to death in the dining room. Wrist slit vertically. Thigh slit laterally. Xanax-girl was very specific.

"Your sister?" Aaron asked.

"My foster sister, I'd only been with them for three weeks. She did it because of me."

"Why do you blame yourself?"

"Because of the cuts. She sliced her radial artery, like I showed her."

Aaron decided not tell her it might have been a cephalic vein, which were much easier to access than the deeper arteries. "You showed her? What about the cut on her leg?"

Xanax-girl spoke evenly. "She cut her femoral artery. Just like I showed her."

"And you found her," Aaron stated instead of asking. "That's too bad."

"Why?"

"Because you had to clean up the mess. I mean, those arteries must have spurted!"

Xanax-girl laughed and Aaron knew she was making up the story. Probably read some medical journal at her foster parent's house. Sometimes when the Caller was too specific, he knew they were either delusional or simply a creative teen, as if there was a difference.

Aaron accused her of lying, one of his common tactics. At first, Xanax-girl denied then finally admitted to making up some of it. Even though Aaron doubted many parts of her story, he knew that within every lie is always a painful truth. Xanax-girl was isolated and felt very alone. Yet, in her stories she expressed how she could help her friends even when she couldn't help herself. She'd been told so many times she was worthless, unwanted, unimportant. And somehow, she survived. She found strength by reciting a little motto to keep her going.

The Xanax-girl who sounded like Zoë said, "Every night, before I go to bed, I tell myself to have Ache-ooh-pee-eee."

"It aches when you pee?" Aaron asked. "You might wanna get that checked out."

"No, silly. The letters of hope."

"Ah, an acronym."

"Yeah, whatevs. H-O-P-E. As in Hang On, Pain Ends."

Aaron laughed, "That's cute."

"But do you think it's true?"

"Sure, pain ends. Not forever, but at least it gives you a break. More like pain subsides."

"Sub what?"

"You know, it goes away for a little while."

"Like the ocean," she said. "The tide comes in and out."

"Exactly."

"But," she asked, "the pain ends when you die, right?"

"Maybe. Maybe not. Ask Hamlet. You're a kid, what do you know about pain?" Aaron immediately regretted his rhetorical question. After thirty-one foster families, she probably had a good grasp of suffering.

"And you're just another asshole telling me to smile, be happy, and get over it. You've never been a teenage girl."

Obviously, Aaron thought, she'd seen *The Virgin Suicides*. He was happy to hear the energy in her voice and said, "You're right. I have no idea. But take your own advice about hope and believe it."

"Like my little sister from the forty-second foster home who believed in hope? Well, you can shove that hope right up your ass!" screamed the girl who sounded like Zoë.

Suddenly, Aaron wasn't so sure she'd made up the bit about her sister bleeding to death on the hardwood floor. After the call ended, her residual tone left Aaron missing his daughter. He popped two Ketamine, swiped from the Crisis Center's emergency stash, and left work early.

Later in the evening, when Zoë came home late from soccer practice, Aaron stood in the hallway and hugged his daughter. He held on for so long that she became uncomfortable and finally asked him, "What's wrong?"

"Promise you'll talk to me first. Before you do anything."

"Not this talk again, Dad. I'm fine."

"But I'm not."

"You wanna talk?" Zoë could be a real sweetheart sometimes, Aaron thought. "I mean, I have a lot of homework but I've got a few minutes. Hey, what's for dinner?" And then again, she was still a teenager.

"Had a tough call today." He told Zoë that the acronym for HOPE was Hang On, Pain Ends.

Zoë's quick-wit emerged while she opened the fridge. "High On Pot Everyday!"

Aaron countered with, "How about a teen-support group? Help Our Parents Endure."

They laughed and created different variations of HOPE until dinner was ready. Cold spaghetti from the previous night and two burnt pieces of toast. Aaron didn't have the strength to make a proper dinner, and Zoë didn't have time to care. They ate standing in the kitchen since the table was littered with overdue bills.

After Zoë went upstairs to study, Aaron contemplated the connection between hope and pain as he sat on the front porch listening to the bug zapper. The death chime of tiny insects reminded Aaron that many of the phone calls he received every day had one aspect in common. *Weltschmerz*, or a world-weariness expressed by an overwhelming sadness that the world never matched up with people's expectations. Aaron simply suspected the world-as-pain phenomenon existed because the human heart was unaligned with the mind.

The phone quacked, and Aaron was relieved to speak with Lena. She worked as a stock broker and even though Aaron didn't understand the financial complexities of world markets or how she managed not to get fired while constantly inebriated, he enjoyed their little chats. Without an introduction, she launched into a soliloquy of conspiracy theories. Aaron knew that Lena's existential ennui had been building since 2:04 p.m. which on the East Coast signaled the closing of the New York Stock Exchange plus exactly four additional minutes to confirm traded commodities, but corporate policy dictated the office remain open until 4:30 local time, requiring her to stay busy for an additional two hours and twenty-six minutes before the close of business. Lena enjoyed the mind-numbing numerical Assistant's position at C&E Brokerage, P.C., LLP, requiring her to manage the financials for multimillion-dollar corporations. The boredom of her final two hours of work each day were spent sipping from a flask and trolling the bowels of the Interwebs, which only served to compound the *Weltschmerz* of global suffering. Hilariously, her confusion of world pain emerged in wonderful malapropisms of conspiracy theories.

"You up?" she asked without waiting for an answer. "I just read that the African Ebola crisis was funded by the grey Reptilian elites whose secretive landing site underneath Denver International Airport serves as an intergalactic alien landing zone, two accidentally crashing into the 9/11 towers, and the constant atmospheric UFO traffic is responsible for puncturing a hole in the ozone layer resulting in global warming which recently caused flooding in Battery Park and droughts in Des Moines leading the local Iowa bovine population to produce an excess of methane gas emitted by consuming gluten-infused grain feed, the same corn ethanol fuel used to power the staged lunar rockets, and as if the fabricated Mickey Mouse moonrock wasn't proof enough of the faked moon landing, I've uncovered images in the background photos of Neil Armstrong bounding over giant elongated skulls. Skulls, I've seen it! All covered up by some joint CIA and Smithsonian Institute collaboration only a few years after the CIA was busy training Paul McCartney to assassinate JFK. I heard McCartney died back in '66, and they created a robot to play his songs on stage. Anyway, the government constructed Area 51 which is not in Roswell, New Mexico, but actually on Plum Island in New York where Nazi scientists created the HIV virus from the Candida Dubliniesis fungal bacteria inside a secret incubation laboratory. This invention led to the rise of anti-Semitism because people blame the Jews for creating AIDS."

"Stop," Aaron interrupted her.

"What?"

"I quit listening after Ebola."

"Whatever."

"Did you know Zoë asked me about her period? She had two this month and got worried, wish she would ask you about this kinda thing."

"She doesn't call me. What did you tell her?"

"I dropped some comic book knowledge."

"You're the worst."

"Told her how the new Ms. Marvel, a Pakistani teenager named Kamala Khan, gets shot in the stomach which represents the latent powers of menstruation. She becomes a polymorph, meaning she can stretch her body in weird and silly ways. Just like what's happening to our daughter."

"I'm sure she found that helpful," Lena said sarcastically.

"Which reminds me," Aaron continued, "have you seen the new Captain Marvel movie? She's named after a real person."

"Really?"

"Ms. Marvel Crosson was a famous pilot who died in the 1929 Women's National Air Derby. She was the first female to earn a pilot's license in Alaska."

Aaron tried to bring the conversation back to his concern about Zoë, but Lena drifted into more obtuse, quasi-historical conspiracies. Aaron put the phone down on the railing of the front porch and went inside for a glass of water. He cleaned a few dishes, used the restroom, messed around on the computer, then remembered he'd left his phone outside.

Opening the screen door, he heard Lena continuing to espouse her outrageous theories. "And that's why the floating island of plastic in the Pacific is directly responsible for the cancelation of the show *Firefly*." Aaron agreed with her on that one because such a ridiculous explanation seemed to be the only logical reason for drowning the greatest sci-fi television show ever produced. Sadly, television was an integral part of Aaron's connection to world-pain.

When Aaron was six years old, on the exact same afternoon as his journey into Norton the Breathing Forest, he witnessed the first live broadcast of a suicide. Christine Chubbuck, a Florida news reporter, shot herself on live tv right after saying, "In keeping with channel Forty's policy of bringing you the latest in blood and guts, and in living color,[112] we bring you another first, an Attempted suicide." Every day since then, Aaron found it increasingly difficult to tell the difference between reality and illusion.

This inability plagued him through the years, a low-point occurring during the first week in his new apartment after meeting Lena at the concert. Aaron, utterly devastated and suicidal because Lena had not called him back despite leaving 36 voice messages on her answering machine, unleashed his anger on a television set. To be exact, he had grabbed a shotgun loaded with triple-aught buck and shot his television at point blank range.

Not a smart decision in retrospect because he was living in a basement at the time, surrounded by cement walls. Aaron had been watching a television show which he thought was staged, as in a fake-reality show like the first ones that aired on MTV called *The Real World*, and so he had switched the knob in his mind to FICTION and viewed any violence as not real, thereby making it acceptable. In the show, a woman was being interviewed in a graveyard and the words "Telemundo Network" and "Occurio" scrolled across the bottom of the screen. The woman was visiting the gravesite of her fifteen-year-old daughter who had recently completed suicide. Aaron watched with vivid interest because, at that moment, he was holding a twelve-gauge shotgun in his lap and seriously considering, for the third time that morning, putting the barrel under his chin and pulling the trigger. As he watched the grieving mother stand at her daughter's headstone, her ex-husband approached from behind and shot her in the head with a revolver. At that moment, Aaron looked outside and noticed the sun was in the same position as the sun in the television show. Suddenly, the knob in his mind switched to REAL because he had just witnessed a murder on live tv. He turned the shotgun on the television instead of on himself to kill the illusion of reality.

The loud bang woke the neighbors who called the police, and before Aaron was arrested and placed in a psychiatric ward, he frantically searched his bookcase for a poem called the "Land of Illusion" from the Chinese classic Hónglóu Mèng, translated as *Dream of the Red Chamber*. The meaning of the poem had always eluded him,

> *Truth becomes fiction when the fiction is true,*
> *Real becomes unreal where the non-real is real.*

But as they dragged him away, everything made sense. He had learned that when anyone watches a movie or a television show or a stage play, they are subjected to drama. Drama usually includes a mugging or a beating or a rape or a murder. However, the emotional response is identical even when the audience knows it's fake because simulated violence is always real. There is no knob between FICTION and REAL.

Even at the age of 40, Aaron still had a difficult time piercing the veil of mirage.

Sitting on the front porch, Aaron continued to listen as Lena rambled about how the ancient astronauts were responsible for splitting the atom when she suddenly dropped an old-fashioned bomb.

"Listen, my lawyer said I don't have to give you any more money."

Aaron clenched his gut. "What?"

"Zoë will be eighteen soon, and that's it for child support. I could have stopped paying alimony years ago. But you've been taking such good care of her, and I know you were spending the money on her."

"Wait a minute, you know I can't afford to live without your help."

"You'll figure it out," she said.

Aaron retched a few times, spitting bile over the railing of the porch and before he could attempt to dissuade Lena, a call from the Center came through. "Gotta go," Aaron said while hanging up.

Xanax-girl had decided to call back. Aaron quickly transferred through The Process to forget Lena's cruel decision and rinsed his mouth with water.

The Xanax-girl re-told the story about her foster sister with a few twists. First, the sister had not died in the dining room, but rather in the garage. Secondly, Xanax-girl admitted that the sister had not cut her wrists. Instead, she'd cut off her own head.

"How is that even possible?" Aaron asked. "This isn't the French Revolution."

"Probably an accident."

"Come again?"

Xanax-girl's voice tightened, "The garage door fell on her."

"Garage doors aren't sharp enough to decapitate a human."

"She got pinned under it. You've seen those windows on garage doors, right? The glass shattered and a piece sliced her head right off."

"You saw this?"

"We were playing in the garage. Dressing up her dolls, switching their hats and skirts, changing the legs and arms and heads."

"Then what did you do?" Aaron asked skeptically while searching the Internet for related newspaper articles. He often fact checked a Caller's unbelievable story in order to dissolve their illusions and confront them with their underlying problem with reality.

"She was lying next to her own severed head. Like one of her dolls. I tried to put it back on."

Aaron dismissed her story and wrapped up the call by telling her to journal about the incident. A few minutes later, Aaron found the article with vivid details. Almost a year ago in a small, mid-Western town. Her reality had been his fiction. He should not have doubted Xanax-girl's story because world-pain always found a way to break him.

And without leaning on Lena's financial help, soon he would be broke. Decapitated.

Chapter 16

The Long Con of Paternal Intimacy

Panicking, Aaron rummaged through the house for a dose of medicine. He found a few sedatives in a pill container and realized his stash was dwindling. He wrote a note to himself to pick up Marilyn's prescription so he could pilfer a few tabs of her latest medication. He craved a mood enhancer for his sudden anxiety attack induced by Lena's revelation and looked for his ancient cure—The Green Herb.

When he made the conscious decision to try and live a sober life when Zoë was twelve, he'd tossed out all the marijuana from his hiding places. With no stash in the house, Aaron grabbed his keys and drove to the weed store. He loved Colorado for the two reasons that lead to death, one slow and the other fast: legal weed and legal suicide.

He parked in the back alley behind Chong's Bong, a marijuana dispensary situated between a run-down Liquor Mart and a yellow-painted Smoker's Friendly. Since he didn't have any cash, he walked around front and waited until a tourist begged Aaron for his driver's license. Since the laws dictated that out-of-town residents were charged an additional 5% tax, tourists were keen on buying as much weed for as little as possible to gloat upon returning to some Southern prohibition state like Texas where they still jail Black men for SWB, Stoned While Black.

An emboldened tourist wearing faded jeans, white socks and a pair of $49 ASICS, asked Aaron, "Hey bro, hate to stop ya but could…" Tourists usually said *bro* or *brah* or *brotha* or some derivation of *my brother* because of Aaron's long hair, as if their decision to smoke legalized weed was somehow equivalent to Aaron's hatred of the Establishment[113] manifested by growing out his hair in his early twenties after the reality-bending consequences of the shotgun-television incident.

After stuttering, the tourist continued. "…could I use your license to buy a little, ya'know," glancing worriedly over his shoulder as he whispered, "some *marijuana*?"

Aaron didn't mind the request for his in-state driver's license, in fact he was counting on it, but the guy's tone bothered him. This tourist was the kind of guy who whispered the word "marijuana" the same way white people say "Black" when in uncertain company. Such whispering in that Southern twang convinced Aaron that the tourist was indeed a personification of the Low-Key Grandma Racist. Aaron had worked and partied with plenty of LKGRs over the years. These LKGR-type of racists were not overtly explicit but rather subtle like anyone's grandma might have been while reading the newspaper about a shooting on the East Side and mentioning something about "those damn coons," but said in such a way that everyone in the room sort of sighs, "That's just Granny."

Aaron asked the tourist, "Alright bro, how much? I'll buy it for you."

The tourist handed him a hundred-dollar bill. "This enough to score a whole ounce?"

"No prob, I'll be right back. Give me about 20 minutes."

While waiting in line, he received a text from Debz inviting him to the football game at her house. She often watched sports with her family and sometimes Aaron joined them, on the rare occasion when he acted sociable. A few minutes later, Aaron was seen by a bud-tender and quickly bought the cheapest, bottom-shelf ounce of grass for $85. He slipped the owner a fiver who let him out the back door. Aaron ran to his car in the alley and purposefully circled around front to wave at the tourist. With the window down and the brown baggie held aloft like a stolen trophy, Aaron cried out, "Thanks bro!"

With the extra ten bucks, Aaron stopped at a liquor store and bought a six pack of beer. He didn't drink but he knew the cardinal rule of football—men don't show up empty handed. On the way to Debz's house, Aaron suddenly regretted his actions. He didn't feel bad because he'd ripped off a gullible tourist, but rather that he was tempted to smoke weed again.

Debz met him at the front door where he handed her the bag. "For you, found it on the way over. You know I don't smoke. Beer is for your fam."

She opened it, buried her nose in the sack and smiled. "For reals? Some dank weed here. You sure?"

"Positive." He sat down to watch the game but Aaron felt so disconnected after nearly succumbing to the temptation of green ganja that his interaction resembled a telephone conversation. He only noticed when Debz's family members whispered racist remarks and he realized they were all Low-Key Grandma Racists.

LKGR-uncle-who-voted-for-Trump for reasons of personal empowerment, spoke up before the first quarter of the football game: "The only football players that are taking a knee..." and looked over his shoulder before saying, "are the *Black* ones. I'm not a racist but you don't see white men kneeling for anyone. Except for Jesus."

LKGR-dad-who-voted-for-Trump but is upset because he lost his Medicare, mentioned during the second quarter: "Who brought the fried chicken? I like it bout as much as..." and shrugged his shoulders before whispering, "those *Blacks*. I'm no racist but Blacks eat fried chicken and watermelon because you don't need utensils. Savages."

Even withdrawn contemplating his internal struggle with sobriety, Aaron knew any words following such a loaded preposition as *but* often proved to be subversively racist and laced with toxic masculinity.

LKGR-brother-who-voted-for-Trump for theological reasons, announced during the third quarter: "I wouldn't date your sister for all the scuba gear owned by..." turns around to look over his shoulder, "*Black* people. I'm not a racist, but er'body knows they don't have pools in the ghetto."

LKGR-grandpa-who-voted-for-Trump, just like ten percent of all Black men over the age of 65, mumbled in the fourth quarter for the win: "I woulda voted for Obama a third time. Er'body knows there's good N-words and bad N-words," whispering *N-word* each time, actually using the abbreviation and not the full, racially-explosive curse with an *A* or an *AH* or the blatant *ER*.

Aaron, coming to his senses near the end of the game, leaned forward while sitting on the plastic-covered, leopard print couch and said, "N-word? Don't you mean the N-bomb?"

LKGR-grandpa rocked back in his chair. "N-bomb? What do nuclear bombs have to do with anything?"

"You keep saying N-word, but it's not a word. It's a bomb."

LKGR-grandpa: "Hey, I'm cool, man. I've got *Black* friends," whispering the key word. "I even dated a *Black* chick in college."

Debz jumped in. "Even, Grandpa? You *even* dated a woman who was and probably still is Black?"

LKGR-grandpa scratched his head. "Such a long time ago."

"Listen," Aaron said, "it's a bomb because the N-word is not a word, it's a racist weapon."

LKGR-grandpa pounded his cane on the ground. "I can't be a racist!"

Aaron tried to explain, hoping to calm the elderly man. "I don't mean to curse, but *fuck* is given the socially-acceptable euphemism *F-bomb*, so why shouldn't a slave word that has verbally exploded in the face of Black men and women since the day they were born not be called the *N-bomb*?!"

LKGR-uncle jumped on the couch and yelled, "Those Eagles beat the Patriots, can't believe Tom Brady lost to a bunch of...*Blacks*!"

Aaron, unable to change minds, stepped outside on the porch for a smoke with Debz. "Seriously, your family is a bunch of racists. Especially your grandpa!"

Debz, while holding a plate of ham hock and black-eyed peas with a side of collard greens, a fried chicken leg, a slice of cornbread, two large pieces of watermelon while smoking a Pall Mall menthol cigarette, looked at him and said, "Whatcha talkin bout, Willis? Didn't you know there's no one more racist than an old Black man?!"

Aaron threw up his hand and drove home, feeling conflicted about Debz's racist African-American family. No wonder her sense of humor was so warped. Her own family distrusted Black people more than a good old-fashioned Dixiecrat, but Aaron could relate to that type of self-loathing. His own self-hatred stemmed from voluntary male isolation. As a boy, Aaron had rarely hung out with men and he grew up to distrust them since the only feat men had ever accomplished was to hurt the women he loved.

Reclining on his own golden couch with a book of poetry[114] in his lap, Aaron thought about the men at the football party and the tourist he'd ripped off. He drifted off to sleep and dreamt of his father.

Reverie I. The Griot

Aaron did not dream of his actual father retired down in Florida, living at an elaborate golf-resort retirement community for New York Jews escaping brutal winters and exclaiming to each other, "What I wouldn't do for a decent pastrami on rye." Rather, Aaron dreamed of a white-bearded Santa Claus-Zeus-Yahweh-God type of father, except more James Earl Jones as Mufasa, King of the Lions, with a rich, baritone voice. Even more like John Amos as older-Kunta Kinte, long after he was held up to the sky by his father to "Behold, the only thing greater than yourself."

Aaron's dream-father was a French African named Cemillòn, pronounced like the French wine Sémillon but with a bitter "C" upon the lips and a smoother finish with a strong, grassy aroma. Cemillòn was an imposing, older man from Cote d'Ivoire with a salty beard. His single-roomed thatch hut had a wooden mailbox out front with towering antelope horns and the word *Griot* hand-carved on the side. In his dream, Aaron journeyed upon a dusty red road and found Cemillòn standing by the door, his milky eyes squinting under the African sun. They sat down on hand carved, four-legged Senufo wooden stools beneath a thatch roofed porch. The blind man had trouble finding the stool and Aaron helped position the old man correctly.

"What's written on your mailbox?" asked Aaron.

"Griot," he said, elongating the initial Greee-oo. "I'm the local storyteller."

"You tell stories?

"Not tell, sing."

"You're a singer?"

"I'm a nganga. A marabout. A griot."

"And you're blind?"

Cemillòn sighed. "Blind to the present, but I can see the past. Unlike you."

"Hey, don't blame me," Aaron said defensively. "I'm like most people. Blind to the past, I can only see the present."

"Humph," the large man shuttered his shoulders and rocked back and forth on the wooden stool. "I sing songs for a living. How do you make a living?"

"I work at…"

"Not work," Cemillòn interrupted. "How do you live?"

"I'm not sure. Save lives, I guess."

"Saving lives of people who do not want to be saved?"

"I know. Seems pointless. I don't care anymore."

"Is there music in your life?" the old man asked. "For what is life without music."

"I have my Zoë and she sings. Angsty, teenage emo-pop, but it's music. Ever heard of Tay-Tay?"

"My neighbors usually request *Song of Our Children*. Maybe you've heard this one." Cemillòn lifted a 21-stringed goat-skinned kora from the wall and strung a few chords. His rich, mahogany voice echoed off the earthen floor:

> *You are our eyes*
> *You are our mirror*
> *You are our hands and legs*
> *That we use to walk*

When Aaron did not sing along, the griot paused. "This song is about you, my child. Sing with me, young man. Lift up your voice with me. Together in song we become sacred."

"Um, I can't sing. Maybe we can talk?"

"Then what shall we talk about?"

"Anything, but please no songs. And no fatherly lectures. It's confusing because you speak in circles."

"A potter's wheel spins clay, a poet's wheel spins love."

"...and a DJ spins records. But I have no idea what you mean."

"Dear boy," Cemillòn said. "I'm blind but even I can see how your nerves lay atop your skin. Not caring about people who call for help every night? Liar! You care too much. Indeed, my son, you feel. Without fail."

Without fail. The words echoed through the rondavel as Aaron looked around the grass-thatched hut. "Do you live here?"

Cemillòn laughed, "Of course not. This is only where I come to think, to write, to sing. I've got a house in the city. With a pool guarded by a swarm of piranhas, in case anyone tries to jump in while I'm away in the country."

"Swimming with the piranhas? I'd like to see that."

"Ha! I don't know how to swim." Cemillòn turned his head upwards and squinted at the sun. "The pool is for my guests. Limits their stay."

"Why are you squinting?" Aaron asked. "You're not blind?"

"I sense the warmth on my face, but it hurts my eyes. My vision is gone but sometimes, I can make out shadowy shapes."

"Shadows?"

"Shadows of the past still haunt me."

"Like when mother left us?" Aaron asked.

"Yes," Cemillòn paused. "Your mother, she's like the wind. Blowing from place to place, your Mother the Wind."

"And temper like a storm."

Cemillòn turned towards Aaron and gently strummed the kora. "I was an old man when I had you, but younger than I am now. Oh, to be eighty again, that'd be a real gift. I lived alone until your Mother the Wind appeared one night and asked me if I wanted her body, her mind or her heart."

"And you chose?"

"What any young man thinks a woman wants to hear. I wanted all three and she laughed such a gust that my neighbor's hut flew into the sky."

"Full of bluster, sounds like her."

"Your mother told me that if I chose her body, I'd have her for a day. And if I chose her mind, then I'd have her for a year. But if I won her heart, I'd have her forever."

"Tempestuous, that's Mom alright."

"After you were born in the year of a long summer, your Mother the Wind left us to wander the desert hills. As a little boy, you asked me, 'Mother left us, how can I ever love again?' Your sorrow was immense like a river but youth made it shallow. Cried yourself to sleep every night for a month."

Aaron gazed at the space between his feet. "I don't remember."

"I tried to cheer you up. I offered hope because the wind always returns. I told you that lost love has a way of healing and over time you'd feel the soft breeze on your cheek and not dwell upon your Mother the Wind."

"I found my own wind," Aaron said, thinking of his daughter.

"I promised the spasms of love would rekindle your tender heart. And was I right? Did your daughter heal your broken soul?"

"She did."

"And forgetting your Mother the Wind, life got better."

Aaron looked coldly at Cemillòn, "I've never forgotten my Mother the Wind. I've only forgotten you."

"Why?"

"Because she came back. As for life, it never gets any better."

"Without fail," Cemillòn ended with a final strum on the kora.

*

Aaron awoke with the song echoing around his mind and off his heart and into his soul. Without fail, he'd have to continue showing up for Zoë. Without fail, he'd have to stand by Eve's bedside every day until she died. Without fail, he'd have to take suicidal calls and offer hope to the despondent. He didn't have a choice. Without fail.

Aaron peeled himself from the amber couch, took a sip of water directly from the faucet, and checked the mailbox. He leafed through the water bill, past due, as well as a brochure from the Jewish Defense League, a subscription renewal letter from the ACLU, and a newsletter from the Compassionate Dharma Cloud Monastery that Aaron and Zoë had stumbled upon while looking for Red Rocks Amphitheater last year. Zoë and her friends had wanted to see Taylor Swift but Aaron mistakenly took them up during the "Reggae on the Rocks" weekend where they heard the peaceful vibes of Matisyahu, a cosmic event that undoubtedly led to his daughter's interest in the Rainbow Gathering. He threw the mail in the trash and returned to the sofa. He laid down and dreamt in black and white. Oddly, red was the only color that vibrated through his dream, a 60s era film with his father playing the lead role of a famous senator from Virginia.

Reverie II. The Red Backpack
or Dreams of a White Savior

Early 1960s. The law office of a retired senator from Jamesville, Virginia.

Scene opens with the Senator ordering bagels on the phone from Morty's Deli, telling him to send the *colored* boy with the delivery. Ms. Whitney, a red-headed secretary, sits at the front desk.

Enter Marcus, a lanky 14-year-old boy, carrying a bag of onion bagels, cream cheese and lox.

The Senator tips Marcus fifty cents and tells him, "Now make sure your mother gets some of this. Heard report cards came out today. How're your grades? I'll give you a quarter for each A you've earned."

Marcus pulls out his report card, proudly displaying straight As except for a D in history.

On the Senator's wall, there is a framed Law Degree, two University diplomas and photos of the Senator shaking hands with Presidents Truman, Eisenhower and Kennedy. Also, on the wall are scores of slightly faded, hand-written school report cards, assembled in rows of six, one for each year of middle school and high school. At the end of each row is a photo of a young Black man or woman in a graduation cap and gown. Over the years, the Senator has been following the academic careers of many local Black students.

"Who's your teacher?" asks the Senator.

"Mr. Cracker teaches history."

"I know him, he's not too bright. Why'd you get a D in his class?"

"I did the work, mister. Always do. See, look at my book report here. Read a book about the man who made the first clock here in America. But Mr. Cracker says 'Ain't no negro gettin a good grade in my class.' That's why we all got Ds."

Senator makes a copy and hangs the report card on his wall, and pays Marcus for each A grade. Together, they step into the back of a long, black Lincoln Continental. Ms. Whitney, as the Senator's official driver, climbs behind the steering wheel. She blows through three stops signs on the way and slams to a screeching halt directly in front of the school.

The Senator storms into the principal's office with Marcus in tow. "Get Mr. Cracker in here!"

The Senator's reputation as a firebrand is well known, and the history teacher cowers in his presence after being summoned. The school secretary and Ms. Whitney peak through the blinds of the office window while the principal tires to placate the Senator.

"You know how these lil negro children are," the principal says. "They don't perform well here in this new integrated school. The Blacks should go back to their own school. I don't know why you care so much about them. Always givin em dimes for good grades."

"Quarters," the Senator says, correcting the principal. He turns to Mr. Cracker and says firmly, "This boy here says he did the work. Showed me his book report on Benjamin Banneker. Why'd he get a D in your class?"

"His people didn't contribute to history," Mr. Cracker retorts. "No reason for this boy to learn it."

"Listen, ever hear of Timbuktu? Great Ruins of Zimbabwe? Pyramids of Giza? Astronomy? Mathematics? Hieroglyphics? Never mind, I'm saying if the boy does the work, then give him the grade. He's earned it. Don't interfere!" demands the Senator, slamming the door on his way out.

After leaving the school, Ms. Whitney drops the Senator and Marcus at the boy's home. The Senator enters and nods hello to his parents. They know of each other but since they are Black and he is white, they cannot be friends. They are very worried that a white man is in their house. The Senator mentions that he has high hopes for Marcus because he sees what every man beholds in a bright boy— potential. He asks where the boy studies and Marcus points to a dark corner in the living room near a blaring radio and three screaming siblings. The Senator spies an unused, small table covered by a broken sewing machine.

"Who's using that table?"

The mother says, "I was planning on fixing the machine, maybe make a little money mending clothes."

The father interrupts her, "Darn thang broke two years ago."

"How about I take that machine off your hands and get it fixed? Meanwhile, the boy can use the table to study." The Senator clears off the table and places an old lamp in the middle. "You need light to do your homework."

The parents agree. Marcus gets to work as the Senator and Ms. Whitney drive off.

Later that afternoon, Ms. Whitney receives a call from her cousin. Apparently, Marcus and a white boy named Craig Johnson are fighting in her front lawn.

(Flashback to the Senator hiring a secretary. He interviews a stream of pretty, blond typists but then in walks Ms. Whitney DuVray, older and frumpy. The Senator asks about her parents, and discovers she was born and raised in Jamesville. She carries on about her friends, neighbors, and who married whom and who's cheating on whom and who got fired last month before the Senator suddenly stops her and says, "You're hired!" As a semi-retired lawyer who once was a sitting U.S. Senator, he wants the scoop on his constituents and future clients).

Ms. Whitney hangs up the phone and marches into the Senator's office. "Your colored boy is gettin in a fight with Mr. Johnson's boy."

The Senator and Ms. Whitney race off in his 1959 Lincoln Continental Mark IV with shiny chrome trim and white-walled tires. Ms. Whitney speaks with wild gesticulations and barely keeps her hands on the wheel or eyes on the road. The Senator seems relaxed because Ms. Whitney is in total control of the huge vehicle, swerving easily around chickens and stray dogs, as she informs him about the bully Craig Johnson and his drunken father. They arrive in a billowing cloud of dust as the car slams to a halt, alerting the crowd around the fighting boys. The boys are being pulled apart by a white adult. The man is jabbing a finger at Marcus and scolding him.

The Senator knows the man because Jamesville is a small town where everybody knows each other. He smacks the man's hand away and says, "Damn it, Fred, get your finger outta that boy's face!"

Fred steps back when he realizes it's the Senator and says, "That negro boy started it!"

"Hold on now, Fred, let me ask the boys what happened." The Senator assumes a prosecutorial air and cross-examines the boys, first asking Craig what happened. The white boy complains how Marcus was acting, in his words, "all-uppity and what-not."

The Senator then asks Marcus what happened. "Craig was pickin on Darnell. Everyone knows that Darnell's got a bum leg. I was standing up for him." The Senator looks over and sees a young, Black boy leaning against a tree with a swollen eye and rubbing his leg.

Meanwhile, Craig Johnson's father staggers onto the scene and screams at the Senator. "Gotta let these things sort themselves out. These negros get outta hand sometimes, you know how they can be."

The Senator looks him up and down, "Johnson, you reek of whiskey. I remember your father Clarence, look just like him."

"Well, that's mighty kinda ya, thanks. My pa was good man."

"He was a no-good drunken bum and looks like you'll amount to exactly the same." The gathering crowd laughs. "Now then, Ms. Whitney tells me you've been beatin on your boy Craig here. Is that true?"

"I never laid a hand on my boy. And if I did, that's my own business. He's my son!"

The Senator lifts Craig's shirt up, exposing yellow, faded bruises on his ribs. "You didn't get these in the fight, now did you, boy?" Craig lowers his eyes.

The Senator turns on Mr. Johnson. "I should have you tarred and feathered! There's no law against smacking your boy, but I could get you arrested for public drunkenness."

"But he's MY son!"

"The cycle of fatherhood, right? A father beats his son and the son does the same. I'm tellin you, it ends right here. That's why your boy is beating on Marcus. He doesn't know any better. But I'm going to fix that."

"What'cha gonna do, mister?" Mr. Johnson raises a fist, but Fred and a few other men in the crowd hold him back.

The Senator smiles. "I'm taking them out for ice-cream. Come along boys."

Ms. Whitney revs the engine and then opens the rear door. The boys look uncertainly at each other, but given the promise of ice-cream, they jump in.

Mr. Johnson mutters defeatedly, "Aww, hell with em."

The two boys, Ms. Whitney and the Senator venture out for ice-cream and the boys shake hands afterwards. On the way back, with Ms. Whitney careening around corners and screeching the tires, they drop Marcus off at his house.

Marcus asks the Senator, "Why'd you bring Craig along? He's the one who started the fight."

"Because he'll keep coming at you. Listen, you're gonna need allies in this fight."

"What fight?"

"The fight to get outta this town and make something of yourself. But first, you gotta survive this town."

"Is that why you want me to get good grades?"

"The good grades are not for me, son, they're for you. And remember, any bully can be turned to work *for* you instead of *against* you. Discover their weakness."

"And use their weakness to defeat them?"

"No, help them overcome it."

Marcus nods. "Like you did with Craig?"

"Exactly. You're not his enemy, but he thinks you are. His father is the real enemy and I've protected him for a little while. Listen, you two could be friends."

"Maybe. Doubt it."

"Why not?"

Marcus shrugs his shoulder. "He's too white to be trusted."

Later around dusk, Ms. Whitney gets a call and runs into the Senator's office. Utterly in a panic and out of breath, Ms. Whitney exclaims, "Lucy Williams was washing clothes down by the river and got raped. Sheriff caught two negroes and has em down at the jail. We've got ourselves an angry mob!"

With Ms. Whitney at the wheel of the Lincoln, they rip through four traffic lights in the fading tempo of early evening. The smell of burnt rubber announces their arrival as they force their way through the crowd. In the center stands the Sheriff roughly holding Marcus and Darnell by their collars.

The Senator demands from the Sheriff, "What happened here?"

The Sheriff explains how the boy Darnell raped a girl named Lucy. The crowd responds with horrified lunacy to the tale as the Senator asks Darnell, "Did you do it, boy?"

Sobbing and snot-nosed, Darnell sways on his bum leg and looks up at the Senator. "She told me to meet her down by the river after school. Said she wanted to show me somethin." He points to a girl standing several feet away.

The howling crowd parts as Lucy steps forward in a torn dress with her parents standing behind her. While the father stares murderously at the gimp boy, the mother only looks down at the small bump in Lucy's belly.

Lucy screams and points at Darnell. "He raped me! Why don't y'all do something about it?!"

Darnell attempts to defend himself with the truth. "Lucy and I, well, we've been sneakin down to the river for months. Few hours ago, she told me she's pregnant, but I said I wasn't gonna pay for an abortion because I wanna keep it. That's when she tore her dress and promised to tell her father that I'd done raped her."

Mr. Johnson staggers up alongside Lucy's family and slurs, "That's a lie! My boy Craig was just tryin to protect her honor." Lucy's parents and several other neighbors join in with further accusations.

Sadly, the truth does not protect Darnell as the crowd surges in. "Hang em before he tells anymore lies. The girl's honor has been spoiled! He's gotta pay!!"

The Senator asks about Marcus, and the Sheriff explains. "When we went to arrest Darnell, this boy here was with him. Figured he was guilty, too."

Marcus holds up his backpack with books. "We were just doing homework together. I didn't know about nothing else."

Fred, the white man who had broken up the fight earlier in the afternoon, knocks the backpack out of Marcus's hands, school books spilling out on the ground. He says angrily, "Negroes shouldn't be readin no how. He ain't gonna amount to nuthin."

"We'll see about that," the Senator replies. He turns to the Sheriff, "Guilty by association? Alright, if they're under arrest, then put them both in jail."

The Sheriff points to the crowd. Some have shotguns and torches in the fading light. "You know as well as I do what's gonna happen here."

The Senator fights and screams, but the crowd holds him back. He realizes there is nothing he can do to halt the lynching. Eventually, he calms down and bows his head in defeat. Then he grabs Marcus by the arm. "Fine. But not him."

Mr. Johnson, Mr. Cracker, Fred and a few other white men concede to the Senator and take turns saying,

"Alright, you can have the boy."

"But make him watch."

"He's gotta learn his lesson."

"He's gotta learn his place."

The Senator cries out, "Y'all won't be getting away with this for much longer. They're called Civil Rights. LBJ is making laws against this sort of terrorism."

"I bet he will," the Sheriff says, "but not today." He signals to the others, "Alright, let's get this over with."

A few men throw a rope around a low branch of a large oak tree in front of the jail house.

Darnell sobs quietly. The Senator struggles again to reach him, but a white farmer puts a shotgun in the Senator's face. "Settle down, you can't do nuthin about it."

The Senator turns away and addresses the crowd. "You hang this boy, and we know nothing will happen. Life goes on as usual round here. But shoot a senator? Every single one of y'all will be hanging up there next to him."

The farmer lowers his shotgun as the Senator continues. "And Marcus won't be watching." The Senator covers the boy's eyes and holds him tightly to his chest. "I'll watch for him."

The crowd proceeds with their ugly business as they add another piece of strange fruit upon the hanging tree.

Afterwards, as the crowd lingers to take photographs, the Senator sees a red satchel used by the post office laying on the ground outside the county jail. He and Marcus pick up the boy's school books from the ground, filling the red satchel.

The Senator storms through the crowd holding Marcus by the arm. They reach the Lincoln with Ms. Whitney at the wheel, revving the engine. The Senator points to the red satchel on Marcus's back.

"If you won't respect this boy here or the boy over there," pointing to Darnell's swinging body, "then at least respect the U.S. postal service. Hell, seems like mail got more rights and more protection than Black folks. From now on, when you see him going to school with this red satchel…"

"What the hell is a satchel?" a voice asks from the crowd.

"A damned backpack. Y'all know what a backpack is!?"

"Yep," several people nod.

"When you see a red backpack, don't mess with them, alright?"

"Why not?" asks the Sheriff.

"Because it means they're a real student. It means they are the best and brightest. It means I'm watching to make sure they get good grades, like I've been doing for years. It means I'm watching over them."

The Sheriff puts one hand on his hip and the other on the gun holster. "You can't protect all of em."

"They don't need my protection. They simply don't need you messing with them. That's all I'm asking, don't interfere with their studies. Let them learn in peace."

"And then what?" asks the Sheriff skeptically.

"Then they go to college, maybe even come back and help us out. Maybe one of them will even take my job as Senator. You'll see."

Flash to a year later. Children walking to school.

All with red backpacks.

*

Aaron woke up sweating on the honey-colored couch and flushed the dreams from his memory before heading upstairs to bed. His father had not been a West African griot nor an actor playing a well-respected Senator. In real life, Aaron had heard stories of how his father had been surrounded by Klansmen while traveling with the Freedom Riders back in the Sixties. As a believer in Martin Luther King, Jr.'s quest for civil rights, and as a proponent of non-violent civil disobedience, his father had travel south by bus and fought against members of the KKK.

In real life, the final scene had played out differently than Aaron's dream. The boy being lynched was not Darnell but rather a local boy named Claude Neal who had been accused of sleeping with the white girl next door, Lola, also known as Lily-May. The boy's horrific dismemberment included cutting off his genitals and making him eat his own balls. In the final scene, while Mr. Neal was undergoing the most brutal form of an elongated death sentence, he had to confess to a crime to which he had no part. He knew in his mind that the love of his life, sweet Lily-May, the girl next door, had been murdered and that he would not be rescued in a last-minute, Hollywood-ending type of effort led by a posse of the descendants of Nat Turner or liberal, white lawyers emboldened by National Guardsmen led by a miraculously saved Lily-May riding on a white horse, charging in to cut him down from the tree. No, there would be no rescue, only the horrible realization that he would be murdered by the very same white uncles that had murdered Lily May. Because she had fallen in love with a Black man.

Aaron's father had intervened during the lynching and when the sheriff threatened him with a shotgun, Aaron's father grabbed the sheriff in a headlock and punched him repeatedly in the face. The crowd was stunned and horrified by this unexpected white-on-white aggression than by the actual lynching. In between every blow, the sheriff asked, "I (*whack*) thought (*whack*) you (*whack*) guys (*whack*) were (*whack*) pacifists?"

Needless to say, Aaron's father was not invited back by SNCC for further outings to sit-ins and peaceful demonstrations. Because the white savior is a myth.

Chapter 17

Lost in Memory

Daybreak opened with a yawn. Not quite ennui, but lethargy plagued Aaron, hints of immobility laced with a disposition lacking self-worth. Lena's decision to stop alimony payments had wrecked him with impending worry. He had been roused by Zoë leaving for school, but he spent the next five hours in a prone, pillow head-covered posture that tenderized his left hip. He was finally roused from bed when Zoë came home for lunch and yelled at him from downstairs.

"We got anything to eat around here?"

Aaron limped into the kitchen. "Sorry, haven't gone shopping yet."

"I'm starving. The food at the school cafeteria is nasty, and it's too expensive."

Her tone irritated Aaron. He snapped at her and said, "Listen, life is expensive."

"Chill, Dad. Can I get some money? I'll get something on the way back to school."

Aaron decided to be honest with his daughter. "I'm broke. I've missed too many days from work. The only way we survive is because your mother gives us money every month, did you know that?"

"Yeah, she told me last year. She called you a bum. She was drunk, I yelled at her. Told her you're a good dad because at least you show up to my soccer games."

"You shouldn't yell at your mother."

"Why are you always protecting her?" Zoë asked.

"Because she gave me you."

"Well, that's not enough. She should help out more."

"She does," Aaron said. "Until yesterday."

"What?"

"She's cutting us off."

"Why?"

"I don't know," Aaron lied. He knew exactly why but was too ashamed to admit it. "Maybe they'll help me out."

"Who's they?"

"Marilyn pays for the roof over our head. And Aunt Jocelyn brings us food. You and your friends eat a lot." Aaron instantly regretted telling his daughter.

Zoë raised her voice. "We don't have to hang out here. My friends and I can eat over at Crow and Thyme's house."

"That's not what I meant. I want you here. This is your home."

"You've got a job. Don't you make enough money at work?"

Mortified to tell his daughter that he was unable to provide for them, Aaron panicked under his daughter's revelation of paternal disappointment. The father inside him withered and his defense was typically masculine. He began to lecture.

"Listen, men define themselves by their job. They say, 'I am a mechanic' or 'I am a doctor'. I've never been able to do that. I have a job, but I am not my work. It's the difference between the copular verb *to be* versus the auxiliary verb *to have* which implies possession…"

"Shut up!" Zoë screamed. "I seriously can't take any more of your bullshit. Just be honest with me."

Aaron continued to confess. "Even Eve slips me a little cash now and then."

"You take money from your dying grandma?"

"It's sad, I know."

Zoë's look of pity crushed him. She asked, "Why can't you pay for stuff by yourself?"

Aaron picked at the old scab on his knuckle. "I've never been very good at caring for myself."

"Mom was right," Zoë said as she collected her keys. "You are a bum. I can't live here anymore."

Zoë slammed the door as she stormed out of the house. Aaron collapsed on the floor and began crawling for the table. He wasn't sure he'd make it out this time.

Suddenly, the phone rang. He forced himself to stand up and answered immediately when he recognized the Poinsettia's number because he never ignored a call from Eve's nursing home. He nodded twice and simply said, "I'll be right there."

*

The hospice nurse met him at the door and said, "It won't be much longer now."

Aaron hoped the nurse was right. Eve had been dying slowly for months now, a guest in her own home. Dementia retained her body but evicted her mind. After cracking her hip on the dining room floor, the nurses had increased Eve's morphine from thrice daily to *as needed* which wasn't enough for Marilyn's liking. Jocelyn stopped by daily to help with the physical therapy, both of them doing what they felt was necessary to aid in Eve's comfort. Aaron only wanted a quick passing for her instead of a long fall through suffering. Had God or mercy existed in the universe, Aaron was convinced she would have passed away months ago. Die, Aaron thought, getting used to the word. She's going to die, he told himself, and I'll have to watch because no one else would and because she deserved to have company near death. Aaron also hated the euphemism *passed away* because life was not a class to fail or pass. Feelings passed, people passed out, footballs were passed around, but death wasn't a phase. Sitting by her bedside, he had often contemplated how life is the beginning of a momentary existence and death is the end. Everything else in between is pain.

The nurse led Aaron into the room he'd been visiting for two years. Beige walls decorated by lavish reproductions of the French painter Manet, potted plants of purple wisteria and English lavender, and a fancy, iron-wrought twin bed by the window with a view of the high desert plains. He looked down at Eve and saw the withering remains of his grandmother. The morphine had removed the pain as well as her hunger for food and Aaron could pick her up with one arm. The skin was pulled back on her face, her once flushed cheeks now dry and brittle, a tired mummy too exhausted to even die. Her hands were bent and bruised, the blood settling in her lower extremities. Aaron stopped kissing her hand last week, the gesture becoming a morbid act. He needed sympathy for the living, not the nearly dead. She was gone, but her body persisted.

Her breathing slowed to about once every thirty seconds. Every time she exhaled, Aaron was convinced this was the last time. He held his breath along with her, desperate for her to stop. But then she'd inhale a long, rattling, asthmatic breath after half a minute and Aaron would re-start his inner clock. Each time he thought, "Is this it? Is she gone?" He'd said goodbye so many times that farewell no longer held any significance.

For seven hours, the boredom consumed him. He read three books about the detriments of white feminism while waiting for death.

Dusk approached, then departed as night settled. He'd seen enough. She'd suffered too long and didn't deserve this, Aaron told himself. Yet, nothing he could do would help her. Until he looked at the pillow under her head and made up his mind.

Aaron waited another hour until the night-nurse came in to check on Eve. The nurse mentioned that she'd return every four hours. No one would come to disturb them. He and his grandmother would be left alone.

Eve's breathing had not changed in many hours. The diaphragm reflexively tightened, automatically inflating the lungs. Aaron focused on the flow of air through her mouth. If he could stop the air, then this would end. She would be free.

Aaron made sure the door was closed and looked out the open window. A cool night breeze fluttered the flower-patterned drapes. The nursing home was silent. Aaron kissed Eve on the forehead. She was cold and her eyes remained closed. She had not opened them in two weeks. Aaron gently lifted her head and took hold of the feather pillow with its tacky, rose-printed pillowcase. He didn't want to hurt her. He convinced himself by thinking,

don't let her suffer; and,

she would want this; and,

I'm only keeping her alive for selfish reasons; and,

do this for her; and,

let her go.

Aaron held the pillow above her. His legs shook, his hands trembled, his heartbeat echoed off the walls. A wave of nausea bubbled in his gut, bile filling his throat. His vision faded. Aaron sat down on the edge of the bed and nearly fainted. He couldn't look at Eve, refusing to confront the choice of this moment.

He had spent his life persuading people not to kill themselves. He'd told atheists that the power of death resides not in our hands, for when we die, we leave the sadness behind. And he told the religiously devout that it's not up to us when we die, it's only up to God.

He grasped the pillow to his chest and sobbed. A stream of tears flowed, crying like when he was a little boy who pleaded with his grandmother to bring his *pitow*, childishly lisping the word for pillow. Crying like when he suffered a concussion in high school and his grandmother brought him a *pitow* while sitting in the nurse's office. Crying like he did when she first moved into the Poinsettia Home and he would visit after a long day at work when she'd say, "Just rest, dear," and pat the *pitow* next to her. Crying like now as he held a pillow above his grandmother.

Above her face.

*

Time passed between the living and dying. Aaron became thirsty from the struggle and decided he needed a drink. Badly. He needed to forget. He wiped away the tears and trembled while retreating to his car. No one saw him leave.

Aaron's hands shook as he drove to the nearest tavern, a dive called the Alibi Lounge. He dared not look at himself in the rearview mirror. A few hours before midnight, Aaron parked in the dirt lot and was lucky to find an empty spot at the bar. He smiled when he noticed the Twins were working because the pair always entertained. He'd stopped in a month ago after Eve had broken her hip and the Twins had cheered him up with their friendly banter.

Claude greeted him with a smile as Aaron pulled up a stool while Claudette washed glasses behind the bar.

"'Sup," Claude said. He was dressed in a white shirt, a black suede vest with a bow-tie and ivory pants. He had a temple fade haircut with sponge twists and a chin-strap beard like Chadwick Boseman as T'Challa in *Black Panther*.

Aaron sat down heavily on the stool. The weight of Eve was oppressive, but he'd had a lifetime of pretending and blocked her from his mind. He automatically engaged in idle conversation like slipping into a neutral gear while waiting at a stop light. "You the bartender here? I'd like a drink."

Claude grinned as he spun a bottle. "Like I was trying to explain to my sister earlier, there is mad difference in what we do behind the bar."

"Do what?" Aaron asked.

Claudette, dressed in a high-collared black dress with shoulders exposed and an unruly afro, reminding Aaron of Zazie Beetz as the lucky Domino in *Deadpool 2*, arched her eyebrows and threw shade. "My brother thinks of himself as a bartender whereas I tend bar."

Aaron took the bait. "And the difference is?"

"We'll show you," Claude said, puffing out his chest. "I've been out of college two years now. I got people pegged. When they stand next to the bar, I ax them 'What'll it be?'"

"And I don't even have to ask," Claudette said without a smile, "Let me guess, cranberry and vodka, right? Short glass, twist of lime."

Aaron was honestly impressed. "How'd you know?"

Claudette reached for a rocks glass. "You were eye-balling that bottle of Absolut, and you don't look like a tonic guy."

"You've got that right," Aaron said, sagging on the stool.

Compelled by a bartender's sense of obligation, Claude attempted to cheer up Aaron and asked, "Yo, why so glum?"

"Experience."

"Hey," Claude said with a bright smile, "I got years of experience. I can tell the difference between red and white wine."

Claudette interrupted and motioned to the front door. "And I suspect that gum-chewing, sorority girl walking in right now wearing Target-brand flip-flops will definitely be sipping on White Zin."

"And the woman behind her?"

"You mean the soccer-mom? She will definitely be hitting up that cheap bottle o'Cab."

Claude nodded. "You right, you right," as they pounded fists.

After serving the two ladies, Claude returned and asked Aaron. "Guess what our number one selling beer is?" He didn't wait for answer. "Bud Lite."

Claudette leaned in towards Aaron, the power-window in the center of her black dress offering a busty view. Aaron didn't look down and met her eyes squarely. He knew the game. "What my brother has failed to realize is the owner here is giving out three-point-two Bud Lite becuase it's cheaper but he's selling it for the same price as everything else. Same can, less alcohol."

"Alright, quiz time, Sis. What's my man drinkin?" Claude pointed to the rear door at a beefy, college guy in a *Tap-Out* MMA tank-top and a backwards Raiders football cap. Three friends in similar apparel followed.

"All Bud Lite. Wait, except for the guy in the Denver Broncos hat, he's a Coors Lite."

Aaron listened as Raiders cap ordered for them all. Claudette had guessed right. For the next hour, Aaron silently watched the scene and drank to forget what he'd done at the nursing home. The Alibi Lounge was a dimly lit one-star restaurant that served burnt burgers and cold fish n' stale chips. The two bartenders were responsible for the drinks ordered by both the customers who walked up to the bar and the seated guests who were served by a pouty-faced, middle-aged, chain smoking waitress who refused to give her name when introduced to Aaron. He watched as Claude measured a precise Jack & Coke using a jigger with exactly two ounces of whiskey. In the same amount of time, Claudette made two margaritas on the rocks with salted rims, one strawberry daiquiri in the blender, and magically concocted a Long Island Iced Tea in a single pour by grabbing all four bottles with both hands.

After the rush of drink orders, Claude polished a Collins glass and said to Aaron, "I always put a lime in a Corona and an orange slice in a Blue Moon. Learned that in college."

"That and an English degree got you a job bartending," Claudette chided her brother. "Even bar flies know that every drink needs the right garnish."

"Get yo garnish game on!"

"Preach brother." She turned back to Aaron and winked. "Trick is to use a carrot peeler for the perfect lemon twist."

An older, mustachioed gentleman in a blue blazer asked for an Old Fashion and Claude reached for the little, red colored edition of Boston's Bartending Guide. Claudette pushed him out of the way and said, "I got this." She splashed a few drops of Woodford Reserve bourbon into a rocks glass, grabbed two ice cubes with her bare hands, added a dash of bitters and threw in an orange wedge, pulp and all. She set it down roughly on the counter without a napkin or coaster.

The gentleman took a sip and complained, "Hey Sugar, where's the sugar?"

Claudette dismissed him over her shoulder as she walked away, "That's how I make it."

Claude laughed as the gentleman wandered away, sadly sipping his sugarless spirits.

Aaron asked Claudette why she had been so rude. She said sternly, "When that old fool gets faded, he won't shut up. Claude will put up with his incessant chatter, but he knows I'll kick his ass right out the door. Worst of all, that bastard doesn't tip. The rule is simple."

"And what's that?" Aaron asked.

"If ya don't tip, ya better skip," Claude explained, vigorously nodding at his sister. "She don't play."

Aaron made sure to tip one hundred percent on the next drink. He was on his second Cape Cod and held a healthy buzz. With every blink, the image of Eve resting motionless lurked behind his eyelids.

Over the next three hours before last call, Aaron noticed a few things. When a customer left cash on the bar after paying for a drink, Claude would immediately pick up the tip and wipe over the spot with a dry towel. He'd give a slight nod and the customer would smile, knowing their gratuity was appreciated. Claudette's approach was quite the opposite. She would completely ignore the tip with utter disdain, as though the amount was never enough. Claudette never smiled and she treated the locals with contempt. Oddly enough, the guys were crazy about her and left bigger tips for Claudette than for her brother.

Claude quickly made one drink at a time and placed it down directly in front of each customer. Claudette would often start making a few drinks at a time before sauntering away to flirt with some cute guy or gal. Later, she'd return to finish the drinks and look around like the customer was the one who had wandered off. Claude always wiped up after a customer left, leaving the counter top shiny. Claudette purposefully kept her end of the bar a total mess, wiping down the counter only when a new customer approached, placing a napkin down as if to say, *I did this for you, bitch!*

Three bar-hopping coeds who had recently turned twenty-one approached for drinks, keenly deduced by Aaron because they mentioned their birthday forty-three times while they smashed their Kleenex-stuffed B-cup bras against the bar, attempting to create cleavage where none existed. Claude, affected by their amateur charm, drooled while the young ladies decided what to order. For Aaron, their uncertainly and awkwardness was painful to watch. Claude asked what they'd been drinking since escaping from the dorms, but they couldn't remember.

Claudette pushed her brother aside and took charge. She asked one question. "Do you like soda or juice?"

The girls replied in unison, "Juice." Claude flirted with the girls while Claudette made the drinks in front of Aaron. She threw a short pull of Malibu coconut rum into a cocktail shaker, added orange and cranberry juice with a splash of Sprite and cherry grenadine syrup. After inserting the straws, she poured the tiniest amount of 151 proof Bacardi rum down each of the straws. Claudette winked at Aaron and said, "Not much liquor, right? It's because they're already jacked up.

Doing them a favor. But the first sip will be that strong-ass rum and then I get my big-ass tip." With a flourish, she added a cherry and lemon wedge.

The three coeds lit up when the drinks were presented and after the first taste, screamed in delightful unison. A string of rapid exclamations pierced Aaron's ears,

"Wow, those are strong!"

"We gettin trashed tonight!"

"Paaar-taaaay!"

"I'm twenty-one!"

"So am I!"

"OMG, me too!"

"Paaar-taaay!"

"I gotta pee!"

"OMG, me too!"

Aaron was surprised they actually said *Oh Um Gee* and not the full *Oh My Gawd* but figured text-speak was in full effect for the next generation. They paid Claude with three separate credit cards before racing off to the bathroom. One of them left Claudette a crisp twenty-dollar bill on the bar. She laughed, "White girls are so predictable."

"How so?" Aaron asked.

"Come on, a twenty for three drinks?" Claudette explained. "She's overcompensating. And she could have put the tip on a credit card, but nope, she's letting me know that she's down, that she's cool. Probably her dad's money. Not like I care," Claudette said as she stuffed the money into a tip jar.

Over the course of the evening, Aaron noticed that Claude gave away only one drink. He actually said, "This one's on the house," to a regular who was downing Fat Tires at a rapid pace to get home before his wife noticed he'd been gone. Claude prepared every cocktail exactly the same way each time, looking up the recipe when someone ordered a new drink. He used only limes for garnish and put a straw or a plastic stirrer in every drink.

Claudette rarely endorsed straws,[115] using a metal cocktail shaker instead of stirring the beverages. She poured heavy, at least halfway up the glass with liquor, and she gave away free Kamikaze shots to most of the ladies. "It's mostly sweet n' sour mix," she explained when Aaron asked about the contents. She charged the price of four beers when serving five and then told every customer in a humorless tone,

"It's always happy hour for you, sweetie." Needless to say, she raked in the cash. Aaron figured they made about $300 between the two of them, and her tips probably accounted for most of it.

When Aaron asked Claudette if tonight was a regular night in terms of tips, she scolded him. "You've never worked in the service industry, have you? Money fluctuates, that's the nature of money. But I always make phat cash."

"How?"

"Because if the customers don't tip, the bar always will."

Aaron's interest swelled, blocking out the nausea roiling in his belly. He'd drunk four Cape Cods and began to slur his words, "Hoz dat work exactly?"

"Old bartending trick. Ring up a five-dollar beer after serving a ten-dollar gin and tonic but leave the extra cash in the till. Do that ten times and when I cash out my singles, I'll pull an extra fifty. Got it?"

"Not really."

Claudette sighed and gave him a disappointing stare, the same kind of look that Zoë had given him before she had moved out of his house. The kind of look that meant, *I expected more from you.*

"We always need singles," Claudette explained, "because when we break big bills, we always give back ones."

"How else we gonna get tips?" Claude said. "If some drunk fool pays for a beer with a hundo, I'm givin him back ninety-seven singles."

Claudette laughed, "My brother actually did that last week. Dude was pissed off with all the singles, so I told him, 'Then just leave the cash on the bar, we'll take care of it for you.'"

Two men, one Black and one white, in Polo golfing shirts both ordered Hennessey and water. They chatted with the twin bartenders for a few minutes and paid separately. They each left a fiver, and Claude swiped up the tip from the white guy, but Claudette slid the other five-dollar bill back at the Black man. He nodded silently.

"Whatz that about?" Aaron asked.

"Don't you know?" Claudette smiled for the first time. "Black people don't need to tip. Their ancestors already done paid."

"Daaaamn!" Claude exclaimed as they high-fived each other. The Twins looked at the clock and cried out in unison, "Last call!"

Aaron couldn't believe 2 a.m. had arrived so quickly. He hoped that he could drive after six, or seven or maybe eight, vodka cranberry cocktails. Suddenly, his gut throbbed from the guilt of what had happened at the nursing home. He ran to the bathroom and retched red liquor into the sink. He rinsed out his mouth, pushed stringy hair away from his face, and cleaned the sink bowl with a paper towel. He refused to look at his reflection in the mirror.

When he came back to his stool, he found three businessmen pleading with Claudette.

"Please, baby, come on. One more drink, just one more," begged the older businessman with a loosened tie and unbuttoned collar. His two friends swayed behind him. "There's like fifteen minutes left."

"Sorry, you missed last call," Claudette said coldly.

He reached for his wallet with shaky hands like a junkie. He slid two twenties across the bar. "This help?"

Her face warmed up. "That'll do." She cracked open three bottles of Budweiser and put the extra cash in the tip jar. She looked at Aaron, "End of night bonus. See, I always close a little early and make these fools beg for one more. Never fails, they always thank me with cash."

Emerging with a case of beer cans to restock the cooler, Claude said, "Like our boy 2 Chainz says, 'Fuck you, pay me!'"

Claudette whispered to Aaron, "Actually, he stole that from *Goodfellas*."

Aaron stood up, grabbed his jacket, and left a tip with his last two bucks. He felt guilty about spending more than his overdue water bill. His legs buckled and he grabbed the edge of the counter.

Claude asked, "You good, my man?"

"He doesn't look so good," Claudette frowned. "Looks like death."

"Want us to call you a taxi?"

Aaron gathered himself and spoke clearly at the Twins, annunciated each syllable to appear sober. "I'm fine. Don't need a cab." He would have accepted the ride but he couldn't afford it. "Let me ask you one last thing. You actually like working here?"

Claude responded first. "Sure man, it's a job. I like it here. Money is decent and the people are nice."

Claudette turned her back to the customers. "You ever hit a light switch and wonder, 'Where does the light go?'" She disappeared into the back room before he could give a response.

Aaron laughed and wished he could be so dismissive of other people. He staggered out the door and threw up two more times on the way to his car. Finally, he climbed in and drove towards destiny.

Aaron circled the Poinsettia three times before pulling into the parking lot. He'd expected to see the lights of an ambulance, a police car or a black hearse from the morgue. However, nothing awaited his arrival. He turned off the engine and sat in the car, metal clinking as it cooled in the night air. Dizzy from the alcohol and horrified of the scene that awaited him inside, he opened the door and puked cranberry juice onto the asphalt. He leaned forward and passed out with his forehead on the steering wheel, the small bumps of rubber imprinting a groove into his skin. He woke up two hours later having sobered up a little and stared out the window.

Suddenly, Aaron found himself immobilized. He couldn't turn his head, couldn't switch on the radio, couldn't even reach for the handle to open the door. He imagined taking the many steps to Eve's room. He could only shift his eyes to the left and right. Panic swelled, a combination of somatic paralyzation and the fear of police approaching the vehicle. He would be unable to lower the window and speak normal words like, "Good evening officer, just sittin here in my car. This isn't Utah, is it?" Motionless, Aaron listened to his breath, to an occasional owl, to the wind. Seconds turned into minutes that became hours, and Aaron did not move. He did not pass out again, he simply waited until the paralysis faded. He only wished he could shut off his mind.

Dawn illuminated the dim edge of distant, purple mountains. Aaron stared at the vast, pointless horizon and compressed the past, present and future together into a single, quiet moment between night and dawn with its subtle inference of hopelessness.[116] Aaron wondered if he would ever be able to move again or would he be bed-ridden forever, like Eve, letting hours slip away into nothingness. Where's my purpose, he wondered? Where's my passion, my creativity, my time? Miserable, he couldn't remember what had happened to these traits since he'd become a caretaker and a parent. Adjustment to fatherhood had taken many years, but the sudden alteration to being a grandson without a grandmother terrified him.

Adjust or adjust, he told himself.

These were the only two options available because stagnation meant death. The conundrum left him miserably confused but happy, because he was only happy when miserable. And waiting to move, unable to make the long journey to visit Eve one last time, he was beyond miserable. He was immobile. And oddly, he'd never been happier because passing through grief meant freedom. Free from what waited for him inside.

The scent of lavender lingered on the wind and Aaron could move again. His fingers at first, reaching for the steering wheel. Then he pushed the radio button. Music, such beautiful music. Well, Aaron smiled, trendy EDM but at least the thumping bass was better than the stillness of immobilized anxiety. He opened the car door, found his feet attached to his legs and functioning properly. He stood up, stretched and took bold steps forward.

The lobby was empty, the night staff yet to be replaced by the morning crew. He snuck down the long hallway, tiptoeing on the soft carpet so as not to wake anyone despite the fact that many of the residents had lost their hearing years ago. When he reached the door to his grandmother's room, Aaron paused. He was unafraid because in Aaron's mind, his grandmother had departed months ago. Only a body remained.

Aaron entered the quiet room. The body was stretched out on the bed, skin pulled back on the face, mouth agape. Aaron did not see his grandmother, he only saw a shell. The body inhaled a raspy breath. The body exhaled wispy air. The pillow was still at the feet where Aaron had placed it before he'd fled for the bar, where he had placed it when he had decided not to smother Eve. Smothering her would have been the antithesis of life's purpose. He reminded himself that this was her body, her choice. Her life was her own, she had brought his entire family into this world and she was strong enough to take herself out of this world. He was only here to watch so she would not be alone.

Then the body stopped breathing. And Eve was finally gone.

Episode 17.5

Yet

Days and nights slipped into the past and Aaron couldn't leave his bed. He didn't sleep or eat or even worry. He barely moved. Silence and dehydration during his self-imposed imprisonment had left his mouth a desert void of life. Even dreams that filled the vacuum of his mind were absent. Aaron had heard a few people banging on the door over the last few days but purposefully ignored them. Zoë had been staying at Lena's house since their fight on the day Eve died. Earlier, he heard Zoë slamming drawers in her room but she had the courtesy not to bother him. She probably needed some clothes since she only kept an empty room at Lena's house. The last time Zoë and her mother had gotten in a fight, a drunken Lena had thrown Zoë's clothes out onto the porch. Aaron and Zoë had returned with two empty laundry baskets only to find Lena sitting atop the pile of clothes and sobbing. She had not remembered the argument, looked up at Zoë and asked, "Why are you running away?" Aaron hoped Zoe's absence was temporary but he feared she was moving out. He feared his daughter was abandoning him.

On the fourth day, Aaron rose from bed but not to splendor or even a mild epiphany about the acceptance of grief or how death is part of life or that Eve was in a better place or any such afterworld mythology. He simply grew bored of staring at the ceiling.

After washing his face, he tried to figure out which of the local mortuaries had picked up Eve's body. Someone had handed him a card but he'd lost it immediately in the ensuing blur of events. He couldn't quite remember the order, had the nurse come in and told him that Eve was gone? Had the doctor come in and verified the time of death? Aaron only remembered sitting drunkenly on the edge of bed until some people asked him to move out of the way. Then he had driven home or so he assumed because his car was in the driveway. Maybe someone had come to collect him, Aaron couldn't recall. He found himself in bed a few hours later, hangover ringing like a death knell, and he had not moved since.

Aaron admitted to himself that he could not serve as the *someone* in this post-death scenario. Someone needed to go through Eve's personal items at the Poinsettia. Marilyn and Jocelyn had probably gone over with boxes mere hours after her death to clean out the room, preparing the way for the next tenant. Aaron envisioned Jocelyn collecting the monetary deposit on Eve's room at the Poinsettia while Marilyn yelled at the staff because they had not, in Marilyn's opinion, offered enough pain medication towards the end. Someone needed to call the church to let the priest know, and call the newspaper to place an obituary, and let Eve's friends know that she had passed away, even though there weren't many left. After 96 years, she'd outlived all her friends.

Someone needed to inform the numerous cousins, in-laws, aunts, and uncles whom Aaron had never met. Someone had to pick up flowers for the funeral, write a eulogy, organize the speaking order at the funeral and where people would sit as well as arrange for the caterers to bring food appropriate for a funeral, nothing too heavy like steak and yet something more formal than mini burgers and more filling than a fruit plate and juice for the kids and definitely booze for the adults, and later someone had to pick up the death certificate.

Someone had to manage all the little details of death and Aaron knew that he would not be that someone. He had been there for her in life, up to the last minute, and he was afraid it might destroy him to be there for her in death. Aaron knew from his decade in social work that it's not the tsunami of sudden trauma that destroy you; instead, it's the incoming tide that erodes your foundation. Bit by bit we fall apart, he told himself. The mundane is murderous.

By the afternoon, Aaron finally managed to check his phone. 112 missed texts and 34 missed calls, voicemail full. He erased all without checking. He assumed most of the messages started with, "Sorry for your loss." I didn't lose her, he told himself. She was taken away. People should instead say, "Sorry your loved one was stolen. Sorry you've been robbed."

Aaron considered eating an apple but found the refrigerator bare. He opened the front door, squinted at the awful sun, took one step out and considered it a huge success for the day. He checked the mailbox and found an invitation printed on a 4"x6" egg-shell stock card with Eve's name on the heading. Jocelyn had sent out funeral announcements, and at the bottom was a quote by Hafez, the 14th century Persian poet:

Even after all this time, the sun never says to the earth,
"You owe me."
Imagine a love so bright, it lights up the sky.

Aaron checked the date and noticed the funeral was planned for later today. She is really gone, he thought. Aaron collapsed on the horribly stained, sun-faded, wobbly, cigarette burned, lumpy, torn, mustard-colored velvet couch before rolling onto the floor and crawling under the table.

The first few hours passed uneventfully, staring at the pleasant wood grain, analyzing the smooth table legs, stroking the soft texture of the beige carpet. The space felt ancient and familiar like a womb. Time passed slowly, as it tends to in dark moments. The weight of panic prevented him from standing. Eve was gone, Zoë had abandoned him, Jocelyn and Marilyn would eventually stop bringing food and paying the rent and Lena was cutting him off.

The first thought of suicide came as a wave of relief. Several hours of sobbing had left Aaron emotionally exhausted, as in his cortisol levels were out of whack, and repetitive shallow breathing had limited the amount of oxygen to his prefrontal cortex. He cognitively understood his condition but could do nothing about it. Once again, he was a victim of immobility.

Under the table, his initial investigation into the possibility of taking his own life sprung from his inability to provide for his family. He wanted to be important, not impotent. Suppressing his anger and disappointment, he contemplated the suicidal methods of a person with similar feelings—such as a mass murderer in a shooting spree.

He remembered six months earlier to the morning at the Denny's restaurant, his first and only on-site crisis call, in which the man had taken his ex-wife hostage and almost resulted in a mass-shooting. Fortunately, Aaron possessed no desire to kill others, he only wanted to end his own life because rage expressed outwardly is misanthropic murder whereas rage expressed inwardly becomes self-loathing, suicidal depression.

While under the table, Aaron heard the landline ring. The first thing he'd done after Eve died was to come home and kick the phone but Zoë had probably placed the receiver back on the base during her visit for clothing. A decade of repetition compelled him to answer.

Before picking up the telephone, Aaron began to worry. He'd seen Zoë reading the Penguin edition of *The Bell Jar* last week, and so under the table with a headful of woe, Aaron followed that fiery path dreaded by every parent when they hear the phone ring. He asked himself, "What if Zoë is dead?" Panic, slow like lava, crawled over him because he hadn't seen her in days, and so Aaron concluded that his daughter must be gone, forever.

Just like Eve. His dear grandmother, suffering no longer. Gone. And such a slow death it had been. Forgetting everyone she ever loved, confused by her own reflection, gasping long breaths until her body had to be reminded that the spirit was gone. His only wished for himself that death would come quickly and that he would not linger in life's shadow.

Don't linger in life's shadow, the same motto Aaron would often repeat to Callers when they were in the act of killing themselves, as in they had the knife/gun/rope to their wrist/head/throat. He would desperately encourage them to succeed and not lounge in the painful aftermath of a failed Attempt. For the chance to offer one last bit of advice, Aaron answered the call and was greeted by a Gaul.

Sobs 1, panicked affect, female, heavy French accent: "You no call ze poe-leece, nooo?"

Aaron, as Finito: "The police? No, this is confidential. I'm supposed to tell you not to do it, I mean kill yourself."

Sobs 1 replied, "But I so sad, my life ess zour."

"Zour?" Aaron didn't understand.

"Like leemon, like veenagar."

"Oh, sour. Got it. You're right, life sucks. Life is like lemons and blowjobs. Sucking leaves a sour taste in your mouth. Alright, if you're gonna off yourself, then do it right."

"*Excusez moi?*"

"Listen here," Aaron said, blending the line between prevention and permission. "Let's compose a list together. Let's write down the top ten easiest ways to kill yourself."

The mental exercise of making a list distracted Aaron from his personal emotional pain and he enjoyed observing the panoptic view of suicide before reducing it to the specific.

"Euh, deez ees berry straaange." Sobs 1 stopped whining. "Maybes I 'ang up now, euh, I dink the baguette ees burning…"

"Make bread later. Here we go. Ready?" he asked, turning the page on the yellow pad to a fresh sheet. For the French Caller's name, he wrote down *Sobs Ahn* instead of *Sobs Un* for purposes of pronunciation. "The first way to kill yourself is to start saving four pills from every opioid pain reliever prescription. Codeine, fentanyl, the good stuff like Vicodin's hydrocodone, or Dilaudid's hydromorphone or Demerol's meperidine. After a few months, grind the pills with a stone mortar and pestle, and mix this fine powder into a 750ml bottle of Smirnoff Raspberry vodka. Chill, add a twist of lime and *Voilà!*"

"Euh, I like vooodka. But I no have doctor to get, 'ow you say, pree-scrib-shawn."

"Alright, got a garden hose? The second way is to connect one end to your car's tailpipe and stick the other end through the window. Bring a pillow for the ride and *Vois là!*"

"I 'ave to turn car on, nooo?"

"Yes! That's how combustion works."

"But ze exhaust smells bad so maybe I rwoll down other veendow, *oui?*"

"That would defeat the purpose," Aaron said slightly exasperated. "Fine, you want clean air? You could buy a canister of helium from the local party store that sells birthday balloons and introduce the gas via half inch rubber tubing into a plastic bag tied tightly around your neck with large rubber bands. You'll die laughing because your last words will sound like a high-pitched clown at a birthday party. It'll sound like *Vwālā!*"

Sobs Ahn laughed and Aaron continued, like most comedians who employ humor to distract from depression. "Or you could find a few yards of rope, static hemp rope not dynamic nylon rope. Tie one end to a tree limb, or a rafter in the garage, and the other end around your neck. It'll help if you can drop a few feet to snap your neck, otherwise you'll struggle while suffocating. *Voicà!*"

"Euh, suffo-ca-ción. Tear-ree-blay!"

"Yes, but here's one even more terrible." He continued with the ridiculous. "Steal ten large T-bone steaks from the grocery store. Sew them together as a meat-suit. Buy a ticket to the zoo and jump into the lion cage or bear den or shark tank. *Bon chance!*"

"Zat smell aah-ful, no? Meet-suit, deesgusting!"

"You're probably right. You enjoy the Olympics?"

"*Oui*, French always ween at badminton."

"That's a real Olympic sport? Good gawd, they're letting anyone compete now-a-days. Anyway, you could dress up in the French national badminton spandex outfit and wait for the Olympic torch to pass through your hometown. Douse yourself with gasoline, charge into the flames and go out in a blaze of glory. *Bon courage!*"

"Soo painful, *oui?*"

"How about something easier. Watch Cary Grant's *Arsenic and Old Lace* on Netflix, pour yourself a tall glass of elderberry wine and spike it with arsenic, strychnine and a pinch of cyanide. *Adieu!*"

"*S'il vous plaît*, can you 'old?" Aaron thought it strange to be placed on hold during a crisis call. After two minutes, Sobs Ahn returned and she asked him to finish the list. "You 'ave *dix*, I mean ten, on dis leest, *oui?*"

"Yep, every good list should have ten on it. Three more."

"Keen you make it queeyck, I 'ave to watch Azz Ze World Turnz."

"The soap opera? Hey, you're the one who called me!"

"*Oui*, but I feeling beetter now."

"Fine. Throw yourself."

"Thee-row?"

"Throw yourself into death. Let gravity do the work. Off a bridge, off a cliff, off a building."

"Zounds boor-ing."

"Ah, the French! Always need to be so damn creative. You want to be original? Fine, throw yourself into a furnace of molten iron like my friend Lead George and become a zombie. *Au revoir!*"

"Le som-bee? Oh, ze valking dead can do le soo-ee-side?"

"You mean if the undead killed themselves, would that be considered suicide? You know, that's the best question I've ever been asked," Aaron said, realizing this might be his last crisis call.

"Are we feenished?"

"Two more. You could throw yourself into a barrel of vinegar. Or dunk yourself inside a huge copper vat of boiling beer. *C'est le mort!*"

"Euh, beer ees deestuisting."

"And what about vinegar?" Aaron asked.

"Veenegar ees zour, like life. *C'est le vie*," Sobs Ahn said before hanging up.

Aaron promptly tore up the *Top Ten* list after his call with the French woman because he would never want Zoë to accidently find a list of ways to commit suicide. Aaron hardly ever worried about Zoë killing herself, although his lack of concern was stressful because maybe he wasn't worried enough. Aaron had read about an overwhelming number of therapists and social workers whose children had ended their own lives. Yet, Zoë seemed happy, outgoing, motivated, and in love with partying, boys and life itself. She laughed while dancing and gave away her restaurant left-overs to beggars outside on the corner. She was one-in-a-million.

Then again, Aaron hoped she wasn't one-in-a-million because the overall, world-wide suicide rate had remained stable for the last two decades at about one suicide for every one million children. Yet, Zoë possessed a racial asset: she was white. At first, this troubled him because Attempting suicide was a white girl's disease, but then he remembered that over the last few decades, the suicide rate had nearly doubled among Black children while it had fallen among white kids. At least Zoë wasn't a Japanese girl faced with the pressures of education. The rates were ridiculously high for Japanese schoolchildren, nearly double everyone else. Every year in the month of September, about twelve Japanese kids kill themselves every day. If going back to school was so awful, Aaron thought, then perhaps Nipponese school boards might reconsider taking a summer break and keep those kids in school year-round. Maybe, Aaron thought, it's tough being a girl in high school. Maybe Clarissa in the *Virgin Suicides* is correct when the doctor tells her, "You're not even old enough to know how bad life gets," and Clarissa retorts with a bland, "Obviously doctor, you've never been a thirteen-year-old girl."

Thoughts of losing Zoë led Aaron to focus on his own self-assisted demise. He worried that were she to die tragically ahead of him, as in a car accident or drug overdose or by the constricting hands of a jealous boyfriend with anger issues or by tripping on a curb in high-heeled shoes or breaking her neck while climbing at a rock gym, then Aaron would immediately die because he'd want their names to be connected, forever. Because he couldn't bear the burden of life without her. He'd want people to say, "Remember Zoë? She was so sweet," and then pause with a big sigh, "Yeah, but Aaron." At some point, they would ask, "Why?" and through his death, the answer would be, "Because why not."

He wouldn't even have to make an Attempt. His heart would simply stop beating. Yet lately, say in the last year or two, as Zoë had begun to fully embrace a high school, teen-aged temperament, Aaron had begun to reconsider suicide and maybe instead of death, he'd endure a long stay within the confines of the State Hospital. Hopefully in a year or two, Aaron might be at a place in life when the loss of his child would only result in a dramatic breakdown that could easily be cured by a weekend stay at luxury resort in Cancún. After his fight with Zoë, he was beginning to understand why men grow cold and grumpy as they age. He understood why men cut their children out of the will. It's not because they don't care, but rather because they care too much and the pain is debilitating.

No matter how life progressed, at some point he hoped to make an honest Attempt, like slitting his wrists in the bathtub because he'd hate to have anyone clean up after him. And this was how Aaron realized he identifies as a woman because he was worrying about the mess!

Since commitment is often expressed by details, Aaron had the deed planned out. When Aaron spoke on the hotline with Laura the Lonely Housewife low on Lexapro or Paul the Painter plain out of Paxil or Exhausted Eric enraged by the effects of an empty ewer of Effexor or maybe someday Medicated Marilyn or Zoloft Zoë, he would ask them in a calm voice if they have a Plan. Not a plan of getting through the day or how to Hang In There or how they were planning to refill their meds, but instead a Plan of how they imagined going through with it. And since Aaron never employed the word *it* to describe suicide, as in "Have you been thinking about it?" instead he jumped straight into, "So, how bloody will the room be after you kill yourself?"

Usually, the Caller-in-Despair either gets angry (men) or breaks out in tears (women) after visualizing the bloody mess they might leave behind. Which was the main reason, Aaron supposed, that women choose to overdose with pills or ingest poison instead of the more decorative and sanguinary firearm method of splattering the drywall with brain matter. Strangulation evacuates the bowels and bladder in a most disgusting manner, leaving a puddle of piss on the carpet below the chandelier. Aaron supposed this was the reason DFW hung himself off the back porch. How considerate, a simple garden hose for clean-up.

The corporeal residue left in the aftermath of jumping from a great height is perhaps why many choose to leap from a bridge. The water below washes away their disfigured bodies emptied of fluids. For therein lies the problem. The body consists of approximately five liters of blood, plus mucus, stomach acid, and food eaten in the last 24 hours, plus a huge dump lining up inside a quivering colon, and every sip of water and orange juice and maybe booze consumed to nudge the person towards the Plan plus half a liter of piss swirling in a nervous bladder and also the grey brain matter and bone marrow and even the tears and snot sliding down the face caused by rushing wind in those four to five seconds of freefall. Talk about messy.

The phone rang again. Aaron answered only because he promised himself to unplug the landline afterwards. This would be his final call.

The woman's voice was familiar. Aaron recognized her voice from the past, but thought she was long dead. The Woman on the Bridge.

Aaron, finally as himself: "Didn't they find your body in the river?"

WomB, parental tone: "Wasn't me. Not yet."

"Glad you're still alive. How you been holding up?"

"Burying my mother today. And my son is falling apart."

Suddenly, he figured out WomB's identity. "Mom?"

"Yes, Aaron it's me."

"Why didn't I recognize your voice years ago?" Aaron asked.

"I had put a sweater over the mouthpiece," Marilyn explained, "and it muffled my voice."

Aaron nearly mocked her technique until he realized she had fooled him. Perhaps from the beginning he'd known that WomB had been Marilyn, but a part of him never could have admitted that his mother was calling him for help. Then again, all women sounded like his mother.

"About what I told you at your birthday party..." Marilyn trailed off at the end.

"Don't worry, it didn't bother me," Aaron lied.

"No, I was wrong. I would not be okay with it, I mean, with you killing yourself."

"I know. I feel the same about Zoë."

"I shouldn't have said that."

"I don't know what to say."

"You don't have to say anything. You're a good listener. Just let me apologize."

"No, you don't need to apologize. You love me, that's enough."

"No, I need to say it. I'm sorry. Let me explain, you saved my life."

"What do you mean?"

"You remember when I called you a few years ago? I knew you'd be working at the Crisis Center. I was in a dark place standing on that bridge. I almost killed myself. I just needed to hear your voice. You pulled me back."

Aaron's mind swirled. Her previous Attempt now gave him permission.

"Anyway," Marilyn continued before hanging up, "See you at the funeral in an hour."

Aaron realized his suicidal urges were genetic. It made his plan that much easier. Committed to making an honest Attempt, Aaron threw the phone down, tore the cord from the wall socket, grabbed a bread knife off the counter and raced upstairs into the bathroom. He removed his drab clothing and placed them in a neatly folded pile on the floor. He quickly polished the sink's fixtures with a strip of clean toilet paper and climbed naked into the bathtub. He decided to skip Eve's ceremony and planned to give the family two funerals . . .

Aaron slipped into a present-tense-in-the-moment-plan-for-an-Attempt. First and foremost, he does not want to leave a mess. That's why the bathtub is perfect, his fluids will simply wash down the drain like Roy Batty's tears in rain.[117] Forgetting an important item, he gets out of tub and runs downstairs. He grabs a bottle of Windex and a roll of paper towels, placing them next to the bathtub in the hopes that the paramedics or coroner will wipe everything down before his grieving family members enter the scene. His only desire is for Lena or Marilyn or Jocelyn to come in, take a look around at the spotless bathroom and say, "Look how clean it is!"

Not matter how hard he tries, Aaron knows his Attempt is going to be messy. He ignores cutting his wrists and decides to make a grand gesture, noble and historic, such as slitting his belly, *seppuku* style.[118] He concedes that the first part will be the worst. Stabbing through clenched stomach muscles will be difficult, so he'll have to place the tip of the blade lower, about half way between the belly button and the pubic crest, where it's soft and slightly pudgy. He'll angle the knife upwards for the ultimate goal—the diaphragm.

Sitting back in the bathtub, Aaron focuses on his diaphragm. He doesn't want to die of blood loss which would take too long and be far too painful. Better to suffocate, Aaron rationalizes. Slicing the diaphragm will prevent him from taking a deep breath or more accurately, prevent him from exhaling. He'll die not a blue-faced fool from lack of oxygen but rather red-faced from too much oxygen in his bloodstream. This specific bodily organ traditionally targeted by disgraced *samurai* and dishonored *ronin* is located directly beneath the lungs. Since Aaron is acting alone without the aid of a trusted friend to lop off his head,[119] he suspects using a long, narrow blade to pierce up through the small and large intestines will leave an utterly repulsive odor. He doesn't want to disembowel himself because, well, the mess!

He decides to plunge into himself low in the belly and aim not for the diaphragm but instead the spinal cord. Although he fears this technique might leave him paralyzed instead of dead, he hopes the ensuing pain and intestinal poison will be enough to cause a blackout and he'll bleed to death before regaining consciousness. He'll have to plunge into his belly up to the knife's hilt and then cut back and forth, as in left to right and back again, hoping to slice the spinal cord which is protected by the tough shell of five lumbar vertebrae. As Aaron imagines slowly sawing into his own spine with a non-serrated blade, he's pleased he brought a bread knife because it could effectively get through the thick wet bone. Looking down at the knife resting across his belly like a flaccid penis, Aaron realizes he is not ready to Attempt.

He steps out of the tub and runs back downstairs to collect the torn-up bits from the top ten list of ways to kill oneself that he complied for the French woman. Sadly, he is unable to find *gutting oneself like a fish* before marching upstairs to climb back into the tub. He decided long ago that he doesn't suffer from mental health issues, because even though he might act crazy, he assures himself that he is not crazy, despite sitting naked in an empty bath tub with a bread knife.

Maybe the craziest thing he's done, Aaron ponders, is not his contemplation of an Attempt but instead his forgetfulness to fill the tub with warm water.

Although his motive may be muddy, Aaron's reason for the Attempt is quite translucent. He doesn't feel cornered with no chance of escape, because he can go outside and breathe in the fresh air; and, he doesn't possess a sense of failure, because Zoë tells Aaron that he's a good father on a daily basis because he changes the ink cartridge on the printer when it runs dry and cuts up slices of apples for a healthy snack instead of potato chips and always stays out of her room and gives her daily hugs, even when she doesn't want them because Aaron knows she may need them; and, he doesn't experience feelings of remorse, because he was holding Eve's hand when she died; and, he doesn't believe in a reward of heaven, although he's not an atheist because he knows that there is no such thing as an atheist because everyone worships something, it's simply a matter of understanding how that worship will destroy you.

Aaron, after fifty-six minutes of lying in the bathtub, stands up shivering and sore from the cold porcelain and steps out of the bathtub, out of his present-tense suicidal fantasy and back into reality.

. . . but instead of an additional funeral, he announced with clear determination, "Not yet."

After dressing in all black clothing, he limped downstairs to the kitchen and replaced the bread knife in a drawer because he didn't want Zoë to use an improper knife while slicing a bagel and accidently cut her finger again.

Aaron, poised to climb under the table, realized his futile excursion to the bathtub was his final Attempt. Marilyn had made it very clear for him. Inherited genetics. She had thought about killing herself which gave him permission to make an Attempt but this in turn meant Zoë would someday copy him. If he killed himself, then she would surely follow. He knew that children of parents who kill themselves are three times more likely to complete suicide. After all, kids always want to be like mom and dad.

Right then, Aaron made a powerful decision. He needed to say goodbye. He left the house and drove past the cathedral and skipped Eve's funeral. Catholic ceremonies were long and cruel enough to send Aaron back into the bathtub. Instead, he went to work. After ten years, he was tired of faking it, tired of pretending, tired of giving a shit about other people's lives. He needed to take care of himself. "Fake it until you make it," quoted another little poster on the wall of Boss Lady's office, and he decided that the first thing he did when he returned to the Suicide Prevention & Crisis Hotline Center would be to tear down all the poster because he was quitting his job.

After thousands of hours on the phone, Aaron viewed the apparatus of telephonic communication as a disjointed affair. The

Process no longer saved him from psychic trauma. He could no longer see and feel people on the other end of the line. He needed a job with personal interaction that was not via a phone or a computer screen. He hated how his life had become like a movie where the vast array of human expressions boiled down to emoting into a plastic receiver.

Aaron marched directly towards Boss Lady's office. He wanted to insult her one last time and get fired, thereby insuring his dismal. Getting fired was easier than quitting, Aaron thought, similar to the way the murderously suicidal found it easier to be shot by a cop instead of cowering in a corner and pulling their own trigger. Luckily, Boss Lady was out to lunch but Aaron was greatly upset that he'd have to terminate himself. A lack of exposure to men in his life meant he was not tempted to massacre everyone in the Crisis Center as a way of expressing his grief. Instead, he slid a note with his signature under her door that simply read, "I quit."

Marching to his desk, Aaron looked over the wall for Debz to say goodbye and heard her singing in the bathroom. Two volunteers yelled at Aaron for barging into the woman's restroom and he heard Debz in a private stall belting out, "Take this job and shove it!" He entered the one next to hers and put the lid down before sitting on the toilet.

"So," Debz said with finality, "today's the day, huh?"

"How'd you know?"

"Well, heard your grandma's funeral was today. Figured you need a change of scenery."

"Right."

"You outta here, son, no need for big drama."

"Later, sweetheart."

"Sorry about your grandma."

"You know, it's kinda nice in this bathroom" Aaron said, hoping she wouldn't try to Normalize and Validate his sorrow. He'd been in the business far too long to be consoled out of sadness. "We shoulda moved our cubicles in here long ago."

Debz laughed. "Gonna miss you, home boy."

"Whatever. Hey, and tell you mom wassup from me. She'll know what I mean. Point!"

Debz threw a roll of toilet paper after him as he exited the bathroom.

Aaron didn't make his way around the office and say goodbye to the Brendas and other social workers in the office because he wouldn't miss any of them. He swiped a cardboard box from the janitor's closet and pilfered three differently colored bottles of cleaning fluid. He taped a handwritten note for Moises on the door, "Exodus requires purification."

Aaron emptied out his desk and placed a huge stack of case files into the cardboard box. Since he had no intention of bringing anything home from the office, he placed the box on Debz's desk as parting gift. He then stole all the staples out of her stapler and stuck them on her chair as a final prank. He sprayed the empty desk and cabinet with blue mist and wiped everything down with a wet rag.

Suddenly, the phone rang and he decided to take one last call.

"You coming home?"

This time he recognized Marilyn's voice. She knew his direct line because she had called him years ago when she was standing on the bridge. And a mother always knows how to find her son.

"We're waiting for you," Marilyn said. "We're celebrating Eve's life. Together."

"I'm on my way," Aaron said.

He stayed on the line because background noises offer the best clues. He could hear Marilyn and Jocelyn talking before the call ended.

"… I know you're trying to be helpful but maybe we're enabling him?" asked Jocelyn.

"I don't care if I'm enabling my son," Marilyn responded. "He's still alive."

Aaron's heart soared, newly unburdened. On his birthday many months ago, his mother's indifference to his life had caused him to feel not only unwanted, but rather unmade. And now, with this sliver of stolen conversation between the two sisters, Aaron glimpsed her true feelings. A mother's love is eternal.

He kept the three bottles of cleaning fluid as his severance pay and proudly left the Crisis Center. After ten years, his own healing could begin.

He drove home slowly, meandering through the strength of hope. From the street, he could see Lena and Zoë chatting on the porch. Marilyn planted lavender in the front yard as Jocelyn served lemonade.

Parking in the driveway, Aaron stared at his family waving to him. Momentarily optimistic, he no longer could summon a motive nor a reason to end his life. Maybe he'd find a job that offered more money so he could pay his own bills. Maybe Zoë would move back in. Maybe he'd cook a meal for his mother and aunt. Maybe he'd stop worrying so much and spend less time under the table. Stepping out to greet his family, Aaron's thought of suicide dissipated as he repeated the two words of a life-saving mantra.

Not yet.

—End—

Appendix

People are suicidal. Death is synonymous with life; the antithesis of life is doubt. An Attempt requires confidence.

This too shall pass.

—or—

People are not suicidal. We endure seasonal cycles and daily rituals of tragic pronouncements, but human nature is not inherently suicidal. Rather, the **events** surrounding our life are cause for life-threatening action from despair.

This too shall pass.

Recovered Fragments from
45-Fists of DàHú GōngFū[120]

2. Idle Iguana

versus Two-handed chest push.

Greet attacker's verbal taunts with a smile. Split attacker's attention with downward glance at shoes and ask, "What are thooose?!" Follow with iron palm to philtrum.

7. Stinking Sushi

v. Right punch, right foot lead.

Left step forward, left parry and right claw to groin. Left arm circles around into rear-naked choke. Check attacker's wallet for small bills.

13. Tormented Termite

v. Two-handed choke.

Raise right fist outside of attacker's left arm while left raises inside their arms. Twist hips inward, snap down to collapse attacker's arm, followed by right cut elbow to temple. Have attacker call his own mother and apologize for being such a difficult child.

17. Cursed Crane

v. Left grab to right shoulder from the right side.

Right backhanded flick to groin, left palm upward chin lift, right chop to throat. First, make sure attacker is not your brother.

23. Sleeping Sloth

v. Low charging tackle.

Step forward to right 45-degree angle. Left knee strike to groin. Review astrological charts to determine if Mercury is in retrograde.

29. Timid Tiger

v. Bearhug from the front, arms are free.

Step back right, double palm strike to ears. Loop fore-arms around neck into guillotine choke. Consult acupuncturist for remedy, discover *dit da jow* liniment cures bruising.

31. Masturbating Monkey

v. Right punch, left foot lead.

Step back right, left elbow block to opponent's right wrist. Left flip wheel to groin. Re-check astrological charts to see if Saturn is in anterograde.

37. Pathetic Python

v. Two-handed grab to both wrists.

Step forward left, right hand tucks underneath to pin both opponent's hands. Raise hips to hyperextend elbow. Ask attacker, "Do you have a date for Homecoming?"

41. Flaming Flamingo

v. Headlock.

Left knee drops, pretend attacker's groin is a speedbag. Trap attacker's left foot. Grab their right arm through legs. Pull down on arm, driving face into ground. Look both ways for bystanders recording with iPhones and ask them to delete.

43. Barking Bhutanese Dog

v. Left grab followed by right uppercut from the left side.

Right step away, left back knuckle to incoming grab at opponent's wrist, circling low with left claw to groin. Parry incoming punch with right hand, left eye flick, right palm to ear. Shuffle, left elbow smash to jaw. Go home and compare definitions of Chinese *wuwei* and Japanese *mushin*.

About the Author, i.e. vacat page

This page intentionally left blank
at the author's request
due to the corruptive nature of biographical surveys,
the postcedent of a hyper-inflated ego
derived from a societally-induced
narcissistic personality disorder,
and herewith subsequent infringement by the publisher of
aforementioned author
may result in severe consequences such as
state-enforced sterilization,
flogging and/or autoerotic asphyxiation;
and hereby the author only admits to currently residing in
Pueblo, Colorado,
a wonderful place to break down and spend twenty years,
and by *break down* he does imply
a troublesome automotive malfunction rather than
permanent residence at the State Mental Hospital.

All endnotes expand Aaron's temporal orientation and the mental segues that occur during conversation.

<u>Temporal Guide for Endnotes</u>

UNDERLINED for history's importance

1) <u>PR</u> = Past Remote
2) <u>PRc</u> = Past Recent
3) <u>PiP</u> = Past-in-the-Present
4) <u>PiF</u> = Past-in-the-Future
5) <u>PY</u> = Past Yesterday
6) <u>PT</u> = Past Today
7) <u>PNo</u> = Non-Past

BOLD for the now

1) **P** = Present
2) **S** = Still
3) **NS** = Non-Still

ITALIC for future's slant

1) *FNo* = Non-Future
2) *FT* = Future Today
3) *FTm* = Future Tomorrow
4) *FiPa* = Future-in-the-Past
5) *FiPr* = Future-in-the-Present
6) *FN* = Future Near
7) *FR* = Future Remote

---

[1] The Still tense is from the Luganda language of Southern Uganda, indicating a continuous action that is still occurring meaning *so far*, whereas the non-Still tense means *not yet*.

[2] [<u>PT</u>] The text: *happy girl   I like it when you come up on the bed please yes* and Aaron thought this the weirdest invitation he'd ever received from his ex-wife and was about to answer *duh fük* when the next text arrived: *oops   talking to my cat   phone recorded my voice* to which Aaron simply replied with the heart-eyed cat

icon, conveying the he cared for his ex-wife in the same way a cat loves its owner, which means slight disdain but covertly dependent.

[3] **[S]** Neither a personal reliance on a past status quo nor a personal expectation of a future normalcy; however, Aaron personally rejects this mode of existence and instead embraces a truthful pessimism that he has not been nor will he ever be *okay*.

[4] *[FiPa]* Aaron had decided his alias on that particular evening would be Federico. During every shift he used a different alias which drove Boss Lady utterly mad because she didn't have enough room on the tiny line for SOCIAL WORKER ID on his reports to type his fake-alias (changed daily) followed by his official alias of Roberto, determined on Orientation Day many years ago. Aaron has never used this fake-alias, although he had a long conversation with Boss Lady in the beginning of his career over the meaning of a *fake-alias*, which Aaron believed gave the false implication to the would-be Caller that he, the would-be Listener, might actually be using his real cognomen. Conversely, the term *official alias* was used which implied he was a government spy, to which both comments were followed by a heavy sigh by Boss Lady and her common response of, "Whatever Aaron, I need to go smoke." The fake-alias was followed by his birth name, first name only, written as ARON because Boss Lady had misspelled it on the Excel sheet and the typo had plagued Aaron through the years since the HR Department was completely helpless in terms of changing the spelling mainly because Information Tech Specialist Richard M. Johnson, aka Dick "Magic" Johnson, (not a fake-alias) working from home in his damp basement didn't think it a worthwhile expenditure of his time, whereas changing the obvious misspelling of his Warcraft avatar level 89 Elven frost Mage named "Dick The Almighty" certainly was a priority, in which he, the IT Specialist, sent many angry electronic missives to Blizzard, Inc., to procure a properly spelled "The" in the middle of his virtual alias. Thus, Aaron remained ARON on

spreadsheets, presently "Federico-Roberto-Aron" or in the recent past "Francisco-Roberto-Aron" whereas in the remote past "Fernando-Roberto-Aron", and looking over the spreadsheets, Aaron had the distinct pleasure of noticing he had successfully, albeit unconsciously, used masculine proper nouns ending in "o", bestowing on Aaron, at least on paper, an appearance very much exotic with a distinguished Latino heritage. He didn't know what to make of the adherence to names starting with F, except that F stands for "fake".

[5] [PR] A man who, by his own account, "would try to inocculate the Indians by means of infexted Blankets," in retaliation for Pontiac's Rebellion.

[6] [PNo] Non-Past footnotes are film, literary, musical, and cultural references that serve as the momentary mental segues we experience-in-the-moment during a conversation. For example, as Aaron is listening to Lord Amherst's descendant, he ponders the cinematic role of thugs, such as Mexicans with bandannas, or Arabs with turbans, or Asians with pointed, rice farmer hats or Blacks with Oakland Raiders caps, because apparently only bad guys wear hats. And if the actor selected for the role of Thug #2 happens to be white, then he's most certainly Russian.

[7] [PNo] Similar to a Level 1 wizard/cleric's spell named "Protection from Evil," an abjuration spell from *Advanced Dungeons & Dragons* with a 1' radius which adds +2 to all saving throws versus demons, devils, djinns, efreets, night hags, wind walkers, xorns and **the chronically depressed**.

[8] [PY] As Dr. Blasey Ford said in her testimony, "Indelible in the hippocampus."

[9] [PiF] Prison rape occurs to about 2% of male inmates. In the US Army, 14,000 men are suspected of being raped every year, which is also about 2%. And that's nothing compared to 32%

of women in the US military report having been raped and 8 out of 10 women report having been sexually harassed.

10 [*FiPa*] This two-fold footnote illustrates how "Future-in-the-Past" operates while also representing Aaron's mental digression during the conversation when he says the word "island". He is suddenly reminded of the dream he had the previous evening entitled *Gilligan's Island, Revisited*. The cast of castaways included Mr. Gregorian Howell, III, a gay, 65-year-old Russian billionaire of a software company; and, Mrs. Willy Chan Howell, a 30 year-old Chinese-American man that works as biochemical engineer (a cross between Mrs. Howell and the Professor) who is transgender and has recently begun the process of transitioning to female; and, Dr. Ginger Johnson, a stunning, red-headed 39-year-old African-American who was Ms. Nevada when she studied at UNLV while earning two PhD's; and, Mary Anne Winterovski, a chubby, 19-year old Jewish internet sensation for her programs "Kosher tastes Great!" and "Yoga Rabbi"; and, Skipper Edward Gumby, a 55-year-old white, overtly racist and misogynistic ex-cop from Cleveland who was fired from the department after shooting an unarmed black teenager and now is the pilot and owner of Minnow Tours Airline Company; and, Gil Egàn, a goofy 26-year-old Latino hipster, video gamer, and web-author on gaming and geek culture. After waking from the dream, Aaron researched the 60s sit-com *Gilligan's Island* and discovered the character Gilligan had no first name. However, the producers revealed many years later on a radio talk show that they (the producers) wanted to portray the Skipper and Gilligan as close friends, having served in the US Navy together, and the Skipper slurred his little buddy's first and last name together so that everyone thought the Skipper was calling him "Gilligan" when in fact his name was actually Gil Egan. And so, the information that Aaron discovered in-the-future had somehow affected his dream-in-the-past.

¹¹ [PR] The ᚒ of Phags-pa script, created by a Tibetan monk for Kublai Khan whose Japanese invasion fleet was destroyed twice by divine winds or *kamikazes*.

¹² [S] *Pan*, the Greek word for "all" depicted here as a global phenomenon, and *Oizys*, the Greek goddess of anxiety and the daughter of Nyx.

¹³ [PR] The ninth letter of the Hebrew alphabet ט, Tet. Although the letter is found in *tov* meaning *good* ("*Mazel tov!*" in Yiddish), the paradoxical nature of Tet and its serpentine form contains a hidden message: *evil*.

¹⁴ [PRc] A Himalayan ethnic group, with unique high-altitude, hemoglobin-binding capacity, who worked historically as farmers until Western explorers appeared in fancy North Face hiking boots and asked, "My good sir, would you mind carrying my backpack to the top of Everest?" And the Sherpas climbed in plastic sandals!

¹⁵ [PRc] After saving England, Alan was accused of the Gross Indecency Act for being a homosexual and forced to undergo government sterilization which resulted in severe depression. In 1954, he committed suicide by dipping an apple in cyanide. Apparently, during the war, he had seen *Snow White* and often recited the Wicked Witch's rhyme, "Dip the apple in the brew, Let the sleeping death seep through."

¹⁶ [NS] Aaron frequently blended fact and fiction, often unable to tell the difference, but he did know that Ian Fleming had been a commander in the Royal Navy's Intelligence Division during World War Two, codenamed 17F instead of 007. Rumored to have briefly dated Agnes Driscoll while she was stationed in London. When asked to describe her, the future spy novelist was recorded as saying, "Hot stuff!"

¹⁷ [FN] The Greek letter Ω, omega, used to indicate the end of Aaron's patience.

¹⁸ [**S**] Because men think they know how to find it (*La Tuñel*), but they always need signs to point them in the right direction.

¹⁹ [PNo] Because what's not to love about a persuasively suicidal Mel Gibson? Suicide conveys commitment in cinema, such as Geena Davis and Susan Sarandon driving off a cliff in *Thelma & Louise*, and Bruce Willis in *Sin City* and Bruce Willis again, portrayed as younger version of himself by Joseph Gordon Levitt in *Looper*, and Denzel in *Fallen*, and a bunch of characters saving humanity from an alien invasion like the pilot in *Independence Day*; and, Private Vasquez and that asshole Gorman clutching a live grenade in *Aliens*; and, Ripley as she plummets into lava in *Aliens 3* while clutching the symbolic representation of an aborted fetus conceived by rape.

²⁰ [PiP] Thus, to survive Cleveland is to refute Grandma Death herself.

²¹ [**NS**] Daily, with consistent regularity, as detailed by the aphorism: "Religion is like a pill, take one a day religiously to keep the sin away." Then again, all pills have side effects.

²² [FN] A desire to revert to one's earliest stage of infancy/helplessness, simultaneously defecating and breast feeding, expressed as the fetish of an adult male wearing a diaper and hiring a recently pregnant prostitute to serve as wet nurse. In Nirvana's *Milk It*, "Her milk is my shit," confirms the logical fallacy, affirming the consequent, with "my shit is her milk."

²³ [PiF] Most likely a Lulu's *Find Me Guilty* halter top dress, oddly similar to the dress that his future lover, not a Brenda, will be wearing when they meet at a conference.

²⁴ [**NS**] Diss, as in disrespect, not to be mistaken with, "Revenge is a diss best served cold." Regardless of gender, often accompanied by, "You got diss'ed, son."

²⁵ [PiP] Aaron hates long intros, thus begins *in medias res* with actors running/screaming/fleeing in terror because the audience knows it's a zombie-flick since they've seen the trailer at least a dozen times.

²⁶ [FiPr] Thematic Analysis, TA, written as notes in the margins of Aaron's screenplay. TA#1 is as follows: The main character's zombie-lead-penis symbolizes how men are led around by their cocks.

²⁷ [FTm] The lead patch symbolizes Male Stubbornness which will slowly fade as George develops a relationship with the film's main actress in the leading role, played by none other than the new Brenda.

²⁸ [PT] Debz had said Kellie probably attended Smith or Mount Holyoke.

²⁹ [S] And other clichéd activities that college girls do in horror/soft-core-porn type films.

³⁰ [FiPr] A very meta-moment in the film, but Aaron decides to go along with it. It's important for Aaron to have the women in his story be aware of their objectification.

³¹ [S] Male preoccupation with automobiles especially the '65 Shelby Cobra, '66 Alfa Romeo Spider, '67 Corvette Stingray and the '68 totally bitchin Chevy Camaro.

³² [FTm] An important part of any modern sex scene is that consent must be explicitly given.

³³ [PNo] Aaron is fairly certain this line of dialogue exists in every horror/soft-core-porn type film, whether being attacked with a kitchen knife or an erection because like the Jane's Addiction mantra, "Sex is violence."

³⁴ [*FiPr*] George has regained a bit of his humanity through his interaction with Kellie.

³⁵ [*FNo*] Yet, the clothing is appropriate for zombie/soft-core-porn type films with the fabric low-cut in the bosom and high-cut in the thigh, such as an extra-small Hooters t-shirt with plunging neckline and a plaid-pleated mini-skirt.

³⁶ [PiF] Basically, a metaphor for the entire college experience.

³⁷ [**S**] Good-hearted men are clueless to the struggles women endure at the hands of corrupt and evil men.

³⁸ [**NS**] Love blinds us from the most obvious flaws in our partner.

³⁹ [*FN*] An example of a cock-block. Literally.

⁴⁰ [*FNo*] Star Trek Voyager, "Death Wish," stardate 49301.2. The episode revolves around an immortal being named Q and his quest to commit suicide, instigating the only double face-palm by a single character contained in one frame within the Star Trek universe. The theme, despite its rampant issues of sexism towards Captain Janeway, equates mental instability with suicidal ideation. More importantly, expressed throughout the episode is the sentiment that freedom is tolerated only when individual rights do not interfere with public benefit. Thus, to kill oneself is not good for the state. Because in the free world, "We've all been the scarecrow," and found it boring.

⁴¹ [**NS**] Here used to signify logical negation, instead of the Boolean algebraic dash with a tail.

⁴² [*FR*] Thirty years older than Aaron is now, which is why college kids think 50 is old but it's a matter of perspective since anyone over ninety would love to be 80 again.

[43] **[S]** In Klingon, *Heghlu'meH QaQ javam*, with emphasis on the "is" when translated because the most regal of copular verbs in the English language, the infinitive form of the predicate *To Be*, was purposefully ignored when the linguist Marc Okrand created a unique language for the Klingons in *Star Trek III: The Search for Spock*. Ironically, the first thing director Leonard Nimoy asked him to translate was Hamlet's *To Be, or Not To Be* soliloquy.

[44] **[NS]** *Kiss Off* by the Violent Femmes: "And two, two, two for my family. And three, three, three for my heartache. And four, four, for my headaches. And five, five, five for my lonely. And six, six, six for my sorrow. And seven, seven for no-no-no tomorrow. And eight, eight, I forget what eight was for. And nine, nine, nine for a lost God. And ten, ten, ten, ten for everything, everything, everything, everything!"

[45] **[NS]** *Yana*, Sanskrit for path or vehicle, as in *Mahayana* (greater vehicle), *Hinayana* (smaller vehicle, now called *Theravada* because "lesser" lacks a certain persuasive marketing tactic), and *Tantrayana* (the sexy vehicle with plush leather, tantric seats). Thus, when California gurus call Aaron late at night with thoughts of passing into the Void, he attempts to figure out their persuasion of Buddhism by asking, "What kind of car do you drive?"

[46] **[S]** To differentiate between fictional dialogue and historical attributions, the individual's final remarks pronounced on their deathbed are delivered forthwith within double quotes as, "**'BOLD'**." Credit to <u>Last Words of Notable People</u> by William Brahms, with the great understanding that most of these men probably died saying, "Uuuungh" or, "About time" or, "Water". However, since these men desired legacy, they composed concise lines of wisdom months before their death and turned to their wife or mother or aunt or daughter or granddaughter because only a woman can be trusted to write it down properly. And a wife never forgets EXACTLY what her husband said.

[47] [PiP] The dagger symbol (†) indicates the individual completed suicide.

[48] [PR] Dying words of the Sleeping Buddha: "'**Make of yourself a light. Rely upon yourself; do not depend upon anyone else'**.'"

[49] [PiP] For Aaron, the line evokes Sgt. James Doakes and the Ť resembles the "T" on the Dexter poster hanging in Zoë's room whereas the Greek letter ὑ, upsilon, signifies going *up* north, the route to freedom taken by Araminta "Minty" Ross, the slave name of Harriet Tubman.

[50] [PiP] Fuenteovejuna (translated by S. Appelbaum). "Well, that's the way men are: When they need us, we're their life, their being, their soul, their heart."

[51] [S] Celsius sign because Aaron's temper is close to boiling.

[52] [S] Cedi sign, the currency of Ghana.

[53] [S] Euro sign, the currency designed to form a global economy run by the Illuminati.

[54] [PRc] Diagnostic and Statistical Manual of Mental Disorders, 4th edition (1994) at 886 pages, and sure, after 20 years they added about 100 pages for the 5th addition, but the difference was minimal. After browsing the aisles like a drunk at last call in 'da club, bouncing from one option to the next, Aaron ends up staring at the latest trade paperback issue of Justice League of America, knowing that a comic book aficionado needs to understand JLA in order to capture the references/inside jokes of the greatest graphic novel ever, *The Watchman* by Alan Moore.

[55] [S] First time said aloud by Aaron, the macron over the capitalized "Ū" means, "Uuuugh".

[superscript]56[/superscript] **[S]** The curse word is absent a letter because one parent is missing.

[superscript]57[/superscript] **[S]** Because Aaron's world is always turned upside down whenever his daughter is hurt.

[superscript]58[/superscript] **[S]** ℂ, the capitulum, indicating an end to Aaron's present-tense deluge and that a new beginning is needed. A symbol more commonly seen by those who failed 10[superscript]th[/superscript] grade English alongside a backwards P with two vertical lines written on the side of their essay. Usually scrawled by the teacher in red ink.

[superscript]59[/superscript] **[PNo]** The five stacks of cards are each labeled on the backside with a different symbol. The *Where* cards have a picture of a treasure map with an "X" and indicate location. The *Why* cards have a "?" and illustrate the reasons for suicide such as depression, tragic loss of child, death of partner, tumor, cancer, old age, break-up, or dog died. The *How* cards are labeled with a "Ω" symbol (ohm sign for electrical resistance, not to be confused with omega, the Greek letter Ω) and explain the method of suicide such as electricity, drowning, asphyxiation, gravity, cutting, gunshot, drugs or poison. The *Tool* cards have a drawing of "empty hands" and express the ways of implementing the method of suicide. The *Tool* cards are combined with the *How* cards to form a Plan. For example: the *How* card of electricity combines with the *Tool* cards of fork in outlet. The drowning card combines with the bathtub, ocean, or pond cards. Asphyxiation combines with rope, belt, or extension cord. Gravity combines with jumping off bridge, leaping from building, or driving car over cliff. Cutting combines with knife to belly, glass to throat, or razor to wrists. Gunshot combines with pistol to head, shotgun to chest or rifle pointed at police. Overdoes combines with heroin, opium or alcohol. Poisoned combines with sleeping pills, arsenic, bleach or fertilizer. Lastly, the *When* cards have the image of a vintage pocket watch on a silver chain and indicate the time of the Plan.

[60] [PNo] The 15-page, 11-point font, single spaced rulebook. Summarized as follows: One player is designated as the Suicidal Player (SP). The other players work together as Prevention Players (PP). The object of the game is for the SP is to make an Attempt once certain criteria are met. The Suicidal Player's character sheet has five (5) skill stats with a sliding scale from 10 to 0: Mood Level, Emotional Stability, Physical Health, Hormonal Balance, and Religious Belief. When all five stats have reached a rating of zero, then the SP moves to a location at a certain time and makes an Attempt. If the SP succeeds, then the game is over.

[61] [PNo] One or more other players serve as Prevention Players (PP). Their character sheets have five (5) different skill stats from 0 to 10: Empathy, Listening, Socializing, Validating and Normalizing. When the Prevention Player's skill reaches 10, they draw a card from the Prevention card pile that increases the Suicidal Player's stats. For example: Brenda completes a mission at the State Hospital tile which increases her Listening skill by 4 points and Empathy by 2 points, but decreases her Socializing skill by 1 point. She now has a Listening skill stat of 10 and draws a card which reads: "You meet SP for lunch and listen to him/her worry about the plight of starving children in the Sudan. Raise SP's Mood Level by 1."

[62] [PiF] Freeze being the third option, but a more accurate description would be the Flight & Fight & Fuck response instead of employing the terminology pilfered from Dr. Seyle in 1936, because history has been dictated by men chasing women (flight), beating them over the head (fight) and raping them.

[63] [PRc] In retrospect, the euphemisms turned out to be true. The first woman he took for a wild ride, the second he played like a fiddle and ripped out the heart of the third, but he vowed never to date three women at once not because of the lies but rather from exhaustion.

[64] [PNo] The Wicked Witch of the East obviously invites her own death, overcome by feelings of remorse for enslaving the Munchkins, because what omnipotent witch can't avoid a falling house? Also obvious is Dorothy's exploratory trip down the Yellow Brick Road as a metaphor about the suicide of her girlish innocence and her emergence into womanhood. She is reborn through a sexual journey when she encounters three men: the limber scarecrow, a portrayal of a young girl's first flaccid lover who can't perform; secondly, the well-oiled man with a long metallic shaft; and thirdly, a real lion-of-a-man with a ferocious, sexual appetite, but also a sensitive, new-age guy who cries after climaxing. And yes, the man behind the curtain is symbolic of the Patriarchy because he hides the truth from Dorothy, an orgasmic liberation finally discovered when she rubs her ruby-red clitoris three times and says, "There's no place like home."

[65] [FN] Actually, the person experiencing a self-harm episode is not inherently suicidal and only needs a little help to make it through the day/night.

[66] [PRc] According to Edwin Shneidman, father of Suicidology, "It hurts to be human."

[67] [PNo] Episode 3, Season 1, of *Gilligan's Island, Revisited*. Mrs. Willy Chan Howell, serving as the only doctor on the island, heals the Skipper who was attacked by a jaguar. When the Skipper announces, "I have B negative blood," the doctor realizes that only 1.5% of the population has that specific blood type and therefore cannot give a blood transfusion via his newly invented needle made from a bamboo shoot and an I.V. bag carved from a coconut. At that moment, Ginger saunters through the make-shift operating room, leans over the table thereby exposing her massive DD fake breasts to the home audience via the camera, and purrs in a sensual tone, "What can I do to help?" The doctor looks at her breasts and says, "Those are fake, right? We can use the saline instead of

blood." To which the Skipper looks right at the camera and shouts out the punch line, "Those tits will save my life!"

68 [*FiPr*] The ç with the cedilla transformed the word into "fushed" and was said by Aaron to convey his intention of gentleness, but only sounded ridiculously flaccid.

69 [PiP] Aaron wanted to explain how pornography made men completely dependent on visual stimulation, ruined their endurance and destroyed intimacy, thus making it easy for men to orgasm. Unless the man was sexually abused as a child and had conflicting emotions about becoming aroused and abused, expressed by the simple equation of Sex=Violence, as in only getting a hard-on when slapped in the face while being choked.

70 [*FiPr*] Aaron said *might* because he knew that women are different not from each other but from themselves at different points in their life. The younger version of a woman will be concerned about pleasing her man, and so will only cum after he is satisfied, whereas the middle-aged version of the same woman knows how to please both herself and her man at the same time, whereas the older version of herself honestly doesn't give a damn whether he's even in the room and can make herself orgasm by squeezing her thighs together.

71 [PY] Rape and the utter lack of consent seem to be common themes throughout *Grimm's Fairy Tales*. The first princess, Sleeping Beauty, obviously gets raped by Prince Charming because well, she is sleeping! Different from sleep-walking, somnambulism, and could be called somnufutuoism or sleep-fucking. She is awoken not by his tender Disney kiss but instead the suckling of her twin babies upon her fingers because she slept through both the rape and also the child birth. The next princess is Snow White who gets repeatedly gang-banged by the Seven Dwarves in one of the remote Pleasure Houses established through the many kingdoms (see Bill Willingham's *Fables*). She serves as a maid, cook and

comfort woman to seven nasty, ill-groomed, tiny-endowed men, hence their being called "dwarves", with nicknames that are clear references to their cocks: Sleepy (can't get hard), Dopey (sorta flops to the left or right), Happy (straight n' erect with no curvature), Bashful (the head is especially red n' bright), Sneezy (pre-ejaculatory), Grumpy (sullen in appearance and refuses to perform like it has something better to do) and Doc (a mishmash of "dick" and "cock"). Next, Cinderella with her glass slipper, representing either her pussy that the Prince slips into or a condom that he slips on, but nevertheless poor ol' Cindy is drilled by her three strap-on, dildo-wielding step-sisters who try to cock-block her from the Royal Palace. Even better are the two little mice, Jaq and Gus, and their sexual experimentation with anal beads in the innocent Fifties animated version. Next, Little Red Riding Hood receives cunnilingus on her way to grandma's house, the house a metaphor for old age which encourages young women to have big-bad, hairy men ride their little, red clitoral hood. Next, the Little Mermaid has no legs but also no genitalia until Prince Eric spreads Ariels' puberty-sprouted land-legs and plows into her with his sailing vessel of sea men, aptly named *Argosy* borrowed from the Agrosy Glacier in Antarctica indicating he is a cold, heartless bastard because he only liked Ariel when she had no voice, reinforcing the oppressive, gender-conditioning stereotype that men only like silent women. Next, in a fairy tale named "The Girl Without Hands" or "The Handless Maiden", the Devil tricks a miller's daughter, but her hands are clean of evil deeds, another way of saying the girl has never given a hand-job. The Devil forces the father to cut off her hands so that she may be abducted by the Devil. But in another version, the brother or father is trying to rape the maiden, thus she severs her own hands to appear ugly and less appealing. Next, Disney princess Mulan might be the anomaly who actually gives her consent but only because she's in drag. Besides, she's from *Zhongguo*, the Middle Kingdom, and everyone knows not to mess with a Chinese dragon. Next, as for Jasmine, that poor girl is forced to confront the horrors of venereal disease. She's locked up in her father's palace because on one of her illicit outings to the marketplace, she picked up the raging tiger of VD known as herpes. She's also contracted the contagious clap, as ear-splitting as Iago the panicky parrot, and she has symptomatic signs of the sinister syphilis from jealous Jafar. Abu's cuddly relationship with Aladdin symbolizes the fake origin story that tells of some African or Jamaican guy (aka Black, male sexual aggressiveness) who screwed a monkey to contract the deadly disease better known as AIDS. Yet, the arrival of Aladdin and his blue Genie's penicillin-in-a-bottle signals relief for Jasmin's venereal woes. And lastly, the white-skinned Goldilocks ventures down from the vanilla 'burbs searching for porridge (heroin) and chairs (social mobility) but is caught trespassing in the chocolate 'hood and forced to perform lewd acts upon three dark-skinned Bears in a tale of inter-racial exploration. Mama Bear's bed (cock) is too soft, Papa Bear's cock is too hard but Baby Bear . . . . ooooh, he's juuuuuuust right.

72 [FT] *The G-Spot, or Grafenberg Spot,* is a small, highly sensitive area located two to three inches inside the vagina, on the upper wall, said to be the primary erotic zone, perhaps more important than the clitoris, named but not discovered by German gynecologist Ernst Grafenberg in the 1940s. The G-spot was most likely discovered by Cleopatra with the first vibrator constructed from a hollowed-out gourd filled with angry bees and thus should be called the C-spot. However, this Dr. G gets credit for finding the G-Spot while conducting research on the mysterious female orgasm, and soon discovered the female's urethral tube is surrounded by erectile tissue that swells when a woman becomes sexually aroused. This G-spot expansion causes a small patch of the wall to protrude into the vaginal canal, the significance of which is lost while performing the missionary position. Historically, the

term G-spot is misleading whereas the more accurate G-zone would be preferable since many women have searched inside themselves, after a glass of chardonnay and a G-Spotter vibrator fresh out of its plastic wrapping, to seek a pleasure button that can be pressed like an ignition switch, for which men would pay an enormous amount to have installed inside his girlfriend/wife's vagina, which is not as ridiculous as it sounds since plastic surgeons and gynecologists have recently teamed up to perform G-spot enhancements by injecting collagen into the G-zone. The difficulty in locating a woman's G-spot led some male gynecological clinicians to perpetuate a vast Freudian-inspired, governmental conspiracy, enforcing the patriarchal emphasis on immature clitoral orgasms. These same male gynecologists were the type of doctors who said to a patient when his finger was halfway up her vagina, "I usually have to take a gal out for dinner and a movie to get this far!" These same male gynecologists who purchased for their frustrated wives the studded, dual-head rotating, 10-inched, curved, plug-in, G-Spotter vibrator by Acme…the same Acme used by Wiley Coyote (a symbol for the clueless, CIS-normative, hetero-male) who spends his life desperately chasing the elusive (G-spot) Roadrunner.

[73] [FT] *The U-Spot* is a small patch of sensitive erectile tissue located on either side of the urethral opening although absent in the small area between the urethra and the vagina which is annoying/painful if messed with, and whose presence is overshadowed by the clitoris. In fact, most regions are ignored including the nape of the neck where the short hairs rise when tickled, the erogenous zone behind the ear, the scalp, or perhaps the most difficult but rewarding area to stimulate—the female mind. Researchers found that when the U-spot is gently caressed by a finger or tongue, female ejaculation can occur which many embarrassed couples think is urine but in fact is fluid from the Skene's glands, remarkably similar to male seminal fluid sans semen, of course. This fluid released by female ejaculation, from a few drops to the perceived freakin' gallon when witnessed the first time by an unsuspecting young

couple who then quickly strip the bed of sheets, blankets, comforter and bed pad so their parents won't see the anomaly and the boyfriend immediately breaks up with his girlfriend because he is convinced from years of porn that he should be the one marking his territory by ejaculating on her and not the other way around, which confirms the ignorance of female genital activity by the general public.

[74] [FT] *The A-Spot, AFE-zone or Anterior Fornix Erogenous Zone or the Epicenter of a Woman's Earthquake*, is a patch of sensitive tissue at the end of the vagina just above the cervix and is the female equivalent of the male prostate which is the G-spot of the male anatomy so often avoided by straight, homophobic men much to their detriment. Direct stimulation of the A-spot spot can produce violent orgasmic contractions and unlike the clitoris, does not suffer from post-orgasmic over-sensitivity as in, "Oh, my gawd! Stop touching it!!" The existence of the A-spot was reported by a Malaysian physician in Kuala Lumpur in the Nineties, claiming that pressure on it produces rapid lubrication of the vagina, and could possibly be probed by a long, thin and upwardly-curved AFE vibrator.

[75] [FNo] *The Clitoris*, most popular of erotic triggers, located at the top of the vulva where the inner labia . . . aw hell, if the location is unbeknownst then woe be onto her or him. In utero, the same cells evolve into a clitoris within a female that become the tip of a penis in a male, which should help men understand the area's sensitivity, for no guy would ever want someone to repeatedly flick the top of his member. The visible part of the clitoris is partially covered by a protective hood, making gas station attendants in films from the 1940s sound lewd when they asked, "Ma'am, need me to check under the hood?" The Clit or Lil' Bald Man in the Boat or her Bean or the Greek island found south of the Mons Venus but north of the Deep Valley, is a bundle of 8,000 nerve fibers, more than a canine's nose, thus the most sensitive spot on the entire female body besides her heart. Many women who do not easily reach orgasm purely from vaginal stimulation find it easier to climax

from oral, digital, mechanical, visual, symphonic, or pedagogical clitoral stimulation which can be quite time consuming. The visible portion of the clitoris is actually just the tip of the iceberg, so to say, as reported by one Australian surgeon who stated the rest of its length, known as the clitoral shaft, lies beneath the surface and actually surrounds the vaginal opening. This means that for years, men have been stroking a woman's shaft. The clitoris can be excited by a rhythmic, downward roll of the pelvis, created by direct friction which requires a more dominant role for the female, as in any of the woman-on-top positions, which are not always socially acceptable. The Patriarchal preference for the man-on-top is represented by the vast multitude of male doctors, male politicians and **male authors** of fiction who strive to mansplain/control the mysteries of female anatomy.

76 [**P**] Serving as a focal point, the first time Aaron hides under the table is one of the few present moments in his life. From this point, he views reality as past and/or future. Other moments exist in the present for him as well: The birth of his daughter (Present-in-the-Past) and the death of Eve (Present-in-the-Future).

77 [**S**] A reference to Sylvia Plath's poem, "The Rabbit Catcher":

> *How they awaited him, those little deaths!*
> *They waited like sweethearts. They excited him.*

78 [PRc] *La petite mort* in French.
Also, Benedict says to Beatrice in Shakespeare's "Much Ado About Nothing":
> *I will live in thy heart, die in thy lap, and be buried in thine eyes.*
Also, a song by Cutting Crew in 1986, "(I Just) Died in Your Arms Tonight."

79 [FT] The song's duration is 5½ minutes. 8 hours is equal to 480 minutes which means he listened to the song 87.3 times.

80 [PiP] *The Adventures of Blind Kät & Bad Døg.* After the divorce, Aaron had drawn crude sketches with crass dialogue and submitted the idea for a graphic novel to Vertigo, a subsidiary of DC Comics. Essentially derivative work that helped him expunge anger towards his ex-wife, Blind Kät resembled a bumbling Mr. Magoo which represented Aaron's nearsightedness regarding his doomed marriage whereas Bad Døg resembled the karate-dawg Hong Kong Phooey which represented Lena's ability to kick-Aaron's-emotional-ass. The editor's assistant to the assistant at DC Comics sent him a curt reply thanking him for his drawings and that was the end of their correspondence, leaving Aaron with the unmistakable impression that he shoulda gone with Marvel.

81 [FNo] An appropriate guide for their journey into the desert. *Muad'Dib*!

82 [PR] Modern, not ancient, referring to the Ming Dynasty around the 15th century, or about 500 years ago if one's not too particular about dates. Thus, more modern than ancient but who would heed the advice of a Modern Chinese proverb? Simply doesn't have the same ring as ancient. Even less effective would be a Contemporary Chinese proverb, something more akin to "Always bring an umbrella to a protest" for those involved in the *Yusan Geming* (Umbrella Revolution). Nevertheless, the ancient proverb relays the wisdom of an old man, naturally, who is worried the Mongols might return but should have been more worried about Manchu bureaucrats. This older gentleman, in his perhaps fifties which was old for those Ancient (Modern) times, and this somewhat middle-aged guy like any father who can easily subtract a good decade or two from his life expectancy due to countless nights of worry, even in those Ancient (Modern) times, such as, "Will my daughter marry a rich acupuncturist?" or "When will my son stop reciting the drunken poems of Li Po and get a real job?" To illustrate the brief version, Old(er) Man is out walking through his flooded rice fields and discovers a bridled mare, saddled but no rider. Claiming

ownership after honestly searching for days in vain for the horse's master [for the Old(er) man must be honest, plain and poor in these stories], he leads the animal home and everyone says, "Oh, how wonderful, you found a horse." And the man says, "We'll see." His son, whose terrible poetry is cause for great concern, having no athletic ability whatsoever since he's a poet, mounts the horse in search for romantic inspiration after drinking rice wine. He falls off, breaking his non-writing arm and both father and son praise the Daoist pantheon of gods. The villagers are overcome with grief for the Old(er) man of Ancient (Modern) times and announce, "Oh, how terrible, your son broke his arm." And the man says, "We'll see." The provincial army arrives the next day, as they tended to do back then, forcibly recruiting the young men, etc., etc., but the man's son cannot go for his lack of a fighting arm and the people cheer, "Oh, how wonderful, your son is saved!" And the man says, "We'll see." This goes on as one can imagine, the story lengthens with great embellishment…the horse kicks a hole in his wall, "Oh, how terrible!" then he finds a sack of gold inside the wall, "Oh, how wonderful!" He rides the horse to the river and hooks a talking fish, "Oh, how wonderful!" but the fish curses him in Classical prose, unable to pronounce the 5th tone and so making Filial Duty sound more like Filthy Booty, "Oh, how terrible!" And so on and so on until finally the original owner of the horse appears, describing the bridle in great detail, including the character for *To Run Off* embroidered on the saddle and the story ends, as do many Chinese tales, unlike Aesop or Grimm, without a moral. Just a sudden conclusion of the owner's fleeing horse, the boy's unmetered poetry and the rice needing to be harvested. Oh, how terrible! We'll see.

[83] [PRc] The 31st President of the United States who presided during the economic coughing and stock market sputtering Crash of '29. Soon after Herbert was born, he contracted Whooping Cough which left him purple and lifeless. His Quaker parents covered the infant body with a sheet and left him for dead until a doctor galloped in on horseback and saved the boy's life.

[84] [PT] The doctor from the film *Reanimator*, based on H.P. Lovecraft's short story published 1922. More importantly, the car had successfully carried Aaron and his posse westward.

[85] [FNo] Governor Gary Herbert of Utah would later sign the "Fireworks Amendment" into law restricting the number of days that fireworks could legally be exploded in July, the Fourth and Pioneer Day.

[86] [PRc] A California serial killer who had killed a number of boys, including four teenagers camping in the woods for apparently "polluting the forest". The murderer believed the sacrifices had prevented an earthquake in the early 1970s.

[87] [PRc] Australian Olympian, set the world record for the mile run in 1958.

[88] [PRc] Top ranked tennis player in 1958, a nice Jewish boy from Brooklyn.

[89] [PRc] Basketball player in the NBA for eighteen years, born in 1958.

[90] [PiP] Following the commentary track on *The Matrix* trilogy narrated by modern mystic Ken Wilber and this century's most eloquent and rhetorical philosopher, Dr. Cornel West, Aaron stayed up late one night while waiting for Zoë to come home from Freshman Prom and while watching all three films, he calculated that Neo in the first *Matrix* film asks 89 questions versus the 41 statements. This nearly 2:1 question-to-statement ratio means that the main character asks twice as many questions as statements, including "Whoa!" and "I know gung-fu." In *The Matrix Reloaded*, the question-to-statement ratio is even at 1:1 whereas in *The Matrix Revolution*, the ratio becomes inverted at 1:2, meaning there are half as many questions as there are statements. This narrative technique substantiates the hero's accumulation of wisdom, and for Aaron, fortunately

caused an insight regarding the film's Socratic Method thereby facilitating the statement from Aaron to his daughter, "I'm glad you're home safely," instead of him asking Zoë at 6 a.m. upon her return, "Where the hell have you been?"

[91] [PRc] <u>Herbert the Brave Sea Dog</u>, a beautifully illustrated kid's book by Robyn Belton, is the true story of a dog who fell overboard and treaded water for thirty hours in New Zealand's French Pass.

[92] [PiF] Ð, as a past-tense signifier, expressing how the contemplation of a previous action directly results in an altered future.

[93] [PRc] The 24-second shot clock, known as "The Rule that Saved the NBA". Since a game lasts 48 minutes, or 2,880 seconds, and an average of 120 shots are usually taken by both teams, then each possession should be equal to 2,880/120 which is exactly 24 seconds.

[94] [PiF] A nuclear physicist who worked on the Manhattan Project, and were he alive today might have been a nominee for the "Public PiMP" award (Photography in Medical Physics).

[95] [PiF] Television producer who directed an episode of *Star Trek: The Original Series* entitled "The Lights of Zetar" which is of no help to Aaron in the ensuing flashlight fiasco.

[96] [PRc] Founder of Dow Chemical Company in 1897. During WWII, as Americans were smoking 400 billion cigarettes a year, Dow recommended adding glycols to tobacco in order to promote a humectant effect in cigarettes. Ethylene glycol is used in antifreeze.

[97] [PRc] Germany's most successful musical artist and film star who starred in the international hit *Das Boot*, a dramatic film set aboard an imperiled submarine during WWII. The technology

of the hydrogen fuel cells from the German U-boats helped spawn the Soviet Union's Project **685** class of submarines.

[98] [PiF] 19th Century English philosopher and sociologist, conceptualized society as a social organism. Influenced Émile Durkheim's *Suicide: A Study in Sociology* published in 1897.

[99] [PRc] He also came up with the expression "survival of the fittest" to explain evolutionary theory after reading Darwin's *On the Origin of Species*.

[100] [PRc] Conductor for the Berlin Philharmonic for 35 years, one of the greatest conductors of the 20th century. He raced sport cars including the 1959 Porsche Spyder and the 1966 Ferrari GTB, in cobalt blue.

[101] [FT] The 1963 VW Beetle would later that day play a significant role for Aaron in learning an important lesson about life.

[102] [PNo] See **Removed Appendix** for a technical explanation.

[103] [PiF] In a momentary Fourth Wall break, Aaron suspected one novel by an Erich Segal was enough for this world and yet he intuitively knew how his story would end . . . with death rather than love.

[104] [S] Insert the word "robbed" for Raped. Exchange the word "stolen" for Raped. Switch the word "ripped-off" for Raped. Add a sense of finality like "perpetually abducted, eternally hijacked, endlessly pillaged & plundered" for Raped and an idea emerges of not only taking but destroying. Her consent is not his to demand. Her virginity is not his to take. Her body is not his to steal. Her choice is not his to decide.

[105] [PR] Criminals, prostitutes, several unburnt witches and the morally ambiguous.

106 [PNo] Aaron imagines that had this been a Dave Chappelle skit with Dave acting as the deranged Corey Moore (reprising his role as Rusty P. Hayes from *Screwed* and assaulting the police chief with a gun instead of a desk lamp) and Dan Carvey as Jimmy Carter ("I got peaahnut butter hair, peaahnut butter shirt, peaahnut butter shoes"). In this skit, Aaron imagines Carter's punch line before hanging up would have been "I'll see whaaat I kin do bout thaaaat" or the even better response, "Well, at the current rate of miscegenation, in a huuundred years all vanilla is gonna have a lil chocolate in it."

107 **[NS]** Aaron's fore knuckle snapped against the man's radial nerve causing the arms to retract and the eyes to tear up and dilate. The palm to the groin was more of a grab-pull-and-rip action, causing the man's diaphragm to seize, the knees to buckle and the sphincter to loosen. The smell was unbearable.

108 [PR] Latin for "felon of himself". An 18th century English common law and archaic legal terminology for suicide. Those found guilty had a stake driven through their heart and buried in secret at midnight near a crossroads, drawing a comparison between the post-mortem punishment for suicide and the preferred method of exterminating the unholy Dracula. The law was abolished in England and Wales by the Suicide Act of 1961, about the same time Christopher Lee started portraying Count Dracula in British produced films.

109 [PR] Latin for "suicide". *Suī* = of oneself (genitive singular of reflexive pronoun). *Caedere* = to kill or to cut, because the Romans knew that cutting is the easiest way to kill. *Sui Caedere*, also the name of a depressive-doom-heavy metal band from Montreal, Quebec, their only album *Thrène*, a tribute to the abyss-damned poet Émile Nelligan who imitated both Baudelaire and Poe. Lamentably, he suffered a severe psychotic breakdown at the age of 19 in 1899. However, the term *breakdown* is used contemporarily as a subjective term since Émile was diagnosed with dementia praecox, today known as schizophrenia. His condition, which led to forced

institutionalization and sadly ended his prestigious poetry career, was best described by the poet himself in the final lines of *The Golden Ship*:

> *So, what has survived this flash of storm?*
> *What about my heart, abandoned ship?*
> *... O, still it sinks, deep in Dream's abyss.*

[110] [PT] Insert aforementioned euphemism.

[111] [*FiPa*] A regional accent with a lazy and elongated tempo, including a vowel shift on T words like "cot" and "bit" to make them sound like "caught" and "bet", or even dropping their T's altogether such as, "plummet down Monument Hill like hittin a ski chute," the Colorado version of a Bostonian Southie trying to, "paak ya caah in Havaad yaad," usually illegal because parking is not allowed in pedestrian walkways, except on moving day for Freshman.

[112] [PN] The broadcast occurred about twenty years before the premiere of *In Living Color*, a Wayans Brothers comedy show that launched the careers of Jamie Foxx and Jim Carrey, with a fly-girl dancer named J-Lo.

[113] [PR] Although in the 18th century, Aaron would have rebelled by having no hair because gentlemen often wore wigs. Both Western men and women shaved their heads because of the abundance of lice in Europe and their enslaved colonies. History is filled with evidence of hatred against men who wore long hair, starting with St. Paul's letter to the Corinthians, "Shame unto a man, Glory unto a woman" and the simple fact that Roman statues of male champions always have cropped hair. In 1066, the Archbishop of Canterbury punished those who grew their hair out "like a girl" and not until the Renaissance did male artists, bards, raconteurs, and poets revive the style that was later picked up by anti-war Hippies in the 1960s.

[114] [PiP] Aaron reads very little poetry, because, well, it's poetry. But he does enjoy LeRoi Jones' *Preface to a Twenty Volume Suicide Note*, written in the late 1950s before Jones became Amiri Baraka. The same Baraka who contemplated those actually responsible for taking out the ceiling of the Twin Towers by hooting like an owl, "Who? Whoo?" Whereas fifty years earlier, LeRoi's main concern was flooring:

> *What can I say?*
> *It is better to have loved and lost*
> *Than to put linoleum in your living room.*

Sure, carpet is nice but linoleum lasts longer than love, as evidenced by the missing patches of linoleum on defaced countertops and scuffed kitchen floors. The same missing patches of a woman's heart after thirty years stuck in a loveless marriage.

[115] [FTm] 500 million plastic straws will be used tomorrow in the United States, a figure guessed at by a nine-year old for his 4th grade science project. However, Aaron requests a straw despite the growing trend to ban straws in public restaurants because he thinks the First World perspective imposed on Third World nations is absurd since the one time he visited Mexico and ordered an Orange Fanta in Ciudad Juárez, he drank directly from the edge of the glass bottle and contracted dysentery.

[116] [S] Lack of hope, a bodily weariness manifested by rapid, social interactions that praise the wicked, or by rabid, unfinished deeds that condemn the honorable. In a word, Aaron was screwed.

[117] [PiF] An improvised scene from *Blade Runner*, the film version of Philip K. Dick's *Do Androids Dream Of Electric Sheep*. As a crisis worker, Aaron has always felt a connection to the detective Deckard because *(SPOILER!)* Aaron knows they would never send a human to kill androids, obviously they'd dispatch another android. Obviously, don't ask a sane person to help the suicidal, instead send in another psycho.

[118] [FNo] Aaron would never be so vulgar as to say *hara-kiri* which is like telling your girlfriend on a second date that you

wanna "hit it" rather than "make love". Sure, it's the same thing but not really.

119 [FNo] Aaron would prefer to have a friend's help because obviously decapitation by sword is extremely difficult by oneself. Also, Aaron wouldn't want his head rolling around on the bathroom floor, severed carotid arteries squirting blood upon recently scrubbed tiles, but who nowadays could be trusted with the *dakikubi* (embraced head) technique when the aforementioned friend, hopefully trained in the art of Kendo, keeps intact the foremost flap of skin on the throat, leaving the head attached but severed from the rear so that it hangs down upon the chest. Unfortunately, it's quite difficult to properly swing a stainless-steel katana within the confines of a 5'x 9' bathroom where the bathtub, toilet bowl, sink basin and vanity take up most of the space.

120 [PR] The origins of DàHú (*big lake*) gōngfū and ShàoLín (*little forest*) kungfu are similar, both stemming from the 5th century Buddhist monk Bodhidharma. The mystic martial arts of the ShàoLín style did not emerge from meditating monks but rather from ex-cons. As with most worldwide religious orders, monasteries have historically provided superb hiding places for those running from the law. For example, Mr. Lee's son robs a bakery (naturally, he's starving and needs to feed his family). When the authorities come searching for Mr. Lee's son, the father shows them the family lineage scroll drawn in ornate calligraphy with the son's name crossed out. When they ask why, Mr. Lee moans, "My son has become a Buddhist monk. His new name is Shàolóng (Little Dragon). He is no longer part of this family." In this manner, the monasteries filled up with convicts hiding from the cops, and many of these thugs were once soldiers or grew up fighting on the streets of Zhengzhou in Henan. These drunken hooligans taught the Buddhist monks their martial skill which is why the Qing government burned the temple, leaving a scorched earth later repopulated by little trees or shaolin, *little forest*. Because from tragedy comes strength.

**More books from
Harvard Square Editions**

www.ingramcontent.com/pod-product-compliance
Lightning Source LLC
Chambersburg PA
CBHW021848010726
47493CB00005B/1598